Sophie Pembroke has been █████████████████ and writing romance ever sin██████████████ Mills & Boon as part of her E██████████████ at Lancaster University, so getting to write romantic fiction for a living really is a dream come true! Born in Abu Dhabi, Sophie grew up in Wales and now lives in a little Hertfordshire market town with her scientist husband, her incredibly imaginative and creative daughter, and her adventurous, adorable little boy. In Sophie's world, happy *is* for ever after, everything stops for tea, and there's always time for one more page…

Karin Baine lives in Northern Ireland with her husband, two sons and her out-of-control notebook collection. Her mother and her grandmother's vast collection of books inspired her love of reading and her dream of becoming a Mills & Boon author. Now she can tell people she has a *proper* job! You can follow Karin on Twitter, @karinbaine1, or visit her website for the latest news—karinbaine.com.

BEST MAN WITH BENEFITS

SOPHIE PEMBROKE

PREGNANT PRINCESS AT THE ALTAR

KARIN BAINE

MILLS & BOON

First published in Great Britain 2023
by Mills & Boon, an imprint of HarperCollins*Publishers* Ltd,
1 London Bridge Street, London, SE1 9GF

www.harpercollins.co.uk

HarperCollins*Publishers*, Macken House, 39/40 Mayor Street Upper,
Dublin 1, D01 C9W8, Ireland

ISBN: 978-0-263-30648-4

07/23

BEST MAN
WITH BENEFITS

SOPHIE PEMBROKE

MILLS & BOON

To anyone who has ever been set up on a blind date…

CHAPTER ONE

THE OFFICES OF Here & Now Events sat in the centre of London, just off Berkeley Square in Mayfair, in an elegant Georgian townhouse that had been converted into three floors of meeting rooms, desks and display and storage space.

It was also an absolute hotbed of gossip.

As Nell Andrews climbed the few steps to the front door one Monday morning, juggling a heavy laptop bag on one shoulder and the cup of coffee she held in her other hand, she just hoped that her most recent gossip hadn't reached the staff yet.

An assistant, hurrying out of the building despite the early hour, held the door open for Nell and she stepped inside into the familiar soft white space, punctuated with occasional pops of bright celebratory colour. Her own office, up in the attic of the building, stuck to just the white walls and some restful neutrals. But they *were* a party and events company, so a little bit of exciting colour mixed in with the sensible, capable and competent office set-up only made sense. At least that was what Nell's twin sister and business partner, Polly, told her.

Nobody paid Nell much attention as she made her way past the reception space on the ground floor and towards the stairs, passing the display cabinets holding endless party supply samples, and the imposing floral displays that flanked them, in front of the meeting rooms they kept set up for impressing potential clients.

The white walls held oversized canvases showing images from past events, all in black and white except for the odd detail picked out in vivid colour.

Nell turned her head as she passed the largest one, right by the stairs, showing the four of them together at the launch party for Here & Now, five years ago.

Polly, Fred, Alex and Nell.

All rendered in black and white, except for the pink party hat on Polly's head, the green bow tie Fred was wearing, and Alex's purple cummerbund.

Even the photographer hadn't been able to find anything colourful about Nell to edit in.

The four of them had met at university, where Fred had fallen head over heels for Polly, and she'd kept him dangling at arm's length while she enjoyed the freedom of student life. Fred's best friend, Alex, had regularly been engaged as an envoy to try and get a read on Polly's feelings from Nell, which had brought him into their circle too—especially in second year, when Polly decided it was time to stop playing hard to get, and admit to what everyone else already knew.

Polly and Fred had been madly in love ever since.

And when they announced they wanted to start an events business, after graduation, it had been only natural to bring Nell, Polly's accountant twin sister, and Alex, Fred's law graduate best friend, in to round out the team. Here & Now had been born over a bottle of wine and an

Indian takeaway in Nell and Polly's tiny London flat, and from there it had only grown.

Now they had the media mentions, the millionaire clients, the constant referrals from happy customers, the central London offices—and the ever-growing staff.

At the top of the stairs, Nell stepped out into the main office floor—every desk filled by one of those staff members. The office had a constant buzz of chatter, excitement even, as they all went about their days. Organising parties for the rich and famous wasn't the kind of work which lent itself to quiet contemplation. Even now, Nell could see someone holding up two different styles of champagne bottle piñatas for a colleague's approval.

Piñatas? Whose party are those for?

Most of their events were rather more classy than that, but maybe a new client had a sense of fun that outweighed their need to impress. That would make a nice change.

The important thing was, the staff all seemed suitably diverted by their jobs and not at all interested in her. Which hopefully meant the news hadn't got around yet—and even when it did, that nobody would care.

It wasn't as if she was a regular topic of office gossip, she reassured herself. Her life—unlike the lives of almost everyone else who worked for Here & Now—just wasn't interesting enough to gossip about. She made sure of it.

Nell had lived enough drama and high emotion in the first eighteen years of her life to last her for the rest of it. All she wanted now was a quiet, boring, content existence.

Something she'd *thought* she had with Paul. Until this weekend.

There was no real way anyone could know about it

yet, was there? Except that the rumour mill at Here & Now was unparalleled, and somehow someone always knew something.

All it would take was Paul telling a friend, who told a friend, who told a cousin, who knew someone who worked at Nell's office, and there it was. Everyone would know.

It wouldn't even have to be Paul. One of her neighbours might have overheard. Or the taxi driver who had to have been eavesdropping on Paul's epic breakup speech, on the drive to the restaurant where, until that moment, Nell had been almost certain he was planning to propose.

Or there was always the other, more exciting, more daring, more *fun* woman that Paul had left her for.

She'd probably told loads of people since Paul had dumped Nell for her on Friday night.

While Nell hadn't quite managed to tell anyone yet. She'd spent the weekend holed up in her tiny flat—the one she used to share with Polly, until the business took off and she and Fred bought their gorgeous house together. She'd stress baked, and watched old episodes of calming shows about country life, where the biggest drama involved whether someone cheated to win the farm show.

And yes, she'd cried. Just a bit.

But not for too long.

After all, if Paul was after excitement and drama, he was the wrong guy for her. Better to know it now than later—after she'd said yes to that non-existent proposal, for example.

She'd picked Paul *because* he was boring like her. Because he was content to stay home on a Saturday night, rather than checking out the latest, hottest club. Because they agreed on everything and never argued. The last thing Nell wanted from a partner was someone who always disagreed with her. Someone she'd spend her life yelling at then making up with.

She wasn't built for that kind of drama. Not like Polly.

Not like their mother or their father.

Nell had always taken after their grandparents more. They would have approved of Paul, she thought. Until now, anyway.

She made it past the dangers of all the desks, and had almost reached the final, narrower staircase that led to her cramped attic office space—away from all the people, sharing the roof space with the storage area—when she heard someone call her name.

'Nell! We're in here! We need you!' Not just someone. Polly.

And when her twin needed her...well. Nell went running. Always had, always would.

She turned and spotted Polly waving at her from the open doorway of the small meeting room they preferred to use for their Core of Four meetings—the term they used for the four of them as owners. And yes, there was Fred, sitting in his customary chair next to where Polly had spread her files and her empty coffee cups across the polished wood of the conference table. And there was Alex too, standing by the window looking out over the leafy street below, his dark russet hair glowing in the weak sun, his hands on his hips, as if reminding them all he had far more interesting and exciting places to be. Because he always did. Always had, even back at university.

Alex McLeod came from money. And land. And possibly some obscure Scottish title.

None of them were under any illusion that he'd agreed to come in on the business for any reason other than his own amusement. He didn't need the income the way normal people did—although Nell supposed it gave him a little petty cash for his regular insane adventures.

She preferred to pay her mortgage and add to her pension, but each to their own.

Fred didn't need the money either, but he did it because this company was Polly's dream, so that was different.

And anyway, she didn't like to spend too much time thinking about Alex. She'd done enough of that in university, and she knew that got her nothing except disappointment. Or embarrassment, and having to avoid each other for one very awkward term, until things had settled down again.

Yes, it was a good job she'd got anything to do with Alex out of her system back in second year. Otherwise working with him would be excruciating.

As it was, she could just avoid him as much as possible, and put a mental lock on that one night where things might have been different.

Nell stepped into the meeting room, sat down in her usual seat and smiled at Fred across the table. Polly, practically vibrating with something—coffee or excitement, Nell wasn't sure—leaned against the back of Fred's chair, hands on his shoulders, as Alex finally deigned to turn around and give them his attention.

'We've got some big news,' Polly said, grinning. 'We're getting married! And we want Here & Now to arrange the biggest, most amazing wedding ever!'

* * *

Alex stared blankly at his best friends and tried to make sense of what they were saying.

'Married. Like…*married* married?' Okay, that didn't even make sense in his own head, and from the derisory look Nell was giving him, he'd just given her another reason to think he was a total waste of space.

He wasn't entirely clear on what her initial reasons for that conclusion were, but he was one hundred per cent sure that she'd made it—probably within the first hour of meeting him at university.

As he recalled, he'd been pretty drunk. That might explain some of it.

And if there had been a time where he thought he might have convinced her otherwise—a time when she might even have *liked* him a little bit…well, that was long past too. He'd ruined that one nice and neatly back in their second year.

But today wasn't a time for dwelling on Nell. Today was about her sister and his best friend.

'Congratulations,' he added, belatedly stepping forward to hug Polly, and clap Fred on the shoulder. 'That's amazing news.'

'It really, really is.' Nell was on her feet too, pulling her twin into a tighter, closer hug than the one he'd given her. 'You'll be settled and together for ever.'

It was easy to forget that Nell and Polly were twins sometimes—they were so different as people. But seeing them with their heads pressed together, matching grins on their faces, Alex was struck afresh by how alike they really looked. Same long dark hair. Same bright blue eyes. Same slender shape and same long fingers clasped together now.

Nell had a dimple in her left cheek that Polly lacked—a dimple Alex had seen but rarely, given how little she smiled in his presence—but otherwise they were identical.

Well, apart from the clothes. There was never any confusion in the office about which twin a staff member was talking to. If she was wearing black, perhaps the odd shade of beige, it was Nell. If there was colour—from a brightly hued silk scarf around her neck to neon-pink high heels, and everything in between—it was definitely Polly.

But now he looked closer, the colours and the dimples weren't the only difference. There was something in the eyes. Polly's held unbridled joy, whereas Nell's…

She was sad. Sad that her sister was getting married? That didn't make any sense.

'So I'm thinking we can really showcase everything we can do through the wedding.' Polly disentangled herself from her sister's arms, settled into her seat and flipped open the first of the folders she'd spread across the table.

Alex laughed. 'We don't even get the engagement story first? Just straight to business?'

Polly rolled her eyes. 'Don't pretend you want all the gory details, Alex. We all know you're fundamentally against the very institution of marriage, but I'm afraid you're going to have to pretend you think it's a good idea for at least a few months, if you're going to be Fred's best man.'

'Which I haven't actually asked him yet, darling,' Fred pointed out sanguinely. It took a lot to ruffle Fred. More than one person in the past—from teachers to women to business acquaintances—had taken that to mean that he didn't care about anything. But Alex knew better than that.

When Fred set his mind on something there wasn't anything in the world that would stop him. He'd fallen in love with Polly the first time he saw her at university, and that had been it for him. He'd never hassled or harassed her, or tried to make her feel guilty for going out with other men. He'd just patiently waited until she came to see the world from his point of view, and realised they were meant to be together.

And now they were getting married.

'Who else would you ask to be best man?' Alex dropped into the fourth chair at the table. 'Nobody else has put up with you for the last twenty-odd years, have they?' Since the day they'd met at boarding school, seven years old and terrified but refusing to show it. 'Anyway, I'm not against marriage *in principle.*'

'Just not for you, right?' Nell's tone was acerbic. Whenever they were all in the same place, Alex couldn't help but feel that Nell thought she saw every inch of his soul and found it sorely lacking.

'Do you really think I'd be an asset to the marriage market?' Alex asked, eyebrows raised, and tried not to be insulted when Polly snorted with laughter.

It *wasn't* that he was against marriage. He truly believed, for instance, that Fred and Polly would have a wonderful marriage. They complemented each other so well, for a start.

People thought Polly was flighty, but she was just creative. Fred helped her focus her ideas.

And yes, they'd had that whole on-again, off-again thing going on at university, and he'd been party to some ear-splitting arguments between them over the years. But they always made up. Always talked it through and came back together, stronger than before.

He'd had to listen to enough of the aftermath, through shared walls, to know that the arguments weren't *all* bad either. They both definitely enjoyed the making up, anyway.

But for him? He'd thought he'd found love once, but… well. He'd been wrong.

These days, he found fun, excitement and adventure a lot more fulfilling than a bittersweet search for an emotion that might never happen for him. Not everyone found their happy-ever-after. And despite what people—Nell in particular—thought, he wasn't so full of himself to assume he'd be one of the lucky ones, riding off into the sunset with his One True Love.

But that didn't mean he wasn't thrilled to be giving two of his best friends that send-off.

Best man. He'd never been one before. He assumed it came with a bucketload of responsibilities, though—those sorts of titles always did. And the one thing he *did* know about the job of being best man was that he got to flirt with the bridesmaids, right?

Bridesmaids. Wait.

'I assume the lovely Nell will be acting as Maid of Honour opposite me?' he said, the pieces starting to fall into place. Oh, she was going to hate that.

'Of course,' Polly replied. 'Who else would I choose?'

'Right,' Nell said faintly. Alex assumed she was realising the same thing he was. That it was going to be a long, and very busy, few months before the wedding—and they were going to have to spend a lot of time together.

More time than they'd ever spent together since that second year at university, and a night that had changed their friendship for ever.

No wonder Nell looked so horrified.

CHAPTER TWO

NELL'S HEAD WHIRLED with all the ways her world had shifted over the last few days.

Not only was she *not* getting married, Polly was. And Nell was over the moon for her—really, really, she was. Marriage would be good for Polly and Fred, she was sure of it. They loved each other deeply, and perhaps the commitment would help them move past the cycle of arguing and making up they seemed to have fallen into.

Polly always laughed when Nell worried about it. She said that real love needed passion, and she didn't want someone who just said yes to her all the time. Besides, making up was the best part.

But that didn't stop the clenching fear Nell felt in her stomach every time Polly appeared on her doorstep announcing that she couldn't bear to be in the same room as Fred for another moment, so they were having a girls' night.

Their own parents had never managed to get married at all—had barely even lived together. But their mother had married—or almost married—enough times since for Nell to know that a ring and a piece of paper never solved anything.

It would be different for Polly and Fred, though. Because, under it all, they loved each other more than they wanted the drama of the fights and the making up. She was sure of it.

She hoped.

And she was going to be Polly's maid of honour. What did that even entail?

Nell felt a small surge of panic at the idea that she might have to organise a hen do.

Not to mention spending more time with the best man.

Look how that ended up last time we tried it.

It had been years, and she still remembered the heat of her embarrassment and the tightness in her chest in that moment. How close they'd been...and how fast Alex had pulled away from her as the door opened.

Don't think about it. He probably doesn't even remember that night.

Her twin sister didn't seem to notice her reticence. Polly bounced a little in her chair as she turned to Nell. 'I want the whole thing to be a total festival of romance! Like, everything for couples. I'm thinking a fairground with a tunnel of love for the engagement party!'

'Engagement party?' Nell said faintly. 'And you'll want me to—'

'Oh, no!' Polly laughed, tinkling and high and only faintly insulting. 'Don't worry, I'm not expecting you and Alex to do any of the organising or anything. Not when I've got a whole team out there who can do this sort of thing standing on their heads!'

'We'll put the whole thing—engagement party, hen and stag dos, and the wedding week itself—through as a project for the company, just like we were normal clients,' Fred explained.

'That's why I want the couple theme,' Polly added. 'It'll be such a great advert for all the wonderful kinds of events we can provide.'

The couple theme. Right. Nell had been trying to avoid that part.

'About the couple theme...'

'I was thinking maybe all our guests could dress up as famous couples from history or film or whatever for the joint hen and stag do,' Polly burst out. 'Won't that be the most fun?'

'I'm sure it will,' Nell said calmly. 'But, uh, what about people who don't have another half to invite?'

'Worrying about me, Nell?' Alex tilted his chair back on two legs as he gave her a lazy smile, and Nell scowled back at him. 'I'm sure I can find *someone* to be my plus one.'

'I'm sure you can too, but—' Nell started, only for Polly to cut her off.

'Not just anybody, though,' she told Alex sternly. 'If they're going to be in my wedding photos for all time as the best man's date, I want it to be someone who will actually still be in our lives in six months' time. Otherwise you can pair up with our mother for the occasion, assuming she hasn't remarried already by then.'

Alex looked less pleased at that idea. 'I'm not dating your mother.'

Polly rolled her eyes. 'Of course not. I just meant... oh, you know what I meant.'

'Seldom, if ever,' Alex muttered, and Nell decided it was time to reclaim control of this conversation.

'I wasn't actually talking about Alex,' she said. 'I was talking about me.'

Alex, Fred and Polly all turned to stare at her.

'But you'll be going with Paul,' Polly said, eyes wide with incomprehension.

'Not so much.'

It took pathetically little time to explain what had happened that weekend. Polly's eyes welled up as she threw her arms around Nell, and Nell tried to wriggle out of them.

'I'm fine, really,' she insisted, even if she wasn't completely. She didn't want anyone—not even Polly, and especially not Alex—feeling sorry for her. 'Just…not going to have a partner for your couple-fest.'

To her credit, Polly didn't even suggest that *Nell* partner with their mother. Probably because she knew what a disaster that would be. Chalk and cheese, her grandmother had called them. Her grandfather had used rather stronger terms.

Neither of them had spoken to Nell and Polly's mother in almost a decade, by the time they died.

Polly clapped her hands together, eyes suddenly shining with excitement again. 'No, this is perfect!'

Fred winced at his fiancée's choice of words. 'Maybe not perfect, Pol.'

'Well, no, obviously not *perfect,* perfect. But still pretty great!' Polly grabbed Alex's hand across the table, then reached out for Nell's.

No. No, no, no. Nell could see exactly where this was going, and she didn't like it one bit. She tried to resist her twin's grip, but it was almost unbreakable when Polly really wanted something.

And it looked like she *really* wanted her couples themed wedding.

I always knew Polly would be a Bridezilla. I just figured it would have more to do with the right shade of flowers or matching dresses than messing with my love life.

'You and Alex can just pair up for all the events!' Polly said gleefully, and Nell's heart finished its long, slow drop towards her shoes. 'That way, he can't bring some date whose name he doesn't even know, and you won't be *alone.*'

The stress she put on the last word made it sound like a fate worse than death.

But it wasn't, Nell knew. It was far, far worse to be with the wrong person than alone.

And Alex McLeod was most definitely the wrong person. She'd learned that years ago.

She couldn't find a nicer way to say it. Couldn't mind Alex's feelings. Couldn't even keep the words in.

'Not a chance in hell,' Nell blurted, too loud and too fast, and across the table Alex laughed at her.

Oh, yes. This really was the perfect day.

'Nell!' Polly sounded genuinely offended on his behalf, which Alex supposed he should be grateful for. But really, it was kind of a ridiculous idea.

'Polly, Nell and I are not going to start dating just to make your wedding pleasingly symmetrical,' he said, as drily as he could manage under the circumstances.

Of course he and Nell weren't going to couple up. If that had ever been going to happen, it would have done so back at university, during that week in second year when they'd…connected. When it had almost felt like there'd been a chance for them. Something between them worth exploring.

But it *hadn't* happened, and that was for the best, given how their lives had turned out, the people they'd grown into. They were polar opposites. Of *course* they weren't going to get together now.

Did Nell really need to sound *quite* so repulsed by the idea, though?

Polly rolled her eyes. 'I'm not suggesting that either of you are likely to fall madly in love with each other in the three months it's going to take to plan this wedding—'

'Three months?' Nell interjected. 'Don't most weddings take, well, a year or more to plan?'

Her twin gave her a withering look. Alex was glad he wasn't the only person who got that one directed at him. 'We're professionals, Nell. And I have some strings I can pull with suppliers and venues.'

'Still, three months…' Nell shook her head, her long dark hair slipping over her shoulders. Alex suspected she was doing calculations in her head—of how much extra they'd pay for the short notice, or the overtime it was going to take.

Even if this was a Here & Now project, Nell would still be handling the money side. His expertise would only be needed for checking contracts—and maybe writing a prenup, if Fred and Polly had any sense. Which, in his experience, they didn't. Not when it came to love.

'The point is, neither of you are likely to find *anyone* to fall madly in love with in the next three months,' Polly went on. 'But I don't want either of you bringing just anybody to my wedding. Apart from anything else, we're planning on a destination wedding out in the Seychelles. If you fall out with your date there it's a long way home.'

She was looking directly at Alex as she said it and he

knew, without having to ask, that she was remembering the time he'd brought a girl he'd just met to their New Year's Eve celebration at some cottage in the hills they'd hired, and then she'd dumped him just before midnight but they'd had to spend the new year together anyway, because they were in the middle of nowhere and everyone was over the alcohol limit for driving.

Yeah, maybe she had a point. He really didn't want to go through that again.

'And you want people who are still in your life in the photos,' Nell said wearily. 'I get that. But I'm pretty sure there's another way round this.'

Lots, probably, Alex figured. But once Polly had got a path set in her mind it was hard to lead her off it. One of the ways she and Fred were alike, he supposed.

God help them all when they picked different paths. The showdowns were epic.

'Three months is plenty of time to find love,' Alex said definitively, even though he had no real idea if it was true. Nell clearly didn't want to spend any more time with him than she had to, and he wasn't exactly keen either. If he wanted to be a disappointment to people, he'd go home and visit his parents more often.

But they were going to have to work together to get out of this. Fortunately, Nell picked up on his theme instantly. 'Some people get engaged within three months. Or even married.'

'And haven't you ever heard of love at first sight?' Alex added.

'Exactly!' Nell said, then frowned. 'Wait...'

'Nell doesn't believe in love at first sight,' Polly said smugly.

'Three months isn't first sight, though,' Fred said thoughtfully. 'I mean, they're not wrong. I fell in love with you faster than that. It just took you a little longer to realise what I already knew.'

Polly rolled her eyes. 'Fine. Here's the deal. Either the two of you pair up for the wedding events, or you *both* find another partner to bring—but no fake dates, and nobody you've just met. It doesn't have to be your forever person—I'm not expecting miracles. But it has to be someone you genuinely believe you have a chance with. Okay?'

Alex and Nell exchanged a quick glance, then nodded. But something about the look in Polly's eye told Alex he was being set up here, even if he wasn't entirely sure what for. She said she didn't expect miracles, but was this Polly's way of trying to get them both as coupled up and settled down as she and Fred were?

Surely she knew him better than that by now? Alex was not the settling kind.

He knew how miserable that could make a man, after all.

'And if you don't have anyone by the time the hen and stag dos are done and dusted, you're coming together,' Polly finished. 'Now, onto more important things. Like planning my wedding! Let's get the whole team in here and share the news!'

CHAPTER THREE

THE STAFF, it seemed, already knew exactly what was going on—because they exploded into the too-small meeting room with trays of Buck's Fizz and the champagne bottle piñatas Nell had spotted before. She kept herself pressed against the wall as the excitement filled the room to bursting point. She had no idea how news had got around so fast, only that it always did at Here & Now.

Fred fired up a slideshow on the big screen, filled with Polly's wedding mood boards, and it was clear by the way the team started shouting out possible ideas that this was going to go on awhile. The brainstorming section of a new project was always the loudest and most enthusiastic part of the process.

Nell was just wondering if she could escape up the stairs to her quiet attic office when she felt a tug on her arm.

'You know, I'm thinking we're surplus to requirements here right now,' Alex murmured, leaning close enough to her ear that she could feel his breath against her skin. She forced herself to repress a shiver at the sensation. 'What do you say we go have a strategy session of our own, best man to maid of honour?'

'Can it be somewhere with coffee?' Nell asked. The

cup she'd bought on her way in was long gone, and she could already tell this day was going to require a lot of caffeine.

'Most definitely.'

Neither Polly or Fred seemed to notice as they slipped out of the meeting room and hurried down the stairs. Nell felt a pang of guilt about leaving the wedding planning session, but only a small one. Polly knew exactly what she wanted, and she had assembled the right team to make it happen, exactly to her specifications. Other than handling the financial and legal aspects, she and Alex were surplus to requirements. And right now it was all about the ideas. Polly would call them in when they got down to the details.

Outside, the spring morning was warm—one of the first truly warm days of the year. Nell was glad she'd left her coat in the meeting room; she wouldn't need it. Or her laptop or files, she supposed—all of which were tucked under the table back at the office. All she had with her was her phone, and it felt strange to be so unencumbered on a work day. Like she was playing hooky from school—not that she'd ever actually done that. But she imagined the feeling was much the same. She hoped she didn't have any video meetings this morning that she'd forgotten about…

She pulled her calendar up on her phone to check, and Alex rolled his eyes.

'Put that thing away and live dangerously with me for a moment, would you?'

'I thought that was exactly what we were strategising to avoid,' Nell replied archly.

'Good point,' Alex said. 'Check away.'

They strolled along the leafy Mayfair street until they reached Hyde Park, pausing at the first coffee stand they came to. Alex bought their drinks, and Nell sipped at hers as they walked.

'Straight black Americano,' she said, surprised. He hadn't asked for her order. 'How did you know?'

'I do notice some things,' he replied. 'And besides. You're a straight black coffee kind of woman.'

'Boring, you mean.' It wasn't as if she didn't know how he felt about her. Had known for plenty of years now.

'No-nonsense,' he countered. 'Now. What the hell is going on with Polly and this couples retreat of a wedding idea?'

Nell sighed. 'I have no idea.' Except that wasn't *entirely* true. She'd been Polly's closest companion and confidante their whole lives—well, until Fred, anyway. She knew how her sister's mind worked. 'I suspect it's that she's happy, and she wants everyone else she loves to have the same happiness.'

'And so she's trying to get us both to couple up. With each other.' Alex sounded sceptical, which was fair enough. They weren't exactly an obvious pairing.

Even if Polly didn't know that they'd already tried and failed before.

'Or with anyone.' She shrugged. 'It's more of an emotional instinct with her, rather than a conscious decision.' That was the way Polly always did everything—on instinct, just like their mother. While Nell, on the other hand, would spend weeks working out the pros and cons, weighing up her options, before making the safest choice.

'Well, I suppose it's nice that she wants us to be happy.'

The doubt in his voice suggested otherwise, but Nell didn't call him on it.

'So all we really need to do is show her that we *are* happy, and she'll leave us alone.' Put like that, it didn't seem so impossible.

'And have dates for her couples-only wedding events,' Alex pointed out. Okay, that part was a little harder.

They walked through the park in silence for a minute, each lost in their own thoughts as they drank their coffee.

'*Are* you happy?' Alex asked suddenly.

Nell, halfway through a sip, spluttered coffee down her top. Thank goodness her signature black sweater didn't show it.

For a moment he'd sounded the way he had during that week in second year, just after Fred and Polly had finally got together and the two of them were left out in the cold. They'd talked—really talked—about things other than her sister and his best friend for the first time. And she'd believed, for a short while, that maybe he was really interested in what she had to say.

One week where they'd connected as human beings. And one night where the whole idea of them as friends— or more—had been smashed to pieces.

It was too late to resurrect that fledgeling friendship now, surely?

'Sorry.' Alex fished a handkerchief—a real, old-fashioned cotton one—from his pocket and handed it to her. 'I just meant…you got dumped this weekend. It would be perfectly normal not to be happy.'

'I did not get dumped,' Nell lied. 'We just realised we wanted different things out of life, so agreed to go our separate ways.' Paul wanted excitement and drama, and she wanted anything but. Easy decision, really.

The fact he'd already fallen in love with another woman was really beside the point when you looked at it that way.

From the pitying look Alex was giving her, she suspected he was seeing it the more traditional way.

'Fine,' she said. 'I got dumped. But it was honestly all for the best. And it definitely doesn't mean I need you to take me to the wedding as a pity date, okay?'

'I kind of got that from your reaction to the suggestion. What was it again? Oh, yes.' He put on a voice that didn't sound a bit like her. '"Not a chance in hell." Pretty clear.'

'Oh, like you'd want to go with me anyway,' Nell replied. 'I'd be your worst nightmare as a date.'

Pausing on the path, Alex looked her up and down, then shrugged. 'I don't see why. You're intelligent, funny when you don't think people are listening, and you're objectively gorgeous. I could do worse.'

Nell ignored the way her heart thumped twice at 'objectively gorgeous'. Yes, she looked exactly like Polly, so she knew she didn't look bad or anything. But where Polly wore her looks with charm and grace and smiles, Nell…didn't. *Objectively* was the key word here.

On paper, she was a catch. In practice…

She already knew how he reacted to the idea of kissing her in practice.

That night lived in infamy in her memory. If she concentrated, she was right back there in his university bedroom, sitting beside Alex on the bed after a week of getting to know each other as more than extensions of Fred and Polly. Maybe they hadn't shared all their deepest secrets, but they'd connected in a way she'd never expected to.

And then they'd connected in another way. Tipsy and relaxed, they'd kissed and kissed, and she'd started to think for the first time that this could be more... Until the door had opened and Fred and a few of his other mates had yelled something about needing his help, calling for him to join them—and Alex had pulled away fast, darting to the door before they saw him with her. Because Alex McLeod didn't kiss boring, sensible girls like Nell Andrews.

Then he was gone, the door slamming behind him. She'd waited briefly, then headed back to her own room, telling herself it was all for the best. Alex McLeod was not a good fit for the life she wanted to lead, anyway. And they'd never mentioned the kiss again.

'Doesn't matter,' she said, knowing exactly how to shut this conversation down. 'You'd never date me, because I'm too boring for you.' End of story.

Except, to her surprise, this time it wasn't.

Boring?

Alex steered them towards the nearest bench and sat down beside her, surveying her in light of her words. From the shiny sleek black hair that flowed over her shoulders, to the intelligence in the light blue eyes behind her tortoiseshell glasses, down over her signature black sweater and trousers, to her polished black heeled boots. Nell, for her part, sipped at her coffee and awaited his judgement.

But this wasn't about her looks, or the person she presented to the world, was it?

It was about who she believed she was, inside.

'You *want* to be boring,' he realised suddenly. 'You are actively trying to be boring.'

Her gaze slid away from his and she shrugged, and the boring black sweater slipped from her shoulder—just an inch or two, before she yanked it back up—but long enough to give him a flash of a bright pink bra strap.

And a memory. Of walking into Polly's and Nell's university rooms looking for Fred, and finding Nell in a tired old bathrobe that wasn't tied quite tightly enough to hide the teal and pink leopard print lingerie she was wearing under it.

He'd thought it was Polly, until she'd walked in arm in arm with Fred. Because surely *Polly* was the twin who'd wear the daring lingerie, while Nell would wear sensible cotton basics.

But apparently not. And apparently there was still some of that girl inside her, even now.

The girl who'd once kissed him like the world was ending. Like he could fall into her and never come out.

Who'd then run away and ignored him afterwards, and pretended it had never happened.

No, Nell wasn't boring. She was a veritable puzzle box he wasn't sure he'd ever understand.

Maybe this wedding was the universe giving him a chance to do just that.

'I'm not trying to be anything,' Nell said, but he could hear the lie in her voice. 'This is just who I am.'

'Maybe who you are isn't as boring as you think.'

Oh, not because of whatever she wore underneath her perma-black outfits—or because of any years-ago memory of one drunken night at university. But because he saw that spark in her eye whenever a staff member said something ridiculous, and he knew she wanted to mock it but didn't. He'd seen her, for years now, standing on the sidelines of life, never quite giving herself to it—but he could tell there was a part of her that wanted to.

He'd spent enough time with her ex, Paul, at events over the past couple of years to have been baffled as to what she saw in him. There was no connection between them, the way there was between Fred and Polly—an intuitive link that even an outsider could see. No obvious chemistry either, from the dry hello or goodbye kisses he'd witnessed. And nothing in Paul's less than sparkling conversation or company to explain it either.

He was good enough looking, Alex supposed, but that had never seemed to be what mattered most to Nell anyway.

Even Polly had been at a loss to explain the relationship, but they'd been together for two full years, so there must have been something. She must have loved him, he supposed.

Now he was out of the picture, would she be willing to let that not at all boring side out?

Alex wasn't sure.

So he went back to the only thing he *was* certain about.

'So, this wedding. If we don't want to go together, we're going to have to find other dates.'

Nell nodded. 'I was thinking about this. They really don't have to be our forever person or whatever, do they?'

'I don't think I even *want* a forever person, let alone to have to try and find one in three months just to look good in some photos.' Alex had always heard that planning a wedding did something to a person's logic faculties, but Polly already seemed to be taking it to a new level.

If he didn't know how madly in love Polly and Fred really were, he'd be thinking this was all a publicity stunt for the company. Not that they needed it.

'All we really need to do is find plausible dates. People they believe we could really fall for,' Nell went on. 'I mean, if she's worried about the photos we could just appear together in those, right?'

'Sure,' Alex said with a shrug. 'If you're sure you can put up with standing next to me long enough for a camera shutter to close a few times.'

Nell elbowed him lightly in the stomach. 'You're taking this way too personally.'

'You not wanting to date me? Why would that be personal?'

'You don't want to date me either,' she pointed out, which was hard to argue with.

'I don't like being told who to date,' he said. 'And it's not like I couldn't find my own date for a wedding.'

'So we'll do just that.' Nell gave him a mischievous smile that made him think of leopard print lingerie again. 'Operation Wedding Date.'

'We're *naming* it now?'

'Whatever it takes to get it done.'

Alex sighed. 'Fine. So we both find another date to take to this wedding as fast as possible—'

'One that fits with Polly's rules,' Nell broke in. 'She'll know if it's a fake date or whatever. I don't know how, but she will. She *always* knows.'

He knew Polly well enough not to argue that one. Her

intuition was scary sometimes. 'A *real* date, then. Someone she will believe could be the real thing for us.'

Maybe he even would be, for Nell. There had to be someone out there better for her than Paul, anyway. Perhaps this wedding would give her the push she needed to find him.

Because Alex was almost sure that Nell was anything but boring, and she needed a partner who brought that out in her.

It just wasn't going to be Alex. That ship had sailed years ago. And maybe she wasn't boring, but Nell didn't want the kind of life he led. And he didn't want any life that meant succumbing to the sort of misery his parents had made of marriage.

'Exactly.' Nell nodded, and stuck out her hand. 'Let's do this, then.'

Placing his coffee cup down on the bench, he took her hand and shook it.

Operation Wedding Date was a go.

CHAPTER FOUR

AGREEING TO OPERATION WEDDING DATE in principle was all very well, but when it came to actually putting it into practice Nell found it easier to, well, not.

It wasn't like her sister was going to uninvite her to the wedding if she didn't have a satisfactory date, she reasoned. Plus, if she found one too soon she'd have to date him for the whole three months until the wedding, and she wasn't sure she was ready for that, so soon after Paul's betrayal.

Trusting a man enough to take him to a wedding was one thing. Trusting him enough to actually date him for real, and imagine a future together…that was going to take a little longer.

So she pushed it to the back of her mind for the next week, and concentrated on the business side of making the wedding happen at all—not to mention the finances for all their other projects at Here & Now.

As a strategy, procrastination was serving her well until she found herself round at Polly and Fred's lovely townhouse for dinner the following weekend. She was happily sitting on the sofa with a glass of wine, leafing through one of Polly's many bridal magazines, when her sister launched her attack.

'So, how is the date-finding mission going?' Polly asked, plonking herself down on the sofa beside Nell, her laptop tucked under her arm.

Nell narrowed her eyes. The laptop was suspicious.

'I've got plenty of time,' she said. 'I don't want to just rush into something. You were very clear that you only want me to bring someone I think I could have a future with, after all.'

Using Polly's own arguments against her was the only way to ever win in a disagreement with her twin, in Nell's extensive experience.

'You're right.' Polly flipped open her computer on her lap, and angled the screen towards Nell. 'You need someone who is totally compatible with you from the start. Which is why I've signed you up to this new dating website one of our clients has developed. It has the greatest accuracy on personal traits and beliefs ever! Fred and I road tested it for them, and it matched us up instantly.'

'Which is more than Polly managed,' Fred threw in from the kitchen, where he was cooking them all dinner.

'You…signed me up?' Nell stared at the screen, and the happy smiling couple on it. They didn't look anything like the way she felt in a relationship. Apart from anything else, they were apparently about to dive off a cliff together.

Without helmets. Or a safety rope. Or any information about the depth of the water below, or possible rocks awaiting them.

'I'm not sure this is my kind of dating site.' She pushed the computer back towards Polly.

Polly pushed it back again. 'Of course it is. It's for everybody! It says right here at the top, see?'

What it actually said was, *There's somebody out there for everybody!* The *Even you, you loser,* was unwritten but still clear.

Nell sighed. 'You already signed me up. Did you do all the questionnaires and things as well?'

'Of course.' Polly grinned. 'You always say I know you better than yourself.'

This was true. But it didn't stop Nell feeling… What *was* she feeling? As if her whole personality and life had been decided for her by some test on a dating site. As if her existence was…static. Unchanging and unchangeable.

Which was fine, really. Nell had decided who she wanted to be a long time ago, and could summarise it easily enough. *Not my mother.*

Not the woman who flitted around the world from one adventure, one lover—one *drama*—to another, leaving her daughters behind with grandparents who resented them. Not the woman who always, always had to be the centre of attention. Who used her beauty and her charm and her vibrancy to make the world love her, even as she used it to her own ends.

Polly had got the best parts of Madeline Andrews. Not just her beauty and her charm, but her openness. Combined with an authenticity and empathy that their mother had never shown, Polly just drew people in and made them love her. If she liked being the centre of attention sometimes, or lived her life with flair and drama, that was okay—because she'd be just as likely to make someone else the centre of things, and use her powers of persuasion and partying for others too.

Maybe that was why nobody was objecting to the over-the-top wedding celebrations they had planned.

But Nell…she'd inherited her mother's looks too, but not the charm to go with them. She had the calculating brain, the way to look at any situation and figure out how to use it to her advantage. She just didn't want to use it that way, so she kept it for spreadsheets and figures.

She didn't want to be the centre of anything. She didn't want a life filled with drama.

She wanted the safety and security that Madeline had never, ever been able to offer them.

'You are actively trying to be boring,' Alex had said. And maybe he was right.

But what was so wrong with that?

She scrolled down the screen to the answers Polly had given for her. In many ways, they were spot-on—her twin really did know her better than she knew herself. But every few questions she came across an answer that jarred.

'My ideal date is a cruise along the Seine?' Nell raised her eyebrows at her sister.

Polly shrugged. 'Paris is romantic.'

'And I'd love to go for dinner at a rooftop restaurant? You do remember I'm afraid of heights?'

'You're afraid of everything,' Polly said, not unkindly. 'But in love sometimes you have to take a chance. Jump off that cliff, so to speak.'

'What if I don't want to?'

'Then you'll have to come to my wedding with Alex,' Polly said.

'Right.' The only thing worse than going on a series of set up dates through a dating site had to be attending the wedding of the year as Alex McLeod's pity date, knowing that everyone else there knew he was only taking her because no one else would.

That was not happening.

Polly obviously read her decision on her face because she said, 'Okay, then. Let's look through these matches. I want you booked on a date every weekend between now and the hen night before Fred finishes cooking the curry. All right?'

And, despite all her many, many reservations, Nell nodded.

It wasn't that Alex didn't want to find a date for Polly and Fred's wedding, it was just that there was no real rush. Three months wasn't long to find someone he'd actually plan to spend the rest of his life with—three years wasn't long enough for that. Or nearly thirty, going on present evidence.

But to find someone compatible enough that he could date them for the couple of weeks between the stag do and the wedding? No problem. He and Nell would pair up for the photos, Polly would be too busy getting married to really care, and everything would be fine.

Really, there was no rush at all. And that was why he wasn't rushing.

And why he was surprised that Fred brought it up at all the weekend following the engagement announcement.

He and Fred had a standing once a month Sunday meet-up. Some months they caught a rugby match, some they met old friends at the pub, and some they drove out of the city and went rock-climbing. This month was a rock-climbing month.

Fred waited until they'd almost reached the peak of the ledge they were climbing before he mentioned it.

'So, do you have a date for the wedding yet?'

Alex, concentrating on getting his next hand hold, and bringing his leg up behind him safely, ground out a succinct, 'No.'

'Time's getting short.' Fred swung himself up over the ledge to sit at the top. He'd been practising, probably at that indoor wall not far from the office. Alex should do that too, except he didn't want to. He liked climbing outdoors, where the risk and danger felt real, far more than indoors with all the safety measures and security indoor walls required.

'There's three months to go.'

'Less now,' Fred said. 'And, well, Polly's getting anxious.'

Ah, so that explained it. *Polly* was worked up about it, which meant Fred had to be bothered too, or she'd take her ire out on him. If he talked to Alex, though, she could transfer all that annoyance to him and spare her fiancé.

Fantastic. So he was the fall guy.

Not a thought he wanted to be having as he hung from a rock ledge, really quite far up off the ground.

He swung himself up behind Fred, panting a little as he sat beside him.

God, he loved this spot. Far enough away from the city that he felt in another world. As much as he loved London's cut and thrust and busy, busy, busy—and, he had to admit, he really loved its restaurants and other entertainments—there was something about being out in the country. About breathing in clear air, watching the clouds pass over trees and hills rather than skyscrapers. About hearing the sounds of nature rather than cars and cell phones.

'So?' Fred asked again, and Alex revised his view of being out in the middle of nowhere.

If he was in London, having this conversation on his mobile, he could duck into the tube and lose Fred instantly. Instead, here he was, actually having to answer questions about his love life.

'I haven't given the matter much thought just yet,' he replied. 'Not everyone looks at a woman and knows she'll be the love of his life, you realise.'

Fred and Polly's story was one of a kind—almost like a movie romance. And Alex had loved watching it, in a way he never liked the *actual* romcoms Polly sometimes insisted on for movie night.

They complemented each other in ways Alex had never really imagined people could. His own experience of marriage and relationships came mostly from his parents' marriage, and he had only come to realise as an adult that that really wasn't typical.

His parents would argue and storm out and refuse to speak for months, his mother relocating to one of their other houses—often with another, younger lover his father pretended not to know about—before returning in a sea of apologies and gifts, usually when she'd run out of spending money. They'd make up—loudly and often in front of guests—before retiring to the bedroom for a day or two. And then it would all start again…

When Fred and Polly had an argument, they just kept going. They argued until they were each blue in the face—but they'd come to see each other's point of view in the end, even if they never actually agreed with it. Eventually, they'd come to a compromise.

And nobody ever left—at least, not for more than a

night, when Polly decided an argument was stupid and she needed a girls' night, and Fred called Alex over to drink beer and not talk about it. Then, in the morning, Polly would be back, and it would be over.

The making up was equally obnoxious, but somehow Alex found he didn't mind so much, when it was them.

Now, sitting on a rock face miles away from his fiancée, Fred sighed. 'Look, you know I don't care about this. You want to be alone for ever, that's fine by me—you can be sad Uncle Alex to my kids one day.'

'Or fun Uncle Alex who doesn't have to worry about the responsibilities of kids or a spouse or anything like that.'

'If you like,' Fred acquiesced easily. 'But for the next three months—just the next three months—you have to pretend like love and romance is the most wonderful thing in the world. For Polly. And for me, because she'll give me hell if you don't.'

Alex sighed. Three months. He could give his friends three months of make-believe, he supposed. 'Don't worry. I'll find a date.'

'You know, Polly set Nell up on this dating site we road-tested for one of our clients,' Fred said. 'She's got dates every weekend between now and the stag and hen party already. I could get you the details, if you wanted.'

Alex wasn't sure what rankled more. The idea that he needed the help of a website to find dates, or that Nell already had a full roster of them. She certainly hadn't wasted any time—which had to be an indication of how much she really didn't want to go to this wedding with him.

For a second, an image of Nell sitting beside him on

that bench, sipping her coffee, as her sweater slipped just enough to give him a glimpse of bright pink bra strap, flashed through his mind—along with a question.

What would it take to get her to give up trying to be boring?

More to the point, what might he discover if she did?

Alex shook the thought away, and pulled out his phone. He'd been there, tried that, and it had been a disaster. Nell had barely spoken to him for the rest of that year, after their kiss, she'd been so horrified by their actions.

'I can get a date any time I want,' he said, scrolling through his contacts. 'Trust me.'

He found the one he was looking for, and hit the call button.

'Hey, Annabel?' he said when she answered. 'Alex McLeod here. We met at that gallery opening last month? I know we talked about getting together sooner, but things have been manic.' He paused to let her say that her life had been the same, and they laughed together at the craziness of London life. They both knew this dance. 'Reason I was calling, I have to fly to New York this weekend for an event, and I wondered if you might like to join me? My treat, of course. Great! I'll send you the flight details as soon as I have them, and arrange a car to the airport. Can't wait.'

He hung up and glanced across at Fred, who didn't look quite as impressed as Alex thought he should.

'See? Easy.'

CHAPTER FIVE

NELL SPENT THE next week alternately panicking about, and trying to think of ways to get out of, the first date the agency had set her up with, on Saturday night. But in the end she decided there was nothing for it but to just go with it and hope for the best. After all, the agency knew what they were doing. Right?

Apparently not.

'It can't have been that bad,' Polly said the following Monday morning, when she cornered her in the office kitchen to hear all about the date.

'It was worse,' Nell replied shortly. 'Now, are you going to let me at the coffee or not?'

Polly moved directly in front of the coffee machine. 'Not until you tell me what happened.'

'You remember that rooftop restaurant idea you put in my profile? I can confirm that it was *not* a good idea.'

Her sister winced. 'Your fear of heights kicked in? I was hoping the romantic atmosphere would distract you.'

'And maybe it would have. If we'd ever got there.' Nell feinted right then darted left, hoping to trick Polly into giving up the caffeine. It didn't work.

Sometimes it really seemed like her twin could read her mind—usually when she didn't want her to. Of course, other times it felt like she didn't understand her at all…

'Are we having the post weekend date chat in here?'

Nell spun around to find Alex lounging against the doorframe behind her. 'Girl talk,' she said shortly. 'Nothing you'd be interested in.'

'Oh, I don't know,' Alex replied. 'After the disaster of a date *I* had this weekend, I'd quite like to hear someone else's tale of woe for a change.'

'You had a bad date too?' It was hard to imagine, really. In her head everything in Alex's life went exactly according to plan. And if it didn't, it was only because a bigger, better, more dramatic adventure had come along.

Alex glanced between her and Polly, obviously taking in the coffee standoff. 'Come on. I'll buy you a coffee and you can tell me all about your weekend.'

Nell considered for a moment. On the one hand, it meant confessing her dating disaster to Alex McLeod. But, on the other, she'd get one over on Polly *and* get coffee.

Put like that, it was a no-brainer.

'Come on, then.'

A short stroll down the road and past the daffodils and crocuses blooming at the edge of the park, and they were back at the same coffee cart they'd stopped at the other day.

'So, what happened?' Alex asked as they waited for their drinks. 'On your date, I mean.'

Nell sighed at the memory. 'When Polly filled in my dating profile, she said that my idea of a really romantic date was dinner in a rooftop restaurant, looking out over the city.'

'Sounds good to me.'

'Then you're obviously not cripplingly afraid of heights.'
He winced. 'Ah. Not ideal.'

They both took their coffees and moved away, almost instinctively, towards the bench they'd occupied last time.

'As it happened, it didn't matter,' Nell went on. 'Because the lift to the top floor broke down halfway up, and we were stuck in it for three hours waiting for the fire brigade to come and break us out.'

Alex spluttered coffee over the path. 'Three hours? In a lift? Wait, aren't you equally not fond of small places?'

'Well remembered,' she said drily. 'A hangover from a childhood game of hide and seek gone very wrong.'

'I suppose at least it gave you and your date time to get to know one another?' Alex said, clearly hunting desperately for some sort of silver lining.

'Not really. Turns out he was claustrophobic too, so we mostly had private breakdowns in our own corners of the lift.' It had been, hands down, the most disastrous date of her life. Not that she had very many to compare it to. But still, it reaffirmed her belief that staying home alone was much safer than 'putting herself out there' as Polly kept insisting she did.

Alex leaned back against the bench, his long legs stretched out in front of him, his face contemplative. 'What?' she asked. 'You've got a look. What're you thinking?'

'A look? Me?' Alex attempted what she assumed he thought an innocent face looked like, and failed miserably. She raised her eyebrows and he gave up. 'Fine. I was just thinking that if I was stuck in a lift with someone I found attractive for three hours on a first date... I'm pretty sure I could find a way to pass the time.'

He meant having sex, Nell realised, heat crawling up her neck. Because in Alex's world, that was the kind of thing that happened. Random sex with a semi-stranger in a broken-down lift, with the fire brigade about to arrive any moment.

It was so far away from her world that the idea hadn't even crossed her mind. And she was pretty sure it hadn't crossed her date's mind either, given the way he'd been whimpering in the corner.

Maybe they should have tried it. It might have distracted them both from their impending breakdowns.

But no. That was the sort of thing that her mother might do. Or Polly and Fred.

Not Nell.

It was…anti-Nell behaviour. And from the smirk on Alex's face he knew that.

Knew it from personal experience too. Although if he'd hung around instead of running off with his mates that night at university, to avoid the humiliation of people knowing he'd been kissing her, who knew what might have happened?

Nothing good, she thought darkly. Well, maybe good in the moment, but not for the long term.

And she wasn't a 'good in the moment' sort of person. They both knew that.

'So what went wrong with your date?' she asked, eager to change the subject.

Alex groaned. 'Trust me, it was way worse than getting stuck in a lift for three hours.'

'Really?' It was hard to imagine *any* date being worse than that one.

'Come on.' He jumped to his feet and dumped his

empty coffee cup in the nearby bin. 'We can enjoy the spring flowers while you mock me for my date from hell.'

Perhaps, Alex had decided, New York had been a little ambitious for his first outing of Operation Wedding Date. But he wasn't the sort of guy to do things by halves, and women loved a big gesture, didn't they?

Like a rooftop restaurant, he supposed.

They'd been unlucky with the lift, but from Nell's expression as she'd told him about it, it didn't sound as if she had any intention of seeing the guy again. There was no coming back from mutual breakdowns on a first date, really.

Still. The part he couldn't get his head around was that the guy had been trapped with *Nell* for three hours and hadn't even got some flirting in. Granted, the claustrophobia probably hadn't helped, but still. Three hours. He'd have definitely tried for a kiss to take her mind off things, or something.

He knew how she kissed, after all.

It made a much better story too.

Far superior to his New York one, anyway.

'So who was she?' Nell asked as they rounded a bed of some purple flowers or another. He'd never really understood gardening, and the seasons came so much earlier down here than they did at home in Scotland, he wouldn't know what to look for when, anyway. 'Blind date? Old friend? An ex?'

'Someone I met at a gallery opening a few weeks ago,' he replied. 'We exchanged numbers at the time and then, well, life got busy, and neither of us called.'

'Until now.'

'Well, Fred was nagging me about getting a date for the wedding. So I gave her a call and asked if she'd like to come to New York with me for the weekend.'

It took him a couple of steps to realise that Nell had stopped walking. 'New York?' she said incredulously when he turned around to find her.

He shrugged. 'It seemed like a good idea at the time.'

'You really don't do things by halves, do you?' Nell shook her head, but started walking again at least. It wasn't quite warm enough just yet to do a lot of standing around.

'I was going anyway,' he explained. 'There was this party... Anyway, it doesn't matter, because we never made it.'

'To the party?'

'To New York.'

'What happened?' Nell's eyes were wide with anticipation, and something about the expression made Alex want to live up to her expectations. To spin a good story—even if the ending was rather pathetic.

He hooked her arm through his and led her around the longer path that would eventually lead them back to the office—just not too quickly. Normally, he was keen to get his work done and clock off for the day to enjoy his free evenings for flirting, friends, partying, or whatever. But, for some reason, today felt like a day to take a longer coffee break with Nell, and work late that evening to make up for it.

Alex decided not to read too much into that feeling.

'So, picture it. It's a Friday night in London, and the rain is lashing down. I pull up outside a Chelsea townhouse in a limo—'

'Because who wants understated on a first date?' Nell interjected.

'Exactly. So I'm in my limo, wearing my best suit, ready to jet off to the city that never sleeps with a beautiful woman on my arm.'

'Because you wouldn't take her if she wasn't beautiful.' There was something in Nell's voice that gave him pause, but he wasn't quite sure what it was. After all, *she* was beautiful. At least he thought so.

'I only meet beautiful women,' he said instead. 'Or maybe I just think all women are beautiful.' That hadn't occurred to him before. But really, it was hard to think of a woman he'd ever met who hadn't had *something* beautiful about her. Never the same things—he wasn't one of those men who had a type and stuck to it with religious fervour. But there was always something.

Like with Nell, it was the waterfall of dark hair over her shoulders, the knowing, mocking eyes behind her glasses, the curved lines of her that ran from her shoulder, in at her waist and back out over her hips...

Okay, maybe Nell had more beauty about her than most women. But every woman had *something*.

'Fine. Carry on.' She didn't sound like she believed him, but since he wasn't sure how to convince her, Alex continued with his story.

'So she stumbles out of her house and the driver grabs her case as I help her into the car, and it's then I realise she is sozzled.'

Nell raised her perfectly arched eyebrows. Another beauty point for her. 'Sozzled? She was drunk?'

'Plastered,' Alex said. 'So I guess that was my first clue things weren't going to go so well.'

'What was your second?' She was looking much more amused by this story now, Alex realised.

'Probably when she raided the limo minibar.'

Nell snorted at that. 'So by the time you got to the airport…'

'About ready to pass out, or throw up on the steward's shoes. Yes.'

'They wouldn't let her on the plane because she was drunk?' Nell guessed.

'Worse.'

It had been excruciating, trying to steer her through the airport. He had access to the first-class lounge, of course, but Alex hadn't really wanted to take her there. So he'd planned to head to the business class one instead, since they were probably more used to that sort of behaviour, he'd reasoned.

In the event, they hadn't even got that far.

'What happened?' Nell pressed.

'We got stopped at security, and when they searched her bags they found some items that are not entirely legal at the best of times, and definitely not supposed to be taken through airport security.' Alex was almost at the point where he could find this whole story funny, he hoped. If nothing else, it was a good tale to tell at dinner parties.

'Drugs?' Nell looked horrified.

Alex didn't blame her. He liked a drink and he liked fun as much as the next person—when the next person wasn't Nell, who really didn't seem that keen on fun at all, in general. But drugs were not something he'd ever found an attractive prospect. He wouldn't give anything that much control over his character or behaviour.

'Apparently.' He sighed. 'So we spent a significant

amount of time with the security team and the police—
because obviously they all thought I'd planted them on
her.' She'd sobered up remarkably quickly to be able to
try and pin the blame on him, really. He'd got lucky in the
end that they'd managed to find nothing against him—
and more against her, including past drugs charges she'd
never mentioned. 'Then eventually they let me go and,
well, I'd missed my flight, obviously. And somehow I
didn't really fancy New York for the weekend any more.'
Or flying anywhere with anyone for a while, really.

'Wow.' Nell stared up at him, eyes wider than ever.
'You know, I think you might be right.'

'Not something I'm used to hearing you say.'

'Yeah, but in this case…your date really *was* worse
than mine.' She smiled impishly up at him and Alex
couldn't help but laugh in response. Nell tugged on his
arm. 'Come on. Time to actually do some work.'

It was only as they turned the last corner back to the
office that he realised sharing disastrous date stories with
Nell was more fun than any date he'd been on recently.

Even ones that didn't end up with a cavity search.

CHAPTER SIX

THE NEXT WEEKEND was Polly and Fred's engagement party. Nell had tried to argue that it really wasn't appropriate to bring a first date to a family event like this, but Polly had overruled her. So Nell put on her first date dress—black, obviously, but with a wrap top and a split skirt that made it significantly more date-like than her usual work dresses—black block-heeled boots and red lipstick, and waited by the door for tonight's date to show up.

And then she waited some more.

When the message belatedly came through, telling her that her date needed to cancel, it was a relief on two fronts. One, she didn't have to go to the party with a stranger. And two, the knowledge that she'd never be able to date someone who was habitually late, anyway. That would just never work.

She grabbed her black suede jacket, her cross-body bag and her phone and headed out solo.

Polly and the team had commandeered—or at least hired—the gardens and ground floor of a London mansion for the party, one they'd used before with great success. Nell hoped they'd got the same caterers in too. Their crab puffs were to die for…

The venue was tucked away off a moderately palatial London street, with plenty of other similarly impressive houses and buildings along the way. On a normal day it would be impossible to guess which one might be set up as an event venue instead of a family home.

Not so tonight.

Tonight, she could hear the music from across the street, and see the lights almost as soon as she stepped out of the nearest station.

Tonight, the place was alive.

She passed the security guard on the gate easily with a smile—possibly they thought she was Polly, or maybe they actually remembered her from previous events. Either worked.

Guests were being shepherded up the steps, past the columns that fronted the entrance, to where both doors were flung open to welcome them in. Inside the marble floored hall, brightly coloured decorations and balls hung from the ceiling and the bannisters of the double staircase, all the way to the huge glass doors which opened up the whole back of the house onto the garden.

Outside, the flashing lights and music were brighter and louder than ever, and the air was filled with laughter and the odd happy scream as people enjoyed the fairground rides and stalls Polly had arranged for the event.

Nell paused at the bar, set up by the open doors, and grabbed a glass of red wine. It was only then she spotted the lit-up signs welcoming them to the Faire l'Amour. Nell stifled a groan at the title, and wondered how many of the guests would be able to accurately translate it—or plug it into a search engine.

Hopefully not too many.

Another one of Polly's little jokes, she supposed. At first glance, it just looked like a Fair of Love, which, combined with the rides and stalls and the occasion, made perfect sense.

But the *actual* translation...

'Interesting name for tonight, isn't it?' Alex's warm voice spoke close to her ear, easily audible even over all the fairground noise.

She swallowed. Of course *he* knew what it really meant.

'Polly's little joke, I imagine.'

'Oh, I'm sure. Fred was always rubbish in French lessons.'

Nell turned towards him, and swallowed at the sight of him in a dark red V-neck jumper and black jeans. He always looked impeccably good in his suits for work, of course, but she'd become immune to that sight over the years.

Seeing him dressed down, but still immaculately, did things to her insides she didn't care to examine.

After all, this was *Alex McLeod.* He'd always been gorgeous. She'd just learned a long time ago that attractiveness wasn't the same as being someone she could like, trust or rely on not to run out on her after they were getting hot and heavy in his bedroom...

'Probably for the best,' she said, and he looked at her in confusion. It took her a second or two to realise that was because he'd been doing the same thing she was—looking her up and down and getting distracted by her appearance, and now the moment for actually responding to his comment had long passed. She jerked her gaze away and cleared her throat. 'That Fred was rubbish at French, I mean. So he won't translate the signs.'

To make love, that was what it meant.

And suddenly Nell couldn't think about anything else.

What would have happened that night at university, if Fred and the others hadn't interrupted them? If Alex hadn't run out—or if she'd waited for him to get back?

If they hadn't both backed away and avoided each other, embarrassed by what had almost happened between them?

Would they have slept together? Would it have been a one night thing? Would they have tried for something more?

They were too different for her to believe it could have ever lasted between them. But still…the curiosity lingered.

Another couple approached the bar, and Alex put his hand at the small of Nell's back as they moved out of the way and into the garden. He pulled it away as soon as they were outside, but Nell had the strangest feeling she'd have a burned palm print on her skin when she took her dress off later that night.

'So, where's date number two?' Alex asked. 'I was assured you had one for every Saturday night for three months.'

'Stood me up.' Nell gave him an easy smile to show how little she cared. 'So I'm a single rider for the fairground rides tonight.'

'I'm not sure that's allowed.' Alex pointed to a sign printed in bright pink letters, propped up beside what looked like a tunnel of love ride.

Couples only. No single riders.

Of course. Nell sighed. Well, Polly had warned them.

'You'll have to stick with me.' There was something

in his voice that made Polly turn towards him, studying his face as she tried to put her finger on what it was.

'Where's *your* date?' she asked, still unsure as to what the strange dynamic between them tonight added up to. 'Don't tell me she's stuck at Customs.'

He laughed, low and hot. 'Not tonight. Tonight, she ran into her ex—who also hadn't got the memo about couples only and had shown up stag. They got talking and, well, when I spotted you at the bar and made my escape I'm not sure either of them even noticed.'

He told the story nonchalantly enough but Nell winced on his behalf, anyway. Maybe for him it was just another story to tell at parties, but she knew if it had been her she'd have run away and hidden for the rest of the night.

Not Alex, though. 'Come on,' he said, tugging on her arm. 'Let's go find some rides to go on before we get stuck into the doughnuts and candy floss.'

Glad she'd worn her boots, she followed him out onto the dewy spring grass towards the rides—and then stopped stock-still as she spotted a familiar face in the queue for the carousel.

Alex made it a step forward before falling back again, following her stare. 'Is that…'

'Yes.'

'Paul?'

'Yes.'

'What's he doing here?' There was a hint of anger in Alex's voice, presumably on Nell's behalf, which she appreciated.

'I have absolutely zero idea,' she admitted.

Why on earth would Polly have invited Nell's ex-boyfriend to her engagement party?

Unless…

'Who is that he's standing with?' she asked, her voice small.

Couples only, that was the rule. Which meant he must be here with another woman.

The woman he'd left her for.

The one he'd told her was more exciting. More fun.

Who made him feel more alive than he'd ever felt with Nell.

The one he'd probably been *faire l'amour*-ing with while they were still living together.

'Oh,' Alex said in the sort of tone that told her she wasn't going to like the answer to that question. 'That's Fred's cousin, Jemima. I didn't realise *she* was…'

'The one he left me for. Apparently.'

Over in the queue, Jemima flipped her long, perfectly highlighted and waved hair over her shoulder and smiled adoringly up at the man Nell had expected to marry.

'Shall we go find Polly and Fred?' Alex asked gently. He must think her so pathetic. Broken, even.

But she wasn't. Not even close.

It would take a lot more than a cheating boyfriend to break her.

Nell stared at Paul and Jemima for one more moment, then turned away. 'No. We came to the fair. I want to go on some rides then eat enough doughnuts to make me sick.'

'Okay then,' Alex replied, taking her arm as he had done in the park earlier that week. 'Then let's go find us a ride.'

Nell vetoed the Ferris wheel out of hand.

'What if it gets stuck?' she asked incredulously when he suggested it.

'Is this because of your lift date?' Alex enjoyed the way her cheeks turned a little pink at the suggestion. 'Because not everything that goes up in the air gets stuck, you realise.'

'I don't like heights,' she admitted. 'And getting stuck at the top of one of those things…' She shuddered and Alex wrapped an arm around her shoulders instinctively. 'It's basically one of my recurring nightmares.'

'No Ferris wheel, then.' Alex steered her away, scanning the fairground for another ride she might enjoy.

It wasn't a *real* fairground, of course—there wasn't quite the space for that, even in the palatial grounds of the London house Polly had hired. Not unless the owners were willing to sacrifice a few trees and shrubs, anyway, which Alex suspected they weren't.

In addition to the Ferris wheel there was the carousel—where Paul and Jemima were currently queuing, so that was out; the dodgems, except Alex worried Nell might be a little too susceptible to road rage given her current state of mind; a ride that seemed to go up into the air then plummet to the ground, which was probably worse than the Ferris wheel and…

Oh, of course.

'Tunnel of Love it is, then,' he told her, changing their course.

There was a small queue so they waited their turn, and Alex took the opportunity to take in the sights and sounds of the fairground. It wasn't quite the real thing, he knew that. But it was still the closest he'd ever got to it.

'There used to be a fair that came to the village nearest our estate most summers,' he told Nell. He wasn't sure why, exactly, except that she looked like she needed the distraction tonight, and telling stories about his life was sort of his default for that.

Usually they were stories that made him sound adventurous, stories filled with drama—or ones that made people laugh, and think he was a good sport.

This wasn't any of those, but then, Nell wasn't his usual audience either.

'I'd look out of my bedroom window at the lights, and listen to the screams and the laughter,' he went on. 'Sometimes I could even smell the frying doughnuts on the breeze. God, I would have given *anything* to go down to the fair.'

He hadn't been totally sure she was even listening, but now she looked at him in surprise. 'You never went?'

Alex shrugged. 'It wasn't an appropriate place for Callum McLeod's son to be seen.'

Was that pity in her eyes? Alex hoped not. There was nothing anyone should pity him for. He'd grown up rich, privileged and wanting for nothing—except possibly a night at the fair.

He knew how lucky he was.

The Tunnel of Love didn't look quite like the ones he'd seen in the movies—probably because this was a small ride that had to be transported around the country. As such, the swan boats that journeyed through the short tunnel travelled on rails, rather than bobbing along on water.

Still, he thought as he helped Nell inside and she tucked her skirt around her legs to stop him sitting on it, the basics were the same. A couple pressed up close together in a small, romantic boat, travelling through a dark space where anything could happen...

Nell flashed him a look as the swan started to move. 'Don't go getting any ideas, now.'

'Wouldn't dream of it,' Alex lied.

The ideas were already there. Had been for years—since the last time he'd kissed her, and returned to his room to find her gone.

And it was hard not to imagine kissing Nell as she laughed at the ridiculous lit-up cupids and glow-in-the-dark hearts that filled the tunnel.

'Only Polly would think something like this is romantic,' she explained when he looked at her. 'All this... For Polly, romance is something you have to show, perform even.'

'She wears her heart on her sleeve,' Alex agreed cautiously. 'She doesn't hide how she feels.' Unlike her sister, he suspected.

'Never mind her sleeve—her heart has a permanent megaphone attached.' Nell sighed. 'I love her dearly, but sometimes I wonder how we came from the same womb.'

Since Alex had been wondering the same thing, he just nodded.

The swan boat jerked around a corner and Nell was jostled closer into his side. Alex wrapped an arm around her instinctively and, when she didn't shrug it off, kept it there.

'Why do you think you *are* so different?' he asked.

Nell looked up at his question, her skin taking on a pinkish tinge from the lights inside the tunnel. 'I don't know. Well, I guess I do.'

She just didn't want to talk about it, Alex read between the lines. But the way she worried her bottom lip with her teeth just thinking about it suggested to him that maybe she needed to.

So he pushed. 'Tell me.'

'When we were growing up... I always knew that, as much as we looked the same, Polly and I were different inside. That's just how we were born. But maybe it was also, well, encouraged by the different ways we reacted to our upbringing.'

'How do you mean?' Polly didn't talk much about her family and, to his knowledge, Nell never did. All he knew was that their father had died when they were very young, and they'd spent a lot of time with their grandparents after that. 'You mean your dad?'

'Partly. I mean, it's not like we saw a lot of him *before* he died. He was an adventurer, did you know that?' She pulled a face. 'As if that has ever been a real job.'

'Polly told me he was a treasure-hunter once,' Alex remembered suddenly. 'Diving old shipwrecks and the like, looking for booty?'

'That's the one.' There was a sour note in Nell's voice he didn't quite understand.

'That's...pretty cool, isn't it?'

She shot him a look. 'What? Flying around the world to search for treasure nobody has wanted or needed for decades, or even hundreds of years, instead of, oh, I don't know, staying and raising your daughters?'

Ah. Put that way, Alex supposed it *wasn't* all that cool.

'We didn't see him for months at a time—even a year once. It was hard to tell the difference, really, when he died searching that wreck.' The lines at the corner of her mouth said otherwise. As much as Alex believed Nell *wished* she didn't care, he suspected that in truth she cared far too much. He wondered how many other things that was true about, and he'd just never noticed before.

'I'm sorry,' he murmured.

'He just left us with *her*. Except she wasn't all that interested either.'

'Your mother?'

'Yeah.' She looked away, even as the swan cornered the last bend at a slight angle, pressing her closer against his side.

Alex thought about his own parents. About his father, locked away in their castle on the hill, the latest in a long line of McLeod men who'd stayed put, however miserable they got. About his mother, storming in and out with her temper and the wind. And about the boy he'd been, growing up looking out at a world that never seemed accessible to him—until he'd finally left for boarding school and discovered it had just been waiting for him to arrive.

'Polly always was more like her, really,' Nell said softly. 'She had her charm. I never did.'

'I don't know about that,' Alex said, his own voice low and almost lost in the crunch of the swan coming to a halt at the end of the ride.

Nell's smile was sad. 'Everyone else does.' She hopped out of the swan and held a hand out to pull him up too. 'Come on. I think it's time for doughnuts. Don't you?'

CHAPTER SEVEN

POLLY WAS OVERFLOWING with apologies about Paul's presence at the party, when they finally caught up.

'I had no idea she was bringing *him,*' she promised. 'I'd have said no if I had!'

'How could you?' Nell asked. 'I mean, she's Fred's cousin and he's her boyfriend.'

'Yeah, but you're my sister and he's your *ex*-boyfriend.' Polly's arms were folded tightly across her chest. 'I've already told Fred she can't bring him to the wedding.'

'Except then she won't have a pair, for all the couple stuff,' Nell pointed out. 'So unless you're going to uninvite Fred's cousin...'

A frown line settled between Polly's eyebrows. 'If I have to.'

Nell sighed. 'No. Don't do that. I don't want to make a big deal about it, have Jemima cause a scene or anything. Just...don't seat them near me at the wedding breakfast, okay?'

'Are you sure?' Polly asked, and Nell nodded. 'Okay, then. But they're definitely not coming to the stag and hen do, though.'

'Agreed.'

Nell had hoped that being the reasonable one, and not

making a big deal about her ex being at the wedding, would buy her some time in Polly's good graces. Time that might be spent not having to continue her search for her own date for the big day.

But the goodwill her magnanimity bought her didn't last anywhere near long enough for Nell's liking.

'You're running out of time, you realise.' Polly's voice was arch and when Nell looked up from her computer screen she saw her twin leaning against her doorway, eyebrows raised and knowing smile in place. 'A girl might think that you'd abandoned the idea of finding anyone other than Alex McLeod to go to my wedding with after all.'

'I have another date tomorrow night.' Nell tried to sound rather more enthusiastic about that than she felt. 'One of these set-ups has to actually go well eventually, right?'

'If you let them,' Polly replied, before drifting away, back downstairs to where the action happened. 'Just let me know what name to put on the seating plan,' she called back over her shoulder.

Nell tried to turn her attention back to the numbers on the spreadsheet that filled her screen, but they all seemed to blur to one. Instead, so dropped her head in her hands and wondered how she'd ended up here.

Probably it was Polly's fault. This sort of thing usually was.

The worst part was she'd been doing exactly as they'd planned. She'd been on a damn date every single Saturday night for the past month, since her no-show at the engagement party. And every one had been an unmitigated disaster.

Polly thought she was sabotaging them. Her reasoning seemed to vacillate between believing that Nell was still hung up on Paul—whose relationship with the perfect Jemima seemed to be going from strength to strength, damn him—thinking that she was just trying to prove some point to Polly, or suspecting that Nell really did want to go to the wedding with Alex after all.

All of which was nonsense. Especially the last one.

Okay, maybe they'd shared a moment riding that stupid swan at Polly and Fred's engagement party.

And maybe the best part about all her stupid dating site set-ups was sharing how awful they were with Alex over coffee in the park on a Monday morning, while he told his own horror stories about his attempts to find a date for the wedding.

She sat back in her chair and smiled as she remembered all those Monday mornings. As the daffodils had faded and the first summer blooms had begun to appear, they'd shared tales from dating hell and laughed so much that even the most excruciatingly embarrassing stories didn't seem quite so bad any more.

Like the riverboat cruise down the Seine with the man who'd whisked her away to Paris. As the water had started coming in from the sides and they'd all been evacuated in blow-up boats, she'd thought that Alex would never be able to top that one.

Then it turned out his date had stolen his car.

Week after week, failed date after failed date. And Monday morning coffee with Alex was the only bright spot in the whole endeavour.

But that didn't have to mean anything. Did it?

She was sure it wouldn't to him. It hadn't last time, after all.

And she wasn't about to make the same mistake again, that was certain.

Her date the next night was 'a surprise'—which meant the guy was already off to a bad start, as surely Polly must have put in her profile how much she hated surprises.

All the same, Nell slipped into a black wrap dress and tall boots, opting for her leather jacket on top this time, and headed out to meet him on the South Bank. At least it was far enough from St Pancras station that there was little chance he was going to take her on another water-logged adventure in Paris.

One of these dates has to stick, she reminded herself as she hurried to meet the guy.

If it didn't, her only option would be to succumb to being Alex's pity date for the wedding, and she couldn't face that—even if, after the last month or two, she suspected they'd actually have fun together.

That wasn't the point.

The point was...

What was the point again?

She recognised the man leaning against the railing by the Thames from his photo on the dating site and headed towards him, still trying to order her thoughts. He was dark-haired, tall, handsome...and he reminded her just a little too much of Alex.

Not that she was thinking about Alex tonight. Except about how she didn't want to be his date for the wedding.

Because she was better than a pity date, that was the point. Alex would take her, she was almost certain, because it turned out he'd grown up into a nicer guy than she'd expected. And they had more fun together than she suspected either of them would have predicted.

But it wasn't the real thing. Neither of them thought for a moment that the pair of them made sense together. He was all about adventures and drama and tall tales. And she was very much not.

She wanted a guy who'd stay home and live a quiet, boring life with her. The sort of life she'd imagined she could have with Paul.

And that just wasn't how Alex lived his life.

They'd both known what a bad fit they were for each other back at university, when they'd swerved to avoid a train wreck between them before it ever really happened. Yeah, she'd been mad at him for walking out when things were just getting interesting between them, but after that had faded she knew he'd made the right choice. They just didn't match up, so better not to try.

Nothing had changed in the years since then to make that equation add up now.

Everyone at the wedding would know they weren't really together. That Alex had taken pity on her and paired up with her rather than bringing his own date. And she couldn't bear people talking about her like that.

So, she'd better hope this guy was the one.

Pasting on a smile, she marched over to the railings and introduced herself.

Her date, Richard, returned her smile with a warm one of his own, and even instigated a hug hello. He seemed charming, and unlikely to have a panic attack in a lift or book a boat with holes in it.

And, up close, he hardly looked like Alex at all.

This could work.

'So, what's the plan for tonight?' she asked, still smiling.

'Have you ever been on the London Eye?' Richard asked, and Nell felt her stomach sink.

Richard had paid for some sort of special ticket that meant they didn't have to queue at all, and they had their pod almost entirely to themselves—just a few other couples. There was a table set up in the middle, laden with champagne and chocolate-dipped strawberries, and waiting staff to serve them. Really, it was all very romantic and thoughtful.

Nell made her way to the edge, step by shuffling step, and held on for dear life to the railing that ran around the pod.

Everything is glassed in. It's perfectly safe. What's the worst that could happen?

She heard voices behind her as the last couple was admitted to the pod, but she focused on Richard standing beside her, rather than their companions.

The pod moved slowly, slowly upwards.

It wasn't really like a Ferris wheel at all, Nell reassured herself. It didn't spin, or race around. It wasn't even a ride. It was a tourist attraction, designed to showcase London in all its glory.

At night, the lights of the city were mesmerising. Nell focused on staring outwards, far over the river, listening to Richard lecturing her about everything they could see—or couldn't, since it was night-time. Not very much of it went in, but then she'd lived in London her whole life. It wasn't as if she didn't already know where things were.

Her stomach dropped a little as they reached the top, but at least that meant she was closer to the end than the beginning, didn't it? Richard had gone quiet—perhaps intuiting that she wasn't actually listening to him at all. But she'd be more fun once they got off the wheel of death. Not a lot more fun, admittedly. But maybe enough that they could get a nice dinner together.

This was all going to be okay.

Then the Eye jerked, shuddered...

And stopped in mid-air.

Alex had recognised Nell the moment he and his date stepped onto the London Eye. No one else had that shimmering black hair combined with that defensive, determined stance as she stood staring out over London.

She hates heights, and has a fear of Ferris wheels. What idiot would bring her here for her first date?

The idiot, he reasoned, must be the man standing beside her.

Another Saturday, another date from that damned dating site.

For his own date, he'd brought a friend of a friend of a friend. Mollie—his actual friend—had been trying to persuade him to listen to her advice on who to date for years. She'd been thrilled when he'd finally taken her up on the offer. And he'd been pretty pleased with the situation when he'd picked up Eva for the evening too. She was blonde, beautiful and not high, drunk or likely to steal his car.

That made her a winner by his current, admittedly low standards.

Eva tucked her arm through his and tugged him over to the far side of the pod as they started to move.

'So, are you going to tell me all the things we can see?' she asked with an indulgent smile. As if that was what people did on dates on the London Eye.

Maybe it was. Alex had never brought anyone here before.

He looked out at the pitch-black London night sky, dotted with lights of buildings, planes and stars, the lit-up landmarks he could make out so obvious that no Londoner would need them naming. Then he glanced back at her and shrugged. 'It's night-time. You can't see much of anything. Champagne?'

On the other side of the pod, Nell's knuckles were white as she clutched the railings. Alex could see them, bone-white, even at a distance.

'God, she has to be hating this.'

'Who?' Eva looked up at him in confusion. 'Hating what?'

Alex nodded towards Nell. 'That's a…friend of mine. She doesn't like heights. Or Ferris wheels.'

'Then why on earth did she come on here?' Eva asked.

'So she wouldn't have to go to a wedding with me.'

Nell's date had stopped prattling on in her ear and had taken a step aside. Alex was just wondering if he should go over, let her know he was there and check she was okay, when the whole Eye shuddered to a halt.

With their pod right at the top.

This is literally her worst nightmare.

Okay, so it wasn't quite like being stuck at the top of a Ferris wheel, like she'd told him she feared. The London Eye pods were all enclosed, and they were wandering around drinking champagne and eating chocolate-dipped strawberries, rather than dangling exposed from a rickety metal chair.

But if we were on a Ferris wheel, I could put my arm around her like I did on the swan boat in the Tunnel of Love. I could keep her safe.

Right now, she didn't even know he was here.

'If you want to go look after your friend, that's okay,' Eva said, sounding genuinely amused. 'I'm sure there are plenty of other people here who can explain the London skyline in the dark to me.'

She was already eyeing up Nell's wandering date, he realised. Well, good luck to them both. With a nod to Eva, he headed over to Nell, making sure she saw him, knew he was here, before he settled an arm around her shivering shoulders.

'Okay?' he murmured softly.

'Of course I'm okay. Why wouldn't I be?' The sharpness in her voice was fear, he realised, rather than disdain. But if he hadn't known about her Ferris wheel nightmare, he'd have assumed the latter.

How many other times in the past had he done that? Taken Nell's defensiveness as dismissal, rather than vulnerability?

Probably too many.

Like that night at university when he'd kissed her, then been dragged away—and she'd been gone when he returned. He'd always assumed her coldness towards him after that night was because she'd realised what she'd almost done while drunk and hated him for taking advantage of her that way.

But what if it was something else…?

He shook his head. That train of thought was going to lead him away from what Nell needed from him tonight, which was, he guessed, distraction.

'Apparently the done thing on a night date on the London Eye is to describe the skyline we can't actually see very well. Would you like me to try?'

That earned him a laugh, at least. 'Richard has already done that, thanks. I wasn't really listening though.'

Alex glanced back across the pod to another two heads, pressed close together, looking out over the skyline. 'And now I believe he's telling Eva. My date.'

'How romantic,' Nell said drily. 'Guess this is another failed date for the books.'

'Oh, I don't know. It doesn't seem to be going so badly for Richard and Eva.'

'True.'

They both stared out through the glass of the pod as they waited for it to start moving again. It didn't.

'Why do you date such boring men, anyway?' Alex asked, already anticipating the glare she would send his way. If she was angry she wasn't scared and, in his book at least, that was an improvement.

'Boring is all a state of mind,' she retorted. 'I prefer to think of my preferred sort of date as stable, reliable and reassuring. All things this piece of steel and glass isn't.' Her glare was redirected to the centre of the London Eye.

'Still. Don't you ever want a little more adventure?' He waggled his eyebrows to try and make her laugh. 'I mean, as long as it doesn't end with you stuck in the air in a confined space, or sinking on the Seine?'

Nell didn't laugh. 'You're thinking of my parents, or Polly. They're the adrenaline junkies, remember?'

'And you have to be contrary because you can't want what they want?' He'd started this conversation as a distraction, but now Alex found himself invested in the answers.

'No. Because I'm a different sort of person to them. And I don't think love is what *they* think it is.' A waiter passed with a tray, and she grabbed a glass of champagne and practically downed it in one. Belatedly, Alex reached for one of his own—only for Nell to take that one from him too.

At least she didn't down that one. But he suspected the situation was getting to her rather more than she'd admit.

'What do they think love is?' he asked.

Nell shrugged. '*You* know. All drama and tension and arguing and making up and running away and coming back. High romance and drama.'

'You mean passion,' he replied. 'There's nothing wrong with some real passion between people who care about each other.'

His own parents were proof of that. His mother might leave, but she always came back.

They had passion. That was the important thing. If they didn't fight and make up, how would anyone know they loved each other?

'Passion?' Nell shook her head. 'That's not passion. That's drama. It's just that some people prefer that to the real thing.'

'People like Polly and Fred?' he asked, mostly to distract himself now from the fact he'd always thought passion and drama *were* the same thing.

Well, what did he know? At least one ex-girlfriend had told him he'd never know real love if it slapped him in the face. Maybe they were right.

Nell's expression softened at the mention of her sister. 'No, Polly and Fred are the real thing. They just like the drama too.' She frowned for a moment, and when she spoke again it was with the surprise of realisation in her voice. 'I guess maybe it's possible to have both.'

'Maybe,' Alex agreed. 'Or maybe you and I know nothing about love.'

Finally, that got him the laugh he'd been angling for. And as it echoed off the glass of the pod, the wheel finally started turning again, resulting in a loud cheer going up from all the people in it.

'Would you want to?' Nell asked, her tone serious again.

'Want to what?'

'Know about love?'

Alex didn't have to think about his answer. 'Doesn't everybody?'

'I suppose so,' Nell said thoughtfully.

He just wondered if either of them ever would.

CHAPTER EIGHT

HAVING SPENT THEIR Saturday night together, stuck at the top of the London Eye, there was no real need for a Monday morning debrief over coffee—which meant that Nell and Alex both made it to the Start the Week staff meeting early for a change.

'So?' Polly asked as they took their seats. 'How were your respective dates this weekend?'

Nell glanced over at Alex, who was already looking at her.

'Safe to say, I don't think either of us are planning to bring our Saturday night dates to the wedding,' he said drily.

Fred gave them both a sympathetic look. 'That bad?'

'Mine took me up the London Eye,' Nell explained. 'And it got stuck.'

Polly winced. 'Not ideal.'

'No.' She sneaked another look at Alex. 'Luckily Alex was there to talk me down.'

'Oh?' Polly hopped to the edge of her seat, leaning her elbows on the table as she looked between them. 'How come?'

Alex lifted one shoulder in a casual shrug. 'The London Eye's a classic, right? I just happened to be there with my date too. I knew Nell doesn't like heights or big wheels, so... Anyway, my date was more interested in *her* date's explanation of the London skyline. It all worked out.' Another shrug, which somehow had the effect of making his laidback sprawl in his chair look less casual.

Polly narrowed her eyes. 'So it was just a coincidence?'

'Completely,' Nell assured her. The last thing she needed was her sister getting ideas at this point.

'Or fate.' Polly's lips twisted up in an amused grin. 'I'm definitely putting my money on fate.'

'And I'm putting mine on us running out of ways to have lousy dates every weekend, just to fulfil your couples only wedding nightmare.' It was cruel, and she regretted the words almost the moment they were out of her mouth—and definitely by the time the hurt showed on Polly's face.

Fred, ever the peacemaker, stepped in.

'Don't worry, Nell,' he said in an earnestly reassuring voice. 'I'm sure you and Alex will both be able to find a date at the stag and hen do—someone who's already coming to the wedding anyway would be perfect, right? And Pol did say you needed a date by the *end* of the stag and hen weekend. Besides, there's bound to be plenty of people you both know.'

'People we haven't already dated?' Nell asked caustically, thinking of Paul and Jemima at the engagement party fairground.

'That's a thought.' Fred turned to Alex. 'I think Caitlin is going to be there, Alex, and I'm not sure she's said who she's bringing yet.'

Caitlin, Nell's foggy memory reminded her, was Alex's last but one semi-serious girlfriend, who had left him high and dry after walking out of another wedding four years ago, when Alex had been best man. They'd had a huge argument in the vestry before the service, as she recalled. One that every single guest in the church heard every word of, until the organist stepped it up a notch.

Always with the drama, these people.

Alex wasn't keen on the idea of a reunion anyway, if the sour look on his face was any indication.

And neither, it seemed, was Polly. 'Fred! He's not dating Caitlin again.' Nell imagined she remembered what had happened last time too. Not what she'd been hoping for at her own festival of romance wedding.

Fred gave her a confused look. 'But I thought we were *supposed* to be helping them find dates.'

'Not that one,' Polly replied shortly.

But someone. The idea that Alex *wouldn't* find someone to take to the wedding, even in the now shortened timeframe they had left, was laughable.

'Well, at least we know someone he's dated before is someone he's attracted to,' Fred pointed out. 'And we know he *really* doesn't want to go with Nell!'

Fred—good old slightly oblivious Fred—laughed. Then stopped when he realised no one else was.

The slight burn at the back of her throat, the sting in her eyes…they weren't caused by tears, Nell told herself. Because why would she want to cry at that? Fred was absolutely right. Alex really *didn't* want to go to the wedding with Nell—and she didn't want to go with him either. She didn't even want him to *want* to go with her, because she wasn't the kind of person who enjoyed that kind of drama power trip.

Alex didn't want her now, any more than he'd really

wanted her when they were back at university. And she was fine with that.

She just wanted to find a date for this wedding, and so did he. And maybe Fred was right, and the hen and stag party was their best shot at doing that.

They should both be open to that possibility. Encourage it even.

And she really, really needed to stop remembering that moment on the London Eye, when she'd felt like all she could do was curl up in a ball and cry, until Alex had come over and distracted her from her fear.

She wasn't going to think about how he'd known instinctively exactly what she'd needed. Or even the fact that he'd remembered about her fears at all.

It didn't mean anything after all. Just that Alex McLeod was more of a decent human being than she'd always assumed.

Nell pushed her chair away from the table and stalked to the door. 'I assume we're done here?'

They hadn't actually talked about work, she realised. But apparently everyone realised that they weren't going to, because nobody tried to stop her.

She considered stopping by the kitchen for a coffee, but decided she couldn't face the chatter and the gossip. So instead she headed straight for the narrow stairs that led to her attic office, and prepared to spend her day dealing with numbers rather than people.

They made much more sense, in her experience.

And her spreadsheets wouldn't ask her why, if she didn't want to go to the wedding with Alex McLeod, she kept thinking about that night on the Eye together, or their evening at the fairground, and remembering how much more like a date they'd felt than any of the set-ups she'd been on through the dating agency.

If she got really lucky, her spreadsheets and numbers might even distract her from the fact that she'd liked that feeling.

A lot more than she'd meant to.

When Polly and Fred had asked if it would be possible to hold the joint stag and hen party at his family estate in Scotland, Alex hadn't been able to find a reason to say no.

Well, actually, he'd had a hundred reasons ready to go. But none that weren't horribly selfish, or required a lot more conversation about his childhood and his relationship with his parents than he was willing to enter into.

Which meant that, in the end, he'd said yes. And now teams of Here & Now staff were descending on his family home, setting up what was sure to be the party of the year.

'Are those hot-air balloons, darling?' His mother stood beside him, peering out of the window at the industrious activity going on across the West Lawn.

'Apparently so.' Alex had tried to persuade his parents that they might prefer to be somewhere else this weekend, but to no avail.

'Nonsense!' his father had said. 'We love a good party as much as the next person, don't we, Shelly?' His mother had, of course, agreed.

And Alex had given up.

Because he knew it wasn't just the party his parents loved. It was the noise and the drama, and they never could stop themselves getting swept up in it.

Ah, well. His mother hadn't stomped out of High Dudgeon House—as it had been nicknamed by Fred when he came to stay one summer in their teens—for at least eighteen months. She was probably due.

And he'd spend the next few months reminding them both how much they actually loved each other, and him, and the life they had together, until she floated back in and they were sickeningly adoring again—until the next time.

He'd been through this far too often to expect them to stray from the formula this weekend. So he just steeled himself for the inevitability, and reminded himself that this was how his parents showed their love. It was demonstrative, over-the-top and, yes, time-consuming for him. But they were still together, after all these years, despite everything.

This was love. Passion. Drama. Just like in the movies.

Who was he to argue with that? Even if he didn't want it for himself.

Fred and Polly subscribed to the same show-your-love-with-excess school of thought as his parents, although hopefully without the breakups and makeups. Which was why there was now a small fleet of hot-air balloons scattered across the West Lawn and the fields beyond.

Who threw a party in hot-air balloons?

Alex pitied the poor DJ, who had to make the music work across all the balloons. Not to mention the balloon operators—were they called pilots? He should ask, it would be polite—who would have to deal with all the partygoers. Alex knew most of them. That wouldn't be easy.

In fact, as best man, he really should be helping.

Making his excuses to his mother—who declared she needed to go and get ready for the party anyway—Alex made his way outside to see how things were going.

'Ah, there you are!' Polly beckoned him over with expansive gestures. 'I know we said you wouldn't have to do much as best man—'

'Except let us use this magnificent venue,' Fred interjected, and Polly acknowledged the point with a nod.

'But we did rather hope you'd actually be here,' she finished. 'Where have you been hiding?'

'Just paying my respects to the parentals,' Alex explained.

Fred pulled a sympathetic face. 'And how are they?'

'Looking about ready to pull their latest greatest drama,' Alex admitted. 'Don't worry, I'll try and keep it off-stage for your party, at least.'

'It would be appreciated,' Polly said drily. 'I would rather like my wedding events to be more about Fred and me than your parents' drawn-out foreplay habit.'

Alex winced at the description, but he had to admit she had a point. 'It's romantic? In a way?'

Polly gave him a look. 'If that's what you think romance looks like, no wonder you haven't got a date to our wedding yet.'

Alex thought back to his discussions about love with Nell on the London Eye. 'Your sister said something similar the other night.'

'Where is the maid of honour, anyway?' Fred asked. Polly looked to Alex for an answer, and he shrugged.

'Why would I know?'

'No reason,' Polly said airily. 'I just thought… Anyway, she texted me earlier. Her train was delayed.'

'Why didn't she fly up here like everyone else?' Fred's brow was furrowed in confusion.

'Afraid of heights. And flying,' Alex said absently, and

shrugged when Fred gave him a strange look. 'We've spent time together.' Enough that he suspected Nell's delay might have more to do with hoping to miss the hot-air balloon ride at the start of the party than anything else.

'I noticed.' Polly's eyes narrowed. 'Well, as part of your best man duties, I'm putting you in charge of the maid of honour for the evening, okay? I'm going to be too busy with my guests.'

Alex raised an eyebrow. 'Are you under the illusion that *you* have been in charge of Nell before now?' From his own observations, it most often seemed the other way around. Nell tempered Polly's flighty enthusiasm, brought her down to earth when she threatened to fly away. Although he supposed Fred had taken on more of those responsibilities over recent years.

Still, it was impossible to imagine *anyone* taking charge of Nell. She was her own woman—and a competent, brilliant one at that. She didn't need looking after that way.

Polly flapped a hand at him. 'Oh, you know what I mean! Just make sure she doesn't freak out too much about the balloons.' Her expression turned suddenly sly. 'You seemed to do a good job of distracting her on the London Eye, after all.'

Before Alex could question what she meant by that, Polly had already dragged Fred away, towards the largest of the hot-air balloons in the centre of the lawn. The other assembled guests, having been shown to their rooms earlier and given the opportunity to change into their finest evening gowns and dinner jackets, were now being herded towards the balloon baskets—or lured in by the trays of champagne that awaited them.

Alex had to admit that the sight as the balloons started to take flight was spectacular. The sun just starting to sink behind the mountains, the sky filling with brightly coloured hot-air balloons, the music playing magically between all of them—including the one still on the ground, waiting for the last few guests.

Polly might have gone over the top with her wedding plans, but she'd definitely proved that Here & Now knew how to put on a show. Alex predicted a whole rush of hot-air balloon parties on their books next year.

He turned back towards the house and saw a figure running down the path towards him. *Nell.* Her dark evening gown billowed out behind her, revealing the boots she was wearing underneath. Her silky black hair streamed out over her shoulders in the early evening breeze as she clutched a camel-coloured wrap around her.

He could see the flush of pink on her cheeks before he could make out the brightness of her blue eyes, and he knew—somewhere deep in his gut that he usually tried to ignore—that he was in trouble tonight.

Not because she was so beautiful. Not because of the romance of the night. Not even because she was here, in his homeland.

But because she was Nell. And it turned out that meant so much more than he'd ever realised back at university, or in any of the years since.

She finally reached him, and smiled—and Alex felt his heart contract.

'Did I miss the balloon part?' Nell asked hopefully.

'No such luck, I'm afraid.' Alex reached out a hand to her, and she took it. 'There's one balloon waiting just for us. Come on.' She hesitated, and he felt her pulse of fear. 'You can keep holding my hand if you're scared.'

She straightened her shoulders at that. 'Of course I'm not scared,' she said, even though they both knew it was a lie. 'Come on.'

Nell stalked towards the last balloon with a look of grim determination on her face.

But she didn't let go of his hand.

CHAPTER NINE

OBJECTIVELY, NELL HAD to admit that the view from the hot-air balloon was gorgeous. She felt as if she were floating, weightless, in the early evening air as the sun started to set.

Somehow, Polly had managed to get classical music piped into each of the baskets, and the melody lulled her as she looked out over the rolling hills, lochs and the roof of Alex's home castle.

In fact, the views and the music—and the champagne—were almost enough to help her forget her fear of heights, or all the ways she could die horribly if something went wrong with the balloon.

But they still weren't enough to distract her from the heaviness in the air between her and Alex, or the way she could sense every tiny movement he made, as if he were touching her, even when he was keeping what distance it was possible to keep in a balloon basket.

She recognised that feeling. Remembered how it had ended last time too.

What would make this time any different?

'How are you doing?' Alex's voice was low and rumbly in her ear, only just audible over the noise of the balloon and the music. He still wasn't touching her, though—even if all the hairs on her arms stood up in anticipation of it.

'Finding it hard to believe that you grew up in an actual castle,' she admitted. 'I know you always said it was, but…well, the crenellations were a bit of a surprise.'

He chuckled at that. 'It's something, that's for sure. You know Fred calls it High Dudgeon House?'

'Why is that?' She'd always assumed it was just another of those inside jokes that Alex, Fred and Polly shared—and that she'd always be on the outside of. She'd grown used to those over the years, as she'd pulled back from them.

'Because my mother has a tendency to storm out of there in a high dudgeon, as we call it. Then it takes a lot of expensive gifts and humiliating begging when she returns—or on my father's part to get her to come back in the first place. Once he's decided to forgive her, anyway.'

'Sounds exhausting,' Nell said. Like dealing with her own mother, in lots of ways.

'It is.'

The balloon banked a little to the right, and Nell stumbled a little as she tried to find her footing. But suddenly there were strong arms around her middle, and the scent of Alex—clean and fresh and just a little bit spicy—surrounded her too.

She swallowed, hard, when he didn't let go.

'Did you know, the pilot has practically no control at all over where the balloon goes, or where it lands,' she said. 'I was reading up on hot-air balloon rides on the train up.'

'Of course you were,' Alex murmured. Then he raised

his voice, and she felt him turn his head towards their pilot. 'Is that true?'

The pilot hummed agreement. Really, Alex should just trust her research skills.

'He just has to look for a suitable field, when we get closer to landing time,' she went on. 'Polly's arranged for four-by-fours to meet us wherever we land—I guess they're following us now—and drive us back to the house for dinner.'

'As long as we don't drift off McLeod land, we should be fine,' Alex mused. Nell twisted her neck to give him a questioning look. 'We've got a decades-old feud going with the neighbours.'

'Of course you have.' More drama. Naturally.

Alex laughed. 'What's that supposed to mean?'

'That just seems to be your life—all high emotion and drama.'

'But not yours?'

She shrugged. 'I like the quiet life.'

'Always?' The question in his voice seemed somehow more meaningful than the word suggested.

'As a rule,' she said casually.

But she was hyperaware of his arms, still wrapped tight around her waist, and the way her body responded to his closeness. A moment like this, with a man she had, until recently, if not despised, certainly avoided as being the opposite of everything she wanted in her life—she had to admit there was a certain drama to it.

Especially since they were flying in a private hot-air balloon above his family's country estate.

This wasn't quiet. This wasn't boring.

This was so far out of her comfort zone she didn't even know how to get back.

'Does this feel quiet to you?' His whisper seemed to bypass her brain and go straight to her nerve-endings, setting everything tingling.

'No,' she admitted, her voice hoarse.

'Me neither.'

That surprised her—enough that she turned in his arms, leaving the view behind her and focusing on his face instead.

There, deep in his eyes, she saw something she hadn't expected. Something she felt reflected inside herself.

Heat.

Not just the gentle warmth of familiarity or fondness she was used to feeling with Paul or any of her other ex-boyfriends.

This was something different. Something new. Or something old, perhaps. Something she hadn't felt since the night she ran away from his room at university.

Something she thought might burn her up from the inside and leave her a different person altogether.

Would it burn away her fear? Or just leave her more things to be afraid of?

Nell didn't know.

But in that moment she wasn't sure she cared either.

She'd spent all her life trying to avoid the kind of drama her mother courted, the sort of high emotion that had made her childhood such a misery. She knew that wasn't a life she wanted for herself—or any children she might have herself, one day.

She wasn't the same sort of person as the rest of her family—or as Alex and his family either.

But maybe, just this once, she wanted a taste of how that passion felt. For real, this time.

A taste that wouldn't leave her wondering for years again afterwards.

'Nell,' Alex said, and she could hear the restraint in his voice. He was holding himself back, from her. *For* her.

Because this was madness—they both knew that. It would be hard to find a less compatible pair than the woman who wanted to stay home every Friday night in her slippers and the man who thought nothing of inviting a woman he'd only met once to New York for the weekend for a first date.

But tonight—here and now, drifting over the Scottish Highlands as if she were flying—Nell wasn't sure she cared.

'Alex.' Her voice didn't even sound like her own. Whose was it? Polly's?

No. Polly's voice held laughter and teasing and excitement.

This woman's voice was darker and warmer, a voice filled with passion and possibility.

She liked it.

It seemed as if Alex heard it too, because he let out a small groan as she said his name.

And then he was reaching down—or was she stretching up?—and they met in the middle, her lips burning as they touched his and she finally, finally tasted his kiss.

How could it feel like he'd waited millennia for a kiss he hadn't even realised he wanted until tonight? Okay, maybe a little longer—but not much.

He wanted Nell Andrews. And that might be the most

surprising thing that might ever have happened to him in a lifetime of unexpected adventures.

More surprising than the date that stole his car, even.

Except…maybe it wasn't. Because he'd wanted her before, once, long ago. Maybe they were always heading back here.

They were unfinished business.

He pulled back just a little, to check Nell's eyes, her smile, to make sure she was there with him this time. From the soft smile and slightly glazed eyes that looked back at him, she was.

'You know, this is where you usually run out on me,' she murmured. 'Any moment now Fred is going to come calling, and you're going to rush off before your mates can see who you're kissing…'

His chest tightened. Looked like he wasn't the only one of them living in their past tonight. 'That's not… They needed me for something.' He couldn't say that wasn't what had happened, because it had. Yes, they'd needed his help, but that wasn't why he'd gone. They'd called and he'd run, spooked by the sudden shift in the world that had occurred when he'd kissed the most unlikely girl of all. He'd needed time to process, that was all. But then… 'You were gone when I came back.'

She shrugged. 'I realised what a ridiculous idea it was.'

And so she'd ignored him for the rest of the term, avoided every chance to be alone with him so they could talk.

Alex studied her carefully, took in that same defiance and defensiveness he'd seen at the top of the London Eye, and realised the truth. 'You mean you were scared.'

When she met his gaze with her own, she didn't try to hide the vulnerability behind it. 'Weren't you?'

He swallowed. 'Yes.'

How many years had it taken them to have this conversation? Too many.

There'd been something between them, something real, back then—and they'd both been too afraid to find out what it was. Maybe it was just chemistry, maybe it was really friendship—he wasn't sure either of them would accept anything more, even now. Still, he wondered if they could be any braver this time around.

'Are you scared now?' he asked.

'Terrified,' she admitted.

'Me too.' He tightened his arms around her waist. 'But I'm not going to run if you don't.'

Her lips curved into a smile as she reached up to kiss him again, and everything that had been tight and painful inside him seemed to relax at last.

Alex sank into their embrace, marvelling in the feel of Nell's sharp angles softening against him. He brought his hands up into the silky lengths of her hair, cradling the back of her head as he deepened the kiss, and wondered what luck or fate had brought them here again and given them a second chance at this.

Then the world jolted and Nell broke the kiss, and when Alex turned he saw the pilot trying—rather unsuccessfully—to hide his amusement.

'I did try to tell you we were landing,' he said. 'You were…preoccupied.'

Nell's head was buried against his chest. He had a suspicion she might be laughing.

Well. That or crying. He was hoping for the laughter.

'Nell! You made it!' At the sound of Polly's voice, Nell pulled away completely and Alex felt a chill in his chest at the loss.

Someone had brought over the steps for them to climb out of the basket, and Nell was gone before Alex could even speak to her. Even the pilot looked sympathetic as Alex hurried to follow. Was she running again? Really?

Nell glanced over her shoulder and caught his eye in the fading light, just before she reached her sister and her fiancé. And in that look Alex read everything she hadn't said.

No drama.

Right. Of course. Whatever this was, they weren't going to be making a big deal about it—especially not tonight, at Polly and Fred's engagement party. Probably not at any point between now and the wedding, if Alex knew Nell. And he hoped he was starting to.

If this was going to be anything at all, it meant doing it according to Nell's rules. The last thing he wanted to do was spook her and remind her of all the reasons this was a crazy idea.

As long as she wasn't running from him this time, he could deal with everything else.

So he followed her over to meet the happy couple, and then onwards to his parents' house, and hoped that everyone could keep the drama in check tonight.

Because, that way, he might get to kiss Nell Andrews again. And honestly, right now, that was the only thing he could think about.

Nell hurried away from the hot-air balloon, her heart still pounding. She'd love to blame it on her fear of heights, but she knew it was caused by something else entirely.

Or someone.

All these years she'd been pretending to herself that he was the one who'd run away from their kiss, their closeness, back at university. But she knew that she was the one who'd run really. He'd tried to talk to her after, tried to regain that easy conversation they'd found that week—and she'd turned him away.

But she wasn't turning him away now, even if she probably should.

This is still as ridiculous as it was back then. We're still completely the wrong people for each other.

'Nell? You okay?' Polly wrapped an arm around her waist as they walked together towards the castle Alex called home. 'I'm sorry, I know heights aren't your thing, but I've *always* wanted a sunset hot-air balloon ride and—'

'It's fine,' she reassured her sister. 'If I really hadn't wanted to go, I'd have been even later than I was and just missed it. Besides, Alex kept me distracted.'

Polly looked between them suspiciously, but they both managed to keep their expressions innocent of exactly *how* Alex had been distracting her.

Nell sneaked a quick glance at Alex once Polly had looked away and caught the corner of his smile, the heat still smouldering in his eyes. She turned away.

Beside her, Polly was chattering on about the balloons, the guests, the late dinner they still had to eat. Nell listened with half an ear, but the rest of her brain had turned to something else.

Yes, she and Alex were incompatible in terms of a long-lasting, for ever love affair. That was undeniable.

But neither of them were looking for that, were they? They were looking for a date to the wedding. That was all.

Okay, maybe not all. Maybe she was looking for someone to remind her that she was desirable, or to show her a little fun after Paul's desertion. And maybe they both needed to exorcise some of the ghosts from their past. Find a little closure.

Maybe it didn't need to be anything more than that. Maybe she could have this—could have him—just for now, and without it needing to be a big drama. Or, actually, anyone else knowing about it at all.

Would that be so bad?

It's not the sort of thing Nell Andrews does, her brain reminded her.

But surely I'm *the only one who gets to decide that.*

Perhaps, just this once, and just for now, Nell Andrews could tiptoe along the wild side, without anyone else finding out.

And then she'd go back to looking for what she really wanted in life—stability, security, a predictable future.

Once she'd worked Alex McLeod out of her system.

'Ready for dinner?' Polly asked.

'More than ready,' Nell replied.

It had taken her years. But she was finally ready to give in to what she and Alex had discovered between them all those years ago at university.

Then she'd be able to move on.

CHAPTER TEN

ALEX HAD ALREADY resolved to give Nell some space before trying to talk to her about the kiss. He knew how she ran when she was cornered, and he wasn't going to make the mistake of spooking her again.

To that end, he threw himself back into the festivities for the time being. The hen and stag do featured a reduced and refined guest list—something that Alex was profoundly grateful for. Fred's cousin Jemima and her new boyfriend—Nell's ex, Paul—hadn't made the cut, so that was one less thing to disrupt things. Of his own ex-girlfriends, only three were friends with Polly in their own right. Teyla, who he'd dated in university and was now married to an investment banker, merely gave him the occasional disappointed look, as though he'd lived down to everything she'd always known he was capable of, so that was easy to deal with. Caitlin he avoided completely, which was definitely best for everyone, whatever Fred thought.

The third ex, Ursula, however, was a very different proposition. In fact, her propositions were exactly what he was trying to avoid, by the time they reached dessert.

'Do you remember the last time we were here to-

gether?' Ursula asked, while Alex silently cursed whoever had sat them together for dinner.

Both the stag and hen parties had been mixed together
for the formal dinner in High Dudgeon House's main din-
ing hall, sitting at long wooden tables that looked like
they belonged in a historical movie. Much like many
things in his childhood home, including the plumbing
and the electrics.

It wasn't that they didn't have the money to fix those
things. It was just that they were dull and boring, and his
parents always had more interesting things to focus on.

That had never annoyed him before he'd got to know
Nell again, these last few months.

Was boringness catching?

'Alex?' Beside him, Ursula nudged him with her pointy
elbow. 'Do you remember?'

He blinked, and tried to cast his mind back. 'Last time
we were here together was the night I introduced you to
my parents.'

He'd thought he was introducing them to the woman
he was going to marry. He'd planned to ask for his grandmother's ring the next day. There'd been a proposal plan
all worked out, with a little help from Polly and Fred.

But it had also been the night his parents had invited
their friends, the Hunters, to dinner—along with their
son Patrick, who just happened to have gone to university
with Ursula. One thing had led to another and...

*You didn't really think I was going to marry you, did
you, Alex? Oh, you did. Oh, sweetie.'*

His parents hadn't been surprised when Ursula had
left that weekend with another man.

'The perils of passion,' his father had said.

'The highs and lows of love,' his mother had added.

For them, a little heartbreak was all part of the game—and that was how he'd come to see it too, since then. These days, he was more likely to be the one walking away without much of an apology. He played the game the same way everyone else did. High drama, high passion, a little adventure and a lot of fun—but nothing more.

And if he'd watched Fred and Polly sometimes and wondered how they managed to have both, he'd never admitted it to anyone. Until Nell, perhaps.

But the part he hadn't understood that weekend with Ursula, and wasn't sure he really understood now, was why. Why not him?

He glanced at her now, blonde and beautiful and smiling as if all of life was just a game. And beyond her he saw Nell, across on the other side of the table at the far end. Her hair fell like a black satin curtain, hiding half her face, but he could tell she wasn't having fun.

He wished he was sitting with her, rather than stuck here confronting his past.

But since he was…maybe it was time to ask the question that had been haunting him ever since.

'I remember you told me that weekend…you said, "You didn't really think I was going to marry *you*."'

'Did I?' Ursula at least had the grace to look ever so slightly embarrassed by that.

'I always wondered…why not? I thought we were happy together. Why were you so certain that we couldn't be happy for ever?'

'Because you didn't love me, Alex,' she replied bluntly. 'And I had a little more self-respect than to plan to marry a man who didn't love me.'

He blinked at her for a long moment. 'Of course I loved you.'

She shook her head and gave him a pitying smile. 'No, you didn't. Maybe you thought you did, because you grew up here, with your parents, and the only love you ever saw was based on grand gestures and blazing rows and performative reconciliations. And maybe that's what you were looking for. But it wasn't love, and it wasn't what I wanted.'

Alex rocked back in his chair as he absorbed the truth of what she was saying.

He *hadn't* loved Ursula, but he'd wanted to. He'd thought that the way they argued and made up was a sign of their mutual passion—of how much they cared.

Maybe it had really been a sign of their incompatibility.

Across on the other table he saw his parents glaring at each other as they bickered quietly. Soon, he knew, they'd stop being so quiet. After that, the whole room would know the details of their disagreement, and from there the old familiar pattern would continue.

The one they'd always told him was a sign of the depth of their love.

And for the first time Alex watched them and wondered if it was really a sign that they'd have been happier married to other people.

Then he saw the corner of his mother's smile as she took to her feet and denounced his father, and he knew they wouldn't be. They loved this, the drama, the passion, the way everyone was watching. This *was* love to them. The way he'd assumed it needed to be for him.

But maybe…maybe there was a different sort of love out there for him. Although as yet he had no idea what it might look like.

It definitely wasn't Nell's idea of love—never disagreeing about anything and never caring enough to even discuss it. He still wanted passion, and adventure.

Just…perhaps he could have that, without the high dudgeon and drama of his parents?

Something to think about, anyway.

'You genuinely look like I've rocked your world tonight,' Ursula said. 'Far more than I ever did when we were together. What on earth is going through your head?'

He looked away from his parents, and meant to turn his attention to the blonde at his side—but his gaze got caught on the silky curtain of Nell's hair, and the way her hunched shoulders told him she was hating every minute of this dinner.

Okay. That was enough waiting.

'I'm thinking I don't want to stay for the after-dinner entertainment.' He pushed his chair back, stood up and went to grab Nell and finish what they'd started in that hot-air balloon.

Alex didn't seem to be having as much fun as he usually did at these things.

It wasn't as if Nell was in the habit of watching him at parties, but…okay, fine. Sometimes she watched him at parties.

He just always looked as if he was having so much fun. As if being around all those other people and talking too loud and getting talked into doing stupid things made him feel more alive.

It was a habit she'd got into at university, back when they were invited to a lot more parties anyway. Well,

Polly and Fred were, and they'd drag Nell along, and Alex would just always be there because he knew *everybody*.

And he was always easy to pick out of a crowd, with his dark russet hair, tall frame and piercing blue eyes.

Of course she watched him. Most people did. He was very watchable.

And now, as she watched, she saw him push his chair back and stride towards her.

Her heart felt too loud in her chest—surely everyone else could hear it too? Did they all know that she'd kissed Alex McLeod in a hot-air balloon?

No, because if Polly knew that she wouldn't have left Nell's side all evening, and would be demanding all the details right now. So nobody knew.

Except her and Alex. It was their own delicious secret. One she intended to keep close to her chest.

She lifted her head as he approached and met his gaze, warming as his mouth spread into a smile that seemed just for her. A smile full of promise.

A smile that told her he wasn't done with her yet.

She had no illusions about what this was between them. And she'd make sure he knew that too—that she wasn't expecting him to change, or for anything lasting to develop.

They were very different people.

But maybe, if they could just keep it between themselves—low-key, no drama—they might be able to explore all the passion that kiss had exposed between them.

'Get bored with your tablemates?' she asked as Alex dropped into the empty chair beside her. Nell didn't even know where her neighbour had disappeared to; she'd not paid him any attention throughout the meal, too busy watching Alex.

She just hoped he wasn't someone Polly had been try-ing to set her up with, or she might be in trouble with her twin later...

'Polly and Fred sat me next to my ex-girlfriend,' Alex replied. 'The one I thought I was going to marry until she ran off with the son of my parents' friends.'

Nell winced. 'Ah. Not ideal.'

'No. But maybe it wasn't the worst thing.'

A chill settled over her bare shoulders in her gown. Had she completely misread his expressions and his body language as he'd sat there? Had he really come over to tell her that their kiss had been a one-off and could never happen again, because he was getting back together with his ex?

It would be a suitably dramatic Alex thing to do. And yet she couldn't convince herself of it for longer than a second.

'How come?' She kept her voice level and reached for a spare bread roll someone hadn't eaten with their soup earlier.

'I'd never really had the chance to ask her what went wrong between us. Why she didn't want to marry me,' Alex explained.

Nell's eyebrows flew up without her permission. 'You *asked* her? *Tonight?*' Because only Alex could get into a deep dive on a past relationship, with the potential for an utter blowout, at someone else's engagement party. That was just drama waiting to happen.

He gave her a knowing smile. 'Relax. It was all very calm and amicable. No upstaging the bride and groom-to-be tonight, I promise.'

That, Nell decided, was a promise worth having.

'So did she tell you? I mean, you don't have to tell *me,*' she added hurriedly, realising that it might not be the kind of conversation a person wanted to share. 'But…do you feel better after the conversation?'

Alex tipped back in his chair, hands clasped behind his head, and looked contemplative. 'I don't know. I think so? She said… She told me I only thought that I was in love with her probably because my models of what love looks like weren't always top-notch. But that I never really did love her, not the way she deserved to be loved.'

'Was she right?' Nell asked softly.

He looked over at her, his eyes a little sad. 'Probably. I guess… I thought that all the arguing and the making-up, the passion, meant love. But now…' His gaze drifted away and, when she followed it, Nell realised he was looking at Polly and Fred. 'Maybe I have a better idea of what love should look like now.'

She knew how he felt. Polly and Fred, for all their dramas, were solid. There was a respect and a deep, deep love that transcended all of that.

Nell just wasn't sure that everyone was lucky enough to find that. And she wasn't willing to take a risk on something that might turn out to be just the drama, without the underpinnings.

Besides, she didn't want Alex thinking about marriage and for ever right now. She wanted him focusing on the idea of a wedding fling. With her.

'It's hard to imagine you getting married at all,' she said lightly. 'I mean, I wouldn't have thought it would be on your bucket list. Wouldn't a wife interfere with your life of wild adventures?'

'Maybe the right wife would come with me.' He flashed her a smile, but it faded quickly.

She wondered if he was realising the same thing she already had—that she'd never be that wife. She wasn't that person, and she didn't want to be.

Which meant that whatever had started between them in the hot-air balloon had a built-in expiry date.

Still, that didn't mean they couldn't enjoy it while it lasted. Did it?

'Earlier,' Alex said cautiously. 'In the hot-air balloon…'

'You kissed me,' Nell finished for him.

He gave her a look. 'An observer might say that you kissed me.'

'But a gentleman never would.'

That earned her a laugh. 'Nobody has ever called me a gentleman. Scottish castle notwithstanding.'

'True.' She shifted on her chair so she was facing him, her body curved towards his. 'So. We kissed. What about it?'

'Well, I wondered if that might be the sort of thing you'd enjoy doing again,' Alex said.

'The *sort* of thing?' She put on her best naive and quizzical look. 'Are you proposing a different sort of kissing? Or something else entirely?'

Alex leaned closer, his mouth almost beside her ear. 'Nell Andrews, I'm asking you if I can *finally* take you to bed tonight, and ravish you to within an inch of your life.' He sat back up. 'Now. Is *that* something you might be interested in?'

Every nerve-ending in her body was on fire, as if her blood was burning them up as it pumped too fast around her body, fired up by her overacting heart.

She glanced towards the head of the table, where Fred and Polly sat, and noticed her sister watching them curiously. That would never do. The last thing she wanted was Polly getting wind of anything between her and Alex, and deciding that it was True Love and must be stage-managed by her so Nell couldn't screw it up.

If she wasn't careful, Polly would have planned them a double wedding by the time they made it to the Seychelles for the ceremony and celebrations.

Nell pulled her chair back, adding a little distance between her and Alex. Ever sensitive to her shifting moods, Alex did the same, with only a brief flash of disappointment on his face.

'That's a no, then?' he said without censure.

Nell flicked her gaze to her sister once more and, once she was sure Polly was distracted by a conversation with another guest, looked Alex dead in the eye.

'That's a hell, yes, please, if you can find a way we can do it without my sister ever knowing about it.'

The surprised smile that spread across Alex's handsome face didn't do anything to calm her racing heart.

'Oh, I'm sure I can come up with something,' he promised.

Nell thought she really liked his promises. Almost as much as his smiles.

CHAPTER ELEVEN

IT TOOK A little ingenuity—and a lot of patience—to avoid Polly's attention for the rest of the evening. But, just as Alex had predicted to himself, Nell's red line was drawn just before her sister. She didn't want Polly—or anyone else—knowing about things between them, and he had to respect that.

It wasn't as if he didn't understand why.

So, with a smile and a wink, he left Nell alone for the rest of the meal, waiting until the after-dinner mints and coffees were cleared, and the requisite speeches had been made. He rather thought Polly and Fred were testing him for what he might find to say in his wedding toast, so he got all the most embarrassing stories from university out of the way while the assembled company would appreciate them.

Nell, he noticed, was bright red and staring at the ceiling through most of them, as if she were embarrassed to even be associated with them. Which might be the case.

After dinner there was more drinking and dancing planned, with a DJ commandeering the ballroom of the house. His parents, he noticed, had been briefly distracted from their own drama by dessert, and then the cocktail bar Polly had arranged. If he was lucky, they'd forget about causing a scene until tomorrow.

As long as they didn't ruin his plans tonight, he didn't care.

Even with everything that was going on, the night seemed to drag. Alex tried to focus on the fun, but his mind was filled with the possibilities the night held *after* the party was over.

For the most part, he tried to keep his distance from Nell, worried that his thoughts would be written all over his face if anyone—namely Polly—saw them together. But, finally, he couldn't wait any longer.

He brushed past Nell as casually as he could, on his way through the ballroom, and took the opportunity to murmur instructions to her. 'Give it ten minutes, then tell Polly you're heading to bed.'

'You think she'll let me?' Nell asked.

Alex shrugged. 'You've already suffered a hot-air balloon ride *and* my speech for her tonight. I think she'll take pity.'

'And what will you be doing?'

'Giving myself an alibi.' He smirked as he headed off towards the cocktail bar.

He kept half an eye on Nell across the ballroom, while chatting with a group of old university friends, so he knew the moment she approached Polly.

'Ten minutes on the dot,' he murmured to himself, earning a confused look from the woman he was talking to.

He waited until she'd left for bed, and Polly was dancing with Fred, to announce that it was time for shots.

'Just like back at uni!' he declared, as he procured

some solid silver trays from one of the cabinets that lined the walls, and filled them with plastic shot glasses from behind the bar. A couple of bottles of tequila later, and he was handing them around to anyone still standing.

Even Polly and Fred joined in, looking amused at his throwback to their wilder university days.

'Same old Alex,' he heard more than one person say as he passed by with his trays.

He tried to ignore the way the words stung. Hadn't he grown up at all?

Perhaps not. Nell obviously didn't think so.

Nell. That was who this was all about. He had to focus on the endgame, here.

Three trays of shots later, he decided that everyone in the room would vouch that he'd been there all night, causing mayhem. He wondered if he needed something more dramatic to cement the idea that he'd partied to the death in people's minds, but he was too impatient to come up with anything.

After all, Nell was waiting for him.

He knew the castle better than any of the guests so it was easy enough for him to slip out unseen, through one of the doors only the servants really used, since it led directly into the kitchens. From there, he made his way up the back staircase to the first floor, where the wedding party had all been given rooms. He almost wished Nell had been housed out in one of the converted barns or old labourers' cottages with the other guests instead. It would have given them more privacy for everything he had planned…

Oh, well. The stone walls were thick at High Dudgeon House. Probably no one would hear anything anyway.

Because he was determined to make Nell Andrews scream his name tonight.

He crept along the first-floor landing, shoes silent on the runner carpet. He'd done this often enough in his youth to know exactly where the creaking floorboards were. Not that he thought anyone would hear them over the noise of the party downstairs, but at some point it had just become habit.

Nell's room was fortuitously next to his own childhood room, where he still slept whenever he visited. In fact, the room she'd been assigned had once been his nanny's bedroom—which cast up a number of disturbing connotations, but also meant there was a very convenient connecting door between the two.

Alex slipped into his own room, crossed it swiftly and knocked on the connecting door.

Another woman might have answered it in lingerie, or at least some sort of slinky nightgown. Another woman might have just called for him to come in, where he would have found her naked in the bed.

Nell yanked the door open, still wearing her ballgown and a serious frown, and said, 'What did you do?'

He blinked uncomprehendingly at her. 'What do you mean?'

'You said you were giving yourself an alibi. So, what kind of scene did you cause? Does my sister hate you for ever? If you ruined their engagement party just so you could sleep with me—'

Alex stepped forward, put his hands on her bare shoulders and smiled down at her. 'While I would do many things to sleep with you tonight, darling, I know better than to think you'd still want to sleep with *me* if I ruined anything about this wedding for Polly and Fred.'

Some of the tension flowed out of her shoulders, and he felt them relax under his fingers. She really was far too tense. The woman needed a good massage. Or several incredible orgasms.

Maybe he could help with both those things.

'So what *did* you do?' she asked again, more curious than accusing this time.

'I served trays of tequila shots to basically everybody in that room,' he replied. 'Everyone saw me partying hard. Nobody is likely to notice that I've disappeared early—and, if they do, they'll just think I'm sleeping off the tequila somewhere.'

'Oh.' Nell's mouth curved up into a smile. 'That doesn't sound too bad.'

'Does that mean I can come in?' He stepped a little closer, until his body was flush against hers, and was rewarded by the way her cleavage swelled over the neckline of her gown when she breathed in sharply.

God, this woman did things to him. It was quite a relief to see that he did the same to her.

Nell stepped away. 'Come in, Alex.'

He took a breath, glad he'd only had one of those tequila shots.

He wanted to remember every moment of this night.

Just in case he never got another one with her.

Nell stared at Alex across the room, and wondered at the incredibly weird sequence of events that had brought them here.

They were going to have sex.

In a Scottish castle.

At her sister's engagement party.

And this was the strangest one…

Together.

She was going to sleep with Alex McLeod. Finally.

And however outlandish and unpredictable that idea was…suddenly she couldn't wait a moment more.

Reaching up behind her, she tugged down the zip of her ballgown and let it fall.

It was over-the-top, slightly awkward and maybe a little dramatic—and it made Alex's eyes widen to saucer-size. So that made it worth it.

'You still wear the best lingerie,' he said, his voice husky, and Nell felt the heat hit her cheeks as she looked down at herself.

The strapless corset had been almost a necessity under the off-the-shoulder ballgown. The fact it was zebra-print…well, it was still black and white, wasn't it? Just like all her other clothes.

And the matching thong just made sense.

Alex stared at her a moment longer, until she started to worry he might have changed his mind.

Then he lunged forward, crossing the room in the time it took her to blink, and suddenly she was in his arms and…

Everything else faded away.

The drama of the moment, the fear and the tension, the worry of all the ways things could go wrong, the lingering doubt about whether any of this was a good idea in the first place—even the nagging feeling that Polly was going to knock on her door at any moment and catch them.

The moment Alex's lips touched hers she forgot it all.

'God, I've been waiting to do that again all night,' he murmured as he rested his forehead against hers and smiled down at her. 'You looked beautiful in that ball-gown, in case I hadn't mentioned it.'

'You hadn't, actually.'

His lips twitched as if he were holding in his laughter. 'Well, you look even more amazing in this.'

Alex ran his hands up the side of her corset, over the boning that kept everything in place, and Nell shivered.

'Want to see what I look like out of it?'

Alex groaned. 'God, yes, please.'

'Then take it off.'

Where had the courage come from to make her say that? To do any of this?

Nell had no idea.

But she wasn't going to argue with it.

Maybe tonight—just this one night—she could give in to the passion, adventure and drama that was her genetic birthright and have wild, unashamed, uninhibited sex with Alex McLeod.

Tomorrow, she'd go back to being cautious, careful Nell. She'd resume her search for stability and surety in her life.

But tonight... Tonight she felt like someone else entirely.

Alex's nimble fingers made short work of loosening the corset laces at her back, looking down over her shoulder as he worked, his chest pressed against hers. She wondered if he could feel her racing heartbeat between them. If his blood was pounding in his ears the way hers was.

Then he stepped back and the corset fell to the floor, leaving her bare except for her zebra-print thong, the thigh-high stockings she'd worn under her dress and the heeled lace-up boots she'd chosen instead of high heels. She swallowed as she realised Alex was still fully dressed, his bow tie hanging loose around his neck, but his jacket still on.

She should feel vulnerable. Embarrassed.

Instead, she felt powerful.

His gaze raked over every inch of her, drinking her in. She gave him a moment to adjust, then stretched out her hand.

'Take me to bed, Alex.'

He met her gaze and she saw his throat bob as he swallowed. 'With pleasure.'

Making love to Nell Andrews was like nothing he'd ever imagined. Not that he'd spent a lot of time imagining it over the years since she'd run out on him—or he'd run out on her. But if he had…he'd have thought she'd have been buttoned-up. A lights off, missionary kind of girl, not that there was anything wrong with that.

He'd have thought she'd find the whole thing embarrassing.

The kisses they'd shared before had been too tentative, too uncertain, to give much away. But tonight…tonight he'd known the moment he'd kissed her in the hot-air balloon that things were different this time. He'd felt the passion surging through her, and known that the two of them together could be something very special indeed.

He just hadn't expected *this*.

He wasn't some fumbling teenage boy. He knew what to do to make a woman's toes curl, how to get her to pant his name desperately in his ear. How to take control in the bedroom and ensure that everyone had a fantastic time.

Except…

From the moment she dropped her ballgown and revealed the lingerie she was wearing underneath, Alex didn't feel in control at all.

In fact, he'd never felt so out of control.

'You're wearing too many clothes,' she murmured, reaching for the buttons on his shirt.

How could he have never realised there was this side to her before? They'd known each other for a decade. All that time, this woman—filled with passion and possibility—had been hiding behind the boring rules she imposed on her own life.

He should have known. He should have realised the first time he'd seen her lingerie drawer. The first time he'd kissed her, when they were idiot teens.

But he knew now, and he wasn't going to waste another second.

Together, they stripped off his shirt and jacket in one go, and as she sat on the edge of the bed and moved on to dealing with his trousers he eased off her boots, then her thong, leaving the stockings in place. Then he stepped out of his boxers, and looked down at the glory of her.

'What?' she asked, stretching for him on the bed.

What little blood there had been left in his brain fled to where all the rest had gone, and he knew he'd never been this hard, this desperate for a woman before.

'I'm just trying to decide where to start,' he said. 'I want to kiss every inch of you before sunrise. Twice.'

She smiled. 'Better get a move on, then.'

So he did.

He kissed down her throat to her breasts, spending precious moments on each—then lingering longer when he heard the sweet gasping noises she made when he did.

Finally, he moved lower, skipping down her thighs to kiss up her calves through her stockings, teasing the place where the silk gave way to even smoother skin.

'Alex, for the love of all things holy…'

'Patience,' he told her.

He'd taken so long to really see her, he wasn't going to rush now.

But eventually he couldn't wait any longer. He shifted closer, spreading her legs as he moved his mouth nearer to where he knew she wanted it. She tensed, just for a moment, though, which gave him pause.

'Okay?' he asked softly.

She nodded. 'I will be. When you get to the good stuff.'

Smirking, he got to the good stuff.

And God, was it good. The way she writhed under his tongue. The sounds she made as he worked her all the way to the brink…then stopped.

'I always knew you were a bad man,' she said, her voice hoarse.

He kissed his way over her belly and between her breasts as he slid up her body. 'I want to feel you come around me.'

She wriggled against him in a way that made him clench his jaw and desperately hold onto his self-control. 'I can live with that, I suppose.'

She might be able to, but Alex was kind of afraid the experience might kill him.

At the least, he already knew that moving on from this night was going to be difficult.

Maybe even impossible.

CHAPTER TWELVE

NELL GRABBED HOLD of Alex's arms as he slid inside her, and experienced the same strange weightlessness she'd felt on the hot-air balloon. As if the whole world had fallen away and she was floating out of space and time.

Then everything came back into focus and she moved with him, catching his rhythm, desperately chasing that high his tongue and fingers had promised her.

'God, Nell.' His voice was hot and harsh in her ear. 'We should have been doing this for years.'

She was beyond the words she needed to respond, but she suspected the noises she did make were enough to tell him she agreed. He chuckled in response, and tilted his hips just so and—

Nell had always thought books were exaggerating when they talked about heroines seeing fireworks behind their eyes when they came.

Apparently it had just been another one of those things that was outside her sphere of experience.

Maybe some things were worth taking risks for.

'You still with me?' Alex asked, starting to sound ragged himself.

'Just about.'

'Want to see if we can get you there again?'

It was on the tip of her tongue to tell him not to bother. That she'd never orgasmed twice in one night, with anyone. That he should just let go and finish this.

Except…

This was her night for taking risks. And maybe she wanted to see if she could.

She nodded, and he started to move again, hot and heavy and wonderful inside her and over her, moving one hand down to the place they were joined, and it didn't take very long at all for her to realise that, yes, actually, this was something else she was very, very capable of. If she just let herself go…

This time, he fell over the edge with her, collapsing half on her, half to the side, after choking out her name. Nell lay beside him, slowly getting her breath back, hot and sweaty and satisfied.

'You're smiling,' Alex said, before sitting up to dispose of the condom. 'Guess I must have done something right at last.'

'Not you,' Nell told him. 'Us. We're good at that.'

He lay back beside her and wrapped an arm tight around her waist. 'We really, really are.'

They lay in contented silence for a while, long enough that she began to suspect he'd fallen asleep. She wanted to do the same, her whole body begging for rest, but she needed to get out of these stockings. And she couldn't sleep until she'd cleaned her teeth, not to mention taken off her make-up. Plus she should really send him back to his own room, in case Polly came looking for her first thing, and—

'Do you always think so loud after sex?' Alex asked, the words slightly slurred with sleep.

'I think this loud all the time,' she admitted. 'You're just not usually close enough to hear it.'

Which was, she knew, a ridiculous thing to say, given that nobody could hear another person *think*. But from the way his lips curved against the skin of her shoulder, before he placed a light kiss there, he seemed to appreciate the comment all the same.

Alex sighed and then, with what appeared to be considerable effort, sat up beside her.

'Go on,' he said. 'I know you want to go clean up or whatever. So, go do that. And then we'll talk about whatever has your mind whirring like a clock.'

She didn't argue. Which might have been a first for them, actually.

It was only once she was locked safely in the en suite bathroom that the enormity of what she'd just done crashed down on her.

She'd slept with Alex McLeod. And it had been *incredible*.

To her surprise, she found she didn't regret any of what had happened at all. Her mind was just hung up on what came next.

Which she supposed was what she needed to talk to Alex about.

She took a moment to smile at her reflection in the mirror—a flushed, relaxed Nell she almost didn't recognise smiled back.

Then she set about cleaning up, and getting back to Alex.

The sooner they talked, the sooner she could sleep.

Alex ducked back into his own room while Nell was in the bathroom, leaving the connecting door open so she wouldn't think he'd run out on her if she came out before he returned. He washed quickly in his own bathroom, and pulled on a pair of comfortable joggers—High Dudgeon House got cold at night, he knew from his childhood.

He was glad he had, though, when he heard a knock on his own bedroom door.

Fred stood on the other side, his eyes a little glassy— probably due to the tequila, Alex assumed. Hopefully the drinks had had enough of an impact that he wouldn't notice the open connecting door.

'There you are!' Fred clapped him on the shoulder with a wide smile. 'We were wondering where you'd got to! Polly thought you might have sloped off with some woman, but I was blaming the tequila—remember that night in Mexico? You and tequila never were good friends.'

Alex forced a laugh. 'Yeah, tequila might not have been my best ever plan. You and Polly had fun though?'

'Of course! Great party.' Fred looked both ways along the landing, then lowered his voice. 'Although you, ah, might want to check on your parents in the morning. Last I saw, your mother was deep in conversation with old Calvin Brooks.'

Alex winced. Calvin had to be fifteen years his mother's junior, and a friend of a friend of a friend who had some- how ended up on the invite list for the weekend despite Polly's best efforts. 'Right. I'll deal with that tomorrow. Right now I just want to—' He jerked a thumb towards the bathroom, remembering too late about the open door.

Luckily, Fred didn't seem to notice it. 'Yeah, sure. And I'd better find my room. Polly's waiting, you know?' He waggled his eyebrows and wandered off.

Alex shut the door and rested his head against the wood for a moment, then turned to see that the connecting door had been pushed almost completely closed.

Only almost, though. That meant he was still welcome, right?

He knocked anyway, and found Nell waiting right behind the door.

'Fred came looking for you?' She looked up at him, chewing on her lower lip.

The stockings were gone, he realised. In their place were tartan pyjama bottoms, and a loose T-shirt that still left him thinking about everything he now knew was under it.

'Yeah. He thinks the tequila got to me and I had to go lie down. Or throw up. Or something.' So much for his reputation as a partier. Ah, well. It had been worth it.

More than worth it.

Nell sat on the edge of her bed, and for the first time Alex took a proper look around the room. 'You know, this used to be my nanny's room.'

She gave a surprised laugh, then covered her face. 'I was about to say that I don't know if that makes things better or worse. But I do know. It's worse. Much worse.'

Alex moved to sit beside her, leaving just enough space between them that he hoped she wouldn't feel crowded. 'If it helps, I never thought about my nanny the way I think about you.'

Nell peeked out from between her fingers. 'And how *do* you think about me?'

'I didn't make that clear enough earlier? Because I can show you again…well, if you give me a little recovery time first…'

'That's not what I mean.' Dropping her hands to her

lap, she took a deep breath, and Alex knew that she'd probably been planning whatever she said next in the mirror before she came out. Which meant that it was important, and he should pay proper attention.

It was just hard to do that when her breasts kept shifting under that T-shirt...

'I had a great time with you tonight,' she said. 'Better than I could have expected. I wouldn't have thought... knowing you and knowing myself, that we could be so compatible. But, well, we were, I think.' She looked to him for confirmation, and he nodded emphatically.

'Hell, yes, definitely compatible,' he said. 'But I know what you mean. I wouldn't have naturally assumed you and I would be either.'

'So I guess what I'm asking is...what happens next?' She looked up at him, eyes wide and her mouth looking strangely vulnerable, still pink and swollen from his kisses. Thank God Fred hadn't seen her, or he'd have known instantly what they'd been up to. 'I mean, we might be compatible here, in the bedroom. But outside it...'

The reality of what she was saying hit hard into his post-coital afterglow. 'We're not.'

It wasn't a new thought. He'd had one very similar just a few hours earlier, when talking to Ursula.

However much he wanted Nell physically, emotionally and personally they wanted completely different things. He was never going to be able to offer her the safe, secure, boring life she wanted. And she had no desire to join him in a life of adventure.

But maybe that was okay. Maybe they didn't need to.

'Well, perhaps we just...lean into our strengths and ignore the rest?' he suggested.

'So we just keep having sex indefinitely and otherwise ignore each other completely?' She sounded, not unreasonably, a little sceptical about the plan. But really, what else did they have?

'Unless you want to cause a scene and dump me dramatically at your sister's wedding?'

She rolled her eyes. 'Does that sound like something I would do?'

'No,' he admitted. 'But neither does sleeping with me in the first place.'

'True.'

He nudged her with his shoulder and she leaned into him, a welcome warmth against his side.

'The way I see it, we have three options.' He raised one finger. 'One, pretend this never happened, and go back to being mere business partners and occasionally friendly acquaintances.'

'Hmm. Seems unlikely,' Nell said. 'For starters, sex like that is pretty hard to forget.'

'Agreed. Which brings us to option two.' He held up two fingers. 'Fall madly in love and try to change each other so we can live in harmony together for ever.'

'With our pet unicorn, I take it?'

'Obviously.'

She gave him a look.

'Taking that as a no, it leaves us with number three.' He added the third finger. 'Try being friends. Perhaps with occasional short-term intimate advantages. At least until after the wedding.'

'More best man with benefits than friends with benefits?' Nell tilted her head as if she was actually considering it, which was, if he was honest, more than Alex had actually hoped for.

'If you like.'

'I suppose it *could* work,' she said thoughtfully. 'Although there'd have to be some ground rules.'

'I never expected anything less.' Nell was the *queen* of rules and boundaries, after all. She was the reason they had the laminated poster with coffee machine etiquette in the kitchen at work.

'Polly and Fred never know.' She gave him an intense, defiant look. 'That's a dealbreaker. Because if Polly found out…'

She trailed off, leaving Alex wondering exactly what Polly would do if she *did* find out. Disapprove? Try to marry them off? Something in between?

Whatever it was, it was enough to worry Nell, so he agreed. 'Okay. What else?'

Nell bit down on her lip as she looked up at him. 'It's only until after the wedding. Okay? I just… I don't want to risk either of us getting too comfortable in an arrangement that can't last.'

'That makes sense,' he replied, even as a sinking part of his heart realised that the wedding was only a few weeks away. Why had they wasted the last couple of months dating other people? 'We can get it all out of our system between now and then.'

'Exactly,' Nell said firmly. 'Then we can both get back to trying to find real dates we might have a future with.'

'Great,' Alex said.

Even though the idea of Nell with another boring date who didn't understand her turned his stomach.

Maybe he could just blame the tequila.

CHAPTER THIRTEEN

POLLY SWEPT INTO the meeting room on Monday morning looking for all the world like she'd spent the weekend relaxing at a spa, rather than drinking and partying on her hen do, as Nell knew she actually had. The sheer quantity of empty bottles at the end of the weekend had surprised even Mr and Mrs McLeod.

Separately, of course, since they weren't speaking by that point, and Mrs McLeod had her cases packed by the front door with everyone else's as they were leaving.

According to Alex, that was par for the course. Nell had no idea how he lived with it.

'Well, I think that went well, don't you?' Polly said, glancing around the table with a fond look for her fiancé, and satisfied ones for Alex and Nell. Until she frowned. 'Except neither of you has a date for my wedding yet, do you?'

Nell pointedly did not look at Alex as she shook her head.

'I had high hopes for you, McLeod, after you disappeared on Saturday night,' Polly went on. 'But Fred tells me you were in your room alone, recovering from the tequila shots you insisted on. Which probably serves you right, but doesn't get you any closer to a date for the wedding.'

'Sorry to be such a disappointment,' Alex said drily, and just the sound of his voice made Nell clench her thighs together to avoid shivering.

When she risked a glance up she saw that Fred was giving her a funny look, so she reached for her notebook and started leafing through the pages, as if she might find a date inside.

No need to tell the bride and groom that she already had one. They wouldn't understand, anyway.

It had been a relief to realise that she and Alex were on the same page there. They were too different for anything between them to grow beyond the inevitable heartbreak that would ensue when they both accepted that.

Giving themselves the deadline of the wedding removed that risk. And made the next few weeks all the more intense…

At the head of the table, Polly sat down with a dramatic sigh. 'Well, that's it then. You're just going to have to pair up for the wedding. I know you don't want to,' she said, holding up a hand to forestall the expected objections. 'But I can't have the maid of honour and best man going solo at a romantic, couple themed wedding!'

'Everything *is* planned for twos,' Fred added solemnly. Nell suspected he found this whole thing as ridiculous as she did, but had decided to go along with it for the sake of peace and harmony.

Of course, she also suspected that Polly had only planned it this way in the first place to showcase the agency's best work, but now it seemed to have taken on a life of its own.

With a sigh, she cast a careful look in Alex's direction. 'What do you think?'

Leaning back in his chair, Alex shrugged, his expression bland and emotionless. 'Doesn't make much difference to me at this point. *You* were the one who refused to partner me to the wedding in the first place. *Not a chance in hell,* were your exact words, as I recall.'

Nell bit the inside of her cheek to keep from laughing. She really had said that, hadn't she? 'I don't think I was exactly your first choice either,' she pointed out.

'Well, apparently you're my last.' He sighed. 'What do you say, Andrews? Think you can face putting up with me for the wedding week?'

'We don't have to share a room or anything, do we?' she asked Polly in mock panic.

Polly laughed. 'Even I'm not that cruel. But I will have to put you together in one of the two-bedroom beachfront villas—it would just be a waste, otherwise.'

'Fair enough, I suppose.' Nell tried not to sound too enthusiastic about the idea, but inside she was cheering. They wouldn't even have to sneak around between rooms if they were sharing a villa!

Polly went on, 'And Alex, I'd appreciate it if you could manage not to split up any of the other couples over the wedding week.' When he pulled a wide-eyed, innocent look, she added, 'I saw how chummy you and Ursula were getting again over dessert. But she's coming with Damien, and I have high hopes for the pair of them, so don't go ruining it.'

'My little matchmaker,' Fred said fondly.

'I just want everyone to be as happy as we are.' Polly took his hand across the table and gave him a frankly sickening smile.

Nell exchanged a quick glance with Alex. 'As long as

you're not making any plans for us two. This is strictly a wedding-only arrangement.'

'Over the moment you two jet off on your honeymoon,' Alex agreed.

'Yes, yes, I know.' Polly flapped a hand in acknowledgment. 'Frankly, I've given up on the two of you. Alex will never risk settling down long enough to find love, probably because he doesn't want to end up like his parents, which, having witnessed them this weekend, I suppose is fair enough. And Nell, you'll never risk your safe and boring life to fall properly, deeply, irrevocably in love, even if you leave your flat or your office long enough to find someone!' She took a deep breath and looked around at the others, who sat in stunned silence. 'What?'

Fred squeezed her hand. 'Maybe a couple too many home truths for a Monday morning, sweetheart.'

Polly looked mulishly unrepentant. 'Well, if I don't tell them, who will? They're never going to be happy at this rate.'

Alex got to his feet. 'And on that note, I think I'm going to take my unlovable self off to get a coffee. Coming, Andrews?'

'Why not? After all, I'll never find love if I hide out in my office, will I?'

'I think the guy at the coffee cart was flirting with you last week,' Alex said.

Nell clasped her hands together in pretend joy. 'Well, thank goodness! My spell in the love wilderness is over at last.'

'You two are being ridiculous,' Polly said sulkily. 'I just meant—'

'Oh, we know what you meant,' Alex broke in. 'And I'm sure we each thank you for the early morning psychoanalysis.'

'But I've got an octogenarian coffee guy to flirt with,' Nell added. 'Bye!'

Leaving the meeting room door to swing shut behind them, Alex and Nell headed down the stairs and out into the bright, early summer London morning.

'Well, I think that went well, don't you?' Alex said as they reached the edge of the park, and what Nell had come to think of as *their* coffee cart came into sight.

'I don't think they suspected anything, if that's what you mean,' Nell replied. 'But I'm slightly concerned that this bridezilla thing might lead to my sister wanting to take control of *everyone's* lives.'

'You say that like she didn't already,' Alex pointed out.

'True.' Nell nudged his arm with her shoulder. 'But this, us…for the next two weeks, at least. That's none of her business.'

'Agreed.' Alex pressed a kiss to the top of her hair. 'It's just us. So, coffee?'

'God, yes, please.'

Neither of them mentioned what Polly had said about each of them. Which, Nell decided later that night, lying in her bed with Alex, was probably for the best.

Why ruin something good with reality before they had to?

Alex awoke two weeks later, warm and content and with thoughts of waking Nell up to see if her train of thought was running the same way his was…when he realised the other half of the bed was empty.

He frowned. He was pretty sure she'd been there when he went to sleep. And, not that he liked to brag, by the time they'd called it a night her legs definitely hadn't been capable of carrying her home.

Who was he kidding? He *loved* to brag about that.

Not that he did or could. Because nobody else could know about them. Their entire relationship was invisible to the outside world.

And now Nell herself had disappeared.

'Andrews?' he called out, into the empty room. They'd gone back to his flat the night before, after eating dinner at some tiny restaurant in a part of London he didn't think he'd ever visited before, and knew Polly and Fred wouldn't. Even so, Nell hadn't allowed him to so much as hold her hand, just in case.

That way, if anyone sees us, we can tell them it was a last minute wedding planning meeting, or something, she'd said.

If he didn't know better, he'd think she was ashamed of him.

But he did know better. Which was why he was pretty sure she was ashamed of herself—for wanting him in the first place. For desiring something so far out of her comfort zone as sex with him.

Just sex. Nothing more. That much had been made very clear.

And it *was* for the best. He knew that.

He just…didn't like to think too much about what happened when the wedding was over.

The wedding.

Wait.

Alex sat up suddenly. 'Nell?'

She appeared in the doorway this time, fully dressed in some stretchy black trousers, a stripy black and white T-shirt and a long black cardigan. She was putting a golden hoop earring through her lobe.

'Why are you still in bed? I woke you up before I went for my shower!'

'You did?' Now that he thought about it, maybe he vaguely recalled her murmuring something into his ear, a while ago.

'Yes!' She rolled her eyes. 'Get up. Get dressed. The cab to the airport will be here in thirty minutes!'

Airport. Yes.

Because the wedding week started today, with their flight to Mahé departing that afternoon.

'Bet you're glad I made you pack last night now,' Nell shot back over her shoulder, before she disappeared into the living room.

Alex hauled himself out of bed, showered and dressed in something comfortable for flying, then joined her.

'What are you doing?' he asked.

'Checking our passports and tickets,' Nell replied, not looking up from the special travel folder she'd placed them in.

'You did that last night,' he pointed out.

'And at least four times already this morning.' She looked faintly apologetic as she said it.

'So we've definitely got them, then?'

'Looks like.' She hugged the wallet to her chest. 'Do you think anyone will notice if I've got your travel documents though? Will they guess?'

He shrugged. 'Probably people will be more worried about their own stuff. And if they notice…well, you're in charge of making sure I don't screw up this week, right?' He was sure Polly must have added that to the list of maid of honour duties once he and Nell were paired up for the wedding.

'That's true. And if I hadn't been here this morning you'd have probably slept through the cab coming, so… yeah, we can probably sell it.'

'Great. That's one less thing for me to worry about, then.'

Which didn't explain why a new weight of worry seemed to have landed in his chest over the last few days.

Was it just the fact that she was hiding everything that was between them from the world? He wasn't built for hiding away—he lived unapologetically out loud, and had never been good at pretending he felt something he didn't, or pretending he didn't feel what he did.

But she could never be happy opening up their feelings to the world that way. And what was the point arguing about it when they already had a built-in expiry date?

Oh.

Maybe *that* was the problem.

They were down to their last week together and…he didn't want it to end. Not yet. Not when they were having so much fun together—secrecy and her desire to organise him to within an inch of his life notwithstanding.

But they'd made a deal, and he wasn't going to go back on that now.

All he could do was make the most of the time they had left, then end things amicably—even happily. Then she'd be free to find someone who could give her what she needed and he…

Well. Maybe he'd get to keep her as a friend, after this.

That had to be better than nothing, right?

'You've got the rings?' Nell asked, and he nodded. 'And your suit?'

'You checked my case twice when I was packing it.'

'And you haven't changed anything since?' she pressed.

'No,' he said. 'You realise that airport security will be a breeze after this?'

The fact Nell didn't even make a joke about his previous dates and airport security told him how stressed she was. 'And I've got my dress, my shoes—you packed shoes, right?—and my jewellery…cufflinks! Did you pack cufflinks?'

'Yes. Because they were on the frighteningly comprehensive packing list you gave me.' He had never been so well organised for a trip in his life.

'Come on, then.' Nell grabbed the handle of her suitcase, their travel folder tucked under her arm. 'Let's get down there and wait for the cab.'

He followed docilely, and it was only once they were in the taxi on the way to the airport that he realised she'd booked it for six hours before their flight.

CHAPTER FOURTEEN

POLLY HAD CHARTERED a private plane to get the bulk of her guests to the island in the Seychelles, where she and Fred would be tying the knot. Ostensibly, this was just another example of what Here & Now could offer their clients, and as such was being dutifully uploaded to all their social media channels. In reality, Nell suspected her sister just wanted to keep all her guests in one place, where they couldn't get into trouble.

There were some guests travelling in from other countries, or arriving later in the week for some reason or another, but it was still a full plane heading out. Nell scanned the occupied seats as she boarded, relieved to see that the two guests she least wanted to spend time in an enclosed place with—her mother and Paul—didn't seem to be flying with them.

'I have never seen a plane quite this…pink,' Alex murmured over her shoulder. 'It's like Valentine's Day threw up in here.'

'I'm not entirely sure on the logistics of that, but I take your point.' Each pair of seats had a double-sized pink blanket for sharing, plus a tiny bag of heart-shaped chocolates wrapped in red foil. The overhead cabins had been decorated with pink hearts, and even the stewards were wearing red waistcoats with pink heart pockets.

'Want the window seat?' Alex asked, and she shook her head.

'The less I can see of the open, empty space below us the better.'

They settled into their seats, Alex sweeping the fluffy pink blanket across both their laps. Nell picked up the card placed in the pocket of the seat in front and surveyed the details of their flight.

'So, we have a choice of several romantic movies to watch, and all our food will apparently be heart-shaped.' She tossed the card to him, and he chuckled as he read it.

'Heart-shaped pancakes I can buy,' he said. 'But heart-shaped chicken?'

She snickered at the face he pulled, then glanced around self-consciously to see who was watching. Yes, they were supposed to be attending this wedding together, but not *together* together, and she didn't want anyone getting any ideas. Or guessing what was actually going on between them.

Which meant they probably shouldn't seem to be getting on *too* well. Or would that make things worse? Like they were protesting too much?

Nell wrestled with the uncertainty all through take-off, which served as a pleasant distraction. And at least she didn't feel too self-conscious about gripping tight to Alex's hand under their blanket.

As soon as the seatbelt sign had turned off, and they were cruising along at Nell didn't want to know what height, Polly popped up beside their seats. 'Isn't this wonderful?'

'It's a pastel pink wonderland,' Alex replied from by the window. 'I'm sure all of your fellow couples are loving it.'

Polly rolled her eyes. 'Okay, maybe it's a little over the top, but I wanted *romantic.*'

'It most certainly is that,' Nell said. If, by romantic, one meant pink and over the top.

Personally she preferred more private, intimate romantic gestures. But each to their own.

'I know it's a little weird for you two,' Polly went on. 'Not being an actual couple. But if you could just *pretend,* just for this week, just for me, that would be wonderful.'

Nell cast a quick glance back at Alex, who gave her a slightly lopsided smile and a shrug, as if to say it was all up to her.

But under the blanket she felt his hand resting on her thigh, his fingers inching up along the seam of her leggings.

'I'm sure we can manage that,' she replied, her mouth suddenly painfully dry.

Polly beamed. 'Thank you!' Then she bounced off towards the next set of guests.

And Alex's fingers inched higher.

Alex watched the back of Polly's head as she moved further down the plane, away from them. Then he teased the inside of Nell's thigh just a little more.

Any moment now he expected her to grab his hand and move it, to glare at him and whisper for him to stop playing games.

But she didn't.

So he ran his knuckles up the inside of her other thigh too, and smiled when he heard her suck in a sharp breath.

'Alex,' she whispered. 'Someone might see.'

He gazed around them pointedly. Every other passenger was engrossed in their own occupation—a movie, a book, conversation with their own partner. More than a few had their blankets spread across them, some napping, some…well, Alex wasn't going to judge what might be going on under them. Especially right now.

He inched his fingers closer to her centre.

'Nobody is looking. Nobody cares. Nobody is thinking about what you and I are up to here.' Or anywhere, for that matter.

Nell seemed to think the sky would fall down if people found out about them, but he wasn't so sure. Would anyone really care as much as she thought?

'We're on a plane,' Nell hissed. 'In public.'

But even as she said the words she tilted her hips just so, giving his wandering fingers better access.

He smiled. 'Do you want me to stop, then?'

He would, if she said the words. Of course he would. But she didn't.

'No,' she breathed, her cheeks pink. 'Don't stop.'

'Okay, then.'

Alex twisted his body, wishing she'd chosen the window seat. It would make doing this undetected so much easier. Still, he'd been right when he said that nobody was paying them any attention.

'Think you can be quiet?' he murmured as his fingertips reached the top of the seam.

Nell nodded, her bottom lip caught between her teeth.

'Good.' He pressed down, just a little harder, and heard her breath kick up a notch. Perfect.

The angles weren't ideal and with the blanket over them he could only rely on touch to figure out what she needed. He wished he could pull down her leggings and get inside, but he had a feeling she'd draw the line before then and push him away.

So he'd work with what he had. Better to touch her this way than not at all.

Better to be a secret than to not have her...

He pushed the thought away. This wasn't their relationship he was focusing on, purely her pleasure. A chance for her to do something adventurous, unexpected and fun.

He'd bet none of her exes had ever made her orgasm on a plane before.

With a renewed sense of purpose, he traced a finger along the seam of her leggings again, and watched her bite down harder on her lip. He smiled, and prepared to take her higher—

'Hi, guys.' Fred leaned against Nell's seat, looming over them. 'Nell, can we swap seats for a bit? Polly wants to run through some wedding bits with you before we land. Okay?'

'Absolutely.' Nell's cheeks were burning red as she slipped out from under the blanket, moving away from her seat without even looking back at Alex.

With a sigh, Alex slumped into his own seat, pulling the pink blanket fully onto his lap to hide his own reaction to their activities.

Fred slid into the seat beside him. 'So. How's being a couple with Nell going?'

'Fine.' Alex sneaked a look up at his friend, and found

a knowing glint in Fred's eye. 'Boring,' he added, not caring how obvious the lie was.

'Right.' Fred didn't even pretend to look convinced. 'Well, that's what I'll tell Polly when she asks, then.'

Relief surged through him. At least Fred wasn't going to tell his fiancée his suspicions—which meant Nell might let him live another day or two.

'Great.' Alex reached for his headphones. 'Now, if you don't mind, I've got a trashy movie to watch.'

'Sure. Just…' Fred hesitated, and Alex looked up at him again. 'Just be careful, yeah? For all our sakes.'

Alex grunted agreement, and turned his attention to the film playing on the screen in front of him.

But when Nell returned half an hour later, in time for the meal service, he couldn't even have said what movie he'd been watching.

'What do you mean it's not here? Can you check again? Please?'

Nell rubbed the back of her hand across her forehead as she leaned heavily against the marble counter of the hotel reception desk.

Fourteen hours on a plane, then a transfer by car and—horrifically—helicopter to their private island, and Nell was at the end of everything. She couldn't even muster much enthusiasm for the incredible location Polly and Fred had picked for their wedding.

Alex had stumbled away to check the bridal villa was ready for Fred and Polly, who'd been whisked away for a relaxing welcome drink by the wedding planner, and then she imagined he'd be passing out asleep in his room for the next eight hours. She knew he hadn't slept on the plane, because after she'd returned from her conversation with Polly he'd stayed up to distract her by watching stupid movies with her and keeping a running commentary going, whispered by her ear, so she didn't concentrate on the fact they were miles up in the air in a metal box that could crash at any moment.

Naturally, she hadn't slept either.

She'd planned to head straight to her room and crash out too, but before she did she'd just wanted to check one simple thing.

That Polly's wedding dress, sent ahead by a specialist courier company, had arrived.

'I'm sorry,' the slender young lady behind the reception desk told her, looking very apologetic. 'It doesn't appear to be here. Perhaps you could try contacting the courier company.'

'I will do that. Thank you.'

As she turned away the luxurious hotel lobby started to spin, and she reached out for something to hold onto— only to find that someone had hold of her.

'Okay, I think you need to sit down,' Alex said, guiding her to a nearby chair.

She sank into its plush cushions gratefully. 'I thought you'd gone to sleep.'

'Without you?' He gave her a soft smile. 'I've only got one more week with you, and I have no intention of wasting any of it.'

She couldn't help but return his smile at that, before she even remembered to check that no one was watching them.

Alex sat back in the chair opposite her. 'So. What's the problem?'

'Polly's wedding dress hasn't arrived.'

Alex winced. 'Okay. What do we need to do?'

'I need to call the courier company, see what's gone wrong.'

'They're based in the UK?' Alex asked. Nell nodded. 'Then they won't be open for another couple of hours. I'll send an email to our London office and get someone to follow up on it the moment they get in. And you can get some sleep. Okay?'

It sounded so simple when he said it like that.

'I don't think my brain is working right now.'

'That's because this day has lasted approximately seven thousand hours.' Alex stood up again, rather creakily she thought, and held out a hand to pull her up too. 'Come on. Email then bed. Okay?'

She nodded and took his hand—then stopped, as the hotel doors opened again and two familiar people walked in.

Alex glanced back over his shoulder to see what she was looking at. 'Paul and Jemima?'

Nell nodded.

'You knew they were going to be here,' he said. 'Come on. You don't have to talk to them.'

But she did. Because she was the maid of honour and Alex was the best man, and part of their duties was greeting the guests when the bride and groom weren't there to do it.

Pasting a smile on her face, she crossed the lobby towards her ex and his new girlfriend.

'Paul, Jemima, so lovely you could make it.' She held out a hand to Jemima. 'I'm Nell, the maid of honour, and this is Alex, the best man. Shall we get you both checked in? I think you're staying in one of the gorgeous rooms here at the hotel.' Polly and Fred had booked out the place—plus the twelve private villas on the beach-front—for their guests.

She ignored any attempt from Paul to start a conversation, and instead listened to Jemima chattering on about all the things she wanted to do while they were in the Seychelles—including hiking, surfing, snorkelling…

'And of course I'd *love* to dive with sharks,' she said.

Nell couldn't resist a glance at Paul, who she happened to know had a deathly fear of most sea creatures. He was, she was pleased to note, looking rather green.

'Sounds like you've got a wonderfully *adventurous* week planned,' she said as she handed them over to the staff on the front desk. 'I know how keen Paul is to live a more adventurous, risk-taking life, after all.'

That was what he'd told her when he dumped her.

Served him right if he got eaten by a shark.

'That was fun,' Alex said as they walked away. '*Now* can we go to bed?'

'Definitely.' The adrenaline of dealing with her ex had worn off fast.

They made it all the way to the walkway that led to the private villas along the beachfront before they spotted the next arrival.

There, stepping out of a car in a wide-brimmed sun-hat that must have annoyed everyone on the plane, was Madeline Andrews.

Her mother.

Nell froze as she watched the staff dancing attendance on her, rewarded by smiles and compliments, as Madeline was led towards the main lobby. Give her ten minutes and Nell knew that everyone on the island would be halfway in love with her mother.

Everyone except her, anyway.

She *had* to love her because she was her mother. But that didn't mean she had to like her.

And if she tried to talk to her now, for the first time since—wow, when was it? Two Christmases ago, maybe?—it could only be a disaster. She needed sleep before she faced Hurricane Madeline.

'Bed?' Alex asked, following her gaze.

Nell nodded. 'Yes, please.'

'Your wish is my command,' he said, and put an arm around her shoulders as he led her off to their private villa.

At least she could just take a few hours to rest in his arms, before she had to deal with her ex, her mother and a missing wedding dress.

CHAPTER FIFTEEN

ALEX WASN'T ENTIRELY sure why dealing with the missing wedding dress had become his responsibility, but there was no way he was waking Nell up to deal with it and, since she didn't want to panic Polly unnecessarily, nobody else on the island—barring the receptionist—actually knew it was missing.

So when the London office emailed back later that afternoon with the latest from the courier—insisting that the wedding dress had definitely been delivered on schedule as Polly had paid a lot of money for—he left Nell dozing in their bed and headed back to reception to instigate another search of the hotel.

'I'm sorry, sir, but there really is no sign of it—and no record of it arriving at all,' the receptionist said.

Alex sighed. 'Right. Any suggestions? Ideas?'

She looked around to check they weren't being listened to, then leaned across the counter. 'As it happens, my aunt is a seamstress on the next island. She does very nice work…'

'Right. Thanks.' Alex wasn't sure Polly was going to go for that one, given the amount of time and money she'd spent choosing her dress in the first place. 'You'll call me if the courier actually shows up, right?'

'Immediately,' the receptionist promised. 'You know, the courier might just have decided to wait until after the storm to fly it over from the mainland.'

Oh, good. Something else to worry about. 'Storm?'

She nodded. 'Apparently there's a tropical storm brewing. It probably won't reach us here, but...' She trailed off and shrugged.

'A tropical storm. Isn't it the wrong season for those?' He was sure he'd read something about them happening in January in Nell's guidebook.

She shrugged again. 'Weather.'

'Indeed.' A tropical storm. Just what this wedding needed.

He pulled out his phone to check the weather forecast as he turned away from the counter and almost walked into Jemima and Paul, who were approaching.

'Alex! Everything okay?' Paul sounded a little desperate. 'Did I hear something about a storm? Should we batten down the hatches?'

The weather app at least was reassuring. 'It's probably going to miss us,' Alex said.

'Oh, good.' Jemima beamed up at him. 'I'm just about to book some trips for us tomorrow! I'd hate for them to be cancelled. What first do you think, baby?' she asked, turning her attention back to Paul. 'Diving or jet-ski tour of the islands?'

'Up to you, uh, darling.' Paul, Alex suspected, would rather have his wisdom teeth pulled than do either.

Served him right for thinking he could do better than Nell.

'Right, well, I'd better get back.' Alex waved vaguely in the direction of their villa. 'Have fun you two.'

Jemima was already at the desk enquiring about trips, but Paul hung back a moment and when Alex started to leave he reached out and grabbed his arm.

'Everything okay?' Alex stared at Paul's hand on his shirtsleeve until he let it go and stepped back, looking awkward.

'I just wanted to ask… You and Nell,' Paul said, stammering slightly to get the words out. 'I saw you together at the engagement party, and I wondered…'

Alex raised his eyebrows. 'Are you asking if we're together?'

'You just don't seem like her usual type, that's all,' Paul said stiffly. 'I was surprised.'

'Jemima hardly seems like yours either,' Alex pointed out. 'Everyone likes a change of pace sometimes, don't they?'

Paul shook his head. 'Not Nell. She likes things to stay exactly the same as they've always been, ever since she was old enough to take control of her own life. *You* are not the same.'

A part of him desperately wanted to tell Paul the truth—or a version of it, at least. That he and Nell *were* together, and no, things weren't the same, they were better than ever, and even though it seemed impossible, they *fitted*...

But he couldn't.

Because Nell didn't want anyone to know. Because, actually, things weren't different. She had every intention of going back to her little cocoon of boringness and security the moment this wedding was over.

She was basically using him for great sex, and while Alex had been fine with that when he was doing the same to her, now…

Something had changed. And he wasn't sure he wanted to examine too closely what that was, when there was nothing he could do to change the ending to this story.

So he stuck to the party line instead.

'No, we're not together,' he told Paul. 'Polly paired us up for the events as best man and maid of honour, that's all. We've got one of the two-bedroom villas on the beachfront as a reward.'

The relief on Paul's face was obvious, and it stung.

Is he going to try to win her back? Or does he just not want anyone else to have her, in case he needs a fall-back plan?

Either way, it made Alex hate Paul just a little bit more.

'Alex?' Jemima called from the reception desk. 'Do you and Nell want to join us for a jet-ski tour tomorrow?'

Paul laughed. 'Nell would never do that sort of thing.'

'Maybe not. But Alex would,' Jemima said, eyeing him speculatively. 'I've heard stories about him.'

'Who hasn't,' Paul muttered, with an ominous glance in Alex's direction.

He ignored it.

Usually, he'd jump at the chance to try or do or see something new. To hang out with new people, who were open to new experiences. If it was dangerous, or at the very least exhilarating, that only made it more appealing.

But this week he had other priorities.

'Sorry, best man duties,' he said. That sounded better than *I don't want to leave the woman who won't admit she's sleeping with me*, right?

He made his goodbyes and was heading back to the villa when he recognised another guest in the bar—Nell's mother.

As best man, he should probably introduce himself. Even if Nell had made it clear she wanted to keep her distance for now. He didn't know the whole story of the twins' relationship with Madeline, but while Polly obviously wanted her here for her big day, it was just as obvious that Nell would have been happier if she wasn't invited.

It was the sort of thing he'd ask Nell about, if their relationship was anything more than a short-term fling. As it was…he wasn't about to risk anything that might make her decide to end things earlier than planned.

Didn't I used to be the risk-taker in this not-a-relationship?

Before he could decide whether to introduce himself to Madeline, she was joined by another man—somewhere between Nell's age and her mother's, he guessed. When the man bent in to kiss Madeline, he decided that introductions could wait.

Madeline was clearly having a lovely time. Now he had to make sure that her daughter was too.

Guests continued to arrive all that day and into the next. Nell managed to coordinate things mostly from her villa, via the phone—including tracking down the courier, who had *clearly not* delivered Polly's dress as he claimed.

'It'll be there before the wedding,' he promised. 'Just relax and enjoy the island!'

As if relaxation was really an option, when her sister was getting married in just a few days, her mother was loose somewhere on the island doing heaven only knew what, and Nell herself was embroiled in a best man with benefits arrangement that—

Well, that was kind of wonderful, actually. Which was at least part of the problem.

Because it had to end. Really soon.

Before she got any more attached than she already was.

Nell knew that this wedding was littered with Alex's ex-girlfriends—somehow, he always managed to stay on good terms with them, and plenty of them had been part of their friendship group at university, so it was inevitable they'd see each other again. But the last thing Nell wanted any of them knowing was that she—sensible, stable, determined-to-be-boring Nell—had fallen for the same charms that the rest of them had.

Or that she was going to be cast aside the same as all the rest, for that matter.

It wasn't that she was embarrassed by her connection with Alex—she knew for a fact that it would improve her standing in the opinion of nearly everyone attending the wedding, in truth.

Especially her mother.

And *that* was what she wanted even less than a missing wedding dress or the humiliation of being another one of Alex's exes.

She just couldn't bear her mother telling her that she was a chip off the old block after all—falling for the handsome, daring, unpredictable best man. This fling was *exactly* the sort of thing Madeline would do—and Nell had spent most of her life fighting to be defined as the anti-Madeline.

Of course, Mum had actually run off with the best man at *her own* wedding once, which was far worse. And only meant that she'd lecture Nell about how she couldn't even rebel with the same style and panache as she did.

No. Madeline Andrews could never find out about Nell and Alex—and neither could anyone else.

They didn't need to. It would be over soon enough.

Shaking away her less than cheery thoughts, she headed out across the strip of sandy beach towards the main reception, to see what else could possibly go wrong with this week that she'd be required to fix.

This was why the world needed boring people, she decided. So they could put things right while the more adventurous and dramatic people were off having adventures and not caring about the basic but important stuff.

Like whether the bride had a wedding dress or not.

In fairness, it had been her decision to keep the news of its loss from Polly. But it did mean that her twin was now having a lovely time at the spa on the next island, while Nell had spent all morning on the phone to various couriers around the islands, and Alex…

Where was Alex, anyway?

As she approached the reception building she spotted him, leaning against the wooden post of the jetty, staring out at the ocean. His broad back faced her, and she could tell his arms were folded across his chest. He looked… contemplative, which was not a state she was used to thinking of in combination with Alex McLeod. He was all action and movement and doing before thinking…at least in his personal life. She'd always assumed that he used up all his patience, methodicalness and calm in his work, so had none left for his private life.

But there he stood. Contemplating.

And Nell knew she had to find out what he was thinking about.

'You look very thoughtful,' she said, coming to stand

beside him. 'Contemplating our tiny existence in an un-
believably large universe, or watching those girls in bi-
kinis on paddleboards?'

'Neither.' Alex wrapped an arm around her waist and
pressed a kiss to the top of her head. For a moment, she
wanted nothing more than to lean into his touch, but then
she remembered that everyone on this island was there
for Polly's wedding, and the last thing she needed was a
report getting back to her sister—or mother—about her
getting cosy with the best man.

So she stepped away. 'Then what?'

'They said at reception that there was a storm coming in. It probably won't reach us here, but some of the
guests were going out on a tour around some of the outer
islands and, well, they're not back yet.'

Nell sighed. 'Guess we'd better go inside and start
making some more phone calls then, huh?'

'Looks like.' He gave her a lopsided smile and offered
her his arm as they walked inside.

And, despite all her reservations, she took it. Because
he wasn't out there adventuring with the others—he was
here, helping her fix things.

And maybe, just maybe, that meant something.

It turned out that the guests who'd gone on the adventure tour of the outer island had got themselves a little
bit stranded. The receptionist looked grateful when Nell
and Alex showed up to help with the phoning around
to find someone willing to brave the storm to get them
back. The storm was threatening to linger for a few days,
and if they didn't get back in time for the wedding Polly
would be livid.

'Did you not want to go with them?' Nell asked in a lull between phone calls, while they waited to hear back from someone who might be willing to make the trip. 'A jet-ski adventure tour of strange islands in a tropical storm sounds exactly the sort of thing you'd be jumping to sign up for.'

'They did invite me,' Alex admitted, wondering why she'd asked. Had she *wanted* him to go? Or was she hoping he'd changed his ways?

Or was she worried he'd stayed for her, when she didn't want him to?

'You turned them down?'

He shrugged. 'I had things to do here.'

'Very responsible,' she said, eyeing him with something unreadable in her gaze.

But then the phone rang again and the moment was over.

Eventually, they managed to get their wayward guests back to the island—looking a little tired and windswept, but otherwise none the worse for wear. Alex and Nell were there to meet them—and the courier finally delivering Polly's wedding dress—in the reception space.

'Well, at least we've got a great story to tell about our trip,' Jemima declared, laughing, as she strolled through—her hair windswept but her make-up still somehow flawless.

Paul followed behind her, looking significantly more dishevelled and, if Alex wasn't mistaken, rather disillusioned with the spirit of adventure he'd been courting when he left Nell for Jemima.

From the slightly smug smile on Nell's face when he turned to look at her, she saw it too. And in that moment he could feel any chance at a future with her slipping from his grasp.

What future? I don't want a future with Nell Andrews. Just a fling. That's what we agreed.

But Alex had never been very good at lying to himself.

With all the guests back where they belonged, and Polly's dress safely hung in the bridal suite, Nell slipped her arm through his and stretched up on tiptoes to whisper in his ear. 'I reckon we've got another couple of hours before the rehearsal dinner. Think they can manage without us out here for now?'

'Definitely,' Alex replied.

The future might be out of his grasp, but the present was very much in it. And hadn't he always preferred to live in the moment anyway?

Right now, at this moment, Nell was still his.

And he intended to enjoy every moment of that while it lasted.

CHAPTER SIXTEEN

FOR THE REHEARSAL DINNER, Polly and Fred had arranged a spectacular beachside event—one that had, thankfully, been facilitated by the tropical storm passing by the outer islands and moving back out to sea, without ever coming close to their venue. Nell wasn't sure her sister even knew of the storm's existence—she'd spent the day at the spa with her other bridesmaids, accepting Nell begging off only because she knew how much she hated sitting around and gossiping with most of Polly's other friends.

And since Nell had spent half the day rescuing guests from the storm, and the other half in bed with Alex, she'd decided that made the scales just about even.

Okay, maybe tipped slightly in her favour. Or a lot.

The chemistry between her and Alex still continued to amaze her—and the most surprising thing of all was that it didn't seem to be sizzling out over time.

If anything, it was only getting hotter.

So by the time she met Polly down at the beach before the dinner, to do a final check of the set-up, they were both relaxed and happy in their own ways.

'It looks beautiful.' Nell placed her hands on her hips and looked out over the carefully placed tables with the ribbon-wrapped chairs and the tropical flower and fruit centrepieces. Tomorrow, after the beach wedding itself, they'd be in the large courtyard in the centre of the hotel complex, with a fully catered five-course dinner being served from the kitchens nearby. There'd be musicians and a bar and a hundred other details Nell couldn't remember.

But tonight, the rehearsal dinner, was supposed to be lower key. Not all the guests on the island were invited, just the wedding party and close family—the rest had a buffet going on in the main restaurant. They had a guitarist and singer on a small dais near the tables, and a cocktail bar set up on the sand. The water lapped against the shore, calm and tranquil now all signs of the storm had passed.

Everything was perfect.

Polly clapped her hands together with excitement, her smile contagious. 'I can't believe we're really here, Nell. All the planning and waiting—'

'It's only been three months since Fred proposed, Pol,' Nell couldn't help but point out. Her sister ignored her.

'And now we're finally here! Tomorrow I'm getting married, and Fred and I will be together for ever, no matter what.'

Nell forced herself to keep her smile in place. 'You really will.'

She believed her words, that wasn't the problem. Maybe their mother had never managed to make a marriage last, and their father had had no interest in getting married in the first place, but Polly and Fred would make it. She was sure.

She just couldn't help but wonder if, just as Polly had got all the charm and adventurousness from their parents, she'd got the love and happiness quota that they should have shared too.

Nell had never truly been jealous of her twin before. But imagining her spending her life with the man who loved her beyond everything, and who she loved back just as fiercely—despite any disagreements or drama—that, well. That was worth envying.

She looked up and saw guests starting to arrive, and shooed Polly off to get changed into her dress for the evening. Nell was already dressed in her own, black dress, sparkly silver sandals her only concession to the occasion, and the beachfront setting.

She smiled and welcomed Fred's family, relieved when Alex joined her as he knew them better than she did, so was more relaxed around them all. From Polly's side of the family, there weren't many people to know; most of her invite list had been friends rather than family, and tonight was meant to be family and wedding party only. Other than herself and the five bridesmaids, there was only an elderly great-aunt—the sister of their father's mother—and her daughter, and Madeline.

Who was, of course, late.

'She's probably waiting to upstage the bride and groom,' Nell told Alex when he asked where her mother was.

'She'd do that?' Alex sounded surprised. Which, given his own parents' behaviour at the engagement party, seemed rather naive.

'She lives for that,' Nell confirmed.

Just then, she saw two figures stumbling towards them. One was using the rope of fairy lights the hotel had used to mark the path as a rather insufficient hand rail.

'Here we go,' Nell said.

The figure gripping the fairy lights was male, and not anyone she recognised from the wedding party. The woman, however, in her lipstick-pink dress and high heels that sank into the sand, was instantly recognisable as her mother.

'Who's the guy?' Alex asked. 'Wait, I saw him kissing her in the bar before. Did we know she was bringing a date?'

Nell frowned. 'She didn't. She arrived alone.' And there definitely hadn't been a plus one on her invitation; even Polly wasn't as trusting as that. She'd paired Madeline up with Fred's widower uncle for all the wedding week events, since neither had made the engagement party or the hen and stag dos.

Leaving her post, Nell stepped forward to intercept them. 'Mum.'

'Nell! I haven't seen you yet!' She threw her arms around Nell's shoulders, and Nell smelled the alcohol on her breath. 'Nigel, this is my other daughter—the one who isn't getting married.' She dropped her voice and put a hand to the side of her mouth. '*Probably ever.*' They both laughed.

Nell's jaw tightened, but she ignored them, aware of Alex standing at her side. She didn't want to make a scene, although she knew her mother would love it if she did. That way, she'd be the centre of attention—which was just the way Madeline liked it.

'Mum, the rehearsal dinner is for family only,' she said firmly. 'If you want to say goodbye to your new friend now, Alex will show you to your seat.'

'You're with Fred's uncle Roger, Madeline,' Alex said, offering her his arm. 'He's looking forward to getting to know you.'

Nell hoped Uncle Roger was deaf. Otherwise he was

going to know the whole life story of Madeline Andrews—probably heavily embellished to include extra name-dropping—before they'd reached dessert.

She'd expected Madeline to latch onto Alex as a younger, more handsome and eligible man—that was her usual modus operandi. But instead she took tighter hold of her companion's arm.

'But darling, Nigel *is* family! Or he will be, soon enough.' Madeline looked up into Nigel's eyes, every inch the besotted new lover. 'We're getting married, you see. Right here on this island! I just can't wait to tell everyone tonight. Or do you think we should save the news for the toasts at the wedding tomorrow?'

Nell felt her heart sinking down into the sand, and wished she could follow it.

This was what she'd been afraid of. Why she'd hoped Madeline wouldn't have been able to make it to the wedding for some reason.

Because of course her mother would want to make Polly's wedding all about her.

Never once, in all their childhoods, had anything been about them. Everything had to be about Madeline.

And now she was trying to steal Polly's most precious day from her.

Well. Not on Nell's watch.

And from the steely look in Alex's eye, not on his either.

'We absolutely cannot let Mum ruin tonight,' Nell hissed to Alex, as Polly and Fred approached the rehearsal dinner and the guests all stood and clapped. 'Or, more importantly, the wedding tomorrow.'

'Of course we won't,' Alex replied. 'But how, exactly, do you intend to stop her?'

From the little he'd seen of Madeline Andrews, she didn't seem to be the sort of person who took a hint. Or a direct command. Or any interest in what anyone else cared about or felt at all, actually.

How had such a woman created someone as sensitive and caring as Nell? It really made no sense.

'Okay,' Nell said after a moment's thought. 'This is what we do.'

They averted the immediate crisis by a strategy of divide and conquer. Alex led Madeline over to sit by Uncle Roger, and had an extra seat added to the table so he sat on her other side, where he could keep an eye on her. The staff from the hotel restaurant didn't look too happy at the unexpected addition, but he promised to eat whatever they had left over.

Nell, meanwhile, dragged Nigel into Alex's original seat beside her, so she could keep tabs on him. Polly gave them both a slightly odd look as she took her own seat, but she didn't immediately question it. Alex shot Nell a relieved look across the tables between them, and she returned it.

By the end of the meal Alex knew far more about Madeline Andrews' varied and self-centred existence than he'd ever wanted to—and thought he might understand a little more about Nell because of it.

He'd assumed her need for security and boredom came from being abandoned by her adventurer father, but it seemed her mother was probably just as responsible. If she'd been present at the assassination of JFK, Alex was pretty sure Madeline would have told the story purely in the context of how she got blood on her favourite dress.

And while he was certain she *hadn't* been present that fateful day in Dallas—if only because she'd definitely have told the story if she had—she did seem to have a way of being in the right place at the right time. Well, if what she was looking for was drama, notoriety and stories to tell about famous people, anyway.

If the right place and time meant being with her daughters growing up, not so much.

Nell didn't want her own kids to grow up like she had. She wanted to give them a stable home with a boring, dependable dad. He could understand that.

And he could also understand why she wouldn't see him in that role. Hell, he wasn't even sure he wanted kids, if it meant putting them through what he had to put up with from his own parents.

So, all in all, the rehearsal dinner had just been another depressing demonstration of why he and Nell had to break things off once the wedding was over.

Less than forty-eight hours and we'll be on the plane home.

He glanced over at Nell again and wished he was sitting with her, as the table plan said he should be.

He didn't like wasting the last of their time together.

They made it through the meal without any last-minute declarations from Madeline or Nigel—something Alex put down to Nell's mother deciding the actual wedding would be a more dramatic occasion to announce things, anyway.

Alex made his way across to Nell the moment Polly and Fred had symbolically separated for the night. From here, they wouldn't see each other until they met at the altar.

'Do you need to stay with your sister tonight?' The bridal suite—where Polly and her bridesmaids had been set up for the night before the wedding—was on the second floor of the main hotel, and had the advantage of two bathrooms plus a dressing room, with plenty of space for the hairdressers and make-up artists to do their work.

Nell shook her head, and Alex's spirits rose just a little. 'She knows I don't always play nicely with others, so she said she was fine if I wanted my own space tonight—as long as I put on the stupid maid of honour dress tomorrow.'

'Not black?' Alex guessed.

'Not even slightly.' She sighed. 'But she's my sister. So I'll wear it anyway.'

That was Nell all over, Alex thought. She knew when things mattered, and when they didn't, and she gave her attention to the ones that did. It was one of the things he loved most about her.

Wait.

Not loved. Obviously.

Liked.

In a friendly way.

'You're a good sister,' he said, swallowing the sudden panic rising inside him.

Nell gave him a curious look. 'It's just a dress. And it's Polly's wedding, not mine. This whole thing…it's not about me.'

And that was the difference between Nell and her mother, he realised. He wanted to tell her as much. To tell her why she didn't have to worry about ever being like her—she couldn't if she tried.

He wanted to tell her so many things. But how could he, when this all ended the day after tomorrow?

Nell glanced around, then frowned. 'Where's my mother? And Nigel, for that matter.'

'They were right here...' Alex looked around too, but there was no sign.

'We need to find them.' Nell's eyes were wide with panic. 'What if they've gone to tell Polly they want a double wedding?'

'They wouldn't,' Alex said, before realising, yes, they probably would. 'Or they're planning to elope tonight and announce it tomorrow,' he suggested, and Nell groaned.

'Okay, I'll go check the bridal suite and the hotel bar; you go check the villas and the beach bar.'

'What do I do if I find them?' he asked.

'Just...make sure they're not causing a scene. And get them back to Mum's room as quickly as you can. Okay? Then I'll meet you back at our villa later.'

'I'll see you there.' With a quick check to be sure no one was watching, Alex ducked his head to kiss her, just once, on the lips. Then he turned to go and fix this latest wedding problem.

Because Nell had asked him to. And he was coming to realise there wasn't much he wouldn't do for her.

Which meant there might be another, more important, conversation they needed to have in the future, perhaps.

Nell trudged back to the beachfront villa she shared with Alex, her sandals in her hands. She'd searched the whole hotel, and both bars, but there was no sign of her mother and Nigel. At least she'd also had the opportunity to check that Polly was having fun with her friends, and share a glass of champagne with them before bed.

Maybe it would have been nice to spend the night before Polly's wedding with her sister but, on balance, Nell knew she'd rather spend it with Alex—especially if it was the last night they got together. She'd never really gelled with Polly's friends anyway.

Now she just had to hope that Alex had found Madeline and Nigel, and averted any last-minute nuptials, or anything else that might cause drama on Polly's wedding day.

She paused outside the villa and looked out towards the ocean. Whoops of laughter floated towards her on the air, and when she squinted she could see people out there in the waves.

She moved closer.

Not just people. She recognised that bright pink dress. The one that a woman had just pulled off and thrown into the sea.

'Madeline!' She recognised that voice too. Laughing, not scandalised.

Alex.

Well, she'd told him to take care of her mother, she supposed. She couldn't blame him for doing whatever it took. She'd known her mother would like him. And that Alex would like her.

They were two of a kind. The adventurous, fun-loving kind.

The opposite of her.

Of course they'd connected.

Ignoring the burning sensation at the back of her throat, Nell turned and headed inside the villa. But she found she wasn't ready for sleep just yet, despite the late hour. Too many thoughts, perhaps.

Fixing herself a cup of herbal tea, she took it out to the small covered porch at the back of the villa, away from the sea. The porch was equipped with two light chairs and a small table between them. Placing her mug on the table, she took a seat and prepared to enjoy the peace and quiet before the chaos of the day ahead tomorrow.

The porch area looked out over a wide garden that her villa shared with all the other beachfront accommodation. Tropical flowers bloomed bright and proudly, standing out and drawing attention in a way that English wild-flowers never did.

Nell could see why Polly had chosen this incredible place for her wedding; it suited her and Fred down to the ground. But she'd felt out of place since the minute she arrived.

She missed London.

She missed how simple things had been there, even after she and Alex started their fling.

It was strange to think she'd be going back to a whole new world—one where Polly was married and she and Alex were barely even friends, just business partners.

Could they really do that?

She wasn't sure any more.

Although since he'd gone night swimming with her mother and who knew who else, maybe he was already getting ready to move on, back to his old life, without her.

Maybe she needed to do the same. Focus on the life she really wanted to be living, and find a way to make it happen.

She took a sip of her tea and stared out at the garden

again. In the middle there was a path which led eventually back to the hotel, and it was lit up by torches all the way. She tried to think of them as way markers, points along her life's journey, places she wanted to stop.

One of them burned brighter than the rest somehow, and she knew that one had to be Alex.

But what came next? Maybe dimmer, less exciting lights, but ones that took her where she wanted to go.

To a future with safety, security, predictability, just as she'd always wanted. The opposite of the life her parents had led.

A future she could trust to always be there. That was what she really wanted, wasn't it?

But as she stared at the path, she realised suddenly there was someone walking along it, towards her.

Someone she knew.

'I was hoping I'd find you still awake,' he said as he drew closer.

Nell got to her feet, frowning slightly. 'Is something wrong?'

Paul shook his head, a knowing smile on his lips. 'Quite the opposite, in fact. I feel like I'm thinking clearly for the first time in months. May I join you?'

Nell gestured to the empty chair beside hers, but he shook his head.

'I won't need that,' he said.

'Okay.' Nell frowned. Obviously he wasn't planning on staying long, which was fine by her. But *he'd* come to *her*. Why?

Nothing about tonight seemed to make any sense at all.

Then Paul dropped to one knee in front of her on the porch, and she felt her heart stop.

CHAPTER SEVENTEEN

IT WAS LATE—very late—by the time Alex had finally managed to get Madeline out of the ocean, into a towelling robe he'd borrowed from one of the beach huts, and back to her room. They'd lost Nigel hours ago, possibly in the beachfront bar where he'd found the pair of them after the rehearsal dinner.

'It's too early to call it a night!' Madeline had declared. 'Come on. I want to go skinny-dipping!'

Alex had wanted to just leave them to it, and hope that the lifeguards were working as late as the bar staff. But he'd promised Nell he'd make sure she didn't cause any more trouble tonight, and that meant sticking with her until he'd got her back to her room.

Which, finally, he had. He'd even stuck around just long enough to hear her snores start to reverberate around the landing outside, before heading back to the villa he shared with Nell.

Coming from the hotel, it made sense to cut through the gardens to the back entrance. Madeline's room was at one end of the hotel, though, so the nearest exit led him along the outside of the garden rather than down the well-lit middle path. Which meant he was almost to the villa before he saw them.

Nell, hands clasped to her mouth as she stood over a man on one knee, holding out a ring.

Paul.

He'd known the idiot had seen sense, the moment he'd trailed in after Jemima following the storm debacle. He'd tried the adventurous lifestyle and decided it wasn't for him. Of course he'd gone back to dependable, wonderful Nell.

The only question was whether she'd take him back.

If he'd been asked the question a month ago, he'd have said no way. Nell had a healthy sense of self-respect, and she was hardly likely to come running just because her ex had decided that spreading his more adventurous wild oats wasn't for him after all.

What had changed? What caused that niggle of doubt, the fear in his chest, that she might say yes?

He wanted to believe it was because he knew her better now, and knew from personal experience how much holding out for the right, stable and boring future mattered to her. A hell of a lot more than he did.

Despite all the chemistry between them, and the fun they had together, he knew that she wouldn't even consider giving a relationship between them a chance—because she still had her heart firmly planted in that future she'd been planning her whole life.

A safe, secure one that no parent or anyone else could whisk out from under her.

He'd like to think that Paul having done exactly that already, just a few months ago, would be enough for her not to fall for his act now. But if she wanted it badly enough…he knew she might.

And what right did he have to stand in the way of that

future? She'd never promised him anything beyond to-morrow, anyway.

The surprise in her eyes that he could just make out, even from a distance, not to mention the hands to her mouth suggested she might be considering Paul's proposal, at the least. If Polly had seen it, he knew she'd have been planning the wedding already.

And maybe that was the right thing to do.

What probably *wasn't* the right thing to do was for Alex to slip into the shadows beside the next villa and watch what was clearly a private moment.

He did it anyway.

'I realised this week that I don't want the drama and excitement I thought I needed,' Paul said, up on the porch. 'I want the quiet moments, the peace, the…reassuring sameness you always gave me, Nell.'

Nell, Alex noticed, didn't say anything.

'I made a mistake,' Paul went on. 'Ever leaving you. It's not one I intend to make again. And that's why I'm asking you, Nell Andrews, if you'll be my wife. I can't promise you drama or adventure, but I can give you security and stability. Everything you always said you wanted.'

Everything she'd always said she wanted.

Everything she'd told *Alex* she wanted too.

Everything he couldn't give her.

Suddenly, Alex didn't want to watch any more.

He slipped silently away, back towards the hotel bar.

He couldn't compete with everything Paul was offering, and he didn't intend to try.

If Nell really did want that life, he was the man to give it to her.

If she didn't…

Well.

Alex wasn't giving up hope just yet.

But he would give her the space to decide the future she wanted, without trying to influence it.

However hard the wait was.

Nell stared down at Paul, at the ring box in his hand. Where had he even got that? Had he brought it with him, preparing to propose to Jemima?

She wouldn't put it past him.

'I know you won't want to say anything to anyone until after the wedding is over,' Paul went on, even though she hadn't answered him. 'You won't want to upstage Polly of course—not that anybody could, right?' He gave a laugh, and she remembered suddenly how often he did that—putting down Polly as if she must think the same about her sister really but not say it in public.

She'd always hated that. She and Polly might be different, but that didn't mean she had to disapprove of Polly's life.

But Paul hadn't ever understood that. Hadn't understood how they could be so close when they were so different.

Alex did. She pushed the thought away.

Alex wasn't here, and this wasn't about him, right now. This was about her future. The one she'd just been contemplating when the man she'd assumed, until three months ago, she would spend her life with showed up with a possibly repurposed diamond ring.

'I know what this is, Paul.' Nell dropped back into her

chair, putting herself at eye level with him. 'I've done this myself, more times than I can remember.'

Paul frowned. 'What do you mean? You've proposed to people? Who?'

'No!' Nell laughed, but she wasn't amused. 'That's not what I… What I mean is this. Proposing to me. It's not actually about me at all.'

'Who else could it be about?' Paul demanded.

'What I mean is, you scared yourself—or maybe Jemima scared you,' she went on. 'You thought you wanted the interesting, adventurous life that she leads, but when you tried to live it with her, you hated it. For her, getting stranded in a tropical storm was a story she could tell later. It was a life event. For you, it was miserable. And so you lurched away from her and back towards something safe and familiar. Me.'

'Is that so wrong?' Paul asked. 'Being with Jemima only showed me how perfect what *we* had together was.'

'If it had been perfect, you wouldn't have needed to go off with her in the first place,' Nell pointed out.

She'd *thought* they were perfect together too. Thought that Paul could give her everything she'd ever wanted.

But the last couple of weeks had shown her she wanted things she didn't even know she could want, until Alex came along and gave them to her.

'Look, I know I've made mistakes, but we're both grown-ups, right?' Paul looked eagerly up at her, anticipating her understanding. 'That's what makes you so different from everyone else in your family, or at that company of yours. We make sensible, rational, safe decisions. *You* make good decisions, always. And forgiving me, and moving on, is obviously the right decision for both of us.'

He made it sound so obvious, except Nell knew better now.

Safe, sensible, secure…they meant different things to different people.

For Polly and Fred, their safety was in each other. In knowing that the other would let them live their life—feel their emotions, seek their adventures, act out their dramas—but always still be there in the morning.

For her mother, it was knowing that everyone would always be talking about her—even if she didn't like what they were saying. Nell didn't know what had started that drive in her—maybe it was her and Polly's father walking away because she didn't matter to him. But Madeline needed to matter. She needed to be seen, to be known, to be important—to more people than just her daughters.

Nell hated that about her. But she had to accept it was who she was.

And for Alex…she didn't know what meant safety to him. What meant *home*.

She wasn't sure if he did either.

For her…she'd always assumed it meant a place and a person where nothing ever changed. Where she could rely on consistency and boredom to keep her safe.

But now she wondered.

'I don't think it is the right decision,' she said slowly. 'Not for me.'

'Forgiving me isn't the right decision?' Paul sounded incredulous. 'Nell, you can't honestly intend to hold onto a childish grudge like your mother would.'

He was playing on her fear of turning into her mother, she realised. But she knew now she never would. She wasn't that person.

She was herself. And she *liked* the Nell she'd been since Paul left.

'*Marrying* you would be the wrong decision,' she corrected him. 'For me, anyway. I don't love you, you see. And I'm pretty sure you don't love me either.'

'What *is* love?' Paul asked. She assumed it was rhetorical. 'You and I both know that the grand passionate love affair isn't enough. Love isn't drama and storming out then making up again. It's being sure of the other person, trusting them to look after you, to help you. To know what's really important in life. Isn't it?'

Nell blinked, as a number of things all fell into place inside her at the same time.

'Yes,' she said slowly. 'You're right. It is.'

'So you'll marry me?'

She smiled down at him. 'Not in a million years.'

Because she knew what love was now. She knew what she wanted from her future.

And she intended to get it.

Alex wasn't entirely surprised to find Jemima in the bar, given that the man she'd brought to the wedding was currently proposing to another woman on his porch.

She turned towards him as he approached. 'You looking for a little company tonight too?'

'Mostly just looking for a nightcap.' He hopped up onto the bar stool beside her, though, as he indicated to the man behind the bar that he'd like a beer. What he really wanted was hard spirits, but that wouldn't go so well with getting up and being best man in the morning. So, one beer before bed it was.

Maybe Nell really had been a bigger influence on him

than he'd thought. He sounded positively sensible, even to his own ears. Practically responsible.

To his surprise, he didn't hate it.

Behind them, the bar was open to the beach and he could hear the waves lapping against the shore. This place was, objectively speaking, paradise.

So why did he wish he was back in London, with Nell, and that they'd never come here at all?

Jemima was eyeing him speculatively. 'You're better off without her, you know.'

'I don't know what you mean.' The barman brought his beer, and Alex nodded his thanks.

'Yes, you do.' Jemima nudged him with her elbow. 'I saw the two of you at the fairground engagement party thing, and I knew then. Not to mention this week. The way you look at her…you're besotted. But you know you're not the right kind of man for her.'

'Maybe I could be.' Denying that he wanted to be seemed beside the point now.

'You and I…we're not like them. Paul and Nell, I mean. They're normal—ordinary people who care about… I don't know. Mortgages and pets, or something. We don't care about that stuff. We know that life is about more than paying bills and going to work until you die. It's about seeing things and travelling places and having adventures that people stuck in the corporate cycle could only dream of!'

'You realise I do actually have an office job,' Alex said mildly.

'Do you, though?' Jemima gave him a knowing look. 'The way I understood it, you invested enough money into that company when Fred and Polly were setting up that you'd never need to work a day in your life, just live off the dividends they make you. Maybe you like to keep your hand in by contributing a little legal advice from time to time, but it's hardly a *job,* is it?'

She was right, Alex knew. He also realised he'd spent more time in the office since Fred and Polly announced their engagement than he ever had before. Because he wanted to see Nell. To share tales of disastrous dates. To enjoy their budding friendship.

To see it become more.

If she married Paul, he knew he'd be avoiding the office again for the foreseeable future.

'I know it can be tempting.' Jemima had shifted closer, her thigh pressed against his on the bar stool. 'I almost fell for it too. Paul said he wanted an adventure, and I thought I could show him our life and he'd give up everything else to be with me. But he wasn't built for it, the same way Nell isn't. They're made for each other, those two. All they care about is security and living their boring, respectable little lives, where everyone thinks they're perfect.'

'You're wrong.'

'Am I?'

Alex looked away, thinking hard.

Yes, Nell valued security. She'd had an unstable, unloving childhood, and she wanted to build her future in a way that made her feel safe and loved. That was understandable.

And yes, she cared what other people thought and said—if she didn't, she wouldn't have been so worried about their fling getting out. But was that because she wanted to be *respectable,* or because she wanted her privacy, in a way her mother never had?

Because, despite her protestations to the contrary, Nell wasn't *boring.* She just wasn't.

She was fun and entertaining and passionate and intelligent and funny. She knew herself, and what she wanted. She was confident in both those things too.

She was so much more than he'd ever seen, until she'd refused to go to this wedding with him.

And he was in love with her.

Alex stood up. 'Yes, you are.'

And he was going to find Nell and tell her that. Because as much as her decision about whether to marry Paul or not was only hers to make, she deserved to have all the information when she made it.

Except then Fred's cousin came racing into the bar, looking frantic. 'Thank God I found you! You're the best man. *You* need to talk to him if you want this wedding to go ahead tomorrow. Come on!'

CHAPTER EIGHTEEN

NELL WAS UP early the next morning, not least because she'd barely slept. Alex hadn't returned to the villa at all the night before, as far as she could tell—and he certainly hadn't joined her in their bed.

Their last night had passed, and they hadn't even spent it together.

She got up and showered, determined to ignore the ache in her chest at the realisation that her fling with the best man was already over. This was Polly's wedding day, and that was all that mattered.

She'd arranged to meet the bride and bridesmaids in the suite at the top of the hotel bright and early, to allow plenty of time for hair and make-up before the afternoon service on the beach. By the time she made it up there, hoping that the make-up artist could do something about the shadows under her eyes, the other women were all lounging around in short cotton robes and fluffy slide slippers, drinking Prosecco.

'Nell!' Polly jumped up and embraced her as she arrived. 'I'm so glad you're here! Now it really feels like my wedding day.'

Nell forced a smile. 'It's going to be magical.'

And it was. Polly seemed too distracted to notice Nell's

slight melancholy, and the buzz of excitement in the room couldn't help but lift her spirits. In fact, everything was perfect. Even their mother arriving to share the bubbly and tell tall tales about the many times she'd *almost* got married couldn't blunt Polly's joy.

Nell was glad. One of them deserved that happiness, and it was probably always going to be Polly.

Happiness meant taking risks. And Nell had never—would never—find anything or anyone worth taking that kind of risk for.

At least she hadn't ever expected to.

And now it seemed it might already be too late. Unless she was willing to take a really, really big risk.

She wandered over to the window as her mother told the tale of her almost-elopement in Vegas to a gaggle of rapt bridesmaids. She supposed if you hadn't lived the stories the first time around they were entertaining enough.

Nell looked out over the gardens outside the bridal suite, towards where her own beachfront villa sat, and then frowned. Was that Alex, storming out of the villa? Where was he going? He looked like he was heading for the hotel—had something gone wrong?

Then she spotted the other figure, halfway up the garden path, glancing back over his shoulder as he hurried towards the window where she stood.

Nigel. Her mother's erstwhile latest fiancé.

Nell glanced back at Madeline.

'Of course, next time I head to the altar, I know it will be for real this time,' her mother said, her gaze slowly drifting towards the window where Nell stood. 'Sometimes, true love is worth waiting for. You know?'

True love. With a man she'd met less than three days ago on this island, and when she was only planning on announcing her engagement to him to upstage the bride— her own daughter. This—*this* was why Nell hated the idea of playing the world for drama, for the stories she could tell afterwards.

Because someone else always got hurt because of them.

Rage started to boil in her chest, and she was about to turn on her mother when she realised that would only create a scene—exactly what Madeline wanted, and Polly wouldn't. Besides, Alex was still moving, barrelling towards Nigel at speed. Her eyes widened.

'Excuse me, just one moment,' she said, edging towards the door.

Just then, Polly appeared in the doorway, fully dressed in her wedding gown for the first time. 'Well, how do I look?'

'You look amazing, Pol,' Nell said honestly.

Then she used the excited buzz of the other bridesmaids gathering around to dash outside and find out what the hell was going on now.

'Nigel, we talked about this.' Alex stalked behind the older man as he hurried through the gardens. He could catch up and take him down easily, but he didn't want to if he didn't have to. Rugby tackling a second-hand car salesman to the ground was the sort of thing that drew attention, and that was something he was trying to avoid.

Which was why he'd spent the whole night with Nigel in his hotel room, making sure he didn't do anything stupid.

Ever since Fred's cousin had found him the night before, and told him there was a lunatic trying to get in to see Fred and arrange a joint wedding for him and the bride's mother, Alex had been on Nigel watch. They'd assumed that Madeline would be their biggest worry, but it turned out she'd managed to find a new man with an even bigger flair for the dramatic than hers.

Unless this was all her idea, of course, which was a possibility Alex wasn't ready to discount just yet.

So instead of spending his last night with Nell, he'd spent it listening to Nigel talk about his failed first marriage, the kids who didn't want to see him, the way his life just hadn't turned out like the dreams in his head, how he'd always been meant for bigger things—and how Madeline was about to make that happen for him.

It hadn't left him in the best mood.

Still, he'd dragged Nigel with him when he went back to the villa he and Nell shared to change for the wedding ceremony—only for the idiot to make a break for it while Alex was in the shower.

Now he had to get him back inside, where he couldn't cause any trouble, before Madeline, Polly or—worst of all—Nell saw him.

'I need to show them that I truly *love* their mother,' Nigel said, still hurrying along the path. 'I know it's only her daughters holding Madeline back. But if I can show them—with a grand gesture—that my love is sincere, we can all be one happy family! I'll finally have the future I deserve.'

Alex had some thoughts on the future Nigel deserved, and he suspected they didn't match the pictures in Nigel's head.

Apparently reasoning was getting him nowhere, so

Alex picked up the pace and grabbed Nigel by the arm—just as Nell appeared in the doorway from the hotel.

'What the hell is going on out here?' She folded her arms across her chest, and Alex took a moment to appreciate her in the pale blue bridesmaid's dress Polly had chosen.

She looked beautiful, of course. But he preferred her in black. It suited her better.

'Nigel wants to make a grand romantic gesture,' Alex said drily. 'I'm trying to convince him not to.'

'But I need to show you, your sister and your mother, how much I love her!' Nigel insisted.

'Today?' Nell asked. 'On her daughter's wedding day? You don't think that's a little unnecessary?'

Nigel shook his head. 'It's perfect! Madeline said—'

Nell and Alex rolled their eyes in unison.

'Of course she did,' Nell muttered.

'She said that she needed to *know* I love her, and then she'd marry me on the spot!' Nigel beamed. Alex wondered if he was still drunk. It would explain a lot.

Or maybe a woman like Madeline just messed with men's senses.

He didn't know why. She couldn't hold a candle to Nell.

'Do you realise how many other men she's promised to marry over the years?' Nell asked. 'She loves being engaged, but most of the time she never quite makes it to the altar.'

'That's why I need to marry her *today*,' Nigel said, as if he'd played a trump card. 'When it's true love, why wait?'

'Because this is crazy?' Nell said, but Nigel clearly wasn't listening.

Before Alex could make a grab for him, he'd darted forward and started to climb the trellis of tropical flowers that scaled the wall up to the window of the bridal suite. As Alex looked up, he saw Madeline and Polly both looking out of the window—one with glee, the other horror—at the man approaching them.

Alex moved forward to follow Nigel, but Nell's hand on his arm held him back. 'You'll be too heavy,' she said. 'The whole thing will fall. Besides, it's too late. Look.'

She was right, he realised, looking around the gardens. The wedding guests had already come out to see what the fuss was all about—and seemed to be loving the drama of it all. Only Polly, up in the window, and Fred, over by the honeymoon villa, looked unhappy. Polly seemed on the verge of tears, and Fred…well, Alex wasn't sure he'd ever seen his friend so angry.

The only thing Nell had asked was that he help her keep Polly and Fred's wedding day perfect. It was his job—as best man, as their friend and as…whatever it was he was to Nell.

And he'd failed.

Madeline was clutching some flowers from the trellis to her chest as Nigel loudly professed his love to everyone in earshot, and Polly's perfect wedding was ruined.

In that moment Alex hated drama and everything that went with it just as much as Nell did.

But then, just when he thought things couldn't get any worse, the trellis began to creak.

And crack.

And start to pull away from the wall…

Oh, God, the whole thing was going to come down—with Nigel still on it.

Nell called up to her mother to grab Nigel's hands, but

she was too busy shrieking dramatically. Polly reached for him, but a moment too late, as the trellis finally parted company with the wall holding it and it arced backwards, towards the ground, Nigel still hanging on. And screaming.

Somehow, Nell suspected this wasn't quite the romantic gesture he'd planned.

A few guests rushed forward to try and stop the descent, but it was quickly apparent it wasn't going to work. Which was when Nigel decided to jump.

The trellis had been falling so slowly it made Nigel's leap seem even faster, and more sudden. Nell's eyes widened as she watched him fall—and as she realised, too late, where he was going to land.

I need to move.

The thought filled her brain, but she couldn't convey it to her feet. Couldn't draw her eyes away from the falling man, or the inevitability of what was about to happen.

She was frozen, the way she'd always felt as a child, whenever her mother did or said something so awful that everyone stared, and all Nell could do was stand there and be laughed at.

And her mother's awful next fiancé was going to land on top of her.

Except suddenly she *was* moving—and not of her own accord.

Alex swept her into his arms and out of Nigel's path, leaving him to land hard and skid into the middle of a bush of tropical flowers.

Her heart racing, Nell stared up into Alex's eyes. It was exactly the kind of over the top, dramatic rescue she hated in movies—and now the assembled crowd was cheering and whooping for them, as Alex held her in what could only be described as a dip.

He could have just grabbed my arm and pulled me out of the way.

Except…she was glad he hadn't. She was *glad* he'd given her the romantic rescue—and not just because it took attention away from Nigel and her mum.

And before she could stop herself she was kissing Alex, in front of a cheering crowd, and she just didn't care who saw it.

CHAPTER NINETEEN

THE WEDDING WAS BEAUTIFUL, Alex expected. He honestly hadn't been able to pay enough attention to what was going on around him to really tell. He'd smiled, handed over the rings and everything else he was charged to do as best man, but beyond that...

Beyond that, all he could think about was Nell, and that kiss.

After they'd broken apart, she'd murmured something about talking later, then disappeared back up to Polly's room—and he hadn't had a chance to speak with her since. Even now, she stood at the other side of the happy couple, not looking at him.

Did she regret it? Kissing him where everyone could see? She hadn't *seemed* to, in the moment—which gave him hope. And he was pretty sure she wouldn't have kissed him at all if she'd said yes to Paul's proposal the night before. But beyond that? He had no idea what was going on.

Nigel had been carted off to the medical centre to be checked over, but Madeline had declined to accompany him—which Alex suspected might mean the double wedding was off, thankfully. Instead, Nell and Polly's mother sat in the front row of the congregation, dabbing her eyes with a handkerchief as Fred and Polly held hands on the sand and said their vows. He had a feeling the handkerchief might actually belong to the vicar, who was the recipient of many of Madeline's smiles.

He flipped mentally through all the stories she'd told him at the rehearsal dinner. He was *pretty* sure Nell's mother had never been engaged to a vicar before.

After the ceremony came the photos, and the wedding breakfast, and all the other perfect little details Polly had arranged that Alex didn't care about. He just wanted to talk to Nell, except every time he tried someone seemed to thwart him.

Before he knew it, it was time for the speeches. Thankful he'd prepared his weeks before, he pulled his notes from his pocket to look over them again—but stopped when he realised that Nell had taken the microphone.

'It's not always traditional for the maid of honour to make a speech,' she said. 'But Polly asked me to and… it's not often you get the chance to say lovely things about your closest friend in front of people who genuinely care and want to listen, so I thought I'd take the opportunity.'

Alex smiled, and realised that everyone else there was too.

'Our whole lives, no one has ever had trouble telling Polly and me apart,' Nell went on. 'Even though we're identical. We might look the same, but everything else about us is different. If there's an adventure to go on, a chance to take, Polly will take it—and I'll hide away at home. If there's a bright colour to wear, Polly will wear it, whereas I'm always in black—today being a notable exception,' she added, looking down at her bridesmaid's dress. 'It's always worked well for us, that gulf between our personalities. We've never been jealous of each other because we always wanted different things—and supported each other to get them. As much as I love Fred as a brother, I'd never want him as a husband!' The wedding guests laughed, even as Fred pretended to be offended, and Polly buried her head in her hands.

'But for the first time, this week I've been envious of Polly. Not because she's getting married in this beautiful place, and not even because all of you lovely people are here to celebrate with her.' Nell paused and looked around the assembled company, and suddenly Alex felt her gaze on him. 'I envied Polly her courage. Because it takes a lot of courage to fall in love. Love is a risk—it's giving your heart to another person, and trusting them to take care of it. To love it and cherish it and protect it as well as—better than, even—their own. And it's a challenge too, because suddenly you receive their heart in return, and you have to take care of that just as well.'

She held his gaze, and in hers Alex saw universes of possibility. His heart started to swell, and his hopes rise, in return.

He watched Nell's throat bob as she swallowed and looked away before continuing.

'I know that Fred and Polly together are up to that challenge. And I know that Polly has always been the brave one—that's why she found her happy ever after so early, and has gone after it so determinedly. And it's why they're the best couple I know—and I wish them every possible happiness in the future.' She raised her glass. 'To Polly and Fred!'

Alex raised his glass and echoed her words—and knew he had to talk to her.

'And now, the best man!' The master of ceremonies' voice rang out, and Alex got shakily to his feet to make his own, prepared speech—one filled with humour and affection, and nowhere near as much truth as Nell's.

But the moment it was over…he was going to find her.

And they were both going to be brave.

Alex caught up to her on the dance floor, just after Polly and Fred had their first dance. Nell had to admit, she'd been waiting for him.

'Nice speech,' she told him as he swept her up in his arms and out onto the dance floor.

'Yours was better,' he replied. 'Braver.'

'It's a new thing I'm trying.'

They danced for a few moments in silence, and Nell just enjoyed resting her head against his shoulder and feeling his body against hers.

Then Alex said, 'I saw Paul visit you last night.'

Nell pulled back and stared up at him. 'Is that why you didn't come back to the villa? Because you thought—'

'No.' He tugged her close again and swayed them gently. 'I *was* coming back, after I'd given you time to have whatever conversation you needed to have with him. But then Fred's cousin collared me and told me that Nigel was demanding to see Fred to ask for it to be a double wedding. So I spent the night babysitting him.'

Nell groaned. 'If I never see that man again…'

'I know how you feel,' Alex agreed. 'Although, given that your mother is now dancing with the vicar, we might all be spared Nigel as your new stepfather.'

'Thank goodness.'

'So, you turned Paul down?' Alex asked.

'Emphatically.'

'Can I ask why?'

Nell paused in their dancing again, and looked up to meet his gaze.

This was it. Her moment to be brave. If she couldn't do it now, then none of the rest of it mattered anyway.

'Because he wasn't you,' she said. 'Because…everything I thought I wanted—boredom and stability and everything—it wasn't *wrong,* exactly, it just wasn't the whole truth. I wanted those things because I was too scared to ask for more. Too scared to risk anything for love when I knew how ridiculously people behaved for it. Because I thought love had to be drama and arguments and pain and tears.'

'Like my parents,' Alex murmured. 'I thought for the longest time that arguments and drama just meant passion—that a relationship without those things wasn't worth having anyway. But I realised that what mattered most was what was underneath those things. That if you had trust and respect and love, then everything else was just…'

'Drama?' Nell suggested.

He laughed. 'Yes. And I *like* a little drama and adventure in my life. I won't deny that. But what I want more than that is the real stuff. The trust and respect and love.'

'And I *like* a little boredom and stability,' Nell replied. 'But I want the real stuff more too. And if it comes with a little drama…maybe I could live with that too.'

'Really?'

'I think…' She took a deep breath. 'I think I'd like to try. If you'd like to try with me.'

Alex's smile was soft. 'Honestly? I'm so in love with you, Nell, I don't think I could do anything else.'

He loved her. He really loved her. 'Enough to stay home on Friday nights with me?'

'If you'll go out someplace new and exciting with me on the Saturday,' he suggested.

'Deal.' She squeezed his hands, realising they were just standing in the middle of the dance floor staring at each other now. 'Because I love you too, in case I hadn't mentioned it.'

'You hadn't,' Alex said. 'But the kiss earlier was a clue.'

'It was meant to be.'

'Good. So…' He slipped his arms around her back again. 'Are you ready to try being brave together?'

'More than ready,' Nell said, her heart beating double time in her chest at the thought.

And this time, when he dipped her and kissed her, she was prepared for the way the whole room cheered.

This time, she was ready for anything.

Even love.

* * * * *

PREGNANT PRINCESS AT THE ALTAR

KARIN BAINE

MILLS & BOON

For Mum. I wish you could be here
to see my dreams come true. xx

With thanks to my lovely editor, Charlotte,
who helped make this happen.

CHAPTER ONE

'NOT EVERY PRINCESS gets to live in a fairy tale, Gaia.'

'If anyone knows that, Mother, it's me.'

Currently her life was less handsome prince and happy-ever-after, and more unexpected pregnancy and absentee partner. Not exactly the stuff every little girl dreamed of, nor something she was brave enough to tell her family. The consequences of that particular news would be so far-reaching she couldn't face it yet.

The country of Lussureggiante—the name of which literally described the lush green land surrounding them—was a principality located near the Northern Italian border. It might be ruled by the monarchy but the inhabitants didn't always respect them. Gaia knew she wasn't going to gain them any new fans with her current status.

'I'm not sure what a movie premiere has to do with restoring the Benetti name exactly...' She trailed off, sounding more like a surly teen than a twenty-nine-year-old princess, second in line to the throne, but she had more important issues on her mind than the latest over-hyped film.

Even in the dim light of the limousine she could feel her mother's steely grey stare upon her. 'Your grandfather requests it. He wants you to be seen, so you will be accepted as the first female figurehead of the royal family when he dies.'

'No pressure, then.' There was nothing to be gained from another discussion on the subject other than causing her mother more anguish. She'd been through enough lately because of Gaia's father. He was the reason she was in this new media-focused role. The public scandal of the Prince, the future king, severing all ties with the royal family to run off with a married woman half his age had thrown the monarchy into complete disarray.

Not only had he humiliated his dutiful wife, disgraced the family name and caused their popularity to fall to an all-time low, but also now Gaia was expected to step up into his place. It wasn't something anyone had planned for, they simply had no other choice of direct descendants from her grandfather. If she wasn't put forward for the role the next in line would come from some less than desirable alternative outside the immediate Benetti family.

When she was growing up, the idea of one day leading the country had been something for her father to aspire to, not her. Therefore she'd remained mostly in the background, as the women in this family were supposed to do. Leaving the focus on her grandfather and later her father to have the hopes of a nation weighing on their shoulders. It was her duty to marry well and continue the family line. So far, she'd unfortunately endured carbon copies of her father—men who apparently couldn't commit to one woman or be content with their lot. The last no-hoper, Stefan, the vice president of a large banking firm she'd met at a garden party, had seemed a suitable match at the time. Although he would have been considered a commoner, he was descended from royalty on his Swedish mother's side. Good stock was the common perception. Until she'd discovered she was pregnant and he'd shown his true colours.

Not only had he told her he wasn't ready to settle down and have a family, but he'd later accused her of sleeping around when she told him she was keeping the baby too. It was apparent he wasn't going to be involved, and with that attitude she'd decided she didn't want him in her life any longer. A relief to him, especially when she promised not to tell anyone he was the father. They'd made a clean break, but she was still the one left to deal with the fallout.

Gaia wanted her baby. Being a daughter instead of the son and heir her father had desired, she knew what it was to be considered worthless, and would never purposely inflict that cruelty on her own child. Yes, she'd prefer her baby to be born into a warm, loving family with two parents, but she'd do her best to love enough for both parents.

A child would give her life real meaning, making her a mother, someone her child would be completely dependent on. She needed to be needed, to give and receive unconditional love she never truly believed she'd had in her life. Her mother had tried her best but Gaia knew her heart was completely devoted to her father. She'd been a disappointment to them both and probably the reason there'd been a rift between them since the beginning of their marriage.

Although she'd made the decision before her father abdicated, thinking becoming a mother would give her the purpose she didn't have in life, she wasn't going to change her mind. Even if she now had a dual role to fulfil.

She knew she was privileged to be in such a position, and she would do her utmost for her baby and her country. It simply would've been more comforting to have a supportive partner by her side.

This pregnancy hadn't happened in the best of circumstances, but she never wanted her child to feel the way she had growing up. It would be easier for her not to be pregnant for her and the family's sake, but the sheer joy she felt knowing there was a baby growing inside her was something she would not give up.

She could only imagine the joy of finally getting to meet this little one and having the privilege of raising him or her, introducing them to all the wonderful things in the world, and protecting them from the bad stuff. Being a good parent was as important to her as the other role being lined up for her future and she wasn't going to let anyone take that away from her.

Right now she was under pressure to be a good princess, deserving of the new position her grandfather was prepping her for. One which would break with family tradition in a constitution which had only revered the male members of the family, but her grandfather was resilient, if not 'modern'. With his son's behaviour so prevalent in the headlines, things had to change, and what better way to prove the family could be forward-thinking than to pass the crown on to a woman when the time came? That way the focus would be less on the rich privilege they were granted in their position, which her father had abused, and on a new enlightened monarchy granting equal rights for the men and women in the family.

For it to come out that she was on her own and pregnant would not make a good impression. She could be accused of following in her father's footsteps with loose moral behaviour when nothing could be further from the truth. All she was guilty of was picking the wrong men, like her mother.

'If you do not accept the position your grandfather is graciously bestowing upon you, the alternative is Antonio, who would surely collapse the monarchy with his disregard for tradition or decorum.'

Her distant cousin would be next in line and would be unacceptable to her grandfather and the rest of the country when he was frequently in trouble with the law. Definitely not the saviour of their reputation needed in the wake of her father's mid-life crisis.

She wasn't prepared for this new position or the expectations which came with it. Her only hope was for her grandfather to live for ever or her father to repent and be reinstated in his royal role. Neither of which was likely to happen.

So here she was, rolling up to a red-carpet event, carrying a secret which could cause almost as much damage to the family as her father in front of the world's press.

A swell of nausea threatened to spoil her sheer white, beaded, halter-neck gown.

Even though it wasn't her fault her ex had walked away, her mother would be disappointed in her. She didn't want to imagine her grandfather's reaction when he was championing her as the saviour of the whole institution.

The car came to a stop and she could hear the crowd outside, see the throng of people lined either side of the red carpet. She swallowed down the ball of anxiety blocking her airway and threatening to suffocate her as the privacy of the car interior was about to be ripped away from her.

'Who's in this film, anyway? Anyone I would know?' With this engagement thrust upon her at the last minute she hadn't been given much information and she didn't want to go in blind. If she slipped up on a name or didn't recognise the important people tonight it would be a faux pas she wouldn't be allowed to forget.

'Niccolo Pernici. I know you like that dance film he did a while back. You were always watching it.'

Gaia blushed undercover of the semi-darkness. It was true, she'd loved the film, but she watched it for one particular sexy scene which her mother would not have approved of if she'd seen it.

'I thought he'd been cast out into the wilderness after all those rumours. Something about fraudulent business practices, wasn't it?' She'd been disappointed at the time, reading about the dodgy dealings alleged by his ex-girlfriend in the papers. It had taken the shine off her crush to think he wasn't the honourable, upstanding man he portrayed in the movies.

Yet there'd been no arrest or court case and the furore had seemed to die down after a while. He'd remained off the radar and she had imagined perhaps that he'd grown tired of this superficial world, as she had lately.

She could relate to having a supposed private life splashed all over the papers with no opportunity for comeback, advised to remain silent and dignified until things blew over.

'Apparently this is his baby and the critics have been raving about it. Which is why we want to be seen here tonight. This is his comeback, and your debut as a more prominent member of the royal family.'

'Isn't it going to look strange having two female members of the family in attendance?' Traditionally they were there merely to look pretty on the arms of the men, who were there in a position of more authority. Nothing more than clothes horses whose make-up and hair would be judged and critiqued the world over. Apparently the men added more of a sense of gravitas, or something equally sexist.

'Your grandfather isn't in good enough health to sit through these things, and your father…well, his presence is equally unlikely. Yes, it goes against tradition, but that's exactly why we should be here together. Everyone needs to get used to the idea that this will no longer be a male-dominated monarchy.' Her mother almost sounded proud of her. As if watching her daughter ascend through the ranks could erase the humiliation and shame of what her husband had done. Gaia only hoped she wasn't going to add to her mother's woes.

'Thank you for the support.' Gaia reached out and took her hand, surprised to see tears in her mother's eyes. She'd always been a rock, standing steadfast through all of her father's indiscretions, which he'd never bothered to hide, still carrying out her public duty and serving her country. All the time putting up with the emotional abuse Gaia's father had directed at her.

'You're lucky you married into this family. Without me, you're nothing,' was something she'd heard repeatedly used against her mother when objections to his behaviour were raised.

It was so ingrained in her Gaia thought it about herself too. She wasn't the longed-for male heir but a useless woman who didn't deserve her place in the family, or his time.

As far as Gaia was concerned, her mother had been the perfect princess, always acting appropriately and showing compassion for those less fortunate than herself. She could see the pain that caused her now, still having to put on a brave face when inside she was still devastated by her husband's public betrayal.

There was no more time to console her mother as their chauffeur opened the car door and the glare of cameras and lights blinded them.

As they had been taught to do, Gaia and her mother slapped on their smiles before facing the crowd.

'At what point can I leave?' Niccolo whispered to Ana, his agent, who was his plus one for the night.

'It's your premiere, Niccolo. This is Niccolo Pernici's great comeback. There will be no sneaking away.' She emphasised the last three words with a tap on his chest with her folded fan, a much-needed accessory inside the movie theatre on this balmy evening.

'You know best,' he sighed, resigned to the fact he'd spend the rest of the night smiling and posing for photographs when all he really wanted was to be alone.

'I know these past two years have been tough, Nicco, but I always believed in you. By the look of tonight's turn-out, your fans do too. All of those things Christina said about you were unproven because they weren't true. I still don't know why you didn't sue her for defamation of character after the damage she did to your reputation.'

'Because that's what she wanted—drama, attention and, most of all, a reaction from me.' His ex-girlfriend had accused him of being emotionless, a robot incapable of actual feelings. It wasn't true; he simply found life easier to get through by keeping his emotions at bay.

The death of his mother at a young age had devastated him to the point where he'd stopped talking altogether. No one had thought to tell him about the cancer which had taken her, making it more of a shock to him than anyone else when she went away for ever. It had taken a lot of therapy and counselling for him to recover, with little assistance from his father other than arranging the appointments. He hadn't wanted to talk about what had happened, just wanted his son to be 'normal' again. Niccolo's grief had consumed him and the only way he'd been able to move on and make his father happy again was to lock those feelings away. He'd been doing that ever since.

He could see why Christina had thought him cold, but the truth was he simply hadn't loved her the way she needed him to. That was what had prompted her tirade after he'd broken up with her, refusing to commit to their moving in together. She'd insinuated to anyone who would listen that he was involved in conning people out of their life savings for investments that didn't exist. In reality it was his father who mixed in some dubious business circles, always putting money before people. However, an ex scorned didn't care for trivial details such as the truth and had a ready-made audience in the press, who were all too keen to knock him off his top-billing perch. There was nothing the tabloids loved more than to build a man up, only to watch him fall back down again.

He'd been a box-office surety, thanks to his roles in crowd-pleasing romantic comedies. Then, when Christina had spread her poison, he'd suddenly found himself *persona non grata* in the industry. Offers and scripts had begun to dry up along with his chat-show requests. His refusal to take Christina to court had helped make him look guilty and cost him all of his endorsement deals, not to mention his so-called friends.

His decision to deny everyone some high-profile mud-slinging was because he didn't want to be exposed in what would've been a show trial put on for everyone's entertainment but his. There'd been a possibility the stress would've proved too much, that he would've broken down, not through guilt, but from an explosion of all the emotion he'd been fighting since the day he'd told Christina it was over. Within a few months he'd lost everything he'd ever worked for and he didn't want the world to see him broken, didn't want to let his pain win through for fear of never being able to rein it in again. It would've been a very public breakdown waiting to happen.

Instead he'd locked himself away working on his own projects, since no one seemed inclined to offer him any more work. He'd invested what money he had left, called in favours from people still willing to give him the time of day, and come up with an emotional, one-take monologue about a man coming to terms with a terminal cancer diagnosis. Based on not only his mother's last months but also his own emotional fragility at the time, it was a piece far removed from anything he'd ever done before. No one was more surprised than he when it had been lauded at film festivals by critics prior to this premiere and everything was riding on its being a success.

It was difficult to suddenly bounce back simply because the buzz around his film had made him hot property again. Especially when it had been filmed during one of the worst periods of his life. He wasn't sure he could watch himself unravelling on the big screen, all too aware it was real, raw and unflinching. No acting involved. The last time he planned on ever being that vulnerable again.

'Anyway, you should go and line up with the other subjects for our princess to cast an eye over.' Ana opened her fan with an expert flick of the wrist to rival that of any Edwardian heroine and sauntered into the screening with the rest of the crowd.

Niccolo had no choice but to fall into the greeting line. It was a royal premiere after all. His premiere. All he had to do was smile, shake hands and pray this film was a success so he could get his life back on track.

'Lovely to meet you.'

'Hello.'

'I've heard it's a wonderful film.'

He watched Princess Gaia make her way along the short line of crew who'd worked with him on the project, shaking hands and reducing them to gibbering fools. Usually he didn't put any store in their monarchy when they seemed like any other dysfunctional family, only with extra privilege and influence. However, great things were expected of this woman and he had to respect the grace with which she was dealing with the pressure. He knew what it was like to have the spotlight shining so brightly it was almost incapacitating.

As they'd been instructed to do by those more experienced in royal etiquette, he bowed and only shook hands when the Princess offered hers.

'Mr Pernici, it's an honour to meet you.'

'Likewise, Your Royal Highness.' There was no doubting her beauty, with chestnut curls falling in silken waves to her shoulders, unusual amber-coloured eyes and lips so full he imagined she was the poster girl for every red-blooded human on the planet.

He was still holding her hand, and, though it probably went against all sort of protocol, he couldn't resist lifting it to his lips for a kiss. The flash of cameras lighting up told him it was going to be a watercooler moment tomorrow, but somehow simply shaking her hand hadn't seemed enough. This was the future monarch and he might never get another chance to meet her. He'd wanted to make an impression on her and, judging by her little gasp, followed by her coy smile, he'd done just that.

'Don't you think we've dominated the headlines for long enough between us, Mr Pernici? Anyone would think you were purposely causing a scene.' She was trying to hide her smile but her eyes were blazing with amusement at the stunt he'd pulled. Maybe she liked a rebel who didn't behave exactly as he was told to do, or perhaps she was enjoying something different from the norm. Whatever it was, she clearly knew who he was and what he'd been through.

'That wasn't my intention, Ma'am, I assure you. I'd prefer it if no one else was around.'

'You and me both,' she sighed, letting that polished smile momentarily slip to give him a peek at the emotionally exhausted person behind the glamour. In that moment it seemed they'd made a connection, recognising each other's recent hardships and how much it had cost them to come here tonight to face the world again. A secret club no one else would want to be part of.

Niccolo wondered, despite the entourage of security and advisors around her, if she'd felt as lonely as he had when her family name had been dragged through the mud. She might not have been directly involved in her father's scandalous downfall but he was sure she'd felt the shame and the pressure to clear her name just the same. Had she had support from family or friends, or, like him, had she dealt with it all on her own? There was something about the way she carried herself that made him think the latter. That she portrayed an air of strength to protect that inner fragility he was sure he could see beyond the carefully styled royal. A similar outfit to the one he was wearing tonight, playing the Hollywood superstar to the crowd, kissing a princess without permission, while secretly terrified this could all come to an end again.

If only they had some space away from the cameras and the watching crowd they might be able to confide in each other, compare their troubled lives, perhaps even find solace in one another.

He realised he was still holding her hand and decided he'd clearly been without company too long when he was imagining forging a relationship with the future Queen based on this brief interaction. Realising herself that the introduction had gone beyond the normal polite greeting, Princess Gaia pulled her hand away.

She stepped closer, looking as though she had something to say. Niccolo leaned in so she could speak directly into his ear.

'I guess it's time for us to put on our game faces, Mr Pernici.' She nodded an acknowledgement before moving on but the eye contact between them lingered a little longer than perhaps it should have.

There had been something in that recognition of one another making it impossible for Niccolo to take his eyes off her. His reward came a few moments later when she turned back to catch his eye once more. He smiled and placed his hand on his heart, afraid he'd lost it so quickly and easily to someone so out of reach.

Niccolo had known it would be too much. Watching his portrayal of a man on the verge of a breakdown was too close to home for him to remain in his seat. The last thing he needed was to burst into tears at his own movie.

'Ana, I think I'm going to duck out for a while,' he whispered to the one person who'd truly stuck by him through the worst time of his life.

'But Niccolo, this is your night, your masterpiece.' Her voice gradually got higher as she extolled all the reasons he should keep his butt in his chair.

'I've seen it. Overrated if you ask me.' He dropped a kiss on her head and did his best to leave with the minimum disruption.

Head bowed and knees bent, he crept past the other viewers, and took one last glance at the Princess sitting in the front row. She seemed so engaged in watching him fall apart he should've been proud of his work. Instead, his stomach and his pride plummeted into his expensive leather dress shoes that she should be witness to his actual mental decline.

'Excuse me.' He pushed past the bemused security behemoth at the door, almost gasping for air. To him, the auditorium had become a freak show with the VIP guests invited to ooh and ahh at the downfall of a once-loved actor now reduced to humiliating himself for a pittance. He'd done all that was expected of him so hopefully he could go home as soon as the movie itself had ended.

It was ironic that the budget production, only in existence because no one would touch him, could now herald the resurgence of his career. He couldn't help but think it had come at too high a price.

This was different from the romantic comedies he was famed for, or the few action flicks he'd been lucky to play a part in. For someone infamous for not displaying emotion in his real life, it was all up there on the big screen for the world to see. He wasn't suffering a terminal illness or contemplating his imminent death like his character, but he knew he'd been channelling those overwhelming feelings of his own grief and helplessness to make his character believable. That was why it was a difficult watch for him. It wasn't fiction; it wasn't a performance. It was a man grieving for the life he'd lost through no fault of his own, hiding in plain sight.

He wondered if Princess Gaia could relate to the pain and that powerlessness of the world continuing to spin even though one's life had come to a standstill. If she saw past the story and the character and instead was watching the real Niccolo Pernici reveal a side to him he'd never shown anyone before. That thought was more disturbing than the worry his fans would be turned off by his change of direction.

It wasn't often that Gaia was starstruck. Getting doe-eyed over a film star was not becoming for a princess, or so her mother had reminded her with a sharp elbow to the ribs back at the greeting line.

Given her current circumstances, she never thought she would as much as look at another man. They'd caused enough turmoil in her life to date. There was something about Niccolo Pernici in that short encounter that she'd found…intriguing. A connection between them that she'd been unable to put from her mind. Perhaps it was because they'd both been in the headlines recently for all the wrong reasons, but she'd felt a kinship, a familiarity in him, though they'd never met before. And an attraction she definitely could not afford to indulge in.

To date her relationships had been 'arranged'. Men from the 'right' families, 'good stock', appropriate matches for the daughter of the future King. That hadn't turned out so well when she had a type, leaning towards privileged narcissists as her mother had.

Now she was the future Queen she suspected her choices would be even more limited. In her current position she might not get a choice at all. It was part of the reason she hadn't shared her not so happy news yet. Once the establishment heard she was pregnant they would want her married off to the next available socially acceptable suitor, and she didn't think she had the option to object. An illegitimate child in line to the throne would be unheard of, even in a progressive country which, so far, seemed open to the idea of a future female monarch.

Although she'd done her best to stay away from the press, she knew there had been debates on TV and radio about changing the rules for her. As always, there were those in favour and some against the idea. Either way, she was in the spotlight and under pressure to be a good role model until she got the chance to experience the power and status of her ascension to the throne. Not that she was expecting an easy ride then either. She would have a lot of prejudice to fight, both inside and outside the palace, from traditionalists who wanted to maintain the status quo no matter what.

The only glimpse of happiness she could see cracking through the gloom was the actual birth of this baby. Someone who wouldn't judge Gaia for her choices or her status. At least not until he or she was a teenager, when all bets were off. By the time her bundle of joy was born she expected to have sorted things out with her family and at least have some peace of mind on that front. Until then she had to keep her worries and secrets to herself. Something to keep her awake at night and keep her nerves constantly on edge.

That was why, despite Niccolo's phenomenal portrayal of a man on the brink, she was getting antsy sitting here. She didn't need to be further depressed, and if she was honest she wasn't enjoying watching him fall apart before her eyes. Not when she'd just experienced his charisma first-hand.

What she needed was his usual smouldering, smart-ass romantic lead to make her forget her own tragic love life. She did not need to see him broken and wonder if any of it had been an act, or if she was seeing the toll these past two years had taken on him for real.

Their lifestyles and their reasons for being in the headlines were very different, but they'd both suffered at the hands of the press and the rumour mill. That pain etched on his handsome face she'd seen reflected in the mirror every day her family's name was dragged through the mud, their very existence brought into question. It was no wonder he hadn't been able to watch himself.

She'd noticed him slipping out and he hadn't come back yet. It wasn't so easy for her with Security positioned at every exit and her private bodyguard shadowing her every move. Much needed precautions in the days of terrorist attacks and people who simply bore a grudge against the royal family, but it didn't make their presence any less stifling.

Her bladder was no longer working alongside those societal rules that dictated she shouldn't be seen as a mere mortal who needed such basic amenities as a bathroom either.

'Excuse me, Mother. I'll be back in a few minutes.' She ignored the pointed look and made her escape with her entourage practically announcing her bathroom break to the audience as they got ready to move with her.

'I'm sure Raimondo will suffice for now,' she told them, exasperated by the whole palaver of simply going to the bathroom. Her head of security nodded, telling the rest of the team to back down.

It was a small concession, very much appreciated. Although she still had to wait for a security sweep of the private cubicle before she was allowed a moment of privacy.

A few minutes later, whilst washing her hands at the sink, she heard voices outside the bathroom door.

'So you're, like, the Princess's bodyguard? That's so cool. Do you know Niccolo too?'

She heard Raimondo grunt in response to whom she assumed was some starry-eyed groupie hoping to find a way to reach her movie idol.

When Gaia peered outside, her big, burly security was paying more attention to the blonde twirling her hair around her finger and feeling his biceps than to his charge. This was her chance for a moment of freedom, some time to breathe without the world watching. She eased the door closed behind her, hitched up her dress and hurried down the corridor like a runaway bride having second thoughts about the man waiting for her at the end of the aisle.

In a way she supposed that was what she was, if her future role as a monarch was the groom in this scenario, with the country waiting for the happy ending. After all, what did she know about running a country? She hadn't been prepped for it the way her father had been. This responsibility had just been dropped on her from a great height, a weight so great she could barely breathe and would possibly leave nothing more of her behind than a dark smudge of the person she'd used to be.

She let herself into a side room where chairs were stacked around the walls and old movie posters lay discarded on a threadbare jazzy carpet. Perhaps once an office, it was now little more than a store room, but to her it represented freedom. That strong need to breathe in fresh air sent her hurrying to the window and wresting the wooden frame up until the cool draught from outside breezed across her skin.

'It is rather oppressive back there, isn't it?'

The deep voice coming from somewhere in the room made her yelp. Now she realised how foolish it had been to ditch her security team and run off on her own. She'd left herself vulnerable to whatever weirdo had been hiding in here, and no one knew where she was. A glance around for a makeshift weapon left her clutching a nearby paintbrush.

'Who's there?' she demanded, thrusting her brush dagger forward.

'What are you going to do—paint me to death?' the voice mocked from the shadows.

'My—my security team will be here soon.'

'I hope not. You look as though you need time out and I don't fancy taking on that hulk of a bodyguard you usually have by your side.' Shadow man stepped out from behind a stack of chairs and Gaia was able to lower her weapon.

'Niccolo? What are you doing here?'

'The same as you, I imagine. Escaping.' He lifted a silver hip flask to his lips and took a swig before offering it to her. She shook her head.

Mr Movie Star didn't look quite as composed as he had during the line-up minus his jacket, his sleeves rolled up and his bowtie hanging loosely around his open collar.

'But it's your movie. Everyone is here to see you.'

He glanced at her through narrowed eyes. 'To see me, or to watch me?'

'Isn't it the same thing?'

Niccolo moved across the room to disarm her, setting the paintbrush back on the bench where she'd found it.

'There are some people who have come with genuine interest in the film, curious to see if it lives up to the hype, but...' He took another drink from his flask and she could smell whisky on his breath. 'I'm sure there are many more out there who want to see me fail, to gossip about me, to believe all the things they've read about me.'

'Do you really believe that?' It saddened her to think people could be that cruel, or that Niccolo could think that on one of the biggest nights of his career.

'Don't you?' He had an infuriating way of turning all questions back on to her, as though she was a mind reader, or someone who was going through the same thing and not enjoying the attention.

Gaia thought about the reasons she was here tonight, of how afraid she was that the very subtle changes of her two-month pregnancy might be noticed and of the repercussions of that. Her breasts were tender, her belly a little softer, but nothing too noticeable, she hoped, and her mother hadn't commented. Now Niccolo had caused her to worry people had come to watch her, to witness her possible downfall too, and would see those tiny changes heralding her pregnancy.

She shuddered at the thought. It was a shame she couldn't enjoy a stiff drink along with him.

'Are you cold? I can close the window and fetch my jacket for you.' He rubbed his hands up and down her arms and quickly generated an inner heat. It had been a couple of months since anyone had touched her and she was enjoying the feel of him against her skin.

'Sorry. I'm probably not supposed to do that, much less even talk to you, Princess.' He dropped his hands and took a step back, that damned sense of etiquette which followed her like a faithful hound robbing her of a further moment of comfort.

'It's fine. I think we're both in need of a break from social niceties. If it's any consolation, I never believed any of those rumours in the papers,' she blurted out, keen for Niccolo to know he had a kindred spirit in her.

It was nice to be able to drop her guard for a little while and simply have a chat without having to choose her every word with caution. Niccolo had been to hell and back with the tabloids, so she trusted him not to share the details of their unexpected meeting. It was difficult to make friends in her position, always wary that any confidences shared would somehow make their way to the press. Alas, this was the privileged but lonely life of a princess.

He cocked his head to one side as though he was deciding whether she was being honest or merely polite. Eventually he mumbled a coy, 'Thanks.'

Gaia wondered how much his ordeal had taken out of him. She was emotionally exhausted by the constant dissection of her family's behaviour and it wasn't even her who'd caused a scandal. Yet. Niccolo had come under personal attack, his integrity and good character not just called into question but completely eviscerated.

Although he had been a tad forward during their introduction, it had been harmless fun and he seemed a nice enough guy, minus the usual ego and swagger of entitlement she'd met in other celebrities. Perhaps that had been knocked out of him by one woman's unsubstantiated claims which had derailed his career. Yet he'd never once spoken out against her, which spoke of his dignity and integrity and incredible patience.

She found herself wondering if a man like Niccolo Pernici would abandon his responsibilities. If he would have walked away from a pregnant partner and left her to deal with the consequences. She wanted to believe otherwise, that there were men out there who could still be counted upon to do the right thing, but she would for ever be wary now of anyone who crossed her path.

'I think this film will remind people what a great actor you are and all of that terrible gossip will fade into memory.' There was always a bigger scandal waiting in the wings. Her father's affair had replaced the columns on Niccolo's alleged misdemeanours. She could only pray she wouldn't be the next target for public ridicule.

'I hope so, but I assume the movie wasn't to your personal taste, Princess, since you left halfway through?' He was teasing her, his deep brown, almost black, eyes daring her to tell the truth.

'You were amazing but I, uh…let's just say things are a little tough for me right now and I wasn't in the right frame of mind to appreciate it.' She had no desire to offend him no matter how unintentionally when he'd surely had enough criticism for one lifetime.

'You mean you didn't want to be depressed any more than you already are? Kind of why I walked out too. Let's hope the whole audience doesn't feel the same way.'

That made her laugh. Something she thought she'd never do again after all the recent heartache.

'Sorry.' She didn't know how to explain her reaction, her discomfort at seeing him emotionally vulnerable when she hardly knew him. An apology was all she could offer.

'It's fine. I realise you've had a tough time lately too.' His warm smile immediately lessened her guilt and increased another emotion. An attraction to someone who seemed at ease wearing his heart on his sleeve, encouraging her to do the same and simply be herself. Something which she really didn't need further complicating her life.

'You could say that.' Though he didn't know the half of what she was going through. No one did.

'Sorry I couldn't give you an upbeat, feel-good, forget-about-the-real-world-for-a-while romcom. I guess I just wasn't in the mood at the time.' He ran his finger through his slicked-back hair, dislodging a few errant curls refusing to be tamed.

'I'm not surprised. I don't know how you even managed to get out of bed, much less make your own movie. Didn't you want to just hide away from the world when all of that was going on in the press?' That had been her reaction to finding out about her father, pulling the covers over her head and refusing to face the world until her mother had intervened. She'd been shamed then by her broken-hearted parent, who'd been directly affected by the scandal and still managed to function, outwardly at least. Whatever inner turmoil her mother had been going through she'd kept it to herself, as always. If there was one thing she had learned from her family it was not to give away what was going on behind the royal façade. That was fine when out in public, but it would have been nice to have someone at home who encouraged her to express her feelings, to have someone to talk to and confide in. She hadn't had that sort of relationship with anyone, including her mother. Emotions were something to be contained. Yet no one had taught her how to work past them, through them, or live with them.

She and Niccolo were both trapped, playing roles they didn't want to be in, longing for normal lives away from the public eye. Unfortunately for her that was never going to be a possibility.

'What would that have solved? I still have to make a living. It's not as though you can wake up in the morning and just decide not to be a princess either. This is simply part of who we are and we have to live with it.'

'You could just walk away. Plenty of actors have shunned the spotlight and disappeared into obscurity. It's not so easy for me.' Unless she caused a scandal like her father, except she was the last in the immediate family line and therefore much more likely to cause irreparable damage to the monarchy if she abdicated her position.

'I could, but I love acting so much, and this film has opened up avenues in directing I'm keen to explore too. Until last year it probably was more about the pay check for me but some time in the wilderness has given me perspective on certain things. As pompous as it sounds, I want to leave a legacy behind. I want to be able to tell stories, inform and entertain people at the same time. I'd be happier doing that than sitting counting my fortune somewhere. Don't get me wrong, money helps, but it's not everything.' Niccolo's laugh was as warm as his smile and just as intoxicating. He seemed so far from the wisecracking characters he often played Gaia could see how great an actor he truly was.

'I did enjoy the film you did about the dance instructor, "One More Tango in Rome".' As well as being romantic and sweet, the dancing in that film had been passionate and downright obscene in places. She'd watched one particular scene on repeat. Not that she could admit that to the man standing in front of her, lest she spontaneously combust through embarrassment.

'Ah, yes, a fan favourite.' He did a quick solo waltz around the floor, causing Gaia to burst into applause.

'Did you do the dancing yourself? I mean, did you learn the moves specially for the film?' Her cheeks became suffused with heat at the memory of the tango sequence which led his character and his partner to the bedroom for some more spectacular moves between the sheets.

'We had a really good teacher on set but I think the chemistry with my co-star helped. Do you dance?'

'Only as a social requirement. The Argentine Tango

is not on the approved list for princesses. Besides, I'm not sure I could do it justice. The steps seem so complicated I'd be afraid of kicking my partner somewhere inappropriate.'

'It's easy once you know the basics. Here, let me show you.' He held his hand out and Gaia took it willingly.

'Sorry, is this allowed?' he asked, after pulling her into hold.

'Not usually, but at present I'm not in my princess guise, I'm just Gaia.' They'd both forgotten themselves and how they were supposed to behave around one another, but it was nice not to have someone treating her as untouchable, and at the same time feeling almost normal for once.

'I'm not a very good student.' She made her excuses in case she made a fool of herself in front of someone who clearly had talent in this department.

'I'm afraid it's a very close dance.' He'd pulled her so tightly against him she could smell the mix of spicy cologne and man sweat clinging to his skin.

Afraid any attempt to speak would come out as a squeak, she nodded her consent and placed one hand on his shoulder, the other interlaced with his.

'It's about fire and passion. A love-hate, push and pull between partners.' He showed her a few steps, leaving her dizzy as he twirled her around with ease.

'I'm not sure I'm wearing the right outfit for this,' she noted, her body restricted as she attempted to recreate his kicks and flicks.

'Mmm, I think you're right.' He knelt down at her feet and lifted the hem of her dress. 'May I?'

Despite being unsure what he was asking of her, she

would have agreed to anything in that moment she was so enraptured with this live re-enactment of his most famous dance.

The rip of fabric sounded through the room as Niccolo deftly made two thigh-high splits in her gown. She gasped as much with delight as shock at the bold move, which wouldn't have been out of place in her once favourite erotic scene. Replaced for ever by this one.

'That's better,' he said, standing up, his eyes and voice both darker than before.

Gaia's mouth went dry as he held her gaze, lifting her leg to anchor his thigh while they spun around. She could feel the hardness of his body pressed against her softness and her heart was racing from more than the physical exertion. It was exhilarating being in Niccolo's arms doing something illicit and just for her.

Suddenly he threw her effortlessly up into the air and she braced her hands on his shoulders as he slowly lowered her back down his body. She was lost in his eyes, in the sensation of sliding along his torso so intimately, and to what it was doing to her inside.

He twirled her around again and dipped her head back, following the arc of her body with his so their lips were almost touching, their breath mingling in the millimetres between.

Then a camera flashed and the moment was captured. Ruined for ever.

CHAPTER TWO

'OH, HOLY HOTNESS!' As Gaia bit into a slice of wholemeal toast she glanced at the bundle of newspapers stacked neatly on the table and, in her hurry to grab them, accidentally bumped the table with her knee.

She immediately jumped to her feet, watching helplessly as her glass of orange juice sluiced over her silk floral pyjamas and the sharp, irrefutable sight of her and Niccolo on the front page.

If she hadn't been so acutely aware of the implications of said money shot, she would've been impressed by how good they looked together. She took more care to clean the juice off the newspaper than her pyjamas, shaking the excess off onto the marble tiles so she could get another look.

Everyone was going to lose their mind over this picture. She and Niccolo knew there was nothing in it—it hadn't been anything more than an impromptu dance lesson. Okay, so he'd got her a little hot under the halter-neck with his moves, but neither of them had acted upon it.

'What is the meaning of this, Gaia?'

She'd known it would only be a matter of time before her grandfather saw the same headlines declaring the greatest love affair of the century, false though they were, but he'd been exceptionally quick to find her out here on the terrace. Unfortunately it spoke volumes of his displeasure and urgency to discuss the matter.

'Good morning, Grandfather, Mother.' Although it was her grandfather who was addressing her directly, her mother was hovering in the background. Both had the same disapproving glare trained on her. Just what she needed first thing in the morning with her spoiled breakfast and tabloid scandal.

'How can you sit there, Granddaughter, as though you haven't a care in the world when you've brought our family name into disrepute yet again?' He slammed his hand down on top of the other newspapers, the same photograph displayed on all of the front pages.

'Because I haven't done anything, Grandfather.' Gaia kept her tone measured and calm even though she wanted to scream about the injustice of the pressure on her and dramatically tip over her breakfast table.

'You can see how it looks, Gaia.' Her mother stepped forward to play devil's advocate.

When Gaia and Niccolo had been caught in their compromising position, her mother had been part of the audience. They hadn't known a search had begun during their absence, caught up in their few minutes of liberation from their stifling existence. As soon as the cameras flashed Niccolo had let go of her and her mother had assumed physical control, rushing her back to their waiting limousine and whisking her away from the furore.

'Niccolo was simply showing me a few dance steps, nothing more.' Except in her head. If she'd been thinking logically she would have realised it was inappropriate, but she'd been too caught up in the moment dancing with the handsome movie star to think about how it would look.

'It doesn't look like nothing.' Her grandfather lifted

another of the newspapers and shoved it in her face so she was confronted by the image of her and Niccolo, bodies entwined, heads so close it looked as though they were about to kiss.

'We didn't do anything.' Her protest was weaker this time because she knew with the evidence provided no one was ever going to believe her.

'The damage is done. The whole world thinks you and Niccolo Pernici are in a relationship. It's what we do about it now that is important.' Her mother's voice of reason did little to control Gaia's racing pulse. She knew what this meant. It was another scandal, more discussions about the behaviour of the royal family as if they were needed when all they seemed to do was bring negative attention. In a different time they might have had the whole country lining up at the palace gates calling for her head. All of which seemed so unfair when she hadn't actually done anything. She tried not to think about what might happen when her pregnancy came to light.

'Why do we have to do anything? People have misunderstood what happened. Why should I have to explain anything when it's liable to simply make me look guilty of something untoward?' Even if they had been enjoying a secret tryst, caught in the midst of a passionate embrace, it should have been nobody's business. They were two single adults. Regardless that everyone seemed to believe they owned a piece of them because of their very public status.

'You disappeared, Gaia, causing a security alert. This…this is how we found you, together.' Her mother's usual composure began to slip, her voice shrill and full of accusation as she took her turn to point at the incriminating photograph.

'I've said I'm sorry. It wasn't planned. I just needed a break and I ran into Niccolo. We got talking…' And flirting, and dancing, but her mother didn't need to hear that.

It was a shame they had been discovered and been made to feel ashamed for having some time out. The memory of that interlude, a few minutes getting to relax and be herself, was something she would cherish. Goodness knew when she would get to have anything like it again.

Niccolo had been understanding of her situation because he'd been through something similar. He saw her need to escape everything and had provided that with his time and patience, showing her a few dance steps. It hadn't hurt that he was sexy and fun to be around, enough to take her mind off her troubles for a while.

'If you were just talking, the whole world wouldn't think you and this Niccolo were a couple. This isn't just intimate, it's damn near pornographic. After your father's behaviour this is going to look as though you share the same moral code. We cannot afford to lose any more respect, Gaia. I thought I could trust you.'

Her old-fashioned grandfather might be overreacting to what was essentially an innocent dance but she could see his point. People were going to assume they were together and with a baby on the way it would be easy to believe Niccolo was the father. In seven months' time this wasn't going to be something she could simply brush off. It needed to be addressed now or there would be implications for both of them further down the line.

The die had been cast, even though it was false. Any denial that they were together would make a liar out of her when the baby was born, with Niccolo seen as an absentee father through absolutely no fault of his own. Her family was right—this was a crisis, bigger than they knew.

'I'll speak to Niccolo. I'm sorry to have caused you both further pain. I'll fix this.' She didn't know how, only that she had to. The future of the family and the country depended on it. Poor Niccolo had no idea what he'd got himself involved in.

'The whiff of a royal romance on top of your critical success means you're in more demand than ever. I've been fielding calls from journalists and movie execs since your escapades with our beloved princess last night.' Ana had been thrilled with the publicity this morning, calling Niccolo at seven a.m.

'It was only a dance.' He hadn't shared her enthusiasm upon seeing the photograph on the front page of every newspaper. Not only had it pulled focus away from his film and onto a non-existent relationship, but it had also captured the very second he'd thought about kissing Gaia.

Looking at himself, lost in the moment, was almost as exposing as seeing himself on the big screen. His raw, naked want for the woman whose soft curves had been tight against him was there on display. There was even something in the way she was looking at him, as though he only had to say the word and she was his, that made the evidence against them even more damning. It was no wonder everyone had lost their minds when it was so clearly more than a dance. Yet their intention had only been to find a little peace away from the crowd.

Neither of them had left that room intending to create a stir; quite the opposite. They'd been oblivious to the commotion surrounding her disappearance until the flash of a camera alerted them to the fact they had an audience for their private dance. Gaia had been whisked away with no chance to say goodbye or anything else. He wished they'd been left alone to enjoy some quiet time and each other's company. Instead now everyone was invested in a relationship that could never be. Even if there had been a spark between them last night, the interest generated would ensure nothing further would happen with the eyes of the world upon them. Given time he knew the publicity would fade away but he regretted letting his guard down and causing them both this extra hassle.

'Well, I think you're going to have to release some sort of statement because my phone is in meltdown with everyone trying to get the scoop. Anyway, I'm calling to say good job on the film and the extra publicity, intentional or not. Let me know what you want to do about addressing these rumours and I'll clear my schedule. You're my number one, Niccolo.' She hung up and, though he appreciated Ana's support, Niccolo knew he was only her number one for today. Ana had been loyal to him during his struggles but she was still a businesswoman and he knew she'd prioritised other clients during that time, just as she would when the public lost interest in this non-event. That was why she wanted him to act now and capitalise on the publicity it had generated to keep the momentum going around the film hype. Except he knew how much it would cost Gaia to draw further interest.

Last night had only happened because she'd been seeking an escape from the attention. Even hinting that there was something going on between them would encourage more of the harassment she had no doubt encountered during the reporting on her father's antics. He would never knowingly invite the sort of pain and suffering he'd gone through these past years into anyone's life and especially not the life of someone like Gaia, who had done nothing to deserve it. On both occasions she'd been an unwitting participant in a scandal, unfortunately caught in the crossfire of public appetite for salacious gossip and men around her who couldn't control themselves.

He blamed himself for this incident, led so quickly into temptation by her vulnerability and beauty. A better man would have taken her back to safety and known his place. Not Niccolo Pernici. He'd allowed himself a flirtation, a physical connection, and an almost kiss, without considering the consequences now facing his partner. Gaia would be judged now worse than ever.

She was the future Queen, with the entire monarchy resting on her shoulders, and he'd jeopardised that for one moment of self-indulgence. He'd wanted her and now the world knew that, could see it for themselves, and had concocted a story around it. It was going to be up to him to give a plausible explanation without destroying either of their reputations. He had no desire to put himself, nor Gaia, through the hell he'd experienced because of the last falsehood he'd been accused of. Even if there was the ring of truth around this one because last night had been about more than a dance lesson. It had been a meeting of minds, two lost souls connecting and finding comfort in one another, along with that flare of passion he was sure came from more than the steps he'd shown her.

Now he had to find a way of putting everything right or risk the wrath of the house of Benetti.

Niccolo's palms had been sweating more at the prospect of facing Gaia and her family at the palace than at his premiere, despite the air-conditioned luxury car which had driven him here.

The very officious call requesting his attendance was not completely unexpected but a nerve-racking experience none the less. He supposed he was a very big part of their current problem so it made sense he should be part of the solution too. Hopefully they could work together to clear up this simple misunderstanding and then they'd probably never cross paths again.

Niccolo experienced a sudden pang, an emptiness opening up in his chest at the very thought. It had been some time since he'd been that close to anyone, physically or otherwise, and if Gaia had been anyone else he might have explored the connection they seemed to have. As it was, he'd be lucky if he was allowed to even be in the same room as her again.

Neither of them had thought that her brief disappearance would cause a full lockdown of the auditorium, with a search team combing all areas, on high alert for a possible breach of security and threat to her life. Needless to say there had been more than a photographer witnessing their passionate clinch and he could still hear her mother's horrified gasp at their discovery. The family and their advisors were going to haul him over the coals even though they hadn't actually done anything other than play hooky from their responsibilities for a little while. Although in their short time together there had definitely been sparks flying, and given the chance they could very well have burned the whole building down with the passion flaring between them. The reality of their very different lives had soon poured cold water over that notion.

So they weren't in a relationship, or even involved in a salacious fling, but there had been something between them. He'd felt it, from the moment he'd dared to lay his hands on the princess in the greeting line. If he was honest he'd thought about what it would be like to be more intimate with her. He'd taken the opportunity in that store room to get closer. Perhaps that moment during their dance, that instant desire had arisen from their understanding of one another's circumstances, that recognition of a troubled soul in need of company and comfort. Gaia was beautiful, there was no doubt, but she also possessed a fragility, an innocence that called to his inner Neanderthal. It wasn't that he wanted to club her over the head and carry her off to his cave, but he had wanted to make her his during that dance, become her protector so no one could hurt her.

Great job he'd done of that. Now not only was she dealing with her family's troubles but also the world's press was screaming about their alleged relationship. It would almost have been easier if it were true. At least then they could have confirmed it and moved on. Here, they were trapped by the truth.

After stripping off his jacket and shoes to go through body scanners, and an intimidating security team who took way too much interest in his person, he was escorted through the halls of the palace at breakneck speed.

'Where exactly am I going? What am I doing here?' he asked, whizzing past oversized oil portraits and elaborate gold-embellished tapestries on the walls.

He'd assumed it was for a crisis meeting to discuss what steps were to be taken to minimise the damage done to the Princess's reputation. The brief call from Gaia's secretary hadn't given much away, simply asking him to attend at the family's request. For all he knew he was on his way to the tower now, to be held there for ever as an example of what could happen to commoners who dared sully the Princess's virtue.

The well-dressed member of staff halted his whirl-wind tour through the palace long enough to look at Niccolo, nis long nose tilted high into the air. 'The Princess has asked to see you in her private rooms. I think you know why.'

He was off again, apparently keen to discharge his responsibility of the latest man to embarrass the royal family. He was sure he would meet with a lot more disdain before the day was over. However, he was relieved that it was Gaia he was coming to see and not facing the entire royal family in its might. She would be upset and regretful but that might be easier to deal with than the King blasting him for his inappropriate behaviour.

'Mr Niccolo Pernici to see you, Your Royal Highness.' Mr Uppity opened a door and announced him to the room with a bow.

'Thank you, Vitale. That will be all for now.' Gaia sounded much more guarded than she had the last time they'd met, each word crisp and thought out.

Niccolo couldn't be certain if this was a direct result of this morning's revelations or if she usually talked like this and their conversations were the exception, where she'd spoken freely. Only time and a further audience with her would tell, but he hoped she knew she could still talk to him.

The reverential Vitale bowed and took his leave, closing the doors behind him and leaving Niccolo alone with Gaia.

'I hope there's no one out looking for you again. I'm not sure anyone would believe us a second time that this was all totally innocent.'

Gaia gave a smile but it did not reach her eyes. 'Please, sit.'

She stood and directed him towards a throne-shaped

armchair upholstered in a sage-green fabric, the arms moulded into golden scrolls. In a modern apartment it would have looked tacky but here it fitted right in. The whole scene looked like something out of a Renaissance painting and he couldn't quite believe he was in the middle of it.

The heavily gilded room, cluttered with large freestanding vases and silk screens, should have drawn the eye, but Niccolo couldn't look away from Gaia. She was wearing an emerald-green trouser suit with a white silk blouse, looking as beautiful and elegant as ever, and, though he'd dressed formally for the occasion in a tailored navy suit, he still felt underdressed in her presence.

'I hope you've been as thorough checking for photographers as your security have in searching me,' he joked again, attempting to hide his nerves. Being here in the palace made things even more awkward between them when he was reminded of Gaia's status and how out of place he was.

Another forced smile as she carefully took a seat, perching on the edge of the love seat—embellished with painted images of flora and fauna—opposite. 'Security is at an all-time high. Grandfather demanded it.'

He could only imagine the heated conversations with her family which must have gone on here this morning. It wasn't fair, especially on Gaia, that they couldn't enjoy one moment of fun without its becoming a national incident.

'I'm sorry I've got you into such a mess. Should I write my last will and testament now or will it give me something to do when I'm imprisoned in the tower for the next hundred years?'

'You mean you didn't get your affairs into order before

coming here?' Gaia gasped, then lapsed into a genuine smile he wished he could keep there for ever.

'So how much trouble are we in?'

She screwed up her face, her nose crinkling like that of a cute bunny snuffling in the grass. 'Huge.'

'Ugh, I was afraid of that.' He slumped back into the chair. Though his playful demeanour had managed to thaw Gaia's initial cold front towards him, it couldn't hide the pain their unexpected dalliance had obviously caused her.

'Grandfather thinks people will believe this is proof I sleep around too. Just like my father.' Her bottom lip wobbled as she spoke, and he would have hugged her if he could be sure it wasn't going to cause her more problems.

'That's ridiculous. It's one photograph, and we're not even doing anything in it.' It would be different if they had been caught in an actual clinch, but it was only a dance.

Gaia dabbed a handkerchief to her eyes before giving permission to any tears to actually fall. 'It doesn't matter, it's what the picture implies. You know people will have drawn their own conclusions.'

Unfortunately he did, and once that happened it was near impossible to change their minds.

'So what if we were an item, what would it matter? You have the right to have a life, the same as I do.' Okay, so it wasn't true, but if they let readers and journalists make their minds up the way he'd done these past two years, how much harm could it cause? It wasn't as though they were being accused of anything untoward, simply of being in a relationship. If they let things play out and naturally fade away from the public interest they could probably weather this.

However, his opinion did little to erase the worry etched on her brow.

'I don't. Every move I make, every decision, is scrutinised, Niccolo. My behaviour reflects on the whole family, just as my father's did. No offence, but you're an actor, not of noble birth. I really shouldn't have been fraternising with you and certainly not alone.' It pained her to say that—he could see it in the red tinge of her cheeks and the way she was almost strangling the handkerchief in her hands—but he wasn't offended by her honesty, he appreciated it.

'You were slumming it, in other words.' The idea amused him, teasing her, even more so, to try and keep things light and all the bad stuff at bay.

'That's not... I didn't mean...' She caught his smirk, grabbed an ivory silk cushion from behind her and chucked it at him. 'You're insufferable.'

'Are we breaking up already? You could release that as your statement—"Niccolo and I are no longer together as I find him altogether insufferable".'

'This is serious, Niccolo. It could jeopardise my position in the family, and without that...'

She didn't need to say the rest when they both knew she'd end up as an outcast like her father, who hadn't been seen or heard from since his departure. It was hard to garner sympathy for a man who'd cheated on his wife and caused his own downfall, but Gaia was different— she was innocent.

'Okay, okay, so why can't we just say what happened? We ran into each other and you expressed an interest in dancing. I showed you a few moves and that's when the photographers arrived.' It was clear they had to address the rumours somehow in an effort to protect Gaia when he should never have laid hands on her in the first place.

She gave a heavy sigh, her lips pursed with blatant annoyance. 'Because no one is going to believe the truth. We will both look like liars.'

The weight of her words settled heavily on his chest as he realised it wasn't just Gaia's reputation and position at risk here. It had taken him two years to fight his way back from the last scandal to befall him. He wondered what it was about him that made people ready to believe the worst of him. Was it his profession, his alleged wealth, or did he simply have an untrustworthy face? Whatever it was, Gaia was right—as far as onlookers believed, they were an item, and to deny it, to walk away, would look cold and callous. He'd probably stand accused of taking advantage of her at a vulnerable time and dumping her when he'd had his fun. If they went down this path he stood to risk everything again.

He'd poured his heart and soul into making that film, which had managed to get him his life back. It wasn't something he'd be in a hurry to lose a second time and he doubted making another successful solo film would be easy to do. Next time he mightn't be able to claw his way out of the darkness, a place he never wanted to be again. Alone, afraid of what his future held, and unable to share his feelings with anyone. It was fear which kept him captive, the worry that if he showed his emotions he might not recover from it. That he might end up like that grieving child who'd barely made it through the loss of his mother.

He'd been lucky his film had been a success but in the future he might not be as strong, a recovery impossible. As Gaia had said, this was serious.

'We could fake a relationship, go along with the idea that we're a couple for a few months, make a few public appearances together, then split when interest inevitably dies down. It will be an amicable, mutual separation, ensuring there's no story for the press to follow up on.' He was animated, bouncing in his seat with enthusiasm for the plan which had suddenly sprung to mind. It wouldn't cost either of them anything to go with the flow for the time being and it wouldn't be any hardship to spend time with Gaia. If anything it meant he could get to know her a little better without worrying about the usual hurdles in a relationship. Yes, faking it was the way to go.

'That's not going to work.'

'I know it's not ideal, nothing about this situation is. But everyone already thinks we're together. Where's the harm in a little white lie now to save both of our skins?' Was the idea of even pretending to be with him so repellent? Maybe she hadn't been completely convinced of his innocence in the rumours his ex had created. It was not only a blow to his more fragile than usual ego, but also a personal slight when he thought they'd made a genuine connection. Despite all the trouble, he'd got the impression Gaia might even like him. After two years of emotional turmoil his radar for such things must be totally malfunctioning.

When Gaia didn't respond, he knew he'd got things completely wrong and tried to backtrack.

'It was just an idea. I know lying is the very thing you want to avoid doing, but—'

'It's not that.' Her eyes darted around the room as though she was expecting a photographer to jump out from behind the curtains or the fireplace.

'Well, what is it, Gaia? Whatever it is we're both in

this together and I promise not a word of this conversation will leave this room. Maybe we don't say anything and just avoid each other? After all, our paths hadn't ever crossed until last night.' It would be a shame if he didn't get to see or speak to her again when she'd been the first person he'd met who could relate to his lifestyle and the impact negative press could have on a person.

'That's not going to work either.'

He was racking his brains for a solution along with the possible reason why she was convinced they were set to fail.

'We could always go out on a date. At least that way we wouldn't be lying and we might actually—'

'I'm pregnant,' she cried, leaving them both in a state of shock.

CHAPTER THREE

'I KNOW IT was a sexy dance but I'm pretty sure you can't get pregnant that way. I would've thought your private royal tutors would've taught you about the birds and the bees by now.' Apparently humour was Niccolo's go-to response to her life-changing news.

'Niccolo, don't you see? There will be consequences for both of us when this gets out.' Sitting ever so still now, she appeared more delicate than the china figures posing on the mantelpiece above the fire.

Despite his feeble attempt to lighten the mood, the gravity of the situation was becoming increasingly apparent. Gaia was next in line to the throne, unmarried, and pregnant. With the incriminating photograph of them in a compromising position plastered over the papers and the television it would be impossible to persuade anyone he wasn't the father to her unborn child.

'Yes. I'm sorry. Forgive me. You must be under tremendous strain. I hope your family are supporting you.' He was trying to console her, understanding why this was such a big deal and why none of his solutions were feasible. No matter if they denied, faked or began a relationship, people would put two and two together and come up with a baby daddy. Unless the real father was on the scene and ready to accept responsibility. Judging by the now sobbing Princess, he doubted that was the case.

'I haven't told them yet.'

Another hurdle for her to overcome and she really needed someone in her corner. He knelt down at her side and took her hand.

'I'm sure it will be all right. It will come as a shock but in this day and age it doesn't have the same stigma to have a baby outside of wedlock.'

'This is the royal family we're talking about.' Her liquid-gold eyes implored him to understand her situation.

'I know you're not married but there's still time for the father to step up.' So far there had been no mention of the man she had been in a relationship with. Surely he was the one who should be by her side supporting her and taking the flak from her family for ruining her reputation. Although she shouldn't have to feel shame, as though sex and pregnancy were new concepts. Especially to the royal family.

It was a bombshell now but he was sure everyone would get over it eventually. In his case, two years had been sufficient time to suffer before the world moved on and he was supposed to forget it ever happened.

'People are going to think it's your baby, Niccolo.'

He looked at her, words refusing to form in his head or on his lips, his brain working overtime to process what she was saying.

'But it's not.' It was the only argument he could come up with, and one which wouldn't easily win him a place on the debating team.

'I know that, and you know that, but that's how it's

going to look.' Her smooth forehead was now worried with frown lines.

'And how will the actual father feel about that? Won't he be keen to set the record straight?' If Gaia was his partner, pregnant with his baby, he wouldn't want anyone else claiming paternity. Nor would he stand back and let speculation run rife, causing immeasurable suffering to her and her family, without saying anything.

'He doesn't want to be involved, with me or the baby. I realised too late he didn't want anything serious.'

'You don't get more serious than being a father. It's not something which should be taken lightly, and if he was that concerned perhaps he should've taken precautions to stop it happening.' He may have been crossing the line but it was a touchy subject for him when his own father hadn't been keen on taking responsibility for his child either. When Niccolo's mother had died his father had acted like a born-again bachelor, whose traumatised child had been more of an inconvenience than someone who needed his love and comfort. Not so much these days, when his offspring's celebrity status was something he exploited for the benefit of his love life as well as his business dealings.

That was why Niccolo preferred to keep things light and casual in his personal life, trying to avoid complicated entanglements, because he didn't want to get to the point where a rejection would cause him further irreparable emotional damage. Unfortunately Christina had failed to accept his boundaries and caused more drama than he'd ever anticipated.

'A mother doesn't get a choice. At least, not one I'm willing to consider.' There was a steeliness to her words that already made her a natural mother and he admired her strength in the face of such an uncertain future. She might accept the situation but it was going to be difficult for her family and the nation.

'I'm sure you'll be a great mother and when the baby gets here everything else will be forgotten. Everyone will see how strong and capable you are. A more than suitable leader for this modern country.' He believed everything he said because she came across as such a genuine, down-to-earth person who cared about doing the right thing. Gaia would be an amazing mum, raising a child and simultaneously running a country, defying convention and proving her place in society. He could tell by the way she cared so deeply about people, especially the little one growing inside her. Not everyone might have been so resolute in the circumstances.

'This affects you too, Niccolo. The press think we're together. How is it going to look if we go our separate ways and I have a baby a few months down the line?'

He listened to everything she was saying, saw the picture of them so clearly in his mind it would be natural to believe there'd been a pregnancy as a result. It was easy to imagine the follow-up news article, once again painting him as a villain: *Movie Star Leaves Princess Heartbroken and Pregnant.*

The truth didn't matter when the headline would sell millions worldwide. So much for his comeback. More bad press, especially if it involved hurting the country's beloved princess, would finish his career for good this time.

The gut punch knocked him onto his backside, his legs outstretched on a priceless antique rug. He dropped his head into his hands. Apparently he didn't have to do anything for people to believe the worst of him. Despite his attempts to avoid emotional entanglements, he couldn't seem to escape them.

'I'm sorry, but how did this become my problem? We were only together for a few minutes and, though that's all it takes in some instances, we both know nothing happened. I like you, Gaia, but I'm not prepared to stand back and watch my life fall apart again over another false rumour. You need to put this straight. I know the father doesn't want to be involved but neither do I. That might sound heartless, but being a parent was never in my plans, even in error.' Niccolo was aware that his voice was getting louder but the injustice of what was happening was too great for him to simply stand back and let it overwhelm him again. He was in danger of letting his emotions get the better of him for once, the royal palace an unusual and untimely place for the events of the past years to finally catch up with him. It wasn't Gaia's fault, it wasn't his or anyone else's fault. His life was simply a catalogue of unfortunate events.

'I'm sorry. I know none of this is your fault, Niccolo. You're right, I'll deal with it. I'll get the car to take you back.' Gaia reached for the phone to call Niccolo's getaway vehicle.

It was too much to ask of him; he hadn't done anything, though she had noted the part where he'd said he liked her. Not enough to stick around and support her apparently, like the other men in her life. A shame when she thought she'd found someone who understood her, who saw through the façade and understood her. She'd thought Niccolo was someone she could talk to but it was apparent he wanted to distance himself as far as possible from this mess. Not that she could blame him—she'd do the same if she could.

Niccolo's hand covered hers before she could dial.

'There's no need for that. I'm sorry for overreacting. It's just a lot after everything else lately. There was so much riding on this movie and, well, I guess you know what it's like to be under pressure.' The apology in his gaze would have been enough but the compassion she saw softening his features was enough to make the tears start falling again.

'I just feel so alone, Niccolo.' She couldn't help it; the past months of worry, of keeping this huge secret to herself, finally caught up with her. Her shoulders were heaving as the sobs ripped from her chest. Up until now she hadn't dared share her predicament with anyone, not ready to see the disappointment staring back at her, or worse, that the information would be leaked elsewhere. She'd only told Niccolo because he would be affected when the news did come out and she trusted him not to tell anyone else in the meantime. It hadn't been her intention to ruin his life, or to fall apart on him.

Yet, despite dropping this baby bombshell in the middle of his life, he was gathering her into his arms and letting her cry all over him. It should have been an awkward hug with Niccolo kneeling on the floor trying to comfort someone he'd only met the night before, but the strength of his embrace told her it was genuine concern, not merely a token act. That was sufficient for her to relax into it, revelling in the warmth and protection of his hard body and the knowledge that he cared. She couldn't remember the last time she'd experienced any of that.

'I'm not going to leave you to deal with this on your own. We'll think of some way of getting through this.'

With Niccolo wrapped around her, whispering words of comfort in her ear, she was inclined to believe him even if she knew it was a big ask. He understood the gravity of the situation because he was still living through what was probably one of the worst times of his life caused by gossip and bad publicity. It wasn't fair to get him involved but that ship had sailed with the click of a camera. Selfishly she wanted Niccolo to be in this with her so she had someone in her corner, albeit somewhat reluctantly.

Eventually, he loosened his hold and sat back on his haunches. Though Gaia could still feel the imprint of his embrace on her skin, it was colder without him. She wondered if there was a position available for a royal hugger to take care of her needs when she was feeling low. He'd never be out of work.

'Thanks,' she said, dabbing at her eyes and knowing it was pointless trying to maintain some dignity when she'd probably cried her make-up off in front of him. 'Sorry. I'm sure I look a sight.'

'You're beautiful, as always,' he said with a warm smile before getting to his feet and taking a seat away from her.

They were words she'd heard throughout her life and never put any store in them. After all, it had been her job to look pretty in the background, mauled and manipulated by stylists paid to make her look her best. But hearing them from Niccolo in one of her most vulnerable moments meant a lot to her. She realised, to further her dismay when it would only complicate matters further, that she still wanted him to like her. There was a part of her that needed to know she hadn't imagined that frisson between them last night before the whole world had crashed in around them.

'Thanks,' she said again, her spirits lifted a little thanks to the charming man who'd had the misfortune to get caught in her messy affairs.

'So…naming the deadbeat dad is out of the question?'

''Fraid so. I made a promise, and to be honest, after the way he's behaved, I'd prefer to keep him out of my life.' Believing Stefan loved her had been the greatest mistake of all. He'd let her think he was someone she could rely on in a world where she had no one. Her parents had their own issues they were dealing with, both personally and publicly, and she was something of an afterthought to them. That changed when her grandfather advocated for her to be the next in line to the throne and she became the focus of attention. Although it still didn't make it any easier to confide her fears about the future when one hint she wasn't coping would have sent the whole establishment into a tailspin.

This new development definitely would.

'Okay, I get that. I sometimes think I'd have been better off without my own dad when he so clearly had no interest in raising me after my mother died.'

'Niccolo, I'm so sorry. I had no idea—'

He held his hand up to interrupt her before they got into sharing stories about difficult childhoods. It was probably for the best when it would be difficult for anyone to empathise with her struggles after being born into a life of privilege.

'This isn't about me. I'm just running through our options.'

She liked his use of 'our'—it made her feel as though she wasn't on her own.

'We can rule him out completely. Best forgotten. Hopefully never to be heard from again.'

Her outburst made him grin.

'Message received loud and clear. I'm guessing we can't call it an immaculate conception either, so…what about we make up a partner? He's dead, you're essentially a widow and don't want to be reminded of your heartbreak so you'll not be commenting any further on the matter.' He looked so pleased with himself she hadn't the heart to tell him why she didn't think that would work either, but Niccolo was the one person she thought she didn't have to mollify for appearances' sake.

'Think of the timing though. I'm two months pregnant. If I had a partner I loved enough to have a baby by and lost him, it's still going to look bad that I hooked up with you so soon. That would have the opposite effect from the one I want. I'm not the kind of girl who sleeps around so I'd rather people didn't believe that of me.' It was important to her what others thought, perhaps too much. If she did have a very active sex life that wouldn't have been anybody's business either but, since she didn't, she'd rather not have that kind of reputation. It wasn't one which would command respect from certain quarters when her time as Queen finally came.

Niccolo's head dropped, as though the weight of it all had suddenly become too much, his body weary from trying to project a strength that was now waning. She knew exactly how that felt.

'Okay, so back to the drawing board. You're not going to be able to hide this pregnancy for ever.'

'You're pregnant?' As if the situation couldn't get any worse, a royal entourage including her mother and grandfather had chosen that moment to enter the room and Gaia knew things were never going to be the same again.

Niccolo scrambled to his feet and bowed. 'Your Majesty.'

Though he was in the palace, the arrival of the King was no less intimidating. The way Gaia was so open with him made him forget who he was actually dealing with, but now he was faced with her family he was reminded what a serious situation he was caught up in.

Gaia too got to her feet, looking so pale and fragile he was afraid she might break. 'Grandfather, this is Niccolo Pernici,' she said, bowing her head in respect.

'I know who he is. I just don't understand how he has the audacity to stand in my home after the very public display he engaged you in last night. And now you're telling us you're pregnant, I assume to this man, unless you're more like your father than we thought?' he boomed, demonstrating why Gaia had been so afraid to tell him the news herself.

'But Grandfather—'

'Gaia, your grandfather has a right to be angry. You know the impact this will have on the country. How could you do this? How could you be so careless and stupid? You know what we've been through.' The tall, graceful brunette Niccolo knew to be Gaia's mother, Princess Amara, moved to her side, not to comfort her but to chastise her further for something she was already beating herself up about.

Niccolo couldn't simply stand back and watch them maul her as though she had committed the crime of the century.

'Your Majesty.' He nodded to each in turn. 'I know the circumstances are less than ideal and this morning's headlines haven't helped, but I don't think berating Gaia is going to fix things either. She needs our support.'

'Do you comprehend the seriousness of impregnating my granddaughter out of wedlock, Mr Pernici?'

Neither of them had dared contradict the King's misunderstanding of the baby's parentage and Niccolo didn't think telling him there was another man involved would placate him in any way. If anything, it would further enrage him and Gaia didn't deserve any more of a pile-on.

'I understand that this is a very delicate matter—'

'Are you going to step up to your responsibilities and marry my granddaughter?'

'Pardon me?'

'Grandfather, no, Niccolo isn't—'

In that second Niccolo believed there was only one option available to both of them. A single deed which could save both of their reputations and save them from any more of the King's ire. It didn't matter what he did to try and distance himself from the whole scandal, as far as everyone was concerned he was involved.

'Yes, we're getting married,' he announced, surprising himself as much as everyone else in the room. He put an arm around Gaia's shoulders and she leaned into him as if he were the only thing keeping her upright.

The only way he could see to salvage his reputation and his livelihood before they were ground into the dirt again was to act as though he *was* this baby's father. It wasn't a role he'd ever wanted, and he didn't know how he was going to fake his way through it. He would have to embrace the part completely. Having an emotionally distant parent was as damaging as losing one. Gaia's baby didn't deserve to feel as though it was a burden, so he would have to come to terms with accepting complete responsibility for this child and not simply be a token father figure. He had no intention of imitating his dad but it wasn't going to be easy raising someone else's child. Especially in these circumstances, where he'd been forced into a corner if he wanted to keep his career and the life he'd just got back.

There was no way of explaining to a baby that he was merely a stunt dad, one for show to replace the real deal. So he had to accept he was going to be a dad for real, along with his role as a fake husband. He'd always been afraid of having children himself in case he kept that emotional detachment which had caused him so much trouble in his romantic relationships. Putting himself in this position was forcing him to face those long-held issues head-on.

Christina's antics had made him question the type of man he was for her to have treated him the way she had. He must have really hurt her to receive such vitriol from her, and subsequently from the press and general public. His actions in the past had been his attempt to avoid unnecessary pain but apparently that hadn't been the case. It was important to him that he wasn't the same heartless monster as had been portrayed in the papers, or the same one as his father, disregarding the feelings of his grief-stricken son. He wanted to get over that inability to forge a meaningful relationship and perhaps he could do that with a baby. Children needed to be loved, and gave love back unconditionally. He shouldn't have to fear rejection from that relationship at least.

That was if Gaia agreed to this whole charade. After all, she didn't know him or his motives for doing this.

It was asking her to trust that he wanted to do the right thing for both of them.

'Niccolo?' She was looking up at him, those big eyes searching his face for answers.

He gave her a squeeze of reassurance that everything was going to be okay. This was for her as much as it was for him, to give her the sense of security neither of them had had for a long time. Though it shouldn't be the way, she needed a father for her baby to keep her family and the rest of the country happy. More than that, Gaia needed a partner who would support her in both her personal and public lives.

'This might just work, Your Majesty.' Another man presented himself in the room from behind the King's intimidating bulk. Tall and waspish, he thrust forward a folder of papers for the King to flick through.

'What is this, Guglielmo?'

'The family's popularity soared with this morning's headlines. It appears the country is interested in a romance between Princess Gaia and this movie star.' He looked down his proud nose as though he was more than a mere royal advisor. No doubt someone else for Gaia to validate her life choices to.

Thank goodness he was only accountable to himself. He expected to give himself a really good talking-to about making spontaneous grand gestures without fully thinking things through. Getting married in this instance didn't seem as big a deal as a marriage based on that flitting ideal of love. This was a means to an end, emotions not included. As long as he made that clear from the outset, and they could raise this child as a platonic couple, they might just ride this out.

CHAPTER FOUR

GAIA GLANCED BETWEEN her fake fiancé and her family. At least her grandfather no longer resembled a bearded tomato. She would never have forgiven herself if she'd caused him to have a heart attack. Her mother too no longer looked as though her only daughter had broken her heart. Even Guglielmo had an uncharacteristic air of optimism about him. It was a shame it was all built on a lie. However, she couldn't bring herself to tell them that. It was much easier to go along with Niccolo's crazy get-out scheme for now.

'How far along are you?'

'A couple of months.' She'd been in denial for most of that time because admitting it meant addressing the matter and she'd been too frightened to do so. It was only with Niccolo's help that she was able to get through this now.

He was probably worried he'd end up in the tower for treason, so he'd concocted this story. Once he was outside the palace gates they wouldn't see him for dust. She'd go along with this version of events until she had a different plan in place, but she knew better than to rely on any man.

'The wedding will have to happen soon. Before you show.' Guglielmo looked her up and down as though he were better than a pregnant princess.

The first thing Gaia was going to do when she came

to power was surround herself with more supportive, forward-thinking aides. People she could trust, and who believed in her. Not flunkeys with a superiority complex. He was part of the establishment and therefore part of the problem when it came to the monarchy keeping up with the times. People of his ilk wanted things to stay the same, under their control. They pulled the strings around here and that was why she posed a threat.

She was a modern woman with a mind of her own. For now she was still trapped by the regime because of the respect she had for her grandfather, but when her time came she was going to shake things up. It was no longer enough for her to look pretty and have babies, she wanted to make a difference. Not be a powerless puppet with the patriarchy still making all the decisions for her.

'Announcements have to be made, arrangements for other heads of state to get here…' As Guglielmo worked out the finer details with the family, Gaia watched the colour drain from Niccolo's usual olive complexion.

This was all new to him, a glimpse into the future he was going to have with her if he insisted on seeing this through.

'You don't have to do this, Niccolo. There's still time to back out,' she whispered to him whilst the others were busy making wedding plans on their behalf.

He considered her words for a moment too long before he smiled again. 'I want to do this. For you.'

'But why? What's in this for you?' She wanted to know why she should trust him, what made him different from anyone else. Whether he was someone she should be with even in a fake marriage.

'Must be my shining-knight complex. I see a princess

in distress and I ride right in there on my trusty steed to save the day.'

She rolled her eyes at the impression he did of said knight galloping to the rescue.

'Naturally, we're going to have to consult our lawyers on this too and draw up some legal papers including a prenuptial agreement and a non-disclosure agreement. You will understand the need for the family to protect themselves in the event of the marriage breaking down.' Guglielmo addressed Niccolo directly with no hint of embarrassment about suggesting this alliance would fail before it had even begun.

Even though the whole relationship had been concocted on the spot, it still stung that the idea of her future marriage wasn't being taken seriously. That it was a risk, a liability, rather than a celebration.

'I understand.' Niccolo gave his approval, and acceptance of the situation, probably to get rid of the royal posse as soon as possible.

Gaia held her tongue until they had all left the room, although she didn't miss her mother's pointed stare. The one that said they would be having a word in private later. She wasn't looking forward to lying under direct scrutiny, afraid her mother would see through the lies and force a confession from her, rendering this all a wasted effort on Niccolo's part. He was being chivalrous to a fault going along with this, at extensive personal cost. The interference from 'the establishment' so far was nothing compared to what he'd have to put up with once he became a member of the family. If he didn't run away screaming first.

'Seriously, I want to understand your reasons for going into this before I do.'

It occurred to her that she still had a choice of sorts too. She could say no to this ludicrous idea of a sham marriage and confess she was pregnant by another man who didn't want to be with her. It could leave her in social limbo and possibly cause the fall of the monarchy but it was an option.

'I wouldn't have made the suggestion if I wasn't going to see it through, Gaia. Marriage has never been something I was interested in when I've seen so many end badly. However, this would be more of a business deal, I suppose. Something which suits both of us. It gets your family off your back and the press off mine. Hopefully once the actual ceremony is over we can both get on with our lives. The marriage would be in name only behind closed doors. If that's acceptable to you?'

Gaia could only imagine the millions of hearts breaking as he proposed this deal. Yes, it was a slap to the ego that a man would only consider marrying her because his career depended on it, but it seemed the most palatable idea right now. This way she got to keep her home, her family and her status, which might not be the case if she was honest about her circumstances.

'What about the baby?'

'I'm pledging myself to both of you.'

'So you'll raise it as your own? I want to be clear from the outset so there's no misunderstanding.'

Niccolo took more time over his answer, which could only be a good thing. It was a big decision to take on someone else's baby and she didn't want him to agree on a whim, only to decide fatherhood wasn't for him when the child was old enough to realise he or she wasn't wanted. She would rather raise the baby on her own in a house full of love, than subject it to the childhood she'd had knowing only one parent cared.

As much as she'd told herself she could do everything on her own, having Niccolo in her corner eased a lot of that pressure on her, took away that judgement she would face from the world. It wasn't as big a story, or scandal, for a married princess to be pregnant. The timing they could deal with later, but she was sure it wouldn't cause as much of a fuss if she was married to who the world assumed was the baby's father.

That was a big tick in the pro column for a marriage she hadn't expected. If Niccolo was willing to be the father Stefan couldn't be, this baby would have the security of two parents. They didn't have to love each other to make a good team and provide a stable home to raise this child.

Of course, this marriage meant she might never have another long-term relationship with anyone else. It was a big sacrifice, yet one she'd be willing to make for the sake of her child. At least then she wouldn't be under any pressure to meet someone else and go through all the associated heartache when she was inevitably found wanting in some way. She could live without the rejection and humiliation that seemed to come with relationships, both hers and that of her parents. Arranged marriages sometimes worked and she reckoned they had a fighting chance when they both knew what they were getting into from the start. It wouldn't hurt that they appeared to like each other too.

'You can put my name on the birth certificate if it will put your mind at ease,' Niccolo replied finally. 'I know what it's like to be treated as a burden and I would never inflict that on anyone else. If I'm in this marriage, I'm in this family, and I promise I will be the best father I can be.'

'Thank you, that means a lot. I suppose this marriage of convenience would at least be one I've had a part in arranging. It appears you've got the family's approval too, so I think you've bagged yourself a wife.' She wouldn't put it past her grandfather to push her into another marriage to suit him better if he knew the real circumstances. He surely wasn't so progressive that he would continue to champion her as the next head of the monarchy as a single mother. At least she and Niccolo had some sort of bond, even if it had transpired because they were victims of circumstance instead of naturally occurring.

Gaia held out her hand for Niccolo to shake and seal the deal. If he was really willing to risk everything to help her out it would be remiss of her not to accept his offer of marriage.

It was only when she experienced that tingle through her whole body again when he touched her, reminding her of everything he'd made her feel when they'd danced together, that she thought she might live to regret her decision.

'So what do we do now?' Niccolo was so far out of his depth his feet were no longer touching the ground. Yes, he'd seen marriage as their only viable option out of this mess but now he was taking on a fatherhood role he'd never anticipated.

A family hadn't been something he'd seen for himself due to his own troubled upbringing. It was the thought of repeating history and turning into his own father which had held him back, along with his inability to commit to a partner. Now there was a baby in need of a loving, supportive father, he knew he had to step up. He couldn't live with the picture Christina had painted of him, even in his own head. Somewhere deep down he knew he was capable of love, or else it wouldn't have hurt so much losing his mother. All he had to do was access those feelings to prove to Gaia, the baby, and himself that he could be a good man, and father. Hopefully he wasn't leaving himself vulnerable at the same time.

It was going to come as one hell of a surprise to Ana, since she'd witnessed their first meeting only a matter of hours ago. Albeit a pleasant one. She would see the publicity of his upcoming nuptials to a princess as a cash and career windfall no doubt, yet he wasn't even sure he'd be able to continue working once they were married. He made a mental note to query that at a later date, though he was sure he'd have a list of other questions by then too. All the other things he hadn't considered when he'd leapt in to save Gaia's reputation. He didn't regret it, he simply wished he'd taken some more time to mull over the consequences of his actions.

Gaia's eyes were wide, as though she was gradually coming out of the same dream he was currently trying to process. 'I don't know… I suppose we wait for instructions. They'll be making all of the wedding arrangements, so I'm not sure how much input we'll have.'

'Hmm. I wouldn't say I'm an expert on marriage but I know a bride usually wants her say on the dress and the décor, at least.' None of this was fair, on either of them, but Niccolo didn't think Gaia should be denied the simplest of joys to be had in this day, no matter that the circumstances were less than ideal.

She shrugged. 'It doesn't seem that important in the scheme of things.'

Niccolo hated to see her so downhearted when he was doing everything within his power to make her happy. He didn't know why that had suddenly become so important to him, only that it had started the moment they'd met. In that second in the line-up at the premiere, there had been a spark of recognition between them that hadn't yet been extinguished, and he knew he would do anything to save a like-minded soul from the misery he'd suffered these past years.

He placed his hands gently on her shoulders and felt her slump beneath his fingertips, as though that simple contact was enough to ease some of the tension in her body. It only seemed natural then to hug her, to let her know that he had her back. Something he wished he'd had when he'd needed it most.

'Hey, you matter, Gaia,' he said and pulled her close, wrapping her in his arms as though she were a burrito. Holding her so tight she couldn't fall apart.

Her little sniff as she buried her head against his chest was the only indication she gave of any emotion, something he was sure she'd been programmed to withhold on account of her high-profile status. He could relate on a certain level when he'd held back for so many years. Still, it was nice to feel wanted, needed, and to provide some comfort in return.

With everything that had gone on with his ex he'd questioned his own character. Perhaps what he was doing for Gaia was to ease his conscience about the way he'd treated girlfriends past, an atonement for the man they thought him to be. Deep down he knew he was as vulnerable as everyone else, possibly more so. He had to be careful that by giving so much of himself to protect Gaia, he didn't leave himself unprotected. Especially when he was about to become part of the royal family, scrutinised more than ever, and accountable to more than himself. He had to be strong for them both because he didn't want Gaia to become overwhelmed by her situation the way he had, not with a baby on the way.

Yes, that was added pressure on him too, becoming a stand-in father for a baby that wasn't his, with a wife he'd never intended to have, but he was sure they'd come up with some way to be happy. Despite the trouble which had followed, that short time they'd had together alone had been exhilarating. He'd felt more like the old Niccolo, carefree and uninhibited by the lies which had dogged him for so long. Gaia never once gave him the impression that she doubted his character, putting her trust in him to lead her in that now controversial dance. The only person since his public character assassination to have faith in him, other than Ana, who was paid to remain by his side. He owed it to Gaia and this child to show them the same support.

When she gave a contented sigh and he was tempted to carry her off, away from everything causing her stress, Niccolo knew it was time to let go of her. Before they got too comfortable.

He peeled her away and held her at arm's length for both of their sakes. 'What did you always dream of for your wedding?'

'Well, it wasn't a maternity dress and a fake fiancé. No offence.' She gave him a wobbly smile that made him want to hug her all the more.

'None taken. It's not exactly the life either of us had planned, but let's make the best of it, eh?' Niccolo wanted to do something to take her mind off whatever her family were currently conspiring for her future, and for them both to have a little fun.

'What do you suggest? A joint stag and hen party?' She arched an eyebrow at him, a smirk playing on her lips when she knew even the thought of it would get them into more trouble.

'I'm not sure either of us is up for a party limousine and strippers.' Perhaps in a different life, before his very public downfall, he might have considered that a good night, minus the impending nuptials. Now, however, nothing about that appealed to him. He'd settle for a quiet drink in a local pub, not that it would be an option for them.

Gaia pouted. 'Spoilsport.'

'I mean, you're a princess, in which case I imagine you can order anything you like, so getting a baby-oiled, out-of-work dancer in a loincloth should be a piece of cake.'

She took a step back, looking him up and down so overtly it was making him self-conscious.

'What?'

'I was just thinking…you can dance, not currently working, and I'm sure I have a bottle of baby oil somewhere…' That mischievous glint in her eye, the smirk which had morphed into a full-blown smile, and even the sound of her laughing at his expense, made her seem more like the Gaia he'd first met.

'You know, I was once offered the lead in a film about male strippers. I did learn a few moves before the funding fell through.'

'Uh-huh?' The way she was looking at him only made

him want to carry on with the flirtatious exchange. To make them forget the serious business of marriage and babies in favour of some fun.

'I can do a full body roll that could make those dollar bills rain down.'

'I'm sure you could.' The breathless reply called straight to his ego, and other parts of him keen to show off.

He began to hum the sexy tune he'd used to get into character and slowly undid his tie, whipping it out from his collar, whirling it like a lasso, then hooking it around Gaia's neck to pull her closer. Her giggle only encouraged him.

He bit his lip and popped open the top button of his shirt, before sliding his hand provocatively down the front of his body. Gaia covered her eyes in mock horror, only to peek out again in time to see him shimmy one arm out of his jacket.

'Gaia, don't forget you have that visit to the local women's group later.' Princess Amara walked in again, took one look at the scene, tutted and turned on her heel.

Once they'd got over the embarrassment of her witnessing their little flirtation, both he and Gaia began to laugh.

He shrugged his jacket back on, did up his buttons and retrieved his tie.

'Talk about timing,' he joked to diffuse that sexual tension which had crept in between them once more.

He hated everything about the circumstances which conspired to quash that spirit he so greatly admired in her and vowed to do everything he could to keep that smile on her face. Even if the way she was looking at him called to that primal part of him that wanted to pick up where they'd left off that night at the premiere, before the rest of the world had crashed in and ruined the moment. Every now and then he wondered what might have happened if they'd been left alone with that obvious chemistry sparking between them.

That in itself was enough to concern him. Even in wanting to explore those feelings he was leaving himself vulnerable again, losing control to his libido at a time when he needed it most. He wanted to be the loyal husband Gaia needed, and the supportive father the baby deserved. To do that he had to access emotions he'd locked away, but with that he ran the risk of letting them affect him too deeply. He had to shut down this attraction now—it couldn't run alongside the emotional connection they already had; past relationships told him that. It was sex or companionship; the two things couldn't cohabit in his world without his risking getting hurt.

They'd been forced together into a marriage they both hoped would save their reputations. They couldn't afford to give in to temptation and let a blaze of passion carry them away for a short time. That was how most of his relationships went, until that spark eventually died and he knew it was time to move on because there was nothing beyond that physical attraction to continue a relationship. This time he'd made a promise, a commitment, to support Gaia, and he wasn't going to let his libido get in the way of that.

'That definitely would've been a box-office hit,' Gaia insisted as he dressed.

'I think my dancing days are over,' he said, his voice dangerously gruff simply thinking about what could have been.

'Shame,' she teased.

'I think,' he pulled his phone from his pocket, looking for a distraction from the feelings he wasn't supposed to have, 'we should have an afternoon planning our wedding. Even if it doesn't happen, I'd like to know what you would've wanted.'

She tilted her head to one side, watching him with scepticism as though waiting for him to tell her he was joking. To prove he was serious, he did an image search on his phone for wedding dresses and picked out the most hideous one he could find.

'What about this one? I think the peach chiffon would suit you and that bonnet is just crying out for a shepherd's crook accessory.'

Her laugh was a welcome sound in a place he wasn't sure had heard much of it recently.

'Okay, okay, crazy man, we'll play make-believe for the afternoon, but only because I'm afraid you'll order this and expect me to wear it.' She grabbed his phone as she walked past him on her way to the sofa.

Niccolo took a seat beside her and relaxed watching Gaia come back to life, picking out her favourite flowers and showing him her likes and dislikes, letting him get to know her better. Something he looked forward to but also dreaded when he didn't need any further reason to like her.

Niccolo had gone home to start putting his affairs in order before he officially became part of the royal establishment. Leaving her alone to try and make sense of what had happened over the course of one afternoon—dropping the baby bombshell which had haunted her for so long, followed by a surprise proposal and an offer of a father to her baby.

She was lying on her bed replaying the events of the day and wondering how she'd got so lucky by running into Niccolo. His generosity of spirit was the only thing helping her get through something which could easily have ruined her life. She just hoped he would get as much out of the deal as she should.

Marriage provided her with someone to accompany her on her royal duties, a sounding board for her problems and ideas. It gave her someone other than her parents to turn to in good times and bad. Most of all, she would have a partner to share parenthood with. She didn't have to be on her own any more.

It was ironic that he was the only one who actually felt like family to Gaia at a time when she should have been relying on her mother's support now more than ever. Though currently her relationship with her parents could be called strained at the very least. She knew she was a disappointment to everyone, but Niccolo's intervention had helped to reduce the size of the mess to hopefully manageable levels. It wasn't an ideal situation but preferable to the one she'd believed herself to be in before his proposal.

After dropping the baby bombshell in front of her family she'd just wanted to hide away. Niccolo had taken charge and turned the whole thing on its head so they were now planning a wedding instead of trying to manage another scandal. She would probably have been content to let everyone else organise the big day around her as if she wasn't really a part of it. In her mind she just had to show up, let them dress her, parade her in front of the media, say 'I do', and disappear again until it was time for her to step into her grandfather's footsteps. It wasn't as though any of it was real. Even if Niccolo's impromptu sexy dance had made her experience very real feelings. Namely lust. Her mother's interruption had probably been for the best before they'd got carried away, but she couldn't help thinking she'd been denied a very special performance.

Despite the circumstances, Niccolo was doing his best to try and make the experience enjoyable for her. As though this wedding was for real.

She supposed it was in a way, when it would be the only one she was likely to have.

This afternoon he'd got her excited about what she would be wearing, looking at wedding dresses and getting to know her style. Something she supposed she should have been doing with a best friend who would be supporting her on the day as chief bridesmaid, but Gaia didn't have anyone close enough to do that with. It was only now she realised how lonely the life of a princess was. The price she paid for her privileged position in society.

Now she had Niccolo, she had someone to talk to who gave her a hug when she needed one, and who ordered mocktails and cake samples to cheer her up. He'd become her best friend in the short time she'd known him. Exactly what was needed in a husband. Except this was supposed to be a marriage of convenience, a career move and a way to save face.

She wasn't supposed to be falling for him.

CHAPTER FIVE

'I'M JUST PLAYING a part,' Niccolo told himself as he waited at the end of the aisle facing the ornate stained-glass window casting candy-coloured shadows across the altar.

He hoped he wouldn't go to hell for trying to do the right thing.

Sweat beaded on his freshly shaved top lip. *He* wasn't actually marrying a princess in front of the whole world and accepting responsibility for a baby that wasn't his. That was Niccolo Pernici's latest starring role.

Except when he cast his eye over his shoulder it felt very much as though it was him everyone was staring at. His father and his latest partner were there too, beaming at him. He'd been forced to invite him at the behest of the royal advisors and Gaia's family to avoid any scandal about a family rift. They'd all agreed that, by giving him a prime spot and keeping him sweet, it would steer him away from trying to make money selling salacious stories about his son. Niccolo wasn't sure that accord would last for ever, but he had called a truce with his father for the sake of his new family. This was the ultimate privilege for his father. He believed his son's need to have him back in his life was as genuine as this wedding. As did Gaia's family and the minister about to perform the ceremony.

He deserved an award for this level of acting, or a prison sentence for fraud.

No movie premiere or red-carpeted event could ever have prepared him for the worldwide interest in this ceremony. The security, the press coverage and the sheer number of people lining the streets to wish them well was overwhelming even to someone used to being in the spotlight. With any luck, once the wedding was over, interest in them as a couple would die down.

In their position it wasn't going to be possible to live a 'normal' life but he knew they both wanted one without their every move being watched and criticised. Though today was not that day.

The cathedral organ began to play, the pipes filling the air with their dramatic vibrations. He heard the communal shifting of people in the pews and a murmuring of wonder, and instinctively knew Gaia had made her entrance.

It seemed an eternity waiting for her to come to his side and remind him he wasn't doing this alone. They were in this mess together.

The anticipation was killing him, waiting for his bride-to-be. If he could just see her face he would be less tempted to run out of here. There would have been tremendous pressure on him no matter who he was marrying, but he was joining the royal family based on a lie. The fallout of that secret ever being revealed would be monumental, and the very thought of being exposed had his heart thumping so hard he worried it might crack through his chest.

He had to see Gaia to know it was all worth it to prevent the baying press tearing them both to shreds. She didn't deserve that any more than he had and, being honest, he hoped this marriage would benefit his career as much as his reputation too. It had been made clear to him that the royal family weren't supposed to work in normal jobs alongside their duties, but his wasn't any run-of-the-mill, nine-to-five career. They'd agreed he could take roles which didn't bring the family into disrepute or interfere with his royal duties, so he would be limited. But he expected after their wedding was beamed across the world that his star would shine brightly in the land of celebrity once more. He'd be a fool not to capitalise on that in case this all ended tomorrow and he was left with nothing again.

In turn for helping boost his profile, he'd done what he could to make Gaia happy thus far.

He thought she should have had some input into her wedding day as though it were the real thing. Getting to learn her likes and dislikes, laughing at some of the outlandish creations proposed to her, eating their way through a ton of cake he'd managed to get delivered to the palace, they'd become close. That hadn't been part of the deal but now it felt as though they were in a private club, a dastardly duo in cahoots to dupe the world.

He glanced back again and a shy smile from his glowing bride was the confirmation he needed to see this through. It would all be worth it if he could make her happy, prove to himself and everyone else that he wasn't the cold-hearted so-and-so his ex had painted him as.

'You look beautiful,' he whispered, uncaring if he was

breaking any sort of etiquette because it was true. He needed to say it and she needed to hear it.

'Thank you,' she mouthed back, appearing every bit as nervous as he.

Niccolo gulped as the minister addressed the congregation, ready to perform the ceremony.

Whatever happened from here, they were in this together, bound by secrets and lies for ever.

Gaia couldn't quite believe they were doing this. That they were actually getting married. Niccolo had carried out his promise. The first man in her life she could remember doing so, though only time would tell if that would last.

In the days since the proposal and the hubbub around the announcement she'd expected him to pull out when he came to his senses and realised what he was getting into. Yet he'd been there for her every wobbly step of the way, reassuring her that things would work out, and banishing that cloud of shame and worry which had hung over her since seeing that positive pregnancy test. She'd come to trust him and was putting her faith in him not to do the dirty on her like her exes or her own father. Men who'd treated her as though her feelings didn't matter, and rejected her when they grew tired of having her around.

The knowledge that she was lying not only to her parents, but also to the whole world, with this marriage, still weighed heavily on her heart. When she'd shared that burden with Niccolo, his answer was to remind her that she was doing this for the future of the country. This marriage was to provide stability not only for the baby, but also for the monarchy as a whole. It might not survive another scandal, but this wedding could bring the country together to wish them well. As proved by the thousands of people waving outside and watching this ceremony live on the television. They didn't realise how much more there was to Niccolo Pernici the movie star, and she was privileged that she did.

'You may kiss the bride.' The minister brought her back into the present, facing Niccolo, eyes wide with disbelief at the situation and the fact they had both gone ahead with this.

It would look odd if they didn't show some affection, so she leaned in for the first kiss with her husband.

The rest of the congregation faded into her peripheral vision as she focused on Niccolo. His eyes centred on her lips, she parted them in anticipation of his touch. He cupped her face in his large palms and her eyes fluttered shut. She wanted to believe this was real, that her handsome groom had agreed to spend the rest of his life with her, raising their baby, out of love. That when his lips met hers it was because he wanted to kiss her and that he was enjoying it as much as she was, regardless of the brevity of the intimacy.

Then the moment was over, the witnesses clapping them as they made their way back down the aisle. Her mother and grandfather nodded their approval. They even looked happy. She offered them a quivering smile in return, guilt darkening her soul.

Despite the people lining their path, offering their congratulations, Gaia felt totally alone. Then Niccolo caught her little finger with his, linking them together to remind her he was right there with her. That small gesture seemed an even greater one than saying, 'I do.'

* * *

'If I'd known my son was dating the future Queen I would have asked for a tax exemption,' Niccolo's father joked to the sound of forced laughter from the guests listening to his cringeworthy speech.

Niccolo prayed for this to be over. Listening to all the speeches praising them and celebrating their love had been excruciating. If he'd had his way they would have been on the first flight out of the country after the ceremony to avoid prolonging the agony, but that idea had been vetoed by 'the management'. In the end both he and Gaia had to accept that, to convince everyone of the authenticity of the wedding, they would have to treat it exactly as any other royal wedding and put up with the ensuing formalities.

Gaia rested her hand on his thigh under the table, letting him know that she was hating this as much as he was, but there for him. It was obvious they were both suffering from nerves, anxiety stealing their appetite in the face of the sumptuous feast laid on for them.

'Are you sure you wouldn't like a glass of champagne?' Gaia's mother asked.

'No, thank you.' With all the secrets he was keeping it was necessary to keep a clear head so he didn't let any slip out. There was too much at stake to over-indulge on his wedding day. Although he wished he'd had some Dutch courage when it came to making his speech.

He got to his feet as he was introduced by the MC and waited for the applause to die down before he spoke. In preparation for the day he'd decided to treat it like a scene in one of his movies, saying things that would have been expected from someone of his new standing, thanking the royal family for accepting him. All the while knowing it was something which had been forced upon them. In other circumstances he wasn't sure they would even have contemplated letting a movie star join their ranks. When it was a choice between that and leaving the future Queen as a single mother, he guessed he was the lesser of two evils.

Every now and then he threw a glance at Gaia, but she kept her head down, avoiding his gaze. It was only when he addressed her personally that she gazed up at him, her cheeks pink from his adoration. Those parts of his speech were the only genuine words that came out of his mouth.

'You're a wonderful woman, Gaia, and I'm glad I met you. Here's to a long and happy marriage.' He raised his glass and toasted their future along with everyone else in the room, not missing the tremble of Gaia's bottom lip as he turned to her.

'I meant every word. I'm not going into this marriage lightly. I'll work every day to try and bring some joy back into your life,' he whispered. They both deserved a break, and if fate insisted on putting obstacles in their way he would double his efforts to get over them. It was in both of their interests to make this marriage a success and he'd do everything in his power to make that happen.

Gaia reached over and hugged him, dropping a kiss on his cheek to a chorus of 'Aw…' from the watching crowd. He knew she hadn't done it for show, it was a gesture, like the leg pat, to show solidarity during this most difficult performance of his life. Her touch shouldn't make him want this to be real, anticipating their honeymoon as a chance to physically express his feelings in private. Making love hadn't been part of the deal. They hadn't even discussed it. Now, knowing they were about to spend time away alone, it was all he could think about.

The end of the speeches couldn't come too soon for Gaia. It wasn't easy listening to lies made up for the guests caught up in the romance of the day. They hadn't come solely from her and Niccolo either. Her father had ignored his invitation, and, while she hoped it was because he didn't want to take away the focus from the newlyweds, it was more likely he didn't care she was getting married. To save face her grandfather had stepped in and given his speech about how proud of her they all were and how much they were looking forward to having Niccolo as part of the family. All lies. Just as much a show for the audience as the ceremony had been.

It was Niccolo's words she had taken to heart, his promise that she would be happy. Oh, how she wished that to be true. Crucially that hadn't been part of their deal, but if he was willing to genuinely be a husband to her beyond appearances' sake, it was more than she could have dreamed of. It gave her a flickering ember of hope inside that some day she might be happy again, not simply existing.

That feeling was further stoked when they took to the floor for their first dance. As they swayed together on the floor, Niccolo making her look good as he led her in a traditional waltz, she believed this was more than a business deal to him.

'Thank you for a wonderful day,' she mumbled into his neck in her trance-like state.

Her chest was pressed so close to his that his laugh

reverberated through both of their bodies. 'You're welcome. Although I think next time we should go to Vegas.'

Niccolo made her smile even in the most trying of times. 'I mean it. Despite the circumstances I'm glad you're the man I'm marrying.'

'Well, thank you. There's no other princess I'd rather be saving,' he whispered into her ear, making the hairs on the back of her neck stand to attention, and goose-pimples ripple across her skin.

His apparent affection for her, combined with all the amazing things he'd done to get them here, was an aphrodisiac she didn't need when they were about to go on a sex-free honeymoon.

'I thought we'd never get to be on our own,' Niccolo said as he closed the blinds in their honeymoon villa.

'You'd better get used to it,' Gaia sighed, brushing away the rose petals so she could lie back on the massive bed. She appreciated the gesture, but in this case it wasn't necessary to set the mood, along with the champagne and burning candles. The chocolates she pulled closer, sure she would have a need for those later.

They'd agreed on taking the trip more because they knew they'd need a break from reality than to keep up the public façade.

'It's a shame I'll never be nominated for any awards after this.' He helped himself to one of the chocolate-covered strawberries sitting amongst the harvest of fruit on the huge glass table.

A generous bite later and she was watching the juice squirt over his bottom lip, his tongue sweeping out to lick it away. Clearly her hormones were raging out of control, making her crave more than the sweetness of the chocolate and the juiciness of the berry.

'Would you like some?'

Yes, please, she thought, watching him saunter over to the bed, his shirt unbuttoned and showing off his taut, tanned chest. It was one thing seeing him practically naked on the big screen but totally hotter to have him here in the bedroom with her. The irony wasn't lost on Gaia that she was crushing on her own husband but she was sure it was simply because he had shown her a kindness. Not only was he prepared to play father to a baby that wasn't his, but he'd made it through the pomp and ceremony of the wedding ceremony with a smile on his face for her.

She'd never felt as though she had a place in the world until today. Her ex hadn't wanted her, and neither had her father, and she was never meant to step into his shoes, so this new path to her reign was alien to her. There was no way of testing how much the public respected her, and she worried when she did come to the throne the only place she was comfortable was with Niccolo. She didn't have to pretend who she was around him. He was aware she was a frightened, pregnant, jilted, reluctant heiress to the throne and he was still here, feeding her chocolate-dipped strawberries.

She took a bite, savouring the tang of the juice and the bitter sweetness of the coating. Niccolo caught the small piece of chocolate clinging to her lip with his thumb, pausing before sucking it off. Gaia wondered if he was thinking about the tender kiss they'd shared at the altar before he'd walked away again.

She was being silly, getting carried away by the ro-

mance of the day and the location of their Bali honeymoon. Some time together realising what they'd got
themselves into would surely knock any such notions
out of her head. Her father, along with all her previous
partners, had promised her the world at one time or another. Only to ditch her when someone more exciting
came along. She was sure, despite appearances, that Niccolo would do the same at some point. He hadn't committed to her personally, or sworn his undying love, so
there was more chance of that happening than she wanted
to think about.

'I'm sorry things moved so fast. I'm aware your offer of
marriage was to get me out of a sticky situation with my
family and you likely never imagined you'd end up here.'

'You're right. If I'd known I'd have to spend a week on
an island with a beautiful woman to convince the world
we were a couple I would have demanded a pay check.'
The teasing did the job of reminding her this was a business arrangement and a rushed one at that.

The family might have insisted on Niccolo signing pre-
nups and non-disclosure agreements in case the marriage
ended, so the money and family secrets were protected,
but they hadn't made their own personal arrangement
legally binding. There would be nothing to stop Niccolo
walking away at any time and they hadn't laid down any
ground rules about what they expected from one another.

'It's not too late for us to put something down in writing about our personal arrangement. I'll understand if
you'd like to get some legal advice on the matter.' They
hadn't thought this through properly. All she'd seen was
a way out of her personal crisis, a temporary solution to
a permanent problem.

In hindsight, a marriage based solely on circumstance could bring on its own set of problems.

'I don't think that's necessary. I mean, we can do that if it would make you more comfortable, but I'm happy to take one day at a time.' Niccolo popped the cork on the bottle of champagne chilling in an ice bucket and slurped the escaping fizz before decanting into two glass flutes.

She probably would have been happier with a signed contract saying he'd never leave or hurt her, but that was wishful thinking. It was pure good fortune on her part that he'd come this far with her.

'I guess I'm wondering what will happen when the baby gets here. It's not going to be easy for you.'

'I went into this with my eyes open, Gaia. I'll be here for you and the baby. It's not as though you conned me into marrying you for love. I suppose this was a career move of sorts for both of us.' He handed her a glass of champagne, but even if she hadn't been pregnant she didn't feel much like celebrating. It was literally only Niccolo preventing her from spiralling into a dark abyss of despair due to her past mistakes. She could only hope she wasn't making another one.

Loving her wasn't one of the conditions of their deal. She needed him to keep telling her this was a business arrangement in case she started to believe in her own fairy-tale ending.

'Just a sip to celebrate our nuptials,' he said, assuming her reluctance was because of the baby.

Rather than give him extra reasons to fret about their future too, she accepted the glass.

'To us.' Niccolo clinked his champagne to hers.

'To us,' she said, forcing a sip and a smile, praying they could make this work for the baby's sake if nothing else.

'So, what are the sleeping arrangements?'

Gaia spluttered, shooting champagne bubbles up her nose. 'I—er—hadn't thought about that. As you say, we should probably take one day at a time and just see how things go between us.'

She didn't think sex was part of the deal but she supposed men had needs and some day she might too. They didn't have to be married in name only if they found each other acceptable in that way. It would be preferable to thinking about Niccolo with another woman.

She watched his eyebrows lift skyward.

'That's…uh…' He cleared his throat and took another sip of champagne. 'I meant for tonight. There's only one bed and we might raise suspicion if I sleep out on the beach on our honeymoon.'

Gaia wanted to throw herself back onto the mattress in the hope that she would sink into it and be suffocated by the nest of ornate cushions placed around her. It showed where her mind was compared to his when she was thinking about making love to someone who was still pretty much a stranger to her, despite outward appearances.

One step at a time, she told herself.

They were still getting to know one another and goodness knew what he thought of her now, pregnant and practically throwing herself at him.

'Yes. Of course.' Ugh, now he knew she'd thought about sharing a bed with him. The fact that she was open to the idea might scare him away altogether.

'Don't get me wrong, I'm not opposed to the idea, Princess. It's just, well, we don't know each other very well.'

'You're on the floor, buddy.'

Even though she'd embarrassed herself, she appreciated that Niccolo was comfortable enough to tease her like this. It made things easier.

He gave a bow. 'M'lady was always going to have the bed. I might take the couch instead though. I'm not sure my back could hold out on the floor.'

She gave him the side-eye as she flounced by on her way to the bathroom clutching her nightwear. The whisper of his clothes being removed and the sound of his belt hitting the floor turned her mouth dry as she imagined him getting naked behind her.

She closed the bathroom door and faced her flushed face in the mirror. It was hormone-related, nothing to do with the sight waiting for her out there. She splashed her face with cold water and unpicked the pins holding her hair in its neat prison. Shaking her hair out felt like finally shedding her public princess image. Apart from the fact that she was still wearing the restrictive tailored ivory and black contrast dress she'd changed into before they'd boarded their flight. In hindsight she should have probably chosen something more comfortable, like elasticated lounge wear, for the journey but she was still in that mindset of trying to look good for him. It was ridiculous dressing up in an attempt to impress him when none of this marriage was based on love or attraction, but part of her still needed the validation.

Now that neediness was coming back to bite her on the bum. She reached behind her back to undo the zip to discover too late she needed an extra hand. No matter what shape she contorted herself into she couldn't quite reach the high neck on her own.

Swallowing her pride and whatever other emotion had surged forward upon seeing Niccolo lying half naked under a sheet on the chaise longue, she asked for his help.

'Sure.' He jumped up, letting the cotton sheet slide away to reveal most of his muscular form, save for the area covered by his black boxers, thank goodness.

She spun around, afraid her eyes would linger too long on any specific part of his anatomy, and waited for assistance.

Niccolo carefully lifted her hair and draped it over her shoulder before unzipping the dress in one long, languid motion, his knuckles intimately grazing along her spine. She thought about how it would feel to have his lips follow the same path, to touch her bare skin just as softly and intimately as his fingers.

Gaia bit her lip, attempting to stave off that aching need she was sure would follow that brief connection. It happened every time he touched her. A feeling she was grateful to still experience, yet saddened her to know that there could never be anything more. She didn't want anything to spoil this new chance she'd been given to prove herself as a better daughter, mother and future Queen.

'Thanks.' Her voice was thick with something more than gratitude. This was beyond simply unsticking her from a dress, he was awaking every single erogenous zone with one glancing touch. Even if she was sure a night in Niccolo's arm would be glorious when the slightest brush of his hand melted her, she wasn't naïve enough to think it could solve all her problems, or even last.

'I'm—er—sure you can manage the rest,' he mumbled, stepping back to break the physical connection between them. If he hadn't felt that same pull of attraction he wouldn't have had the need to back away so awkwardly he'd nearly fallen backwards over the settee. But Niccolo had the presence of mind to see the possibility of more as a mistake, ending the frisson before it had a chance to fully take a hold of them both. At least one of them was still in control of their faculties.

She scurried back to the bathroom and slipped on the midnight-blue silk chemise she'd bought specially for the night. Niccolo might not be her lover but she didn't want him to see her in the usual comfy pyjamas she wore to bed. It was their honeymoon after all.

It was tempting to make a dash for the bed instead of giving him time to watch her walk across the room when she was self-conscious about her newly changing body. Judging by the look on his face when she walked by, she might as well have been naked, and she did find some satisfaction as he covered himself with the sheet again.

'We'll have to come up with a better arrangement when we get home,' he growled as she climbed into bed.

'It isn't unheard of to have separate rooms. Though not straight after our wedding. The staff do gossip.'

'The staff,' he snorted. 'I'm not sure I'll ever get used to that.'

'You'll have to, since you'll likely never be alone again.' It was ironic that someone who'd longed for privacy her entire life had never felt lonelier after discovering she was pregnant. At least until Niccolo had tangoed into her life.

'I'm not sure if that's heartening or depressing.'

'What do you think?'

'It can't be all bad. There aren't any bills to pay…people who will do anything you say and clean up after you. It must be like a holiday camp.'

'If you don't mind people watching your every move, can't have any sort of normal life, and have to be careful of every word you utter...yes, it's a joy.' She was aware he was trying to wind her up, to lighten her mood. It was his default setting. Except the restrictions placed upon her because of her lineage were the reason she was spending her wedding night in bed alone with the man pretending to love her sleeping across the room. Given the chance, she wouldn't have chosen this and it astounded her every day that he had.

'You make it sound like prison but, since I'm an outsider, I'm allowed to make waves. I know there are rules but we need space to live our own lives. When we get back there are going to be changes. I don't want you to be unhappy. You've been through enough and it's my job as your partner to protect you, Gaia. I'm not about to start a revolution but I am going to be the best husband and father I can. I take my responsibilities seriously. Now, goodnight, Wife.'

'Goodnight, Husband.'

Niccolo turned out the light, leaving Gaia with a smile on her face. For the first time since peeing on that life-changing plastic stick she fell into a deep, peaceful slumber. Safe in the knowledge that Niccolo was there to keep the nightmares away.

Niccolo listened to the sound of Gaia's steady breathing as she slept. He was glad he'd been able to reassure her things were going to work out, even if he was doubting it himself. It was a lot to take on, marrying a pregnant princess, regardless of its being a marriage of convenience. At least in terms of their careers. Logistically he wasn't certain how convenient it was going to be living under a microscope with a bunch of strangers, any of whom could uncover their secret and run to the press at any time.

He did take his responsibilities seriously, which was why he'd never had any intention of getting married or starting a family. Naively, in his gallant rescue of Gaia's honour, he'd believed that it would be a straightforward transaction. That no emotional involvement would make this relatively easy. Once they'd fooled the world that they were in love they could carry on with their lives.

Now he was beginning to realise what he'd signed up for. It wasn't the lack of privacy which was bothering him—he'd survived the past year in that environment—but the messy complication of emotions.

He'd stupidly convinced himself that night they'd been caught in a moment of flirtation had been nothing more than that. An acknowledgement of mutual attraction. Watching her walk down the aisle had confirmed that attraction and tonight was further proof that he wanted her.

It was proving more difficult than he'd imagined to separate his emotions from a relationship in this instance when that attraction was already so clearly there between them. He was destined for an uncomfortable night, not only remembering the breathtaking sight of her body sheathed in silk but also the warmth of her skin and the hitch in her breath when he'd touched her. All topped off with the less than chaste kiss they'd shared in church. He already had feelings for her. Not a good idea when embarking on a fake royal romance.

With a baby also in the picture things would go from

bad to worse when he cared about Gaia. Despite not being the father he was bound to have some affection for the child because it was hers and because the whole world was under the impression he was the father.

The child was going to grow up believing him to be its father too and he didn't want to replicate his own parent, distant and distracted. Ready or not, he was embarking on a life of domesticity with this strange new family.

The trouble being that success as a family man involved showing feelings and expressing emotions. Something his last partner had fought so hard to get him to show they'd almost gone to court. He couldn't be sure if the past year had changed him as a person but he would be whoever Gaia needed him to be to prevent her from going through the same pain he'd suffered.

A promise had been made, a deal done, and now he had to find a way to live with it. Even if it meant keeping his true feelings to himself.

CHAPTER SIX

THEY'D SPENT THE first few days of their fake honeymoon winding down from the stress of their whirlwind wedding. Breakfast together was a quiet affair on the balcony every morning, followed by lazy afternoons lying by the pool. Other than that it seemed as though they'd been trying to keep their distance from one another, despite their close quarters. Niccolo would pop his ear buds in, stretch out on the sun lounger and close his eyes, listening to music and effectively blocking her out. Gaia buried herself in the stack of books she'd brought with her so they didn't have to make small talk.

At night Niccolo waited until after she'd gone to bed before he bunked down on the sofa. He probably would have stayed out in the lounge if it weren't for the busy staff who seemed to be ever present. Although she should have been pleased they hadn't had a repeat of their awkward wedding night, she did stay awake every night hoping to catch a glimpse of Niccolo getting ready for bed. She put it down to her hormones that she was lusting after him when anything more than that spelt trouble. Especially when they were already dodging acknowledging that chemistry she knew was currently keeping them both awake at night.

'Can I get you a drink, sir?' The sound of their pretty,

young housekeeper filtered across the pool as she approached Niccolo.

He lifted his sunglasses onto his head and gave her his full attention. 'What have you got for me, Cassandra?'

She began to run through a list of cocktails on offer when Niccolo reached out a hand to stop her. 'Why don't you surprise me?' he asked with a smile.

'I'll make you something special, Mr Niccolo. Something strong and sexy. Like you.' The over-familiar member of staff had the audacity to wink at Gaia's new husband before she sashayed away.

Worse still, Niccolo was smiling, encouraging the outrageous behaviour.

Gaia huffed out a breath as she turned the page of her book with such force she almost tore the corner. Still, she held her tongue. It shouldn't matter to her if the hired help was flirting with him, or that he was enjoying it, when their relationship was fake. They'd agreed their marriage was in name only and she had no right to be jealous. Except he looked so good lying over there, his swim shorts riding low on his hips, a drop of sweat travelling between the valley of his pectoral muscles over his taut belly and into that line of dark hair disappearing into his waistband...

She really shouldn't be watching him so closely, or envying the flirtatious housekeeper with the non-pregnant body. Gaia looked at the slight swell of her tummy encased in an all-in-one black swimsuit and for the first time in her life felt unpretty. She knew the physical changes pregnancy was bringing probably weren't apparent to anyone else yet, but it was what they represented which likely made her less attractive than the ever-attentive Cassandra.

Every time Niccolo looked at her he would see someone who'd trapped him in marriage, see the evidence of another man's baby for which he was going to be responsible. It would be difficult for him not to resent the very sight of her when she'd stripped him of the life he'd had, all because of a silly misunderstanding. Therefore it wasn't surprising he should enjoy a light-hearted exchange with a pretty young woman the way he probably had on a regular basis before Gaia had ruined his life.

A mixture of the sun and her guilt was making her uncomfortably hot and nauseated. With Cassandra away to mix up Niccolo his special strong and sexy cocktail, he'd lain down again, eyes closed. So Gaia was free to strip off her loose floral cover-all and walk over to the pool without fear that Niccolo was watching, noticing her every flaw.

It was difficult not to think of herself in that way when she'd spent her whole life being analysed by not only the press but also her own family, who demanded perfection in appearance as well as in her every move. Her partners had been the same, expecting her to act like some living doll, beautiful to look at and not much else. They'd fallen for the idea of being with a princess, not realising she was a woman too, with thoughts and feelings which didn't always line up with theirs. But this was supposed to be her new start and it wouldn't work if she couldn't let go of her old way of thinking. It was time she was comfortable in her own skin, regardless if other people approved or not.

The water was cold at first, drawing a short, sharp gasp as she waded down the steps. Then she launched herself into the pool, the water completely enveloping her. She did several laps before turning onto her back and letting her body simply float on the surface, giving the occasional leg kick or circular motion with her hands. There was something freeing about lying here, simply drifting, with the sun on her face, as though she didn't have a care in the world.

That peaceful world came to a shriek-filled end when Niccolo dive-bombed into the pool, showering her with water and leaving her spluttering as she tried to stay afloat.

'Why would you do that?' she asked, wiping the water from her eyes.

'You looked like you needed cooling off,' Niccolo laughed and flicked more water in her direction.

Gaia's immediate reaction was to get her own back, pushing her hand so hard against the surface of the water she caused a wave to break right over his head. He followed up by diving under and pulling her down with him. She struggled out of his grasp and swam away laughing, Niccolo on her tail until they reached the edge of the pool. With one arm on either side of her, he caged her against the tiles. They were grinning at each other as they fought to get their breath back, their legs entwined in the intimacy of the dance. To anyone on the outside they would have looked like typical honeymooners. They were so caught up in having fun that for a split-second Gaia was convinced he was going to kiss her.

'Your drink, Mr Niccolo.' The outside world came calling and the moment was over.

Niccolo immediately swam away and Gaia could only watch with undisguised lust as he got out of the pool, water sluicing down his body, his shorts clinging to his wet skin. He lay face down on the lounger and Cassandra set his drink next to him.

'I think you need more sun cream—let me help you.' Cassandra squeezed out a dollop of lotion into the palm of her hand with no objections coming from Niccolo's quarter, regardless that the oversized parasol was already providing adequate shade.

Gaia couldn't watch any more. She didn't want to witness her husband being massaged by another woman on their honeymoon. Fake relationship or not, she had real feelings for Niccolo which were already proving an inconvenience. She pulled herself up and out of the pool, grabbed her book from the lounger and went back inside, slamming the door shut in a fit of temper. They were supposed to be a married couple. If this was the way he was going to behave, flirting with every woman who crossed his path, while his wife privately seethed with jealousy and lust, her life was going to be more unbearable than ever.

'Thanks, Cassandra, but I can manage.' Niccolo dismissed his attendant, uncomfortable enough without having a stranger rub sun cream into his back.

Gaia had gone back into the room in a fit of pique, highlighting the fact he'd crossed the line. While they'd messed around in the pool it had been easy to forget the reason they were here. In that moment they'd simply been two people enjoying one another's company, not a couple faking a royal romance to save their reputations. She'd looked so happy, like that night when they'd danced together, and once again he'd wanted to kiss her. Thank goodness Cassandra had made a timely entrance, though apparently too late to cover up his wayward thoughts as Gaia had stormed off, clearly upset by his behaviour.

He rolled over and took a sip of the spirit-heavy orange

cocktail that made him grimace. With another couple of days of living together like this he had no choice but to go and apologise. Hopefully once they were back in the real world they'd have more space from each other. Though they'd still have to keep up appearances, there would be plenty to keep his mind wandering down dangerous paths. He'd be going into a life of public duty, not to mention the parental responsibility he'd be taking on in another few months. With a schedule of engagements to carry out, not to mention sleepless nights with a new baby, he was sure there wouldn't be much time left for him and Gaia to spend alone. It was probably for the best when this growing attraction and affection towards her was becoming too obvious to ignore.

He took another gulp of alcohol to steel himself before he ventured back inside to beg Gaia's forgiveness.

'Gaia? I'm sorry if I crossed the line back there. I promise from now on to be on my best behaviour,' he called through the closed bedroom door. When there was no reply he let himself into the room, only to find it empty.

He was about to leave and search the rest of the villa when he heard a little cry coming from the bathroom.

'Gaia? Are you okay in there?' He knocked on the door, his heart sinking at the sound of her so upset. All because he couldn't manage to keep his feelings in check. He didn't know what it was about Gaia which made him so reckless when he'd spent years perfecting the art of hiding his emotions. Perhaps it was down to the previous troubled years he'd had when he'd been under tremendous strain. More likely it was because of who Gaia was, a kindred spirit who let him be himself when he was around her, and made it easy for him to let his guard down. Whatever it was, he was going to have to be more careful in the future when emotional entanglement wasn't supposed to be part of their marriage contract.

The sound of a faint sob pricked his conscience again. 'Gaia? I'm coming in, okay?'

He tried the door and gave her a few seconds to react, to tell him to get out, before he stepped inside. The fact that she wasn't yelling at him, demanding some personal space, told him she wasn't herself even before he saw her sitting doubled over on the edge of the bath.

'Something's wrong,' she said, tears and fear glinting in her eyes.

Despite the terror gripping him, Niccolo did his best to remain calm for her sake. It wasn't going to help matters if he got into a panic, even though he was equally as afraid as Gaia that something had happened to the baby.

He knelt down and took her hand. 'What's happened?'

'I was sick, but now there's a crippling pain in my stomach.' She was rubbing her belly as if not only trying to soothe the pain, but also to communicate to her precious baby that she needed it to hold on. If he could get a message in there too, he would. Although becoming a father was something he wasn't particularly looking forward to, especially when the baby wasn't his, he didn't want anything to happen to it. It was part of Gaia, a huge part of his future with her, and he was surprised to discover he was already quite attached to the little life who'd caused so much trouble already.

'Okay. Let's get you into bed and I'll phone for the doctor.' Although they were in a private villa, away from the prying eyes of the rest of the world, they had a full staff on call, including a doctor. No doubt someone handpicked by those who'd arranged their honeymoon who would be very discreet, and likely very expensive. Not something he would usually take advantage of but he wasn't taking any chances where Gaia and the baby were concerned.

With an arm around her back, he guided her over to the bed and helped her under the covers. She was openly sobbing now, her fears that she was losing the baby too much for her to hold back.

'Everything will be all right, Gaia. Just relax.' He did his best to soothe her, even though he was dreading the worst too.

'It might be for the best if I do lose the baby. We could have the marriage annulled and you could go back to your old life, without any obligation to me.' Gaia held his gaze, her jaw set with determination, perhaps steeling herself for the possibly traumatic events ahead.

Niccolo knew it was her fear talking and pushing him away. Yet it wounded him. He was as invested in this child as much as he was in her. Why else would he have gone into this madcap scheme if not with the goal of protecting them both?

'Don't talk like that, Gaia. You and the baby are both going to be fine. I'll go and call the doctor now.' He turned away before he let those pesky emotions slip out again and said something which could cause irreparable damage to their 'arrangement'.

What he really wanted to tell her was that he was afraid. That this baby was the only thing keeping them together and he didn't want to lose it, or her. But that sentiment wasn't in keeping with the terms of their agreement, or his need to protect his sanity.

It was easier to distance himself from a partner in a relationship when it was just about sex. That wasn't possible in this situation. Even more so because there was a baby involved. And now there was a real possibility of losing it, he might have to deal with that feeling of loss and grief all over again, along with Gaia's.

She was relying on him to help her through this when he was as out of his depth and worried as she was. It was becoming clear that he might not be the robot Christina accused him of being when he was experiencing genuine emotions he hadn't accessed since he was a little boy. And he wasn't sure how to handle it other than trying to quieten them while reassuring Gaia. He needed to keep her calm and he wouldn't do that if he got himself into a flap about what could happen. It was one thing telling her he'd be there for the baby, but he was beginning to realise that meant an extra person in his life to be worried about. He was going to have to find some way to take care of them all without compromising himself any more.

In the meantime, all he could do was hope that this baby was as strong as its mother, and pray neither of them would have to find out what would happen if their future together was cut short. Niccolo wasn't sure he was ready for their marriage, or this family, to be over before it had begun.

Gaia's mouth was dry, her eyes stinging, and her throat raw from crying. It felt as though she was simply lying here waiting to be told the horrible truth, that her baby and the life she'd envisaged was gone. She was in mourning not only for the baby she'd fought so hard to keep, but also for the fledgling relationship she'd embarked on with Niccolo. If something happened she wouldn't blame him if he decided it was the perfect way out of this mess. Her irrational dislike of Cassandra proved she'd already become too attached to him, and if she lost him and the baby she didn't think she'd survive. They were all she had.

She knew she shouldn't be so reliant on him when he'd promised her nothing but a sham marriage, but Niccolo was the only one who understood everything she'd gone through. He was her sole support and confidante. Even now, whilst the doctor was examining her, Niccolo was by her bedside, holding her hand and promising her everything would be all right. When she was looking at him she was more inclined to believe him.

'Have you had any blood spotting?' the doctor asked, removing the cuff from her arm once he'd finished checking her blood pressure.

'No. Just some nausea and cramping.'

He nodded, his glasses resting so low on his nose she feared they'd fall off. 'Your blood pressure is fine but I'll check in on the baby just to put your mind at rest.'

Gaia clutched Niccolo's hand as the doctor squeezed cold gel over her tummy before moving a Doppler foetal heart monitor over the site. She held her breath waiting for confirmation that her baby was still there and Niccolo placed his forehead against hers.

'Whatever happens, I'll be here for you, okay?'

She nodded, biting back the tears, grateful as ever to have him with her. The whole notion that she could ever have done this on her own had been bravado at a time when she didn't think she had a choice. Now they'd spent time together, bonded over the situation, she didn't want to go through any of this without him.

From the moment she'd seen the positive test she hadn't

had a choice about being a mother. It was something she would simply have to become. At the back of her mind she had worried she wouldn't be good enough, especially when her role models hadn't been the greatest examples of parenting. Would she love the baby enough when its father had been such a disappointment? If she hadn't got pregnant accidentally, would she even have wanted a family? Now she knew for certain the answer to those questions buzzing around her brain was yes. If she didn't love this baby she wouldn't be so terrified she was going to lose it.

When the pounding sound of her baby's heartbeat filled the room, she heard Niccolo's deep intake of breath before she remembered to take one of her own.

'There we go, baby's heartbeat is strong and loud.'

Gaia wanted to kiss the doctor but was more than happy to have Niccolo's lips on hers instead.

'I told you.' He grinned, and for the first time she saw tears glistening in his eyes too. Perhaps he was invested in this baby more than she'd thought. The idea that there should be two happy parents awaiting the arrival of their first-born had seemed so far out of reach not so long ago. Now Niccolo was showing her that, despite the circumstances, he cared about this baby. Maybe even for her too.

She never could have hoped to have someone not only share this pregnancy with her, but also worry about the baby as much as she did. Niccolo wasn't the biological father but he was showing more concern and interest in her child than Stefan ever had. He was still clutching her hand, proving he was with her every step of the way. She wanted to be cautious about getting carried away, yet with every passing day Niccolo became increasingly important in her life. Captured another piece of her heart.

It no longer felt that having a real marriage was merely a fantasy. It was clear he had feelings for her, so it was simply a matter of finding out how deep they ran. Then just maybe she could allow herself to believe they had a chance, a real future together as a family.

Niccolo loved that sound. The quick beat of the baby's heart reverberating around the room was something he could listen to all day, knowing it was evidence that everything was okay. It was proof of that life growing inside Gaia, and as long as they were both safe he would be content. At least for now. He was beginning to see that this marriage of convenience wasn't going to be just a job to him. There were feelings there for Gaia and the baby which he'd let come too far to the surface instead of keeping them at bay as he usually did.

He was supposed to be a fake husband, and a prop dad, but this baby might as well have been his when he was so wrapped up in its development and survival. If he wasn't moved by the situation it would have made him the very monster Christina had told the press he was. He wanted to be a good father, in spite of his own, and he guessed that meant being in touch with his feelings more. It was a relief to know he had them, but also a concerning development for someone who'd tried so hard to protect himself from emotional entanglements in the past. For this fake marriage to work he needed to learn how to separate his feelings for the baby from those he had towards the mother. This baby needed a father to take care of its emotional needs, and to learn from example. The opposite to the upbringing he'd endured with his own father. However, Gaia needed more than another man who would promise her the world and disappear soon after. He didn't want to do what every other male figure had done to her in the past, and if that meant keeping a tighter rein on his admiration for her, then so be it.

'Since you're in your first trimester, you are still in the danger zone. I would advise complete rest. I know it's your honeymoon but you should avoid any further strenuous exercise.' The doctor looked pointedly at Niccolo and he could feel the heat rising to his cheeks, even though he'd done nothing that warranted his embarrassment.

'Of course. I'll look after her, Doctor,' Niccolo assured them both, despite his discomfort. It was only natural that anyone should assume they were any other newlywed couple who didn't stray far from the marital bed. They'd gone to great lengths to make sure no one suspected they were sleeping separately and he would continue to keep up appearances no matter what the circumstances.

'Will I be able to travel back home?' Gaia didn't want any special medical assistance when the time came, making her condition obvious to the world. It was early days in the pregnancy but a scare so soon into their marriage would make it clear she'd been pregnant before the big wedding and give the gossip-mongers a field day. They were waiting to make the announcement after the scan, and the fuss around the wedding had died down. A scandal now would undo their efforts to keep things respectable. The staff here would be discreet if they wanted to keep the royals as guests in the future, but it couldn't be said about every single person they encountered outside of the villa.

'As long as you follow my instructions to take it easy between now and then, and there are no further complications, I don't think that will be a problem,' the doctor told her. 'Now, I'll check in on you again in a day or two, but if you experience any further pain or bleeding don't hesitate to get in touch.' He left his business card on the bedside table, though Gaia was certain Niccolo would have his number memorised already in case something else happened, he'd been so attentive.

'Thank you, Doctor,' both she and Niccolo uttered simultaneously.

'You'll be due your first scan on your return—that should clear any doubts in your mind—but in the meantime…'

'I know, rest.'

Satisfied that the message had got through loud and clear, the medic took his leave, with Niccolo leaving her side long enough to escort him out. He stopped in the doorway to have what seemed to be a very intense chat with her husband before he finally left, with Niccolo looking every bit as serious and intense as he.

'What was all that about?' she quizzed on his return.

'He thought you seemed unduly stressed for someone who's supposed to be relaxing on their honeymoon, but that's my fault.'

Gaia frowned. 'Why on earth would you say that after everything you've done to try and make things better for me?'

As far as she was concerned Niccolo had gone above and beyond his duty as her fake husband, without taking the responsibility of her stress levels upon his shoulders too. Which, without him, would be infinitely higher. If he hadn't stepped up to offer her a way out of her predicament, she would still be trying to think of a way to tell her family she was pregnant and finding it harder to hide it every day. At least that was one problem she'd been able to take care of with Niccolo's help. Now all they had to do was convince the rest of the world they were madly in love to keep up the cover story.

Guilt and shame that the only way she'd got a man to marry her was because a misunderstanding had threatened his career had prevented her from looking at their wedding pics in glossy magazines so far. Another part of her was afraid she'd cry at the images, lamenting the love they were faking for the cameras and in reality would probably never have. For now she'd have to settle for his loyalty and support, which she needed more than ever. It was inconceivable that he could think he was some way to blame for her stress levels when everything which had happened was due to the decisions she'd made. Niccolo had been dragged into her mess through no fault of his own.

He bowed his head before he spoke, as though he was about to confess some terrible deed she was supposed to know about. 'Earlier, in the pool… I know I upset you.'

She was still frowning. 'When?'

He sighed. 'When we were messing around in the pool. I know I crossed the line and that's why you came in here in such a temper. If I hadn't—'

'I didn't come in here because of anything you did. At least not directly.'

Now it was her turn to be embarrassed, having to admit to her own insecurities watching him with other women when she had no right to feel anything about him other than gratitude.

She focused her attention on neatly fixing the bed

sheets across her lap rather than looking at him. 'I was…a tad miffed about the attention Cassandra was paying you.'

'Oh?'

She didn't have to elaborate, seeing the moment he realised what she was getting at manifest in a huge grin spreading across his face. 'You were jealous.'

'No. I—er—we're supposed to be married. Are you going to be flirting with every woman you meet? Not that it bothers me, but, you know, the press are never that far away.' She was rambling and not proud of herself for using the paparazzi as an excuse for the way she'd acted, but she couldn't tell him she had feelings for him. It wasn't Niccolo's fault his act of kindness had made this lonely princess fall for him. He shouldn't be condemned to a life of celibacy simply because she didn't want to share him with anyone else. It was none of her business if he wanted to be with someone, as long as he was discreet about it. She didn't have to like it.

Niccolo stood up and for a moment she thought he was going to walk out on her. Instead, he climbed onto the bed beside her. If this was supposed to make her feel less stressed it wasn't working. Her heart was racing and as he took her hand and cradled it in his she was worried she was going to pass out. They'd spent days trying to stay away from one another, and now he was in bed beside her she was worried something was going to give. Probably her heart at the rate it was pumping.

'Gaia, I married you. I know we're not a conventional couple but I've made a commitment to you, and the baby. I'm sorry if I offended you. Yes, I was flattered by Cassandra's not so subtle interest, but I was never going to act on it. I never will.'

'Who's to say you won't meet someone and fall madly in love? What if you want to marry them? Have a family of your own? My father and every man since has abandoned me. The reason I agreed to this marriage was because I thought that couldn't happen again with a man who'd never loved me in the first place.' She hated this neediness in her voice but she wanted to know now, before they got in any deeper, that he wasn't going to break her heart and run off with someone else.

'I don't need to cheat. I have you. I'm not your father or one of your knucklehead exes who didn't realise what he had. I've given you my word I'll stay with you.'

Gaia so desperately wanted to believe that he was going to stay by her side, supporting her, with no desire to find fulfilment elsewhere. Taking care of her the way no one else ever had.

She knew it was a futile exercise but she liked to imagine what it would be like if this was real and Niccolo had feelings for her beyond sympathy or friendship. It was clear he was becoming more to her than a stand-in husband and father to her baby when she was harbouring resentment towards any woman who showed an interest in him. To have a normal relationship with someone who cared for her, who wasn't a narcissistic cheater, didn't seem like such a big ask, but it was all she wanted. More than wealth and status. She'd trade it in for a regular life with Niccolo and the baby if he could ever bring himself to feel the same way about her.

Despite her protestations to the contrary, Niccolo was certain his behaviour had been partly to blame for the sudden decline in Gaia's health. Even if it wasn't down to his actions in the pool, his brief flirtation with the housekeeper had obviously upset her. Finding out she'd been jealous over the exchange had given his ego a boost, but he wanted her to trust him. So he'd told Cassandra to take some time off and had been doing the chores and looking after Gaia's needs himself.

She certainly looked better, her cheeks a little pinker, her smile a little brighter. Niccolo had thought her lethargic since the doctor's visit when she'd slept so much and didn't seem to have the energy to do anything. He supposed perhaps it was the events of the past weeks finally catching up with her and her body demanding she rest. Now she looked much improved for taking the time out.

He on the other hand had worried constantly about her health, and the baby's, and the consequences if anything happened to them. A new experience for him. It was no longer enough to simply be present in a relationship. Gaia needed him to support her, trusted him to take care of her and the baby. It was a huge responsibility for someone who avoided any emotional commitment, but he found himself wanting to please her. Gaia was worth the uncertainty of what exposing these feelings would bring. She deserved so much more than the automaton he'd become to protect himself.

The way Gaia had reacted to his receiving some attention suggested she was jealous. That the spark between them hadn't been imagined and she might have some feelings towards him too. But he didn't want to ask her outright. He could be wrong and risk not only humiliating himself, but also exposing his own growing affection towards her. Worse still, she might admit she wanted a 'proper' relationship and he wasn't sure he was ready to make that sort of commitment. Confessing their feelings for one another might lead to a physical side to their relationship he was trying to avoid. At least by remaining in the dark he wouldn't have to make any sort of decision yet and they could maintain their current status quo.

Regardless of her take on the matter, he wasn't looking for an excuse to get out of the marriage. He'd enjoyed having someone he could relate to, who understood the world he'd been living in, and who was content to simply be with him, looking for nothing in return except loyalty. Something he'd give her until his dying day.

He'd pledged his devotion to her easily because he didn't believe he'd ever find someone who could compare to Gaia. Marriage so far had not been the prison he'd imagined it to be and perhaps that was because their partnership was not a conventional one. Despite his promise to himself to keep her at a distance, he knew he was falling for her more every day. Holding her as she'd fallen asleep that night after her health scare hadn't helped but she made him feel so protective of her, unlike the urge he usually had to get the hell away. He knew he had to open up in order to get her to trust him when everyone else had let her down. Sharing parts of himself he hadn't revealed to anyone before. However, he hadn't expected the floodgates to open and all these other emotions to start running riot. It was one thing to let her see he was capable of being an interested father and supportive father, but quite another to let himself believe they could be a proper, loving family. Thinking they could have everything, be a normal couple, was madness. And all of these worries about her and the baby, how his actions could affect them, and how he had to keep them safe at all costs, made him feel as though everything was spiralling out of control.

Yet he wanted to be there for her and for this marriage to last. As long as he kept those feelings to himself they could have something special. A friendship, companionship, and a partner with whom to raise this baby.

He'd imagined that if he managed his emotions, stuck to the boundaries they'd agreed in this arrangement, that he'd remain in control. Things hadn't quite worked out that way. This attachment he already felt towards something no bigger than a prawn had thrown him for a loop. Surely that worry, that need to get a doctor to Gaia before the worst imaginable thing happened, said that his heart wasn't the desolate wasteland he'd begun to imagine lurked in his chest. Admitting that, however, also brought its own problems. He was in deeper than he'd ever intended.

He didn't want to upset her, especially now he was aware she harboured some feelings towards him too. If they weren't careful they might stumble into a physical relationship, and sex was something he used to avoid emotional ties. Therefore not a step he wanted to take with Gaia when their lives were already so complicated. What they didn't need was to be even more confused about the part they were playing in each other's lives.

He was attracted to her, wanted her more than he'd ever wanted anyone or anything, but he knew he couldn't have her without consequences. Sex in the past had been a means to an end, a physical release as well as a way of avoiding meaningful discussions with his partner. It would be different with Gaia. Exploring a physical side of their relationship moved them into different territory. It would no longer be a marriage only on paper—consummating it would make it somehow more official. Not only that, but it would also bring expectations from Gaia for more from him, and a pressure to be an emotionally present partner. Something he didn't know how to be because he had no experience of it, and no previous desire to be such.

He had to resist that temptation to act on whatever growing attraction was building between them, to focus on Gaia's welfare and the baby's health.

'I've run a nice, relaxing bath for you.' Tomorrow was the last day of their trip and he wanted Gaia to be ready before they undertook that journey back into whatever chaos lay ahead for them.

'Thank you.'

Niccolo helped her into the bathroom, as she was still a little wobbly on her feet. It was a sumptuous tub, most likely installed to accommodate a honeymoon couple, but he'd filled it with bubbles and rose petals instead. There might not be a need for romance, but he reckoned Gaia still deserved some pampering.

'There are fluffy towels and a bathrobe.'

'Niccolo, this is so thoughtful and it smells divine.'

'Don't worry, I know not all essential oils are good to use during pregnancy, but lavender is safe and supposed to help you relax.'

'Thank you so much.'

Happy that she had everything she wanted, he left her alone with the door slightly ajar so that she had her privacy but he could hear if she needed him for anything. Meanwhile he began packing their bags in preparation for tomorrow's departure.

Gaia eventually stepped out into the bedroom dressed

only in the fluffy white robe he'd left for her, her skin slightly pink and her wet hair hanging around her shoulders.

'How are you feeling now?'

'Good, thanks. I'm even a little peckish,' she told him, collapsing onto the bed like a fluffy white starfish.

'Funny you should say that…if you're up to it I've prepared a little surprise.'

'Oh?' She immediately sat up again, her interest sparked.

'I had the chef prepare us some dinner. I have a table waiting outside.' Since these things were available to him, he thought he might take advantage every now and then for Gaia's benefit.

'I need to get dressed, do my hair and make-up…' Any trace of the relaxed Gaia disappeared as she stood up, frantically looking for her glad rags.

Niccolo stepped in front of the fitted wardrobe doors and handed her a pair of his jogging bottoms and a black hooded sweatshirt. 'You can wear these. I couldn't find any leisure wear in your wardrobe and I want you to be comfortable.'

'But—but the press…' She looked genuinely horrified at the thought of being seen in such casual attire and *sans* cosmetics. Niccolo once again felt sorry for her that she never got to simply be 'normal'. There were always such high expectations of her, even from herself, it had to be exhausting.

He pushed the clothes into her hands. 'I've given the staff the night off. The protection officers are sweeping the perimeter, or whatever it is they do to make sure there's no one spying on us. You deserve a night off. I want you just to relax. Okay?'

Gaia took the clothes with a smile. 'Thank you.'

'I'll let you get changed and see you on the beach.' He left her to dress in private before he forgot this was supposed to be about making her comfortable and went to check on their meal outside.

As instructed, the staff had set up a table and two chairs near the edge of the turquoise sea, the pathway from the villa lit with paper lanterns. It was their honeymoon after all and Gaia deserved some romance, even if it wasn't going to lead anywhere. She should feel cosseted at least once in her life.

'Niccolo... I can't believe you did all this.' Gaia wandered barefoot onto the sand, feeling a little self-conscious without her make-up and wearing elasticated trousers and hoodie miles too big for her. It was just as well she didn't have to impress Niccolo because she was not looking her best. He'd made it clear that there was no romantic interest even if his actions suggested differently.

Not only had he been a rock for her during her pregnancy scare, but he'd shown genuine concern for her too. It had been sweet of him to run her a bath, and now this. A handsome man sitting at a table waiting for her as the sun set fire to the ocean behind him was a picture she wanted to remember for ever. It was just a pity the romantic scene wasn't for a real honeymoon.

Niccolo stood when he saw her coming. 'Strictly speaking, I didn't do it.'

'Well, I appreciate the gesture all the same.' He couldn't fool her—it had been his idea and she wouldn't let him deflect the praise. There were very few people in her life who did anything for her out of the goodness of their heart. Usually any sort of gesture was because they wanted something from her in return. Niccolo never asked for anything, seeming only to want her happiness. It was that thoughtfulness which touched her heart even more than a candlelit bath or a beachside dinner.

'I ordered chicken for you. I hope that's all right. I thought you might prefer something plain and I know seafood probably isn't advisable.' He changed the subject back to their dinner, refusing to accept her gratitude. Another sign of a true gentleman who clearly didn't do such things to make himself feel better. Niccolo had a knack of making her feel as though it was all about her, that she was the belle of the ball, despite currently looking as though she'd been shipwrecked.

'Thank you. It looks delicious.' The chicken breast in lemon butter, teamed with herb-seasoned cubes of potato and roasted peppers and tomatoes, tasted every bit as good as it looked.

Niccolo had a seafood platter which he diligently worked his way through, smacking his lips and licking his fingers. It did her the power of good to see him enjoying himself too. She wanted him to be happy, so that being married to her didn't seem like too great a sacrifice of the life he'd been destined to have again with the success of his film.

'This is so perfect I don't even want to think about going home yet,' Gaia sighed as the waves gently splashed onto the golden sand beside them.

'Is it really going to be that bad?'

'It's just the thought of having to put on an act again for everyone else's benefit. I've enjoyed this time away from it all. You know, minus the whole being ill thing.'

'I know what you mean. I suppose I've only myself to

blame going into the entertainment industry, whereas you didn't have a say in the matter. It can't have been easy.' He thought of everything he'd gone through in his childhood and how much worse it would have been if he'd had to do it in the spotlight. Two years of damaging publicity seemed little in comparison to the royal family who'd had their doubters even before Gaia's father had been unfaithful to her mother and the country. Not everyone was a fan of the privileged lifestyle afforded to the Benettis through the tax payer, and now he was about to become part of that family, keeping secrets which could bring the whole establishment down if exposed. If he was feeling the pressure he could only imagine how Gaia had coped for all these years before they'd met and she'd been forced to confide in him.

'I didn't know any different to people telling me what to do, how to act, even how to think sometimes. And when my father did what he did, well, I suppose I felt a bit lost. He'd gone against all the rules to simply do what he wanted and it didn't matter who got hurt in the process.' It was clear by the catch in Gaia's voice that she had been deeply wounded by her father's hypocrisy. Not least because the fallout from that had impacted on her current situation, making it impossible for her to admit she was pregnant by someone other than her husband and be seen as having the same 'loose morals'. It wouldn't matter to certain quarters that times had moved on and women could have babies without a man in their lives. He'd understood that enough to marry her.

'Never mind the national implications, it was a lot for you to personally deal with.'

'More than you'd think. I spent my whole life being

told by my father I wasn't good enough, a disappointment because I wasn't his son and heir. That women were supposed to be seen, not heard, and just put up with whatever was sent our way. He used to tell my mother she was lucky to even be with him whenever she called him out on his affairs. Yes, affairs, plural. He just happened to make this last one public but everyone has been covering for him for years, because, you know, he was the next in line.' This was the first time Gaia had talked about her family in such a fashion. Until now she'd only talked in hushed tones, afraid anything she said would get back to them. Now it seemed she was opening up, showing him more of the real Gaia. As if he needed to admire her any more.

'Not everyone thinks like that.' He didn't want to be one of those 'not all men' advocates, but it was important for Gaia to realise there were some more enlightened members of society out there, her husband included.

Far from being merely decoration in the background, he thought Gaia one of the bravest, strongest people he'd ever known and her loyalty to her family in the wake of these revelations was even more remarkable.

Her derisive snort, however, disputed it. 'My ex reiterated that idea. He cheated on me too and I thought I should be thankful to even be with him. How stupid was I?'

'You're not stupid, Gaia. Your parents made you think that's what a normal relationship entailed. It's ingrained in us to believe whatever they tell us until we know better.' It was hard not to reach out and hold her when she sounded so alone. It was no wonder she'd got herself into such a mess if she'd been made to believe such nonsense. He could only hope, from the way she was being so open with him, was becoming so emotional about it, that she was beginning to realise how wrong they'd been. She should have been allowed to shine in her own light, not stand in the shadow of the men in her life for the sake of their egos. It made him more determined than ever to protect her.

'What sort of Queen will I ever make, always afraid of what people think of me? Who thinks the only way she'll be accepted is to lie and practically blackmail someone into marrying her?' It was no wonder she wasn't looking forward to going home if she thought she was walking back into the lion's den, but this time she wouldn't be doing it on her own.

'You are loved, Gaia. Not enough people have shown you in your lifetime but I can assure you you'll make a fantastic leader. You've done everything you can to protect your family and the monarchy and I know you'll do the same for your country. As for me...' This time he did reach out, catching her under the chin to tilt her head so she would look at him. 'It was my decision to marry you. One I don't regret.'

The way he was feeling, looking at her now, so vulnerable and fragile, was doing things to him that weren't in keeping with his plan to be the perfect gentleman for her tonight. He needed a distraction.

'May I have this dance?' He got to his feet and held out his hand.

She took it without hesitation. 'You may.'

Niccolo pulled her to him, clutching her close, and began to sway to the music of the waves. 'I think this is where we came in, isn't it?'

'I think that dance was a little more—er—energetic.'

'I didn't want to get your blood pressure too high.'

'Who knew one dance would cause so much mess? I am sorry, you know, for everything.'

'Hey, I told you before there's no need to apologise. I'm living my best life right now.' He really was. Despite what they had yet to face, he was on a beach dancing with a beautiful princess. Two years ago, he couldn't have believed his life would have had such a turnaround and, though the circumstances weren't ideal, there was nowhere he'd rather be in this moment.

Gaia laughed. 'You mean you wouldn't prefer to be at another glitzy movie premiere with someone who didn't look as though she'd run through a jumble sale?'

'Hey, those are my favourite clothes you're wearing. Besides, you've never looked more beautiful.' He meant every word. With her hair hanging in wet curls around her shoulders, face free of make-up and worry, swamped in shapeless polyester blend, she was stunning. Because this was the real Gaia. She wasn't wearing a mask, or playing a role created by her family circumstances, she was simply a woman dancing barefoot on the sand with him.

Perhaps it was because their bodies were touching, that Gaia had opened up to him, or simply that temptation was becoming too great for him to ignore, but Niccolo couldn't resist any longer. He reached down and pressed his lips gently to hers.

'I think I've wanted to do that from the first moment we met,' he whispered, almost afraid to say it out loud. As though by expressing his feelings he might push her over the edge and ruin this moment.

Gaia lifted her hand and stroked his cheek. 'Me too,' she said softly and kissed him back.

Her soft mouth was his refuge and he found solace there, all the noise in his head quietened by the touch and taste of her on his tongue. Here, now, they were two people enjoying the chemistry they'd never got to explore that first night in the theatre. It wasn't the frenzied passion of a newlywed couple, but a gentle, tentative journey together, getting to know one another. There was no pressure for anything more, even though he wanted it. They both knew that to take this to the next level would be a complication they could do without. It didn't mean Niccolo wasn't yearning to be with her in every way possible.

Gaia's sigh seemed to echo his fear and frustration that one kiss should be all they could afford to indulge. He didn't know what the future held for them as a couple or as part of the wider family other than that it wasn't going to be a smooth transition for either of them. Sharing an innocent kiss seemed to be providing them both with some comfort, so it was enough for now.

She laid her head on his shoulder and let out a yawn.

'I must be losing my touch if I can send you to sleep with one kiss.' He hadn't thought about what would happen once he gave in to temptation but he was pretty sure it wasn't this. It was probably for the best, though, given Gaia's current condition and their already complicated marriage.

'Sorry. It's been a lovely night and I've enjoyed being with you, Niccolo. I'm just so tired.' She yawned again, giving him no choice but to sweep her up in his arms and carry her back to the room.

'You need your rest,' he reasoned when she feebly protested against his chest, telling himself that too when he placed her on the bed and lay down beside her.

'I don't want to go back, Niccolo. I'm scared.' Again she voiced her fears, which were clearly weighing heavily on her mind.

'Of what? You've done the hardest part already.'

They were lying side by side staring into each other's eyes and it dawned on him he'd never felt closer to anyone even though they weren't in a physical relationship. He'd had plenty of those which had lasted longer than the relationship he'd had with Gaia so far, but never had he experienced this overwhelming connection with another person. His heart worked overtime as he began coming to terms with that, and what it would mean for them as a couple. Everything hinged on this marriage lasting, and confessing his true feelings could destroy it all. If she didn't reciprocate, if this apparent infatuation was a flash in the pan, or if she decided she didn't need him in her life further down the line, it was a risky move to show his hand. As always it would be better for him to keep those emotions to himself. He was here to play the role of a supportive husband and father, not take his work home with him. Gaia needed a partner, not another man who'd let her down thinking about his own needs.

Apparently satisfied with his answer, she curled into his side, once more showing the trust she had in him, and seeking comfort from him. He was only too willing to give it.

As much as he wanted to make love to his wife and show her how much he cared for her, he chose instead to take her in his arms and hold her until she fell soundly asleep.

CHAPTER SEVEN

THE HONEYMOON WAS definitely over. They'd only been back in Lussureggiante for a few days but lying on that bed together, where Niccolo had made her feel so safe, now seemed like a lifetime ago.

There was a knock on the door of their adjacent bedrooms. Since moving into their own residence they'd been doing their best to keep up appearances but he'd insisted on having his own space behind closed doors. A very big flashing neon sign that he regretted that kiss they'd shared before leaving Bali. Gaia couldn't get it out of her head for a different reason: she was falling for her husband.

In an ordinary world that would have been a pre-requisite to their even thinking about getting married, but this was not a typical relationship. It was based on reputation and careers. Emotions weren't in the contract. That was probably why he'd been a bit distant with her since. A kiss became so much more when it was between two people thrown together in difficult and unusual circumstances. Perhaps it was some form of Stockholm syndrome which had prompted the kiss, and for a moment he'd believed he had feelings for someone who was effectively holding him captive in this supposed marriage of convenience. Whatever had led to it, it had become apparent there wasn't going to be a repeat performance. More was the pity.

Another knock.

'Just a second.' She took a moment to check her reflection in the full-length wall mirror before opening the door, flattening down any wayward hairs with her hand and checking there was no lipstick on her teeth. Still wanting to look good for her husband even if it was a wasted effort.

When she opened the barrier between their rooms she was rewarded with his appreciative gaze.

'You look beautiful as always.'

'Thank you.' The compliment lifted her spirit as well as her confidence knowing that Niccolo found her attractive, regardless of the fact that he clearly didn't want to let things between them go beyond a kiss.

'Did you sleep okay?'

'Yes, thanks. The bed is much more comfortable than the couch I spent a week on.' Niccolo's grin didn't quite reach his eyes and she could see that even this arrangement was taking a strain on him.

It was one thing faking a relationship in a villa hundreds of miles away from real life, but quite another doing it back home with the eyes of the world watching them, likely waiting for them to mess up. Living this way wasn't easy, always sneaking around, pretending to be something they weren't—in love. Lying without saying a word. They'd only been married a matter of weeks but she couldn't blame him if he wanted out already. He'd already holed up in a different bedroom, away from the wife he apparently didn't intend kissing.

Today wasn't going to help if he was already having serious doubts about what he'd got himself into when they were going to be spending it together on their first official engagement as a married couple.

'Are you ready, Niccolo?'

He lifted an eyebrow, looked down at his pristine tailored charcoal-grey suit and held up his hands. 'Don't I look ready?'

'You look fantastic, but I meant are you mentally prepared for this?' On the outside he looked like the handsome prince he was now, primed for his adoring public. Inside, if he was anything like her, he'd be dreading taking this show on the road. Although he was clearly a better actor than she would ever make.

He shrugged. 'So far, so good. I mean, I was always going to have to do my royal duty, so I can't complain.'

'I know, but—'

'I've been briefed on royal protocol and etiquette and everything else which could possibly cause embarrassment to the family if I get it wrong.' He put his hands on her shoulders, the first time he'd touched her since that last night of their honeymoon. The weight of his touch was welcome, a reminder that he was there with her even if he seemed further away than ever.

She bit her lip to prevent any further concerns slipping from her lips when it was clear he wasn't going to share any of his thoughts or feelings with her at present. Whether that was down to his wanting to save her from her ever-increasing burden of guilt, or because of those barriers which had been erected between them since their return, she couldn't be sure. All Gaia knew for certain was that they had a job to do today, officially opening the neonatal unit at the local hospital, that they couldn't, and wouldn't, back out of because she had a serious case of stage fright.

'The car is waiting. I suppose we should go. I don't want to keep anyone waiting.'

Niccolo followed her out of the door. 'Do you have a speech prepared?'

'Yes. I worked hard on it, so I hope it comes over okay.' Her stomach somersaulted at the reminder that she would be giving her first public address since the night of the premiere and the ensuing commotion. Although her engagements in the past had been more for appearances' sake, her standing these days carried more weight. If her rise up the royal ranks hadn't garnered more interest she knew her marriage to a movie star would certainly draw a crowd. Niccolo had a lot of fans who would surely take any opportunity to catch a glimpse of him, even if it was at an event for families of premature babies. As the patron for the charity which had raised the money to build the neonatal unit, she had to be there. However, she'd had a sleepless night, anxious about how she and her new husband would be received today.

Being a wife in public was a different role for her from the one she was used to. She would be in the public eye more than ever, with greater expectations now they'd be viewed as a team. He would have his fans who wouldn't think she was good enough for him, whilst there would be many in the upper classes who would look down on him. She couldn't help but think there were many waiting for them to fail as a couple, and in their duties to the country. The extra pressure and responsibility were preparation for her future position as Queen, she supposed. Although, having Niccolo to turn to gave her some comfort. She had him for advice and support, which meant everything, and she felt stronger with him beside her.

His encouragement and faith in her actions made her feel more prepared for her position in the family than ever.

As they waited out front for the car to pull around, Niccolo flashed her a smile. 'I'm sure it will. I know you will have put your heart and soul into everything you've written. You're a warm, compassionate woman, which is exactly why they chose you as a representative. Without your support they might not have been able to raise as much money as they did, so I'm sure everyone in attendance will appreciate you being there today.'

'I'm not sure that's true, but thank you.' The black limousine drew up beside them and Gaia was a little calmer as she got in, entirely because of Niccolo. If only she'd had his reassuring influence years ago she might not have made so many mistakes and bad decisions. Unlike her family or past partners, he never made her doubt herself, and always made her believe she was good enough. The exception being that one kiss they'd shared and subsequently never spoken about again. It wasn't his fault she'd read more into it and believed it might have led to something more between them if she hadn't been so exhausted. They'd clearly been clinging to each other for comfort in the moment, and got carried away. That should have been the end of the story, but she hadn't been able to stop thinking about it since and how much she'd like to do it again.

Niccolo could tell Gaia was nervous by the way she was fidgeting with her wedding ring. He could spot her tells which would probably have gone unnoticed by people who didn't know her. On the outside she was a quietly confident figurehead, but he'd seen enough behind the scenes to know that she was also someone in need of support. That was what he was trying to be for her and that meant backing away from the other, less selfless, feelings he was developing towards Gaia.

It had been a mistake to act on them and kiss her, not least because it made him want more. He was afraid that by taking their relationship to the next level it would mean the beginning of the end for them, and he'd promised he'd be there for her and the baby. In the past backing away from his emotions had caused the end of his relationships, but in this case he was doing it to save his marriage. This unfamiliar territory was unsettling for him, a loss of control he'd clung to throughout most of his life.

Ironically being married had made it easier for him to let emotions filter into their relationship. It was a more secure environment, a safe space for him to *feel*, because Gaia had signed a contract to be with him. She wasn't going to leave him broken-hearted and alone, risking the same for herself.

But losing that hold he had on his emotions risked his reverting to that lonely child, vulnerable and hurting. Being a broken version of himself wasn't going to do his career or his wife any good.

He was more use to her as a shoulder to lean on than a partner who would let her down when she expected more from him than he was capable of giving. Survival mode for him, and now for them as a couple, was to lock down his emotions.

This marriage was supposed to be about saving their reputations and providing a stable environment for the baby she was carrying. None of which would benefit from what would probably end up being a short-lived physical relationship if they let things develop.

Which was why he'd moved into a separate bedroom, away from temptation. If he ended up lying on a bed with Gaia in his arms again it might not stop at a kiss next time.

Niccolo wondered if he should bring up the kiss, explain why he didn't think it was a good idea to follow up on it. Then decided it would probably make things even more awkward between them.

Thankfully the hospital wasn't too far away, so their journey wasn't as torturous as their trip back from their honeymoon had been. Every time they'd brushed against one another they'd leapt back, as if afraid they'd spontaneously combust from the slight contact. They'd needed to get back to the way things had been before their marriage, when all they'd had to worry about was his career, the monarchy and the parentage of her baby. Not potentially falling for his wife and messing things up with his inability and refusal to open up.

Gaia had shared so much with him. Personal details about her life and the way she'd suffered emotionally because of her family and ex-boyfriend, which suggested real trust in him. A lesser person could easily have sold the stories to the press and made a fortune, and she knew that. It said a lot about him that he hadn't been able to do the same in return. She'd bared her soul, but he'd given her scant details about his own life in an attempt to protect himself.

Divulging those secrets he'd held for so long was diving deep into those emotional reserves when he'd been content paddling on the surface so far. Explaining how he'd caused his ex to go to the papers because of his resistance to making an emotional connection risked her seeing him in the same light as Christina did—a soulless monster who didn't deserve sympathy or love. Except there was a part of him that wanted to be honest with her, to show her who he was inside, and stop being afraid of letting himself have feelings for her.

He didn't know if he'd ever have the courage to do that.

In the meantime he needed to focus on something for him outside of the family and away from his wife. He'd been ignoring the calls and messages Ana, and other people from the industry, had been leaving, because he'd been more concerned with Gaia and the baby. This marriage had supposedly been for his benefit too, so perhaps it was time to look after himself. If there were offers out there for him he should investigate because if all of this ended tomorrow he needed his own career to fall back on. He hadn't gone to all this trouble to save his reputation just to throw it away when there were doors opening up for him again. Going back to his job might take his mind off the more…personal aspects of their relationship.

The car stopped and Gaia took a deep inhale of breath.

'Are you sure you want to do this? I mean, it's so soon after your own scare. We can still send our apologies and go home if you don't feel up to it.' Not only was this a highly emotive subject on its own, but she was still in the danger zone when it came to her pregnancy too. Dealing with families of babies born too early might prove too much for her, and apart from anything else she should probably be resting. Niccolo would never tell her what to do but he wanted her to know he was concerned about her.

'I'm a little nervous, but otherwise I'm fine. I think my experience and my current situation will help me empathise with the families. I promise I won't overdo things, but thank you for asking. I don't remember anyone ever telling me I had a choice, so I do appreciate your concern, Niccolo.'

Her smile was dazzling and full of sadness at the same time. He hoped the genuinely happy part of it was for him, and that he hadn't caused her any of the distress her family obviously had. Nor would he in the future. One of their entourage opened the car doors before they could continue the discussion, with Gaia's mind already made up about fulfilling her duty.

They were whisked through the hospital quickly and efficiently with their royal protection officers in tow. It was a totally different experience from the hype and exhibitionism of the wedding, as it should have been. This event wasn't about him or Gaia, it was to acknowledge the work done by the charity, and the families of the young babies who needed that extra support at the beginning of their lives. Yet again, it proved how much Gaia related to her public. She didn't need the fuss or attention to do her duty when she was invested in people.

Jill, the head of the charity, gave a little curtsey as she introduced herself.

'Thank you so much for coming. It means a lot to the charity, and to me personally, to have you here.'

'You're very welcome. I'm honoured to be here to see all the work you're doing.' Gaia shook hands with Jill, as did Niccolo.

Although this was his wife's venture, he was very supportive and proud of her philanthropic endeavours. There were some responsibilities and titles which had been bestowed upon her after her father abandoned his duties, but he knew this was one of the projects close to her heart. Likely even more so now when she was pregnant herself.

'Thank you for coming too, Your Highness. I know some of the nurses here are very keen to meet you.' The twinkle in Jill's eye told him that, although today was about a very serious matter, there was also room for a little fun. This whole royal protocol might be new to him but he had some experience dealing with fans. Schmoosing he could do and feel that he was being of some use today.

'Well, I'm looking forward to meeting your very hardworking medical team too.'

'They'll be very glad to hear it!' Jill led them to the group gathered outside the new NICU, where they received a round of applause.

Gaia approached some of the families who would benefit from the new unit, whilst he went to say hello to the nurses waiting patiently near by.

'Thank you for all the work you're doing here,' he said, shaking hands as he went along the line. It was strange to have people curtseying before him, and his new princely status seemed to demand people keep a respectable distance. In his day job it wasn't unusual to have a scrum of people vying for his attention, grabbing him for selfies on their phones, and thrusting pens at him for autographs. Although he was appreciative of the fans he had, especially after the last couple of years, sometimes they had no respect for his personal space. He wondered if the security guys had a hand in this new dynamic, or if people generally became more deferential when faced with a member of the monarchy.

Certainly, upon his first meeting with Gaia he'd been very aware of acting appropriately in her presence. At first. It was his subsequent lapse into over-familiarity which had caused all the trouble and brought them to where they were now.

Gaia, well-practised in the art of the meet and greet, gradually made her way to the temporary podium, which had been set up for her to give a speech before the official opening. Jill thanked them both again for attending and invited Gaia to address the families and staff in attendance.

While everyone clapped he watched his wife take a deep breath before stepping up to the podium.

'Thank you, Jill, and thank you to the team for inviting my husband and I to officially open this new unit.' At the first public reference to her 'husband', Gaia smiled over at him, much to the delight of her audience, who gave a little cheer.

The acknowledgement and acceptance, both from Gaia and the assembled crowd, made him stand a little taller, no longer ashamed of the public's perception of him. Even if his current one was based on a lie. But that was the whole motivation behind this sham marriage, though he sometimes seemed to forget that.

'I'm very proud to be patron of this charity,' Gaia went on, 'whose work over the years has culminated in the addition of this state-of-the-art facility for our youngest and most vulnerable members of society. My thanks especially go to Jill and her team, who have tirelessly raised funds in order for this endeavour to finally come to fruition.' She started a round of applause for the team, omitting to mention the work Niccolo knew she'd personally undertaken to secure funding for the project. Not only had she used her personal connections to promote the charity and secure donations, but he happened to know she also made generous financial contributions herself.

Anonymously, of course. Gaia didn't do these things for recognition or brownie points, she got involved in important causes because she cared. That was why the way her family treated her at times was so unfair, and why she'd make an excellent monarch.

She finished her speech by outlining the important role this unit would serve to the community, speaking of the lives that would be saved, and concluding that neither she nor the charity would stop their hard work. As long as there were families who needed their support they would keep fund-raising, keep fighting for those precious babies.

The sound of Gaia's voice cracking was lost against the rapturous round of applause, but he'd heard it and seen the quiver of her bottom lip. Niccolo inwardly swore. They'd treated this as simply one of her duties, but, given recent events, it was no wonder her emotions had got the better of her. He instinctively moved closer to her but with a slight, discreet flick of her hand she urged him to stay back. Realising she was right, if he made a fuss it would draw more attention and cause a scene unnecessarily, he stood down and trusted Gaia enough to know her own mind on the matter, but would make sure to give her a cuddle when they were alone again. Yes, he'd been doing his best to limit personal contact but she would need some comforting.

This was a sensitive issue and only days ago they'd feared she might be having a miscarriage. Everything she was hearing today must have been tough when it made her fears a possibility—she could still have a premature baby. She was taking on board the families' stories of their struggles, and sometimes losses, expressing sympathy when she must have been terrified the same might happen to her. The least he could do was put his arms around her when it was all over.

They were given a short tour of the unit, and, though they'd kept a respectable distance from the families and babies using the facilities at present, Niccolo could see the toll the day was taking on her. He waited until they had a moment alone before he mentioned it.

'Are you ready to leave? I think you've done everything you can today and you need to take care of yourself.' He half expected her to deny she was anything but wide awake and firing on all cylinders, so it came as a surprise when she nodded. The jerky motion looked as though her head had become too heavy for her weary body.

He took the initiative by saying goodbye to Jill, then motioned to the security team that they wanted to leave. In seconds they were being whisked back down the corridor, waving their goodbyes to the people who had come out to see them and witness the opening of the new unit.

'Thanks for that,' Gaia said to him as they walked away. 'I think I underestimated the effect today would have on me, and my energy levels don't seem to be as high as usual.' She was almost apologetic for her compassion towards the families, when that was the very reason people warmed to her. Gaia was genuine, she didn't take her responsibilities lightly, or do them for a photo opportunity. Over the course of his career he'd come into contact with many disingenuous characters who portrayed a certain altruistic persona to the world, but behind closed doors showed their true, ugly, narcissistic traits. She was one of the most sincere people he'd ever met, who should be protected at all costs.

'It's an emotional issue, and you're still recovering,

don't forget,' he whispered lest anyone should discover their secret. Although they would have to make an announcement soon about the pregnancy when it became too obvious to disguise any longer, and the timing would no doubt cause more speculation, they wanted to wait until they were past the danger period.

She leaned her head on his shoulder for a brief moment. 'Thank you. I can always count on you to make me feel better.'

He wished that was always going to be true but he couldn't make any guarantees for the future. Instead of making promises he couldn't keep he put an arm around her waist and gave her a squeeze of reassurance that he would have her back at least.

As they came to the exit and the security opened the door, they were met with a crowd jostling to get near them, all calling out to Gaia.

'How do you feel about your father having a baby with another woman?'

'Do you have any comment to make on the pregnancy announcement?'

'Will this affect your relationship with your father?'

It soon became apparent that during their time inside the hospital, another scandal had broken and now the paparazzi were scrambling to get her reaction to the news first. Niccolo automatically wrapped his arms around Gaia to try and protect her, whilst security formed a ring around them, forcefully pushing past the reporters and photographers to get to the car.

'Get the door open,' he barked to the burly guard closest to the vehicle.

'Niccolo?' Gaia's fearful plea only made him angrier

at the people who had put her in this dangerous position, thinking only of themselves and a scoop, not how terrifying it was to be in the midst of the scrum.

'It's okay. The car's right there, and I'm right here.'

Except just as they reached the door and security made a space for them to get to it, one of the over-zealous reporters managed to grab Gaia by the arm and yank her back into the crowd. She let out a yell as she stumbled back, photographers swarming around her, snapping her distress. Niccolo fought through everyone in his way to reach her, not caring who he shoved aside in the process...all that mattered was getting Gaia to safety. Then he witnessed a paparazzo swing around, his camera bag hitting her in the stomach making her double over, and the red mist descended.

'Everyone, back off! Now!' he yelled, stunning them into silence. Probably because members of the royal family weren't supposed to lose their temper or make a scene, but unlike Gaia's family he cared more about her welfare than appearances.

'You, sort this lot out. Do your jobs.' It was security's turn to take a roasting as he let it be known he was not happy about the way the team had mishandled the whole situation.

Gaia was clutching her stomach and his hand automatically went there too, as if by making contact it would somehow protect the baby more.

'Are you okay?' It was a stupid question when none of this was acceptable, but in his mind her answer was the only important thing in his life right now.

CHAPTER EIGHT

'I JUST WANT to get home,' Gaia gasped, grabbing Niccolo's hand, her lifeline, and let him lead her back to the car through the now slowly dispersing crowd. Her heart was racing like a runaway train, her head spinning from all the pushing and pulling from people trying to get a piece of her. It was only when she was in the car, the door closed tightly against the crowd outside, and she was in Niccolo's arms that she was able to calm down again.

'You're safe now,' he said and kissed the top of her head.

She relaxed into him, his warmth soothing her and making her feel protected.

'W-what happened?' Her teeth were chattering, shock leaving her cold. Niccolo tightened his hold on her, and opened his jacket to envelope her, providing her with more of his much-needed body heat.

'I assume your dear father has caused another family scandal, dragging you into it in the process.'

She recalled hearing something about a baby but she'd been more concerned with her own when they were getting jostled. 'I wish he would give us some warning before he dropped these bombshells so we could prepare ourselves for the ensuing scramble for information.'

'I think he likes the drama, and attention. It's not fair on you though. How do you feel about him having another family?'

'Honestly? I don't feel anything, not towards my father or the baby. I'm sure my mother will be devastated—it's like rubbing salt in the wound. But when those people swarmed around us, my only concern was for my own unborn child.'

'Mine too, and for you, of course.' He squeezed her a little tighter, as though he wouldn't let go of her ever again. At this moment in time Gaia would be happy to stay here for ever.

Niccolo had been her saviour during the melee. She didn't know what she would have done if he hadn't grabbed her by the hand and faced down those desperate for a story. They'd got what they wanted in the end, pics of the new prince tossing protocol aside to rescue his wife. Her grandfather wouldn't be pleased they'd given the press more fodder for their front pages but none of this was their doing. It was her father who'd caused this. Niccolo had simply been there to catch her again when things threatened to get out of control. He was her rock.

'Thank you for getting me out of there. I just froze.'

'You shouldn't have had to deal with that. This day should have been about the unit and your visit, not having to deal with the aftermath of your father's antics again. And I'll be having a stern talk with the head of security about where the hell they were too.' His voice had a steely edge to it she'd never heard before and she knew he was angry about what they'd gone through. More than that, there was a definite sense of his wanting to protect her and the baby. Everything he'd promised when he'd agreed to marry her.

'As will I. I'm glad you were there anyway.'

'Where else would I be but by my wife's side?'

Gaia knew he was teasing, but within it he spoke the truth. So far he'd been true to his word, supporting her both in her public duty, and in private when things were tough.

'It was easier when it was only the two of us.'

'Was it?'

She wanted to ask him what had changed between them since Bali, but they'd already arrived at the palace.

When the door opened she almost expected to see the red, angry faces of her family waiting to express their disappointment over the latest incident, regardless that none of it was her fault. She'd learned details like that didn't matter. The family reputation was everything. Gaia hoped she would be a more benevolent monarch, and understanding parent. She was still human, capable of making mistakes, and she thought that made her more relatable to the general public. Plus, she hadn't actually done anything wrong. Neither had Niccolo, although the photographs taken at the time might suggest differently as he'd stormed through the crowd to get to her. In her eyes he was the ultimate hero, and she was sure his legion of admirers would feel the same way even if her family didn't.

Thankfully, there was no crowd baying for their blood upon their arrival and she intended on getting to their private rooms as soon as possible. Niccolo disembarked first and reached out his hand to help her out. Except her legs buckled when she made contact with solid ground.

'Sorry,' she said as Niccolo was forced to catch her. 'My legs have turned to jelly.'

'That's the shock.'

She was trying not to catastrophise but she realised now that it could have been much more serious than getting pushed about if he hadn't pulled her from the crowd. After all the stories she'd heard about difficult pregnancies and tiny babies fighting for life, she worried about the little life growing inside her more than ever.

'Are you okay?' Niccolo asked, seeing her hands clutching her bump and mistaking the protective gesture as an indication that something was wrong.

'I'm fine,' she insisted, but clearly he didn't believe her, as he scooped her into his arms and carried her effortlessly up the stairs.

'What are you doing?'

'I'm taking you home.' The possessive, growly tone of his voice made her less inclined to protest, as did the way she was curled up against him. Her face was pressed so close to his neck she could smell his spicy aftershave, feel the rasp of his afternoon stubble against her cheek. Exactly where she wanted to be. Only Niccolo had the ability to make her feel safe, protected, and loved. It might all be fake but for now she needed it, needed him.

Ignoring the stunned reactions as they passed through the house, Gaia enjoyed being the damsel in distress for the short time it took to reach the bedroom. She'd spent her whole life being strong, doing as she was told, and not making a fuss. It was nice to have her feelings validated and accepted. She was tired, frightened, and in need of a little TLC. Luckily her husband was excellent at dispensing it.

'You know we are going to be the talk of the staff after you carried me through the house like a caveman,' she giggled. It wouldn't do their reputation any harm to have people think they were still in the honeymoon stage of their marriage.

'I don't care,' he said, setting her gently on the mattress. 'You're my wife and I want to take care of you.'

He was being so sweet, so tender, it reminded her of that last night on their honeymoon and she couldn't help but wonder why it had all gone wrong between them.

'Niccolo?'

'Hmm?' He was distracted as he pulled back the bedcovers and attempted to tuck her in, but she wasn't too tired to hear an explanation for the emotional distance which had grown between them.

'What happened?'

'It was all a bit of a blur, I suppose. Basically, the papers heard your father got his mistress pregnant and staked us out at the hospital so they could get your reaction to the news first.'

'I meant between us, Niccolo. When you're doing things like this, rescuing me from a crowd and carrying me like Kevin Costner, it makes me think you might actually have feelings for me.' She swallowed down the fear trying to stop her from saying the words out loud and potentially making a fool of herself. It could all be in her head but she found it difficult to believe that kiss and the way he'd defended her today were part of an act.

He let out a sigh. 'Of course I have feelings for you. Do you think I would have risked alienating myself from the press again by shoving them aside if I didn't like you?' Niccolo's admission wasn't the grand declaration she'd been hoping for. Mainly because she'd realised she was in deep herself and wanted him to mirror her feelings to justify them. She'd had too many relationships where she'd been the one who'd loved a lot more than her partner and ended up being the one hurt when it was all over. It would be better to find the truth out now before she caused herself irreparable damage loving someone else who didn't feel the same way.

'Do you kiss everyone you *like*?' She didn't want to sound desperate or needy, but she knew he'd had something of a reputation before their marriage. He'd had a string of beautiful women on his arm before his ex trashed his name, so it wasn't a totally off-the-wall idea. However, they were married, and he didn't seem to do commitment along with romance. The two didn't appear to co-exist in his world, so she needed to know the truth, whatever it was, before it was too late for her fragile heart.

Niccolo thought for a moment, then climbed onto the bed beside her. 'Contrary to popular opinion, no, I don't.'

'So why did you do it, then literally put a wall up between us? Was it that bad?' she joked, hoping it would disguise the hint of desperation she was sure was there in her voice.

Niccolo gave a chuckle. 'No, it wasn't bad. The opposite, in fact, but that's exactly why we can't take things any further. This was supposed to be a no-emotional-strings marriage. That was the only reason I agreed to it.'

'But why would it be so bad for us to admit we have feelings for one another? To act on it? Why are we denying ourselves the chance to be truly happy together?' They were already married, a baby on the way, and to her mind if they loved each other it would be the royal icing on the wedding cake. It was a life, a future, she thought she'd only get to dream about. Her happy-ever-after seemed within reach, if only Niccolo wanted the same things.

'There is no guarantee, Gaia. Especially with me. I do have feelings for you and trust me, I lie awake at night wishing I could act on them. But it's never going to happen.'

'Why not?' She didn't understand. It was clear there was an attraction, a deeper connection than either of them had anticipated going into this so-called marriage of convenience. So why would exploring those feelings be such a bad idea?

'I'm not good at dealing with my emotions. Strike that,' he said, shaking his head. 'I can't *express* my emotions.'

'That doesn't make any sense, Niccolo. I saw you get angry earlier at the journalists and be tender with me. You express yourself very well when you want to.' Maybe that was the point, he didn't want to have feelings towards her. He was forfeiting his bachelor life to save both of their skins, so it was possible whatever had been simmering away between them was simply a need for physical release and nothing more on his part. At this point in time she was tempted to settle for that if it was all he could offer her. It had to be better than sleeping in separate rooms and thinking he didn't want her at all. A future in bed alone every night seemed very bleak.

He scrubbed his hands over his face, an act of frustration accompanied by another sigh. 'Okay, it's certain emotions I have trouble with. Why do you think my ex went to the lengths she did to get back at me? I couldn't give her what she wanted—love.'

'It's possible you simply didn't love her; that doesn't mean you have a problem. I mean, her actions did not seem those of a woman you could ever have had a stable relationship with. In my opinion.'

'That's true, but I always bow out before it gets to that stage. This marriage needs to work and I would be risking everything by getting emotionally involved.'

'I'd say it's already too late for that, wouldn't you? It's one thing saying you're keeping an emotional distance but your actions say differently. The way you comforted me when I thought I was losing the baby, the way you swept in today, suggests more than a contractual obligation to me.' She was pushing him, taking a risk that he would admit his feelings for her rather than walk away, and it was taking every ounce of courage she had in her body. Niccolo sounded as though he needed to get to the bottom of this as much as she did in order to move on. She could only hope he took that next step with her and didn't close the door on her for good.

'But it only causes pain,' he spluttered, and she could see the anguish in his eyes, a trauma hiding in plain sight.

'I know neither of us has been lucky in love but that doesn't mean it can't happen. We have to be open to it at least, bare our scars and hope we don't add to them. Otherwise what else do we have?' This limbo wasn't somewhere she wanted to spend the rest of her life, loving her husband from afar and lamenting their lost chance to have something special. It almost seemed preferable to be on her own than to face that for the duration of their marriage.

'You just don't understand.' He turned away but Gaia wasn't willing to let the shutters come down again.

She placed her hand on his cheek and turned his head to make him look at her. 'Then help me.'

He glanced up at the ceiling and took a deep breath. Gaia held hers, knowing this could be make or break for them, and she wasn't ready to lose the only good thing in her life, besides the baby, any time soon.

That rising tide of anxiety was steadily washing over Niccolo. Even thinking about those bad times made him want to curl up in a ball and block it all out. Just as he had done at the time, his father shouting about how much he wished he'd had a normal son. He knew Gaia's childhood hadn't been a garden party either but he'd never shared the details of his grief with anyone other than a counsellor. It wasn't a time he liked to look back on, or something he was proud of. Gaia would never mock him for how the loss of his mum impacted on him, but she would see him in a different light, she was bound to. To the world he was a confident, motivated celebrity. He'd been strong for Gaia, a rock for her to depend on when things got tough. Once he told her he'd stopped talking after his mother's death, traumatised by the loss, she would only ever see him as weak and pathetic—how his father had described him. Yet he knew if he didn't explain his behaviour now he might lose her for ever anyway.

It was overwhelming as images and feelings stacked up, all vying for space when they'd been denied a place in his head for so long.

'My mum died when I was young. She was my world at the time. There in the mornings to make me pancakes, singing along to the radio, and reading bedtime stories to me at night. Dad was often away "working".' If his father had genuinely been grafting, earning money to support his family instead of sleeping around and making shady deals, he might have understood his absence better.

Niccolo took a moment to check Gaia's reaction, waiting for a sign that this over-sharing was going to do more damage to their relationship so he could end this now. However, she was watching him, hanging on his every word and waiting for him to continue.

He inhaled another cleansing breath to take away the bitter feelings towards his father threatening to erupt. This was about Niccolo and his mother, his father merely an incidental character shouting obscenities from the wings and begging for attention he didn't deserve.

'Anyway, I was too young to understand that she was sick. I don't remember anyone sitting me down to explain what was happening. It was all very confusing when she stopped singing, couldn't stand the smell of cooking, and started losing her hair. I know now that it was cancer, that she'd had chemotherapy and that's what had made her so sick, but at the time...'

'The world you knew was different,' Gaia offered.

'Exactly. I thought I'd done something to cause the change and tried to be the best boy I could to make her feel better.' His throat was already raw with the effort of holding back a sob for that child making cold cups of tea and 'Get Well Soon' cards for the only parent who'd ever shown him love. Perhaps his parents had been trying to protect him by keeping her illness from him, but that not knowing what was going on had only made him fret more.

'Oh, Niccolo.' Gaia did the sobbing for him and he had to look away before her tears made him well up too.

'I woke up one morning and she was just gone.' He gasped for air, that overwhelming sense of loss making itself known again, opening up that hole in his heart where his mother had used to reside. 'I wasn't allowed to go to the funeral… I didn't know what had happened. My father just told me she was dead.'

'That's awful.'

'Yeah. It was only as an adult I realised how messed up that was. According to my father I was supposed to just carry on as normal.'

'It's no wonder you have trouble expressing your emotions if that wasn't encouraged, if your feelings weren't validated.'

'I never thought of it that way. I suppose I was just lost without her. I didn't know what to do, or how to act. I shut down and stopped speaking for the longest time. My father's answer to that was to shout and berate me, but when that didn't have the desired effect he eventually took the advice of his new girlfriend, Alice, and arranged for me to see a counsellor. Yeah, he wasn't exactly the grieving widower.' He anticipated Gaia's disgust at the thought of how quickly his father had moved on. That was what had probably irritated him more about Niccolo's grief manifesting the way it had, because it was obvious to everyone he couldn't simply adapt to his new circumstances the way his father wanted. He'd made Niccolo believe it was his fault, that there was something wrong with him when he couldn't forget about his mother and embrace the new family dynamic. Even if Alice had been the first of a string of girlfriends he'd been introduced to and expected to see as a replacement. Fortunately the look of disgust on Gaia's face matched his own current belief that it was his father who'd had something seriously wrong with him.

'You were traumatised, Niccolo. The loss of your mother without explanation must have been a huge shock, you were so young. I'm so sorry you weren't taken care of better.' Gaia tenderly stroked his arm, offering her support, and he grabbed her hand, grounding himself in the present so he didn't get lost in the past.

'I learned it was best for me not to get emotional where relationships are concerned and to lock those feelings away. Then when it inevitably comes to an end I'm capable of functioning again. I don't ever want to be that lonely child, so broken-hearted and lost without the person he loves most in the world he can barely breathe.' It was ironic that he was pouring out all his fears to the woman who could probably do the most damage to him, because it was obvious he had fallen for Gaia. He was clinging on to that last vestige of denial for the sake of his own sanity, aware that when it was gone he'd be vulnerable once more.

'You can't live your whole life afraid of what might happen, Niccolo. We all get hurt sometimes and yes, it's tough and hard to get over, but in the end we all hope to find peace and happiness. You're not giving yourself a chance, shutting everyone out, and letting fear control your life. Don't you want something more?'

He hadn't expected Gaia to understand but neither had he anticipated her helping him see things differently. Perhaps his reaction as a child to the loss of his mother wasn't as extreme as he'd been made to believe. If things had been tackled differently he might have coped with her death better and learned how to deal with his emotions. Instead, he'd been taught to hide them, pretend they didn't exist, and just get on with things.

Now Gaia, who'd been through so much heartache herself, was telling him that it was worth the risk. That he should be willing to chance the pain if it meant someday he would find a person who loved him and would be with him for ever. There was only woman he'd be willing to open himself up for like that and he was in bed with her now.

'Of course I want more. I want you, I want us, but what if things don't work out?'

'Neither of us can predict the future, Niccolo, but you deserve to be happy, to be loved.' She reached out and stroked his cheek with her hand, the soft warmth of her touch a salve to his troubled soul. In that moment it was easy to believe they could have a future together, that it was all there for the taking. All he had to do was be brave.

He leaned in, watching Gaia to make sure this was what she wanted too. When her eyes fluttered shut and she tilted her chin up so her lips could meet his, Niccolo's last defence turned to dust.

Gaia felt as though she was still flying, being whisked through the air in Niccolo's arms, as he kissed her and sent her heart soaring. This was what she wanted, what she'd been waiting for, and it seemed Niccolo had been too. He'd denied them both this chance for something more because he'd been afraid it would mean too much. It was sweet in a way that he liked her so much that he was concerned taking things further would ruin what they had, but she needed this. Needed him.

Niccolo cupped her face in his hands, his kiss passionate and intense. As though by sharing the details of his tragic childhood he'd finally given himself permission to live in the moment. Not get burdened down by catastrophising about the future. And she was benefitting from this new development.

As her fingers moved deftly to open the buttons on his shirt, she knew he needed more than sex too. He'd spent so long keeping everyone at a distance, denying himself any chance of love, he deserved to know what it truly felt like. If their marriage was going to work they both had to be honest, and that started with being true to herself. She knew she loved him, and even if it was too early to tell him in case it frightened him off, she could show him.

Niccolo was nuzzling her neck, his hot breath turning her whole body to one very stimulated erogenous zone. She shuddered with ecstasy as he kissed his way across her collar bone and over every inch of newly exposed skin he uncovered with every button he opened. Her brain was foggy with desire, thinking only about what he was doing to her, how he was making her feel, that she forgot she was supposed to be showing him the time of his life. As he dipped his tongue into the cleft between her breasts she decided he could wait his turn. After all, they had the rest of their lives to express their feelings for one another.

She'd had a couple of partners, harboured a few crushes in her time, but she didn't remember any man making her as breathless as Niccolo. From the first moment they'd met there'd been a connection, and now as they lay here together in bed it was deeper than ever.

Niccolo stripped away the rest of her clothes, kissing his way along her naked skin, discarding his own clothes in the process. Gaia couldn't wait any longer to be with him, ready in body and soul to take the next step in their relationship.

Breath against breath, eyes locked on one another, they moved together, both seeking that ultimate connection and final release. And when it came, Gaia had tears in her eyes.

'Are you okay?' Niccolo panted, fighting to get his breath back, but clearly concerned for her.

It only made her more tearful. This was the happiest she ever remembered being. When she was with Niccolo she was at peace, no longer doubting herself or her actions, sure of every move. 'I just wish we'd met earlier. That I was having your baby.'

It was the one thing that, no matter how strong their feelings for one another might be, they couldn't change. Although it was what had forced them together so quickly, she didn't think she'd ever stop wishing that part of her life had been different.

Niccolo placed a hand on her belly. 'This is my baby.'

He kissed her tiny bump and the love she'd been afraid to acknowledge for him grew tenfold. She didn't know how she'd got so lucky to meet and marry a man like Niccolo, but now she wanted him for keeps.

CHAPTER NINE

THE NEXT MORNING Niccolo woke up with a smile on his face, seeing Gaia curled up next to him. Yesterday had been a major breakthrough for him emotionally. She'd made him realise that there was room in his life, and in his heart, for love. Perhaps that was why making love to her had been the most incredible thing he'd ever known. He'd finally been able to let down those defences and revel in the feelings he had for her.

There was no point wishing for different circumstances, a chance to erase all of their past pain and heartache when it had brought them here. That wasn't to say he wasn't fantasising that they were in their own apartment in an anonymous life somewhere else. Where going down to the kitchen wearing only his boxers to make her some breakfast wouldn't cause another scandal. Along with getting back into bed and spending the rest of the day showing his wife how much he loved her.

'Morning, beautiful,' he said as she blinked awake.

Gaia smiled and he was sure it was the first time he'd seen her without worry lines etched across her forehead. If this was what made them both truly happy he might barricade them in here for good, away from gossip and lies, and people who would hurt them. Gaia and the baby were his family, finally filling that hole in his heart.

'Morning.' She yawned and sat up, clutching the bed sheet around her body. 'I suppose we should get up and get dressed before people start talking about us.'

'After yesterday I think they already are.' He reminded her of the fracas, only because they'd have to deal with the fallout. Not that he regretted his actions—he'd do it all over again to protect Gaia—but he knew his actions had consequences now. For him and Gaia.

She threw herself back down on the pillows. 'Ugh. Don't remind me. Can't we stay here and have a honeymoon do over?'

Gaia placed her hand on the flat of his chest, and gradually slid it downwards. He groaned.

'It's tempting...' More than tempting, it was literally all that he wanted to do. They'd wasted an opportunity to have quality time together in an exotic, isolated location, instead dodging their growing attraction and letting their personal issues get in the way of their relationship. He would like a chance to have a real honeymoon, to restart their marriage based on love rather than a business deal.

It wasn't something they'd actually discussed. As though admitting they had feelings for one another would ruin what they did have together. After last night he was pretty sure she knew he was in love with her. He'd had to stop denying it himself too when his recent actions around Gaia made it clear he was head over heels for her. Her safety had been uppermost in his mind in the scrum of press yesterday, on top of the pride he'd experienced watching her speech. Knowing his feelings were so wrapped up in hers was what had made last night special, and the world hadn't ended because he'd finally accessed his emotions. If anything, it seemed a much brighter place. He'd tell her in his own time, in his own way, but he wanted to make it special. This change in him, brought about by Gaia, deserved a celebration and he wanted to surprise her with something special to mark the occasion. As soon as he figured out something they could do without an audience.

'Well, then.' Gaia whipped the sheet up over their heads with a giggle so they were enveloped in an Egyptian-cotton cocoon.

He leaned across and dropped a kiss on her still smiling mouth, unable to resist her any longer.

A loud bang on the door soon reminded him that a lie-in wasn't an option, and that they were never alone in this vast building.

'I should have kept my apartment so we could use it for secret rendezvous. Somewhere where we don't have to be anyone but Gaia and Niccolo.'

'It's a nice thought, but there'd probably be a journalist hiding permanently in the bushes somewhere outside.'

'I'm sure we could give them a story to titillate their readers.' He leaned in again for another taste of her sweet lips when the banging on the door sounded again.

'Gaia? Niccolo? Could you please get dressed and come downstairs? We have a lot to discuss.' The sound of Gaia's mother, more disgusted than embarrassed at having to rouse them from the marital bed, soon cooled any ideas of reliving their honeymoon right here.

Gaia groaned and covered her face with her hands. 'Two guesses what this is about.'

'Can't it wait? Do they have a hotline they ring as

soon as the sun rises to find out about the latest scandal they're involved in?' He was still getting used to the nuances of being part of the royal family, but this level of accountability made him feel like a little boy again. The idea of his mother-in-law, along with the King, waiting to give him a scolding wasn't something he was looking forward to and there was a chance it could happen on a regular basis when they set such impossible standards.

'Pretty much.' Gaia threw the covers back, the romantic fantasy well and truly over, and sashayed into the en suite bathroom.

Niccolo watched her naked form walk away and restrained himself from following her into the shower. He was in enough trouble already.

They shared a smile and held hands before walking into the lounge.

'Déjà vu,' Gaia whispered, as they found her mother and grandfather sitting there with the morning's papers spread out over the table.

Niccolo held his hand up. 'I know, I know. I should have acted more appropriately but I was concerned for my wife's safety, and the security weren't up to the job—'

'We've let Raimondo go.' The King cut him off with the update.

'Oh. Good.' For someone in such a high-profile security role the beefy guard had been seriously lax in his duty to the future Queen.

'We have more important issues to deal with. Namely the rumours that Gaia is pregnant.' He pointed to the photographs of Niccolo and Gaia hurrying through the crowd of salivating reporters, both with their hands on her belly.

'She is.'

'I am.'

'But it's the timing, don't you see? People will realise you were pregnant before the wedding.' It was her mother who pointed out the real scandal, at least in her eyes.

'And? We're married. Why would anyone care?' Niccolo was tired of the way they treated Gaia, as though everything she did was wrong. People made mistakes and he knew she had done everything she could to try and fix things. So had he. Now it was about time they were both able to have a bit of peace and get on with their married life.

'We're a traditional family, with traditional values. So are many of the people who live here. This should've been handled differently. We could've said the baby was early...'

'Lie, you mean?' He knew he sounded testy but it was about time someone stuck up for Gaia in the face of her family's constant disparagement.

Gaia placed her hand on his knee, a gesture he took to mean stop talking.

'This isn't how we wanted things to play out but it's not a crime, Mother. Sex outside of marriage isn't unheard of these days. You both want me to be a figurehead for this country and that means you have to start trusting me. I'm a modern woman and I think most people will relate to me better if I show that. We will put out our own statement announcing the happy occasion once we have the three-month scan and make sure everything is okay. Once the news is out there it should put an end to all the speculation.' Gaia stood to take her leave, and her mother, who looked as if she was going to say something else, seemed to think better of it and closed her mouth again.

The King got up at the same time as Niccolo and put his arm on his granddaughter's shoulder. 'Make sure you run the announcement by our team before it goes public.'

He heard Gaia's sigh of relief as her family made their way out of the room, leaving them to make their own decisions for once. Although he thought she'd handled things with them better this time around. Standing taller and looking stronger than in the first meeting he'd been involved in, she'd been clear that she wanted to do things her own way from now on and would no longer be cowed by their judgement. There was a renewed confidence about her as she'd faced them, an inner strength which was now making itself known on the outside too.

'I think you'll make an excellent Queen, Gaia. Just don't let me down,' her grandfather threw over his shoulder before he exited.

'No pressure, then,' Niccolo whispered to make her laugh and take some of the tension out of the room.

'That actually went better than I expected, considering we're still lying to everyone about the baby's parentage.'

'Hey, it's nothing anyone needs to know. Our business, our family, okay?' Since he'd made the commitment, and subsequently developed feelings for Gaia, as far as he was concerned this baby was his. He was going to be the father figure, and a better one than he'd ever had, if he had his way. Being honest about his emotional problems was the start to a happy life, and he embraced one where he could have a wife and baby to complete the picture.

'I've never stood up to either of them before. I think

I've got you to thank for the confidence boost.' Gaia wrapped her arms around him and hugged him hard.

'You just needed someone to believe in you so you could believe in yourself. I'm proud of you. In fact, with this new self-confidence I'm not sure you even need me. I think Princess Gaia could have raised this baby on her own and been a role model for single mothers everywhere.' It was clear Gaia had the courage and strength to fight her own battles and all she'd needed was a little faith. He considered himself lucky to have been here at the right time, and luckier still that she saw him as more than a get-out-of-jail-free card. If he wasn't convinced she reciprocated what he felt for her he'd walk away and let her flourish on her own. Thankfully, after last night, it was clear there was no need for him to do that. They were both on the same page where this relationship was concerned, and embracing this new start.

'Don't even joke about that. I'm willing to stand up to my family because I have you in my life and I want to protect what we have.' She glared up at him, letting him know in no uncertain terms that she didn't want him going anywhere.

Whilst Niccolo was happy to be the other half of this new royal couple undertaking their public duties, he was also getting antsy about having a project of his own to work on. With the latest publicity, and the numerous messages from his agent to call her, it was clear he was in demand again. Gaia wasn't always going to need him to come to her rescue. When the baby came she might even prefer to take some time out to enjoy simply being a mother. It was important that they both lead fulfilling lives to make this marriage work. He would be a husband to Gaia, a father to the baby, a prince to the country, but he needed something for himself too. It had been agreed during the drawing up of their marriage contract that he wouldn't undertake any work which would negatively affect the family in any way. There hadn't been a clause saying he couldn't work at all. He just had to be careful.

Gaia didn't have to know anything until he found the right project. He didn't want her worrying unnecessarily. In the meantime, he was going to hit up his contacts and see just how in demand a movie-star prince was and what opportunities were waiting for him out there again.

Gaia was on a high as she fixed her hair and reapplied her make-up. She'd been in a hurry this morning to get ready so as not to keep her family waiting. After the talk she'd been rejuvenated, ready to take on the world. She'd started by booking her scan appointment and confirming future engagements for her and Niccolo. They could be a real power couple, using their profile to raise funds and awareness for charity. For the first time she was actually psyched about being in the position she was, where she could really make a difference instead of simply being an ornament.

Until now she'd acted on her family's advice, and that of their advisors. She'd worn what she was told to, behaved how she was told to, went out with men they approved of and represented charities recommended to her. She was beginning to realise her life didn't have to be like that. As Queen she would have some power over her own choices, and she would like to start exercising that right from now on. Not only to get used to making her own decisions, but also so those around her would see she could think for herself, and fully intended to do so. Of course she would take advice on board on certain subjects, but when it came to more personal issues she was going to have her say. She was sure that had a lot to do with Niccolo's support and the fact he allowed her to express her thoughts and feelings without judgement.

'Why don't we go out for something to eat to celebrate my journey towards independence? Or we could order in a takeaway and avoid another free-for-all with the paps. I can't have any champagne but I'd make do with some junk food,' she called from the bathroom. 'Niccolo?'

When she didn't get any response she went into the bedroom to see if all the excitement, or the exertions from last night, had caught up with him. Instead of finding him curled up asleep on the bed, she saw the room was empty.

The low timbre of Niccolo's voice sounded somewhere below, so she followed it down the stairs to the lounge they'd left earlier. She was about to walk in when she realised he was on the phone to someone. Not wanting to disturb him, she hovered at the door outside, deciding whether to wait there or go back upstairs. She hadn't meant to eavesdrop and it only cast a dark shadow over her mood.

'That sounds great, Ana. I think everything here's under control, so it's about time I got back to work. Yes, I know my popularity is through the roof—why do you think I called you? I've played my role as Prince Charming long enough here and I want to capitalise on that while I can. No, I haven't lost my edge, I'm hungry for something more in life. I've had all of these messages about projects and scripts people want me to take a look at…it's clear that the wedding has restored my reputation.

I mean, I don't even know how these people got my contact details, so they're clearly keen. I'm back in the game, baby.' Niccolo's laugh was a horrible mocking sound that brought a swell of nausea from the pit of Gaia's stomach.

She stumbled away, winded as though she'd been roundhouse kicked about the body. Not wishing to be party to the rest of the conversation where he'd no doubt lament his decision to marry her and give up his movie-star status to play this role which he was clearly finding unfulfilling. Worse still, it appeared the marriage she'd begun to believe was real was nothing but a job to him. A means to an end. Now he'd done what he set out to do, regained his reputation and career, there was nothing left for him with her. If showing her love for him by sleeping with him wasn't a reason for him to want to be with her then she had nothing left to offer. There was no reason for him to stay and it sounded as though he was making plans to get away already. She'd been taken in again by a man who was supposed to be there for her, only to leave her alone nursing a broken heart.

The urge to run was all-consuming but there was nowhere to go where she could remain anonymous and weep over the idiot she'd been in private. A photograph of her fleeing the palace in tears was the last thing the family needed. The only place she could go to be alone was her bedroom. No wonder Niccolo found it stifling and couldn't wait to spread his wings again.

She practically fell down onto the bed, her legs no longer able to carry her as the world was ripped from beneath her. Only moments ago she'd truly believed she had it all—a loving husband who supported her, a baby on the way to complete their family, and a real purpose in life. Now she was doubting everything. She'd always believed Niccolo to be a genuine guy and only last night he'd shared some of his innermost secrets, told her he was afraid of losing her. That phone call said different. He was bored, needed a challenge apparently, as though that was all she'd ever been to him. The only thing that had changed between them was the fact they had slept together last night. Perhaps now he'd bedded his princess he'd lost interest.

Even if it wasn't as calculating as that, it appeared she wasn't enough for him. Only weeks into their marriage he was seeking excitement elsewhere. It would only be a matter of time before he cheated on her too. That was what the men in her life always did and she'd been a fool to believe he was any different. The only thing she could do to save herself this time was to take control back and make the first move towards a separation.

In hindsight she'd rushed into this marriage because she was afraid of being on her own, of facing her family and the country as a single parent. Niccolo had offered her a lifeline when she'd been drowning, but now she was heading towards the shore perhaps she didn't need to cling on to him so tightly.

They'd both served each other's purpose, his career was apparently on the up again, and she was finally finding her feet and working out her place. It didn't seem fair to keep living this lie. Not if he didn't love her the way she loved him. She couldn't bear to spend the rest of her life feeling that she'd trapped him. It would make both of them miserable and wouldn't be conducive to the happy home she wanted for her baby. Niccolo had no obligation to either of them when it came down to it.

Regardless of what he'd said, the things she'd wanted to hear, this wasn't his baby or his responsibility. Very soon she'd be breaking the news to the world about the baby, and she'd already had the conversation with her family. He'd done everything asked of him and now it was time to free him from the contract keeping them together, at least behind closed doors. For both of their sakes. They'd have to keep up outward appearances until the baby was born to give it that legitimacy which had seemed so important at the time, or this aching hole in her chest had all been for nothing.

Niccolo bounded into the bedroom, unable to keep the grin from his face. The phone call to Ana he'd just finished had proved fruitful, confirming he had offers of work flooding in from all over the world. He'd had to lay it on thick with Ana about his need to get back to work so she didn't think he was focusing on his royal duties instead of his career. Although she'd kept him on her books during the wilderness years, he hadn't been a priority because of the lack of work coming in, and therefore lack of earning potential for her too. He was savvy enough to realise he wasn't anything more than a cash cow at the end of the day, but he needed her too to negotiate these deals. He needed to keep her onside and show that he was ready, willing and able to work, even if he wanted to pick and choose his future roles more carefully. Of course he had different responsibilities and duties now, but he hoped his new status would afford him opportunities which otherwise might have passed him by.

'You won't believe the conversation I just had with my agent…' he started, then he realised Gaia was standing stiffly facing him with a look on her features usually reserved for her family. One that said he wasn't welcome in her room. 'What's wrong?'

'I've been thinking about what you said earlier and you're probably right, I can do this on my own.'

'What?' He laughed, disbelieving that she meant what she was saying. Only a short time ago she'd been clinging on to him, begging him not to leave her.

'We only got married to save face. I was afraid to tell the world about my pregnancy and you needed a career boost. It happened sooner than we envisaged but perhaps that's for the best. At least this way we won't waste too much time trying to force a relationship to work. We don't have to keep pretending.'

'I didn't think we were.' He thought of last night, how amazing they'd been together, and wondered how things had changed so quickly. It was only because he'd been as sure of Gaia's feelings for him as those he had for her that he'd opened up his heart again. Now all of those fears and worries he'd kept locked away for years were unleashed, swarming in the air around him like dark demons ready to steal his new-found happiness and leave him in eternal torment.

'Well, circumstances pushed us together. It was only natural we'd seek comfort in one another but one night together doesn't have to mean for ever. As I reminded my mother, it's not the Dark Ages any more.'

Niccolo was finding it difficult to process the change in Gaia's attitude. Whilst he was happy she had a new confidence in herself, it seemed to have come at his expense. He now appeared to be surplus to requirements. Until this moment he hadn't seen her as someone who would use people and toss them aside once they'd outlived their usefulness. He'd always thought her to be considerate of other people's feelings and someone who wore her own like a badge of honour. All of a sudden she was completely unreadable to him, to the point he didn't know if he'd imagined the look of love in her eyes last night when they'd finally consummated their marriage. Whilst he'd been making plans for a future together as a family, it would seem Gaia had been gearing up to fight for her independence. If only he'd had some warning he might have been able to salvage what was left of his heart.

'What are you saying, Gaia? You want a divorce?' If she was attempting to convince him the feelings they'd shared last night were merely a result of being caught up in this secret about the baby, agreeing to a marriage of convenience that saw them stuck together in confinement, he didn't know where that left them as a couple. It would be impossible to continue on now as though none of it had happened. He couldn't stuff his feelings back in a box and pretend he'd never had them, never shared his deepest thoughts with her because he thought they'd be together for ever. Nor could he imagine a life without her now.

'For the moment I think we should carry on. You do your thing and I'll do mine. When an appropriate amount of time has passed we'll have a legal separation and take it from there. I'm sure you have projects of your own, things you would rather be doing than hanging on my arm.' There was a hardness to her that he'd never seen before. Her jaw was set, her mouth tight, and her arms folded defensively across her chest. For the life of him he couldn't understand the change in her. There was an underlying tone which suggested he was at fault, but all he'd done was support her. If this was her way of saying it was over, that she didn't have any feelings for him, he didn't see any way of fighting it. He couldn't make her love him.

'I was speaking to Ana about an opportunity in Italy—'

'Great. Why don't you go and do that?' She cut him off, not apparently interested in hearing what he was planning, only in getting him to leave.

It was as if last night had never happened. She might regret it, be willing to never think about it again, but unfortunately he would remember every second of it until the day he died.

'Have I done something wrong? I thought we were really at the beginning of something special.'

'You played the role perfectly, Niccolo. Now it's time to move on to the next one.' She gave him a smile that better suited one of those shop greeters who told you to have a nice day and deep down didn't care if you got hit by a bus once you left the store. They were just words, with no emotion behind them. Almost as though she'd become the sort of automaton her family wanted to smile and wave and not rock the boat. This wasn't his Gaia, and she was making it clear she never had been.

'What about the baby?' A big part of the marriage deal had been to provide security for the baby. The idea of going back to separate lives now was stealing that future family away from him and the child.

He was invested in them as a couple, and as a result of that had finally embraced the possibility of his becoming a father. It was a chance for him to be that loving parent he'd had and lost, and to be better than his own father in the process. He hoped he'd be the kind of dad to listen to his son or daughter and encourage them to express how they felt. Not inflict the kind of emotional trauma his father had put him through which had followed him into adulthood and wrecked every relationship he'd ever had. It was ironic that, just when he'd learned to let himself love, Gaia revealed she didn't need him. He might have been better off keeping his feelings on lockdown for a bit longer. Then he wouldn't have had his heart ripped out of his chest finding out their marriage was over, that Gaia didn't love him back. The only consolation he had was that he hadn't spilled his guts out to her, confessing his love and furthering his humiliation. Although discovering she didn't love him was a small, unwanted, badly wrapped gift.

Going back to his day job would give him an interest away from the royal duties, but it was no longer his entire life. Being with Gaia, planning a future around the baby, had given his existence a different depth, given it more meaning. Without them again he didn't know who he was any more.

'We'll be fine without you, as I'm sure you will be without us,' she said, her insistence inflicting further injury, as though she'd just drop-kicked his freshly plucked heart.

He thought he saw her smile waver, then put it down to wishful thinking when she was still staring, waiting for him to leave.

'You want me to go now?' he asked, incredulous that this should be over so quickly without prior warning. Though he supposed it was in keeping with the nature of their marriage—hasty, ill thought-out, and something which was going to be difficult to explain. What could he do but bow out if that was what Gaia truly wanted? He did have some options he wanted to explore work-wise—perhaps that would give him some space to think about what had happened, maybe figure out what had gone wrong. Hopefully it would keep him busy enough to distract him from the massive void Gaia would leave in his life. He wasn't going to have much of a career if he reverted to that traumatised boy who couldn't find the words to express the emptiness left behind after the loss of his loved one. Not unless they brought back silent movies.

'I think it's for the best. You've fulfilled your side of the bargain, so now I'm setting you free.'

It was on the tip of his tongue to tell her he didn't want to go, that this was more than a business arrangement and she wasn't doing him any favours. But he saw the steely determination in her eyes and knew it was no use arguing with her. Gaia had made up her mind to go it alone after all. He just wished she'd done that before he'd fallen in love with her.

'Don't you think you should answer that?' Gaia's mother nodded towards the phone buzzing in her hand.

'No. He'll have to give up eventually.' She'd turned off the sound but Niccolo was persistent. Her voicemail was full with messages he'd left but she hadn't been able to bring herself to listen to them. It had been difficult enough sending him away without hearing his voice again, reminding her of what she'd lost. He might have said it was her who'd thrown away their marriage, but he'd thank her when he had his own life back.

If he'd had so many great opportunities thrown his way she didn't want to hold him back any more.

As much as she wanted the sort of man who'd agree to marry her to save her reputation, she needed it to come from love, not obligation. Somewhere along the way they'd confused the two. Or at least she'd been acting out of love and he'd been a slave to obligation. Either way, it hadn't been fair to carry on the way they were. It was clear to her she'd fallen in love with him, or hearing him tell his agent that being with her had just been a job to him wouldn't have hurt so much. To her, sleeping together had been a culmination of their love, but apparently to him it was still all part of the act. One which he should have won awards for when he'd convinced her he had real feelings for her. It wouldn't have been any life for her, or the baby, trying to convince herself that it was better to have a husband at least in name rather than doing this on her own. She'd realised too late that she did need love, that a marriage of convenience wasn't enough for her. By that time she'd already given her heart away again, but at least by calling things off herself she'd clung on to a little dignity.

It was thanks to him that she had found her self-confidence again and it was that inner strength she was going to dig deep into to see her through the rest of this pregnancy and beyond.

Although since Niccolo's departure her mother had been surprisingly supportive, even coming with her today for the first scan. Still, Gaia had opted not to inform her of the real reason they had split, only telling her that things hadn't worked out.

'I'm not so sure,' her mother said as her phone renewed the incessant buzzing.

In the end Gaia had to turn it off altogether. It was torture knowing that Niccolo wanted to speak to her, but also being aware it wasn't going to achieve anything. Eventually he'd realise he was off the hook and find joy in the things he really loved.

'I'm not giving him any choice.' She threw the phone into her bag so she wouldn't even have to look at it, lest she was tempted to listen to what he had to say and give in to the easier life he was likely offering. It seemed taking the higher ground came at a cost, but she hoped it would be worth it in the end. If nothing else she could teach her child that appearances weren't everything, so this toxic legacy wouldn't continue into another generation. Whilst being part of the royal family dictated decorum and responsibility, it shouldn't mean lying and faking a life that suited a narrative from hundreds of years ago. People fell in and out of love, made mistakes, and got pregnant outside of marriage. They shouldn't be forced into marriage to save face. Perhaps if someone had ended this cycle of deceit her father wouldn't have acted the way he had, and she would have been strong enough to stand on her own. There would have been no need to drag Niccolo into their dysfunctional family.

'Are you going to tell me what happened? I mean, I know the wedding was a rush but I thought you genuinely loved each other. At the end of the day that's all that matters.' Her mother apparently wasn't going to let the matter drop so easily. The split must have come as a shock to her when they'd initially been so gung-ho about getting married in the first place.

Gaia thought about the lies her father had told, the life her mother had been forced to live, and knew it wasn't fair to keep her in the dark any more. What did it matter now that she and Niccolo weren't together anyway?

'The baby isn't his. I mean, he knew that, it's not why we split up. He only agreed to this to save our reputations. Genuinely nothing had happened between us when those photographs were taken, but I knew how everyone would react when they found out I was pregnant.'

'He married you anyway?'

'Yes, well, he's a good man. He knew how bad it would look for me…and him, I suppose. People would've assumed he was the baby's father no matter what we said. We thought a marriage would save both of our reputations, and his career had been in freefall up until the premiere.'

'Okay, so it was a marriage of convenience. That's not unheard of…this family has been doing it for years.'

Gaia was powerless to prevent her eyebrows almost disappearing into her hairline. 'You and Dad?'

It would explain a lot about her father's behaviour if he'd been coerced into a marriage he hadn't wanted, even if it didn't excuse it.

Her mother nodded. 'Although I'm not royalty, as your father liked to point out on a regular basis, I was from the *right* family. We had connections which opened up some very important financial avenues and helped strengthen economic relations with other countries. Your father had a lot of side-interests.'

The double meaning wasn't lost on Gaia when his infidelity had turned out to be as prolific as the international duties he carried out.

'I had no idea. I assumed you'd been in love once.'

'Well, one of us was. I'm not sure your father truly loved anyone more than himself.' She gave a half-smile which only served to make her look even sadder than usual when she talked about Gaia's father.

'I'm so sorry, Mum. You always deserved so much better. But it does prove to me that I made the right decision in telling him to leave.'

'Why's that?'

'Unrequited love in a marriage is never a good thing.'

'Oh, Gaia.'

She found herself swamped in a tight hug, her mother's embrace something she hadn't experienced in a long time.

'It's all right, I've realised I'm stronger than I knew. I mean, that might have had something to do with Niccolo too, but I think I'll be all right. I have the baby to think about and that's more important than a silly crush.'

'He's really not coming back?' her mother said softly, yet the words hit hard, causing tears to mist Gaia's vision.

She shook her head, dislodging a solitary tear rebelling against her refusal to cry any more over the loss of her fake husband. 'I didn't think it was fair on either of us to make him stay. It's not his fault I fell in love with him and he doesn't feel the same way.'

'Did you even give him a chance to have his say?'

'I overheard him on the phone to his agent. Apparently he's highly in demand now that he's a movie-star prince. Reading between the lines, he was stifled here. I didn't want him to get bored and end up cheating on me. For him to take work and simply never come back would almost be worse than never loving me.'

'It is,' her mother said, wiping away the tears that were now flowing freely with her handkerchief. 'I'm sorry we put so much pressure on you that you thought marriage was the only way out. What about the father—is he completely off the scene?'

'Yes. Niccolo was the only man I thought would be a good dad, but parenthood shouldn't be forced on someone any more than marriage should. I was asking too much from him.'

'But he was willing to do it, Gaia. Are you sure there's no way forward? If marrying you and being father to your baby so people won't think badly of you doesn't say love, I don't know what does.'

'I told you, he's a good man,' Gaia huffed, put out that her mother seemed to be on his side. She'd been through all of this in her own marriage and knew how it panned out. If anything she should be applauding her for pre-empting the inevitable heartbreak and taking control now before another child was born into a one-sided relationship. So it didn't grow up thinking it wasn't worthy of love too.

'I saw the way he looked at you, Gaia. I think it was more than that. Don't let the toxic relationship I had with your father cloud your judgement. If he had ever looked at me the way Niccolo looks at you we would never have had a problem. Niccolo loves you.'

Gaia thought of everything he'd done for her and how amazing last night had been. As good an actor as he was, she didn't think he could have faked all of that, but it was clear that the resurgence in his career was a big deal to him. He'd risked it to help her and now this was her way of paying him back. Giving him his life again instead of forcing him into her world. Yet there was a selfish part of her wishing he'd fought harder and hadn't got on the plane. That he was here with her to see their baby.

'If he really loved me, he wouldn't have gone.'

Her mother threw her hands up. 'You've probably confused him about what it is you do want. I'm not sure I know any more.'

'Right now I want to know the baby is all right.' The truth was she wanted it all—Niccolo, the baby, and a happy family—but life had taught her that it wasn't possible and she'd be a fool to believe otherwise.

The sonographer came in at that moment and positioned herself in front of a screen. 'Okay, Your Highness, if you could lift your top up I'm going to put some gel on your belly.'

Gaia complied, wincing when the cold substance made contact with her skin.

'Sorry about that, it's just to help the Doppler move over your bump. Not that you have much of one at this stage.' The woman sounded nervous, something Gaia was used to. People often got a tad tongue-tied when they met a member of the royal family. On this occasion, however, it wasn't doing anything to ease her own apprehension. She would have preferred to have a pronounced pregnancy belly at this stage to put her mind at rest that the baby hadn't been adversely affected by everything that had gone on lately.

'I had a bit of a scare recently. Some cramps and sickness. It's been a stressful time.'

'I saw that in your notes but the attending doctor reported a strong heartbeat. We'll check now to put your mind at ease.' If the woman had put two and two together over the dates and realised Gaia was pregnant before the honeymoon she didn't give any indication. The private hospital was used by the entire royal family and their discretion could be counted on. One less thing she had to worry about.

Gaia held her breath waiting for that tell-tale sound again, her eyes locked on the screen in anticipation of seeing that tiny bean which had caused so much trouble. The only thing keeping her going in the wake of her all-encompassing heartache.

It seemed like for ever before the woman spoke again. Even Gaia's mother seemed to be agitated, standing up to peer at the screen herself, as though she'd be able to spot something before the trained medical staff.

'Is everything all right?' Gaia finally asked, unable to bear the silence and uncertainty.

'I'm just having trouble finding baby...'

It was enough to tip Gaia over the edge. She was wrong, she didn't want to do this alone.

'I want Niccolo,' she sobbed.

Her mother took her hand and squeezed.

The sonographer moved the Doppler device with a renewed determination.

Then the door burst open and Gaia was glad she was lying on a hospital bed because she was sure she would have collapsed when she saw who'd walked in.

'Gaia? What's wrong? Why wouldn't you answer my calls?' Niccolo flew to her side and she could tell immediately by his stubble and the rings under his eyes that he hadn't been sleeping any better than she had in the few days since they'd separated.

'Niccolo? What are you doing here?'

Her mother moved so he could get to the side of the bed, leaving go of her hand so Niccolo could take it in his. It didn't matter how they'd parted, in that moment she needed him here with her.

'I knew it was the scan today. I had to be here, even if you don't want me—'

'There we go. Baby was just playing hide and seek with us.' The sonographer interrupted them with the good news before Gaia had the chance to tell Niccolo that she had wanted him here.

'Can we see?' Niccolo asked, squeezing her hand tight as the sonographer turned the screen for them to see the grainy black and white image, the tiny figure floating in the middle.

'Everything's all right?' She needed confirmation before she'd let herself believe it and get too carried away with the thought that it might all just work out. The fact that Niccolo had come back for the scan, for a baby that wasn't his, gave her a flutter of hope that all wasn't lost.

'Baby seems perfectly happy and well. I'll print out the pictures for you, then I'll give you a bit of time to get cleaned up in private.'

Gaia took hold of the precious pictures of her baby and kissed them.

'I'll give you some privacy too. You have things to discuss,' her mother said, leaving the room with the sonographer so Gaia and Niccolo were alone.

Now was the time for honesty for both of them, it was make or break, but Gaia was afraid by telling him she loved him she was losing the control she had over the situation. She was risking leaving herself open to feeling unwanted again if he told her he didn't feel the same way.

'I'm glad the baby's okay,' he said, unsure of what he was doing here. Gaia had sent him away less than a week ago, telling him she didn't want him, and she'd proved her point since, refusing to take his calls or messages. Yet he hadn't been able to give up on her, or them. Perhaps it was the idea that a family was almost within his grasp because he couldn't believe she didn't love him. It wasn't that he was so conceited he didn't think it a possibility. Rather, he'd spent the last nights analysing their every moment together. He'd worked with the best actors and Gaia would be award-winning if it turned out this was still just a business deal to her.

The way she fitted in his arms so perfectly and readily, the plans they'd had for their family, and the love they'd made so tenderly, said they shared something deeper than necessity. Whilst they might have started out in a marriage of convenience, he'd fallen in love with Gaia. He was a different man to the one she'd married, no longer content to hide away from his feelings. Now he was back to make sure she wasn't making the same mistakes he had in the past.

'Why did you come back, Niccolo?' Her voice was barely a whisper, as though she was afraid of the answer.

'For you, for the baby, for us. Things ended so abruptly I wanted a chance to talk things through properly. To tell you I love you in case you were in any doubt.' It had occurred to him on those lonely nights wondering what he'd done wrong that he'd never told her how he felt. That she might have believed he'd only used her for sex when that night together had been his way of showing her how he felt, even if he hadn't been able to express it in words. The idea of losing her for ever had given him the courage to actually tell her.

'You—you love me?'

'Yes. Is that so hard to believe?' He smiled, hoping to charm her back into his life.

'It's…unexpected.'

'So, you see, I didn't have to leave. I just need to know if you feel the same way, then we can be together as a proper family.'

Gaia shook her head as if she was trying to dislodge that thought. 'It doesn't change anything. You'll tire of us. It would only be delaying the inevitable if you came back.'

Niccolo laughed because she was being completely unreasonable as far as he could see. She wasn't saying she didn't love him, but she was afraid to in case things didn't work out. In some ways he could relate. After all, that was how he'd operated in all of his relationships until he'd met Gaia and had to confront the fact that he wanted to be with her.

'Gaia, we can't live our lives being afraid to take a chance on love. Isn't that what you told me? What makes you think that I would ever tire of being with you when I clearly can't live without you?'

'I heard you on the phone to your agent saying this life wasn't enough. That you were excited about the new job opportunities being offered to you. And don't forget, you went. You didn't even fight for us.'

There was so much to unpack in that statement it took Niccolo a moment to figure out what had happened.

'For a start, you asked me to leave. I thought if you didn't love me that there was no point staying here and upsetting you. As for the phone call, yes, I was thrilled to hear people wanted to work with me but not for the reasons you think. I'm part of this family, of course I'm going to do my duty, but that doesn't mean I'm limited to cutting ribbons and waving at people, does it?'

She opened her mouth to answer but he carried on because he had a lot to say. He was done with everyone thinking badly of him when he'd done nothing to deserve it. Gaia of all people should have realised he wouldn't shirk responsibility.

'I know as a member of the royal family my day job is supposed to take a back seat. I agreed to that when I signed those papers before the wedding. And, to be honest, I didn't think it would be much of a problem when I was still trying to rebuild my reputation. Then Ana started calling to let me know there was a chance for me to still be involved in the industry as a mentor and a patron to a charity for aspiring actors and directors. I thought it was a good opportunity to prove my worth in the family, to show I'm committed to my new role. I went because I wanted you to see I'm not going to be living off your coat-tails for the rest of my days. I intend to earn my keep, and people's respect, on my own merits. And I want our children to grow up being proud of us both and knowing they can make a difference in the world, not simply decorate it.'

Gaia couldn't process everything he was saying, so she focused on that last part promising them a future together. 'Our children?'

'Yeah, well, if we don't completely mess this one up, I thought we might want to extend the family.'

'That sounds nice. Really nice.' After his declaration of love, turning up for the scan, and explaining why he'd been so excited about the prospect of work, Gaia was beginning to let herself imagine their life together again. One without secrets.

'So...does that mean you'll take me back?'

She thought about the life she would have without him in it and it was nothing compared to the one he was offering her now, if she was willing to give him a chance and believe he was different to all the other men she'd had in her life.

'Yes, Niccolo, I want you in our lives.' She placed his hand on top of her belly and hoped their baby would grow up in the safe, loving environment it deserved.

'In that case, Your Highness,' he got down on one knee beside the bed and Gaia had to peer over to see him, 'will you do me the honour of becoming my wife for real? Will you marry me again?'

'I will. I love you, Niccolo,' she said, throwing her arms around him when he stood up again.

The kiss they shared, as two people finally honest about their feelings, was so full of love and a need to make one another happy she thought her heart would burst.

The Princess had her fairy-tale ending after all.

EPILOGUE

Four years later

'EMILIA, WAVE AT the crowd.' Gaia encouraged her daughter to make her presence known on the balcony with the rest of the royal family even though she could scarcely see above it, aware that the throng of people lining the streets would want to see her.

Although she was fiercely protective of her family, on occasions such as the diamond anniversary of the King's coronation they were expected to have a visible presence.

'Do you want me to take Leo?' Niccolo asked.

She nodded and extricated her exuberant toddler from his koala position on her waist. Little Leonardo was too young to understand what all the fuss and noise was about, and once he'd given everyone the photo op they'd been waiting for she would take him back inside the palace.

They were lucky to live away from the city these days. Once Emilia had been born they'd made the decision to live in one of the other royal residences in the countryside to afford them more privacy. It was smaller than the palace but had become their family home, where she and Niccolo had been able to live a relatively normal life. They'd even renewed their vows in the grounds and

Emilia had been delighted to be a flower girl on the day, only witnessed and attended by Gaia's mother and grandfather. That was how they lived their lives these days, out of the spotlight as much as possible.

They carried out their duties as members of the royal family as usual but didn't parade their children in front of the cameras. It was important to her and Niccolo that they had as normal a childhood as possible, not under constant scrutiny as she had been.

'I can put them to bed if you want to stay and watch the show,' Niccolo told her as they watched the stage opposite the palace filling with the latest chart singers, keen to celebrate the King's anniversary in front of the packed crowd.

'That would be great. I'll stay for a while, then you can come out if you want.' They had a nanny to help out when they were required at state functions and public engagements, but they preferred to spend time with their children. Niccolo was an excellent father. He'd worried he wouldn't be able to show those emotions which had caused him so much trouble in the past, but he needn't have worried. The moment Emilia was born he burst into tears, the same when his son was born a year later. He loved nothing more than reading them bedtime stories or playing hide-and-seek in the grounds with them. There wasn't a day that went past without him hugging his children, and his wife, and telling them how much he loved them.

Gaia loved being a mother, and being married to Niccolo. She had so much unconditional love in her life now the happiness had pushed out those negative feelings about herself and her family. Life was too short not to enjoy the precious time she had with her husband and children.

They had their own charitable arms—she worked with many mother and baby groups, and Niccolo had his mentorship with aspiring actors and directors. It gave them some time apart and something to talk to each other about when they were reunited. Those separate interests gave them a life beyond the palace walls and also made them look forward to seeing one another again at the end of the day. They had the best of both worlds.

'Okay, kids, let's go. Wave goodbye.' Niccolo waited until the children gave the crowd what they'd come for, then dropped a kiss on Gaia's lips. Even now he was able to excite her whole body with one slight touch.

The sound of wolf whistles and flash of cameras reminded them that they'd just given a very public display of affection, but her mother and grandfather didn't bat an eyelid in their direction. They were popular now because of Gaia and Niccolo's relationship and the new generation of the family. It had taken some time but her grandfather had begun to realise some of those traditions had kept them at a distance from the rest of the country, and showing they were human after all had helped people warm to them more. They had taken some flak announcing the first baby when it was clear she'd been pregnant before the wedding. Mostly, though, people had accepted she was human and made mistakes like everyone else. Not that she thought of Emilia as a mistake when it was her who'd brought Niccolo into their lives in the first place.

'I'll be in soon,' she told Niccolo and he gave her a wink before leading the children inside. They were sleeping in the guest room in the palace tonight, with Gaia and

Niccolo in the adjoining room he'd once slept in alone. As she watched him walk away looking so handsome in his navy tailored suit she decided she wouldn't stay at the party for too long.

One day she would be expected to rule the country and assume all the responsibilities her grandfather currently undertook. Until then she would spend every second she could with her husband and any dancing they did now was in private.

From now on Niccolo Pernici's moves were reserved solely for her.

* * * * *

COMING SOON!

We really hope you enjoyed reading this book. If you're looking for more romance be sure to head to the shops when new books are available on

Thursday 3rd August

To see which titles are coming soon, please visit

millsandboon.co.uk/nextmonth

MILLS & BOON

MILLS & BOON ®

Coming next month

WEDDING PLANNER'S DEAL WITH THE CEO
Nina Milne

"It's a bike."

"Well done," he said kindly, and she grinned.

"Ha-ha. But… I can't ride a bike. I told you that."

"I know. So I'm going to teach you." A pause. "If you want, that is?"

"I'd love that." Warmth touched her that he'd registered her comment at breakfast the previous day, must have seen the regret, the emotion she'd tried to hide.

"Good. We can do a lesson a day and by the time we leave you will be able to ride a bike."

She blinked, knew it was ridiculous to feel tearful, but she did. She hauled in breath. "Your farewell gift." A reminder to herself.

Carefully she swung her leg over and sat, couldn't help but smile at him as warmth touched her again at his gesture. And there it was like a bolt sent on the sweet-flower-laden breeze, a sudden awareness of his proximity, his scent a kind of woodsy, clean, masculine smell, and she felt almost dizzy with a longing. A yearning that it could all be different, that somehow she and Nathan could be two people without baggage or a past, two people open to… To what?

Love? A future? Her eyes snapped open as she registered the sheer foolish futility of her thoughts.

Between them she and Nathan had enough baggage to sink the *Titanic* if it hadn't hit an iceberg. More than that, she would never willingly put herself in the deliberate path of probable pain and humiliation again.

But she watched him, crouched now on the ground so she could see the powerful muscles of his thighs flex, and then he stood up, right next to her, his hands on the handlebars so close to her she thought she'd combust.

And it wasn't only her, she realised—it wasn't. She saw his jaw clench, saw his fingers tighten around the handlebars. And she was tempted, oh, so tempted, to simply pretend to wobble, 'lose' her balance and tumble into him and then he'd catch her in his arms and…and he'd kiss her and she'd kiss him and…that way lay disaster. Absolute disaster. He would be horrified—that was what would happen—and that horror would etch his face. Or would it? He wanted to kiss her—she was sure of it.

Continue reading
WEDDING PLANNER'S DEAL WITH THE CEO
Nina Milne

Available next month
www.millsandboon.co.uk

OUT NOW!

LET'S TALK

Romance

For exclusive extracts, competitions and special offers, find us online:

f MillsandBoon

𝕏 @MillsandBoon

📷 @MillsandBoonUK

♪ @MillsandBoonUK

Get in touch on 01413 063 232

MILLS & BOON

THE HEART OF ROMANCE

A ROMANCE FOR EVERY READER

MODERN — Prepare to be swept off your feet by sophisticated, sexy and seductive heroes, in some of the world's most glamourous and romantic locations, where power and passion collide.

HISTORICAL — Escape with historical heroes from time gone by. Whether your passion is for wicked Regency Rakes, muscled Vikings or rugged Highlanders, awaken the romance of the past.

MEDICAL — Set your pulse racing with dedicated, delectable doctors in the high-pressure world of medicine, where emotions run high and passion, comfort and love are the best medicine.

True Love — Celebrate true love with tender stories of heartfelt romance, from the rush of falling in love to the joy a new baby can bring, and a focus on the emotional heart of a relationship.

Desire — Indulge in secrets and scandal, intense drama and sizzling hot action with heroes who have it all: wealth, status, good looks…everything but the right woman.

HEROES — The excitement of a gripping thriller, with intense romance at its heart. Resourceful, true-to-life women and strong, fearless men face danger and desire - a killer combination!

To see which titles are coming soon, please visit

millsandboon.co.uk/nextmonth